The
Last Moonlight
Dragon

Book 1: The Moonlight Dragon Duology

Dorothy McFalls

Barking Dog Press

Interior Artwork by Dorothy McFalls and canva.com

Cover Artwork by Laura at thebookbrander.com

Page Edges by Painted Wings Publishing Services

PLEASE NOTE: This book is printed with an internal border that bleeds onto the edge of the page, leaving a design. If your book does not print all of the borders or has other quality issues, please let the bookstore know. These are print-on-demand, and the author has no control over the quality of each individual print.

Dedication

To those who look up at the moon and dream.

Jayden Continent

Chapter 1

The valley used to have dragons. They'd slumber stretched out on the gentle slopes in the morning sun in the perpetually chilly land of Earst.

I missed them.

"What has you thinking so hard?" a gruff voice asked as I made my way from the royal library. I kept walking.

Fingers tightened around my shoulder and spun me around until I was face to face with Aaron Krisp, a royal guard with a face like a bulldog and onion breath. "I asked you a question."

"I-I was just remembering." I hugged the stack of books on dragon lore to my chest and tried to skitter away from him.

Krisp moved with amazing speed for a man as wide as him. He gave me a shove. My head banged against the castle's cold stone wall. "The only thinking you should be doing is pondering ways to please me, Lady Celestina."

I threw up my hands to push him away, sending the library books flying. "I'm a Queen's Lady."

"And I'm a guard? Not good enough for you?" He tsked. His onion breath filled the space around me. "I'm all you've got. Queen Beatrice hates you. And no one in court will look at you."

His lips brushed the side of my face. "You're growing old."

"No!" I yanked his dagger from his belt and swung. The blade sliced a bit of skin from his chin.

"Bitch." He moved with lightning speed, grabbing hold of my wrist and slamming it against the stone wall above my head. His other hand landed on my breast. He squeezed hard enough to bring tears to my eyes. "Accept that you're mine."

"My parents would never—"

"Your parents haven't given a fuck about you ever since Queen Beatrice took the throne. Everyone knows you've been abandoned."

That stung. "I have friends."

He laughed. "I put a baby in your belly, and you'll see how far your friends' loyalty will go." He tried to wedge his knee between my legs.

"Get off me, you big oaf. I'll never lie with you."

"I wasn't asking for your permission." The hand that had been on my breast was suddenly tightening around my throat. Black spots danced in my eyes.

I tried to kick him, but every part of him was smashed against me.

A loud clanging startled both of us. It echoed through the hall, followed by repeated calls to arms. All guards were being called to duty. "This isn't over." Krisp sucked my lower lip into his mouth and bit down until I tasted blood. "No one will protect you."

He pushed me to the ground before lumbering away. Breathing hard, I gathered the books and then sprinted up to my room in the tower. I was usually more careful about moving about the castle alone.

He was right. No one in the castle was watching out for me.

My hands trembled as I climbed onto the windowsill. When the dragons still came around, I would sit there while sipping hot chocolate and watch the younger dragons frolic with each other. Their tussling reminded me of the little princes. The queen had ordered me to babysit them every afternoon following their lessons. They behaved like the young magical beasts I loved. The largest dragon, however, a green beast with a golden sheen to its scales, seemed to be above the brawling silliness of its smaller cohorts. If any of the frisky dragons got too close to the majestic green dragon, it would push them away with its massive claw.

If only the magnificent green dragon hadn't left me. I liked to imagine that it watched me as closely as I watched it, that it loved me as much as I loved it. If only it had flown to my window before abandoning the valley.

If it had, I would have crawled over the ledge and out of the tower. Before anyone noticed I would have been on its back. I would have left behind the queen's cruelty. I would have left my parent's indifference and Krisp with onion on his breath.

"Lawks, Lady Celestina! If that *thing* flew up here, it wouldn't be to carry you off to be cherished in some faraway land," Trisha my lady's maid had screeched after I had once confessed my fantasy that the dragon would rescue me from the viciousness that accompanied court life. "It would come to your window because it wanted to crunch on your bones. That's what dragons do! They crunch innocent maidens' bones."

"I'm not sure that's true," I had said. But maybe it was…

The kingdom was awash in tales of monsters and creatures of the dark that wanted to do us harm. The queen often recounted to her court in grotesque detail how she constantly had to use her magical powers to keep the monsters from attacking her people. And I believed she did work hard to make our lives safer…but the dragons?

They didn't seem *that* terrible.

They never did anything other than sun themselves in the valley for a few hours every day.

But then one day the dragons stopped coming. They'd simply stopped coming.

No one seemed to know where they'd gone or if they'd ever return.

Worried, I'd secured an audience with Queen Beatrice, the lone ruler of Earst, and begged her to send her army to find out what happened to the dragons. *My* dragons.

"Those scaly creatures?" She had tossed her head back and laughed. "The kingdom already has enough troubles with monsters. Why worry about the absence of a few ugly beasts?" She'd said it while flicking away two green lizards that had crawled up the leg of her golden throne and had scurried across her lap. "I don't know why you don't do something different with your hair," she had then criticized with a royal wave of her hand. "You look like a street urchin."

I touched my head. Trisha had braided my light brown hair into intricate loops. It had taken her the better part of the morning to accomplish what I'd thought looked like a masterpiece when I'd left my room to meet with the lovely and incredibly young Queen Beatrice. But I supposed the queen was right about my braids…and the dragons. The queen was, after all, infallible. Chosen by the gods to lead us and all. The last lady to question her word ended up with her head on a pike at the castle gate. Since I would rather keep my head attached to my neck, I bowed and begged her forgiveness while promising to take more time with my appearance.

"You do that," Queen Beatrice had said, her gaze narrowing at me. "Not that it will do much good. No matter how much time you spend polishing a chunk of gravel it'll still never become a diamond."

The other ladies of the court attending the queen had all tittered, even my friends Rechel and Everly. I understood why they'd join the queen and laugh. I also understood why none of them, not even my friends, would dare speak or be kind to me for the rest of the week. Showing me kindness after I'd suffered the queen's rebuke could be dangerous. No one in the court wanted to risk angering the queen, especially when her wrath often turned deadly.

Goddess only knew how I'd managed to survive this long in Queen Beatrice's court. Nothing I did was ever good enough for the perfect, beautiful, regal queen. My eyes were mismatched. My limbs were too long. I was too clumsy, too outspoken, too quiet, too dowdy, and collected too many shiny books and baubles.

Oh, look! A sparkly sequence had fallen off one of the ladies' dresses. I had scooped up the treasure as I hurried down the corridor back to my tower after that meeting with the queen. I had held it up and let the light dance off its metallic folds before pushing the trinket into my pocket.

A few years ago, the queen didn't like the blue color of my dress and in a pique moved my room from the luxurious ladies' hall and into one of the cold, drafty towers.

Honestly, though. That had been one of my favorite punishments. The tower room, unlike any of the ones in the main, well-heated, part of the castle had a clear view down into the valley. Thanks to the queen's punishment, I was able to spend the last couple of years watching the dragons and dreaming of being rescued by that handsome, strong green dragon with the golden sheen.

But as I peered out the arched opening now, the shiver I felt had nothing to do with the bitter cold or the fear I felt from Krisp's attack. Because today, the dragons had been replaced with a different sort of creature in the valley below me.

An army draped with red capes over one shoulder marched across the frosty grass as they approached the castle. The line of soldiers stretched as far as the horizon. And possibly beyond.

The wicked kingdom of Tiburnia was coming.

They'd sent a note warning of their invasion three weeks ago. The parchment had been secured to the head of one of our royal guards with a knife sticking out of the poor dead man's forehead. The note promised that the Tiburnian army would kill our queen and then slay the rest of us.

Where have the dragons gone? The Kingdom of Earst could certainly use them right about now.

Chapter 2

Two Days Later

Where had those mischievous little princes disappeared to this time? With the battle raging outside the castle walls, the tutor had canceled his lessons.

"You canceled them?" I shouted while beating my fists against the tutor's door.

"In case you hadn't noticed, Lady Celestina, there's an army trying their best to kill us all," Gustav Grunt shouted back.

"So, you turned four lively young boys loose in the middle of a war with no one to watch them? They'll be frightened." I hoped they were frightened enough to stay out of trouble. Although I doubted that would be the case.

It wasn't as if any of them were old enough to join the fight or to even help with the weapons. The oldest was only seven and the youngest was three. And the two twins in the middle had turned five a few weeks ago.

The queen had instructed me to keep the princes out of the way. Neither seen nor heard. Not just for the war…but forever.

"Those brats are not my problem!" Gustav shouted. The lock in the heavy door clicked. With the tutor locked in his own chamber, likely hiding under his bed, it was up to me to keep the princes safe.

But to do that, I needed to find them!

The tutor had sent them away hours ago without thinking to fetch me, which meant the boys had been on their own and unsupervised for the past five hours. *Five hours?* A cold wave of dread swept through me. The castle was awash with foreign forces. The queen had appealed to the neighboring kingdoms of Fein and Asteria for assistance against the Tiburnian army. Both kingdoms had sent their best (or perhaps I should say *worst*) warriors to join the fight. The men were large and frightening and most likely dangerous for the children to be around.

All the ladies of the court had been warned to keep as far away from any of the foreign forces as possible.

The two kingdoms' encampments had been set up in the spacious bailey within the castle walls. A place that had been deemed off-limits to anyone who valued their lives.

Since the bailey was surely the most dangerous place for the princes, I imagined that would be exactly where I'd find them. I ran down the winding stone steps toward the yard while praying they were safe. And also praying the boys hadn't learned how to get outside the gates to the battlefield!

I blasted out one of the castle's side doors and hurried around the outside of a small storage hut as I headed toward the foreign army camps. That was when I found them.

All four of the scamps had somehow obtained wooden practice swords and were wearing leather armor that was much too large for their tiny bodies. Worse, the leathers weren't the purple leather the Earst warriors wore, but black. I could only imagine where they'd found the leather armor and swords and how much trouble I was going to face when I needed to return them to their rightful owners.

I grabbed hold of the skirt of my pale pink dress and sprinted toward the boys, hoping to reach them before they noticed me. The princes could be slippery when they didn't want to be caught.

I was just about upon them when to the left of me a hinge in need of oil groaned loudly. My heart stuttered. If a door was being opened to the left of me, it meant someone was opening a door in the outer wall to access the battle outside. Or, or, worse, invite the battle into the castle walls.

It took everything in me not to spin toward the sound. But if the castle walls were about to be breached, that made my need to get to the princes much more urgent.

There was a shout from the groaning door hinge. I ignored it and continued to run.

The youngest prince, Robert, yelped as I scooped him into my arms. "Got you!" I cried, trying to keep things light, hoping they would think I was playing a game. I didn't need any of them worrying I might punish them. I didn't need them trying to run off. I scooped up the twins, Rupert and Ryan. "Got you, too!" They giggled. Thank goodness. "And you!" I leaned down so the oldest, Ronald, could jump onto my back. "Ooof!" I staggered a bit. They were growing like weeds. Pretty soon I wouldn't be able to carry all four of them at the same time.

The fastest path back into the castle was to run past the door with those squeaky hinges. The other entrance, which was much further away, would take me past the foreign soldiers' encampment filled with those large, dangerous warriors. Passing the warriors would surely be just as treacherous as facing a battlefield. It only took a heartbeat to decide. I turned and ran as fast as my legs could carry me past the opening door and toward the castle entrance.

"Celestina!" someone shouted from the outer wall's door. "This way!"

I ignored the gruff voice. That direction was not the way to safety. Not for the princes. And not for me.

"Celestina! Stop!" Grasping fingers dug into my arm. The force of the grip spun me around. It took everything I had to not fall or drop the princes.

My eyes widened when I saw who had latched onto me.

"Father?" He was dressed in red that matched the capes of the Tiburnians. "What are you doing?"

My mother, who was dressed in matching red leggings and tunic was at the groaning rusty iron door. The door was half hidden by the thick ivy that covered that portion of the castle wall. She was struggling to push the ivy aside so she could pull the iron door fully open.

"Stop her!" I shouted. "The Tiburnian army will come in if you open it!"

"That's what we want," my father yelled.

"No!" How could they? How could they? So many in the castle would die if he let that happen.

"Come with us." He tugged on my arm.

"I cannot." I tried to pull away. "I have to get the princes to safety, especially if you're going to let those murderous Tiburnians in here!"

Mother had her hands on the heavy iron loop that was attached to the door and was still fighting with the ivy to get the door open.

My father's strong fingers clamped on my arm with bruising strength. "I'm going to have to insist," he said, dragging me toward the door that suddenly sprang open. Hordes of those red-caped Tiburnians stood on the other side, swords raised.

"They'll kill us!" I screeched.

"No, they won't. They'll keep you and the princes safe." He dragged me closer to the door.

"No!" I shouted. "No!"

The enemy wouldn't protect the princes. I understood enough of royal life to know that. If the Tiburnians took the castle, they would kill every person inside, especially those with royal blood. If they didn't, there would always be the risk that even one of the youngest princes might grow up, raise an army, and one day reclaim the throne.

The moment I passed through that door, the princes were as good as dead. They might be bratty. They might be difficult to keep track of. They might even have put lizards in my bed one too many times. But none of that mattered. They were little boys. And they didn't deserve to die at the hands of the enemy.

I tucked little Robert underneath my arm and snatched the wooden sword from Rupert's hand.

"Hey!" Rupert shouted. "That's mine."

"I'll give it back, Your Highness," I said as I swung the wooden sword and smashed the broad side of it against my father's head. "Forgive me," I whispered as my father staggered from the blow. It was enough of a hit that his hand slipped from my arm. Freed from his grip, I sprinted toward the small side door in the castle keep.

My father gave a shout. "Stop her!"

A mountain of a man dressed in black battle leathers that were very similar to the ones the boys had stolen, only much larger, thundered toward me. He carried a very real and very deadly-looking broadsword. His shoulder-length jet-black hair gleamed in the sunlight. His jade-green eyes glittered with flecks of gold and determination. And his mouth was set in a straight line. No anger. No bloodlust. Just a cold look of resolve to carry out his duty. That look scared me more than anything else.

No. No. No.

I grabbed Ronald off my back and dropped all the boys to the ground. I fell to my knees and covered them with my body. I held myself rigid, waiting to feel the sting of the fatal blow, determined to protect the princes with my dying breath.

The blow never came.

"You thought you could let the enemy in through the walls at this forgotten outer door when we were all engaged at the gate?" the fierce warrior growled not at me, but at my father. "We intercepted the raven you sent. We already know you and your wife are traitors. But you dishonor yourselves even more by attacking a helpless lady and four small children."

I took a peek just as two other warriors dressed in similar black leathers caught up to the first one. I slammed my hands back over my head as if hiding could protect me.

"That is my daughter." My father sounded like a wild animal. "I was getting her and the boys to safety. You have chosen the wrong side to champion, General Kitmun. The Tiburnians are not your enemy."

General Kitmun? I risked another look. That dark-haired warrior who had positioned himself between me and my father was the general leading the deadly Fein warriors? He was the general the other warriors called *the Beast*? His men had a reputation for leaving no survivors on the battlefield, keeping Perth, the goddess of death, breathless as she chased after him from one battlefield to the next to collect the souls of their brutally slaughtered enemies.

As if the Beast sensed my stare, he turned his head and looked down at me. "Your daughter doesn't look interested in going anywhere with you."

"What she wants doesn't matter. She belongs to me!" my father shouted, which was kind of laughable. My parents had barely spoken two words to me since Queen Beatrice had taken the throne. My father, who looked ages older than the last time I saw him, tried to rush toward me, but by this time the Tiburnian army had pushed through the open outer door and were flooding this part of the bailey like blood from a wound. One of the red-caped warriors grabbed my father's shoulders and pulled him screaming out the narrow doorway. My mother had already disappeared. I winced. Although my parents had never taken a real interest in my life or tried to protect me from the queen's capricious moods, they were the only parents I'd ever known, and I would mourn their deaths. Later.

I'd mourn them later.

I didn't have time to do anything now other than fight to keep myself and the princes alive. Swords clashed and metal sang as General Kitmun and his two warriors—*was that tall dark-skinned one a woman?*—took on the dozens of warriors that had rushed through the door. And more were coming.

"It's safe to run now," the Beast shouted to me. "We'll push them back."

Three against two dozen with more coming? I doubted the three Fein warriors would survive for very long. But I wasn't going to let their sacrifice be for nothing. I scooped the little princes into my arms, surely squishing their tiny bodies as I ran back to the castle.

When I reached the wooden castle door and threw it open, I looked back. The Beast had watched my escape. He gave me a quick smile and winked before whirling back around and attacking two warriors who were at least as tall as him as they charged him with their swords raised. There'd be no surviving that melee for them.

I slammed the wooden door closed behind me. And, after dropping the princes, I slid the heavy wooden bar in place to lock it closed. All four of the princes were crying now.

I felt like crying too. General Kitmun was certainly dead by now. He gave his life to save ours.

"Do you remember where my tower is?" I asked the princes. Robert swallowed hard and then nodded. "That's where we're going. Once we're there, I'll tell you all about the last moonlight dragon and the warriors who have risked their lives trying to find it."

"I'd rather hear about the vampires," young Ronald whined. The vampires had become their new obsession after their nursemaid, Frannie, had threatened to feed them to the nearest vampire if they didn't eat their peas. "Do they really drain a person of all their blood?"

"Can they fly?" young Rupert asked suddenly more interested in the tales of vampires than in the horrors happening just outside this door.

"Do they really burn up in sunlight?" Ryan demanded.

"Okay, okay. I'll tell you about the terrible blood-thirsty vampires that used to plague the land after we've locked ourselves in my tower and hidden ourselves under my bed." Perhaps their tutor had the right idea after all.

Hiding did feel like the only sensible thing to do while the armies battled *and died* outside.

Chapter 3

"Back in ancient times when humans hid in the shadows and the magical creatures in the realm ruled the land, the dragons controlled a fifth kingdom. It was a beautiful land of rolling hills, warm springs, and valleys filled with beautiful flowers."

"I thought you were going to tell us a story about the vampires," Robert whined.

"I am. I am."

"Don't sound like it," Rupert said with a pout.

"Have a little patience, Your Royal Highnesses. The vampires will arrive as soon as I set the scene." While I wanted to linger over the image of the warm paradise the dragons once ruled, I skipped over the parts that explained how peace and abundance had filled the sunny land and dove straight into the next chapter of the story, the part I didn't enjoy. "The vampires show up just as the dragons invited the humans to live with them in their Valhalla—that means paradise. Humans, you must realize, at this ancient time, were little more than animals themselves, living in caves and eating what they could pick from the wild or kill during a hunt.

"The dragons, on the other hand, lived in grand palaces that were large enough to accommodate their massive size."

"You still aren't talking about the vampires," Ryan complained with a lisp.

I mussed the boy's hair before giving a nervous glance out the tower window. The battle still raged outside. The screams of war were loud enough that they reached our ears at all times of the day. Because of that, I struggled to tell the dark tales the boys craved when I wanted to cling to the happier tales.

"The vampires were lurking in the dragon's paradise, at the borders, watching, hating. They hate that the dragons are helping the humans. Humans, you remember—"

"Are vampire food," Robert finished for me.

"Exactly. So, having humans under the dragons' protection was a threat to the vampires. They hunted at night because stepping into the daylight would kill them. They hunted the blood of the humans, feeding off our ancestors with their large fangs. They drained humans until they were nothing more than empty sacks of flesh."

The boys shivered with delightful horror at that image. I leaned forward.

"They are tricky creatures," I continued. "The vampire looks and acts just like a human. They'll befriend you just as sure as anyone here in the castle. Their charms are well-known. You'll fall under their thrall before you realize that it's happening. And once it happens, it's too late for you. The vampire will"—I drew my arms up and then jumped toward the boys as I shouted—"strike!"

My fingers wiggling, I tickled my young charges. The boys giggled until they were panting for breath.

"The dragons watched the humans in their land be taken in by the vampires," I said as I sat back on my bed. "Over and over, clans of humans would be left empty as the night beasts moved through, betraying and feasting on the trusting residents. The dragons would not let this crime stand. They took to the air and started hunting the vampires."

"But it wasn't easy," Ronald, the eldest of the princes said.

"That's right," I agreed. "A great war broke out."

"The vampires overpowered the dragons," Ronald said. He stood up straight. "The dragons fled like the cowardly lizards they are. It was up to my ancestor and her magic. She became the first queen of Earst. She was the one who chased the vampires from our land."

I would have added more to his story, but a loud shout came from the battlefield. We all raced to the window and watched in horror as the armies clashed in hand-to-hand combat just outside the castle walls. And it looked as if the Tiburnian army might be close to breaching the front gates.

"Come on." I pulled the boys away from the window. "I think I have some honey cakes stashed in my wardrobe.

The boys' love of honey cakes outweighed their morbid fascination with what was happening on the battlefield.

Thankfully, eventually, the battle turned. Our allies helped push the Tiburnians away from the gates and back into the valley. Hours later, the sounds of war had faded into the background, though the shouts and cries still found their way into the princes' and my dreams.

Finally, five long days after the battle had started, it was over. The Earst army with the help of the Fein and Asterian allies had driven the wicked Tiburnians back over the border into their own cursed lands. From the reports coming into court, the armies left a bloody trail in their wake. The Tiburnians would surely think twice before trying to invade like that again.

The princes had stayed in my room the entire time, watching the movement of troops from my window, playing soldier with their stolen wooden swords, stacking my collection of books into ramparts, fighting over my collection of shiny objects as if the baubles were priceless treasures, and demanding that I recount every tale I knew about the gruesome vampires while they devoured every bite of food the servants brought up for their meals and snacks.

I'd even lured them into occasionally listening to my favorite tales of the mythical moonlight dragons that had disappeared after the war with the vampires generations ago. The moonlight dragons were the only dragons that could defeat the vampires back during the ancient War of the Magics. But the vampires had discovered an enchanted object that helped them defeat the warrior moonlight dragons. And allowed the vampires to take over the lands the dragons once called home. Some say that one day the last moonlight dragon, with her magic of the air and night, will return from the Great Beyond. When that happens, the powerful dragon will rebuild the lost fifth kingdom and destroy the vampires once and for all.

"Why do you always cry when you get to that part of the story?" Ronald demanded.

I wiped away the tears I hadn't even realized had fallen. "I don't know." The story felt personal. Like I was somehow a part of it. But that was silly. I had no place in a tale of magical dragons. I was only ever a spectator, watching from my tower window, pretending. None of the dragons ever noticed me. Now they were gone. And I was still a gangly, plain-faced Queen's Lady who had only ever attracted the attention of a guard with onion breath.

Not long after the battles were over and the boys returned to the nursery, a summons was sent out to all the Queen's Ladies to attend Queen Beatrice in her throne room. Gah! I tossed down the linen missive. The throne room? That meant I had to wear a heavy court dress. I rummaged around in my wardrobe. The green brocade should do.

"You don't suppose the queen intends to turn today into a spectacle?" my maid Trisha asked as she fought to get a comb through my unruly brown hair.

"She'd have us meet her in her private chambers if she was simply looking for company," I said through gritted teeth as the comb tugged at an especially stubborn tangle. "And Her Majesty does relish her spectacles." Not that anyone else looked forward to them.

The queen's spectacles were often rather vicious and bloody.

I pushed aside the breakfast that the kitchen had sent up. No need to risk a repeat of what happened at the last spectacle when I threw up all over my dress. Luckily, no one had noticed since all eyes had been focused on the unfortunate duke being dismembered by the royal guards in the middle of the hall.

The duke had complained that Queen Beatrice was a cruel ruler. Somehow, his criticism had gotten back to our queen. She'd immediately declared that the duke's words were a sign that he was a traitor to the crown. She ordered him killed in public, in a slow and torturous manner, which seemed to only prove the poor duke's point. The queen *was* cruel to her subjects.

The only difference between me and the now-dead duke was that I was smart enough to never dare voice my opinion of her out loud.

Following a busy morning of preparation—after being sure the princes were indeed safely studying with their tutor, of course—I joined the other ladies as we made our way into the throne room. Rechel grabbed my hand. We walked together to take our places to the left of the raised dais that held the tall golden throne. "Who do you think will be sacrificed today?"

"I bet it'll be another bloody one," Everly whispered as she joined us.

Rechel and Everly were both dressed in dark red court dresses. "We picked the color in case things splattered like last time," Rechel explained.

"Oh! I wish I'd thought of that," I said with a shiver. "Maybe the two of you can stand in front of me when the spectacle begins. My parents won't be able to buy me another if this one is ruined by spewing blood and guts."

My heart lurched. My parents were well and truly gone. Dead, most likely. They'd never again be able to give me the money to buy another court dress.

I had no other means of support.

Everly squeezed my hand. "We'll take care of you."

"Of course, we will," Rechel squeezed my other hand. "That's what friends are for. And my parents have more money than they know what to do with. They can afford to support you as well as myself."

I blinked back tears. "I don't know…I don't know how I'll ever thank you."

"No thanks necessary, you silly goof." Rechel nudged my shoulder with her own. "I would have died from boredom years ago if not for you and your charming dragon stories."

I tried to think of a relevant dragon tale I could share while we waited for the queen to make her grand entrance, but none came to mind. I scanned the room, hoping that would help trigger a memory of a story that would please my friends. The regular assortment of courtiers and dukes and barons were all crammed along the room's walls. Representatives from both the Fein and the Asterian armies had taken places of honor at the front of the room, facing the lonely, elevated throne. A jolt of shock made me jump when I saw the fierce General Kitmun standing there. He was alive and filling the room with a presence that seemed to scream he was the rightful ruler of any kingdom he entered.

"Ohhhhh," Everly cooed. "There's the *Beast*." She batted her eyes and gave him a little wave. Not that he noticed. "They say he kills the women he sleeps with."

"If that was true, why would anyone agree to share his bed?" I asked.

"Can you not see him?" Rechel sighed. "I'd make climbing into bed with him the last thing I did if it meant getting to experience his cock between my legs."

"I bet he's huge," Everly said on a trembly whisper.

"I bet that's how he kills all those women," Rechel said with a giggle. "He rips them apart from the inside out."

Both of my friends sighed knowingly.

I glared at them both before turning my gaze back to the general.

There wasn't a mark on his muscular body. Not even a scratch. How was that possible? The two warriors who had fought beside him against impossible odds were standing on either side of the green-eyed general. All three were dressed in black leggings and a black tunic with the royal crest of Fein stitched in gold on the front.

The dark-skinned warrior on his right was definitely a woman. Her black hair hung in a simple braid down her back. She stood with her arms across her chest and her legs braced in a wide stance. It was a similar stance as the blond warrior on the other side of General Kitmun. I must have been staring at her too hard. The woman warrior's haunting brown eyes met mine. Her lip curled as if she didn't approve of my fancy dress or elaborate hairstyle.

Well, the joke was on her. I would rather have my hair in a simple braid and wear those comfortable-looking leggings and tunic. But that wasn't a choice for someone in my position, now was it?

The blond-haired warrior on the other side of the Beast was ogling the ladies and winking at the ones who would smile at him. He was clearly a shameless flirt and fun to watch, but my gaze kept going back to General Kitmun. The general looked younger than I'd remembered. All three of the Fein warriors looked young.

Young or not, I was grateful for them. If not for their bravery, the little princes would be dead. I hoped the spectacle the queen was planning today involved rewarding General Kitmun and his two warriors. And not killing anyone.

I stared hard at the general, trying to catch his notice as I had with his woman warrior. But he kept his hard gaze locked on the empty throne.

My breath got caught in my throat. Why would the Fein Kingdom make an alliance with Queen Beatrice? What would they gain from it? And why would they send an army led by their best general to fight for us? To die for us?

I didn't like how he was eyeing the throne like he felt as if he had a claim to it. Did General Kitmun—*the Beast*—have aspirations beyond helping a neighboring royal? Had the queen beaten back one enemy only to invite another into her gates?

Watching him made me edgy in a way that fluttered low in my belly, and I wasn't at all sure why. I was glad the war had ended so quickly. He'd leave soon and life in the castle could return to normal. The princes would be kept safe. And I could go back to spinning stories for the boys as we all went on imaginary adventures together in the castle while searching for more shiny treasures to add to my collection.

Was that a sparkling button on the floor? I didn't have a sapphire-colored button like that one. I started edging my way toward the button when the whispers in the room fell suddenly silent.

Queen Beatrice entered the throne room with her royal advisers. She'd donned her largest golden crown, the one ringed with tall points studded in rubies. She also wore a heavy necklace with matching fist-sized rubies.

Should she be flaunting the kingdom's wealth in front of the foreign generals? It didn't seem wise. But what did I know?

The queen climbed the tall dais at the head of the room. Once she'd settled into her throne, she looked out over everyone gathered around her. Her gaze lingered for several moments on General Kitmun. Was she considering him as a stud to produce another child? She'd never used a man from outside the kingdom before, but the heated way she looked at him appeared more than a little predatory.

The general, I was surprised to see, had not even shifted under her scrutiny. He remained with that determined glare locked on the throne as if nothing else in the world, not even the queen sitting upon it, existed.

"We have prevailed over the aggressions from the south thanks to our allies to our west and north." Queen Beatrice's royal round tones filled the hall. "I am grateful to both the Kingdom of Asteria and the Kingdom of Fein, and I will bestow a boon to both your armies. But first, there is another matter I must deal with." She sighed dramatically.

Let the spectacle begin," I whispered.

Rechel giggled.

"One of my own betrayed me. If not for the swift actions of General Kitmun and his trusted warriors, our outer walls would have been breached on the first day of the clash with the Tiburnians, and the outcome of the battle may have had a very different outcome. My princes had been out in the bailey at the time. Their lives in grave danger. But thanks to the quick actions of General Kitmun, my boys managed to escape to safety. I am filled with gratitude for that."

General Kitmun's gaze flicked unerringly in my direction before returning to glare at the throne. How had he known where I was standing?

I bit my lip. He must have told the queen that the princes had been in the bailey. It wasn't information I had shared with anyone. And I knew the princes, even as young as they were, knew well enough to keep quiet about having wandered somewhere they weren't allowed to be, especially after having stolen the oversized warrior leathers from the Fein's own encampment.

The queen turned her beautiful head in my direction. "Lady Celestina, come forward."

My stomach roiled at the sound of my name on her lips. I reached out to grab hold of either Everly or Rechel's hands seeking comfort in my friends' touches, only to find that they'd both stepped away from me and were looking at me as if I was a piece of grime on their shoe.

I was mighty glad I'd skipped breakfast.

General Kitmun turned and watched me with an intensity that made my heart race like a hunted rabbit's as I crossed the room to stand in front of the throne. A corner of his mouth creased up. If that expression had happened on a softer man, I would have called it a smile.

It felt dangerous to turn my back to him, but I had to in order to kneel at the foot of the dais before my queen. I lowered my eyes and kneeled prettily and waited for the spectacle to begin.

Gah! I never expected *I'd* be the spectacle! I'd always been so careful. My heart jumped around in my chest even more wildly.

"Lady Celestina." The queen's voice sounded as chilly as a winter breeze. "Your parents are the traitors who attempted to let the Tiburnian army into the castle walls, is that not true?"

"Regretfully, I believe that is true, Your Majesty," I whispered.

"What's that? Speak up!" she snapped.

"It's true, Your Majesty," I had to force the words around a lump of dread that was lodged in my throat.

"And they escaped with the enemy?" she asked.

"Or were killed by the enemy," I said.

"I doubt that," the queen muttered. "And they are now out of my reach. But you, Lady Celestina, are not. And you, Lady Celestina, will pay for the sins of your parents for your blood is surely just as tainted as theirs. So, I'm afraid…" She sighed again. "Well, I'm sure you understand what needs to be done."

Oh goddess, oh goddess.

It was going to be my blood that would be splattering on my friends' gowns.

"Stand," she ordered.

I don't know how I managed to rise on my wobbly legs when the memory of the duke's bloody and agonizingly slow dismemberment had started replaying in graphic detail through my mind.

Oh goddess, oh goddess.

I should have escaped through that opening in the wall with my parents.

"Step forward," she ordered. She held a golden collar in her hands. It was the same kind of collar the gentry liked to use for their personal slaves.

She rose from her throne and climbed down the dais' stairs to meet me at the base. Her cold hands brushed my skin as she fitted the collar around my neck. I felt a tingling as she muttered an ancient language, weaving what sounded like a binding spell. The collar snapped, magically sealing with no lock or seam. The metal fit snug, not tight enough to choke. As she'd spoken the spell that bound it, the wide, gold collar seemed to merge with my skin. It wasn't coming off. It would *never* come off. I struggled to catch my breath.

"Celestina, you will live and die a slave," the queen said, her eyes narrowing as she ran her chilly finger over the metal encircling my neck. "But do not fret. Yours won't be a long life."

For as long as anyone could remember, the royal family of Earst has possessed great magical powers. The powers didn't manifest until adulthood and only in the women. If the princes had possessed powers from birth, I would never have been able to control them. Oh, goddess. The princes. How was I going to explain this to them?

The queen tutted as she looked at me. "A fancy court dress isn't appropriate clothing for a slave, now is it? Turn around."

I felt a zap at her command. It surged through my body, compelling me to obey her. I turned without even thinking about it. The spell she'd cast hadn't simply locked the collar around my neck, it had also robbed me of my ability to be in control of my life.

Her fingers tugged at the tiny buttons that ran down the length of my brocade court dress, ripping them from the heavy fabric. My face felt as if it had caught fire. She was going to undress me in front of everyone.

General Kitmun's two warriors were looking down at their feet as if embarrassed to be witnessing my humiliation. The general, however, kept his intense gaze on me. I felt pinned in place by his brilliant green eyes. No, not just green. They were the same shade of green as my beloved dragon's scales with flecks of gold dancing in his irises.

Would any of this be happening if the dragons still came to sun themselves in the valley? Would my heroic green dragon swoop in and carry me away from this cruel treatment?

The queen had finished with the buttons. She pushed the heavy gown from my shoulders. It fell, puddling around my feet. She then loosened the stays on my corset and inner skirts until they also slipped free and landed on the floor. I was left standing in a short white shift that barely reached my knees and was much too thin to be considered appropriate clothing, even for a slave.

I raised my hands to cover my breasts.

"No," the queen said. I felt another zap as the power of her command shot through me. "You will stand and be on full display." She leaned in. Her cool breath brushed my ear. "This is for letting my boys enter the bailey during the battle, endangering their precious lives."

My hands lowered to my side without my control.

Tears filled my eyes. I hated the feeling of everyone's gaze pressing on me. I hated the awful silence as the court waited to see what horrible thing the queen would do next.

"Now that this unpleasant part is done," the queen said. I could hear the clicking of her heels as she climbed back up the dais steps to her raised throne. "I have boons to grant. The first one will be the life of this slave to one of the two armies. Tell me Prince Dimitri and General Kitmun, what would your army do with her if I were to hand her over to your power? The one who impresses me will be given the honor. Both armies will also be given eight hundred pieces of gold."

There was a murmuring in the court about the size of the reward. But really, what price could the queen put on their services? Without the help of both kingdoms, Earst would have fallen to the Tiburnians. The queen would be dead.

The general of the Asterian forces stepped forward. He was a prince? I'd forgotten that. And to be honest, I hadn't spent any time at all paying any attention to him where he'd stood alone in front of the throne. His presence had been overshadowed by General Kitmun. The Beast's presence seemed to swallow up the entire space. I directed my gaze, which thankfully I seemed to still have power over, to look at Prince Dimitri now. He had oily brown hair and a long, thin face that resembled a weasel. He wore black trousers and a finely stitched silver court coat that would have made me remember he was a member of the nobility if I'd only taken the time to look at him. He was flanked by two black war dogs that were so tall they nearly reached his shoulder.

The way he raked his gaze over my body made me doubly glad I hadn't eaten breakfast.

"There's not much to her, is there?" He chuckled. "If you hand her over to me, I'd let my men slake their battle lust on her. And when they were finished, I'd throw what was left of her to the dogs to finish off." His dogs growled as if eager to get to me.

If I hadn't been magically compelled to stand, I would have

crumpled to the floor and melted into a puddle of tears.

"I wonder," the queen said from behind me, "is that a fitting punishment for a traitor? General Kitmun, what do you think?"

"No," the Beast said, his voice devoid of emotion. His green eyes were still staring with that intense determination. "It is not a proper punishment."

"Indeed?" The queen sounded intrigued. "Why not?"

"For one, if you hand her over to Prince Dimitri, she would be dead before dawn. You fixed that collar on her for a reason, did you not? If you wanted her simply executed, you could have ordered it done in this chamber. I could swing a sword and end her right now. And the prince doesn't need a woman in a slave collar to toss her to his men like he would a bone to a dog."

General Kitmun didn't have a sword on his hip. He couldn't strike me down as I stood here magically pinned like a bug to a board. Even though I knew that, it didn't stop my heart from slamming against my chest as if it was trying to break free from the horror in this room.

"That's very perceptive of you, General Kitmun," the queen purred as if his describing ways to kill me was making her aroused. "What would you do if I handed this traitor, now bound as a slave, to you?"

"The Fein are a private people. Our customs are not known outside our borders nor are our punishments. So, what we would do is not something I will disclose. However, I can tell you that your—" His lips twisted in disgust, revealing his first show of emotion as he said, "*slave.*" He shook his head. "She would not die tonight, or for many moon cycles."

This was worse!

I had thought that being handed over to Prince Dimitri to be raped by his warriors and then torn apart by his war dogs would be the absolute worst punishment imaginable, but the emotionless promise behind the general's words chilled me to the core. My legs wobbled and shivered as they struggled to follow the queen's command to remain standing.

"This is why they call you the Beast, is it not?" Queen Beatrice said softly. "You are a violent man."

"I am," he agreed. It wasn't a boast. He and the two warriors at his side had taken down two dozen highly trained Tiburnian soldiers, and who knows how many more, before they managed to get that iron door closed again. And they didn't even look bruised.

The queen clicked her tongue. "I think you are exactly what the traitor deserves."

His green eyes darkened as he continued to press his intense gaze on me. "I know I am."

The naked promise of violence made my blood run cold. I couldn't breathe. I couldn't breathe. I couldn't breathe. And now I was going to suffocate right then and there and die in the middle of the hall in front of everyone.

"Stop hyperventilating!" the queen shouted at me. "It's so unbecoming."

The zap of her order shook me. I jerked several times as my body struggled to follow her command. I finally exhaled one long breath and slowly lowered my head. I couldn't bear to look at the general a moment longer. I couldn't bear to look at anyone.

"General Kitmun, the Beast of Fein, I gift you my slave Celestina to do with as you wish and to punish her in a way you find fitting to her parents' crimes. I also give both you and Prince Dimitri eight hundred gold coins as well as the kingdom's everlasting gratitude. I am your humble servant."

The queen was no one's humble servant but her saying that she was did make for a pretty ending for her speech.

"I hope you both will stay and celebrate our shared victory with us at tonight's ball. I would personally enjoy dancing with each of you." The queen made that last part sound dirty. I looked up to see if General Kitmun took her invitation the way she'd really meant. To see if he would welcome spending time with her in her bed. Although she already had four children, she still needed to produce that all-important female heir.

"You'll have to forgive me, Queen Beatrice." General Kitmun

bowed, but not so deeply that his eyes still glaring in my direction broke contact. What did he think I'd do? Run away? "I am a warrior, not a courtier. My place is with my army."

"Oh, poo, Beast," the queen said. "I'm surrounded by too many polished courtiers. They all bore me. I would much rather spend time with a warrior, a real man."

He tore his gaze from me and glanced up at the queen seated on her throne. His inscrutable mask slipped just a bit. "I—" His brows furrowed. "I do beg your pardon. Of course, I'll attend to you at tonight's ball."

"Excellent. And you Prince Dimitri?" the queen said.

"It will of course be my pleasure to spend time with such a beautiful queen," the prince said, smoothly.

"Then let's all go prepare for the ball." The queen clapped her hands. "But not you, Celestina. You'll go with the Beast to meet your sorry fate in his camp." She chuckled as she climbed down from the dais. I felt the brush of her hand on my shoulder when she reached me. "I never did like you. Too happy. Too eager. Being around you made me itchy with distrust. I'm glad your parents betrayed me. It means I can finally rid myself of you."

"*Please*," I forced through lips that weren't given permission to speak, "*tell the princes goodbye for me.*"

"Hell, no." The queen walked past me and exited the room, followed by her advisors and courtiers and the Queen's Ladies. None of them looked at me, not even Rechel and Everly who used to be my dearest friends. I was now nothing…*less* than nothing…to them.

I was nothing to everyone.

Chapter 4

I used to tell the little princes that vampires were the most fearsome creatures in all the four kingdoms.

I was wrong.

"Come with me." General Kitmun's order hit me like a punch to the stomach. My legs moved as if they were attached to puppet strings. My body, without my permission, hurried to catch up to him and his two warriors. The trio headed straight for their camp, ignoring courtiers who vied for their attention. My face burned as I was forced to walk through the castle wearing next to nothing. We passed into the bailey, passed the iron door where we'd rescued the princes, and then entered the area where the foreign soldiers had set up their camps.

"What the hell, Soren?" the big blond warrior exploded as soon as we crossed in front of the first ominous black Fein tent. "What the hell are you planning to do with her?"

"Right now?" The general shrugged. The Beast's first name was Soren? I tucked that piece of information away. "Take her to my tent, I suppose."

"And then?" the warrior asked.

"Gray," Soren said with a groan, "I have a damned party to attend tonight. Let's worry about how to deal with her afterwards."

That gave me tonight. I breathed a sigh of relief.

"You're keeping her in your tent?" The tall woman warrior flipped her long braid over her shoulder. "A slave? In your tent?"

"Raya," Soren's voice sounded like a warning.

"And the queen? She expects you to kill her?" Raya persisted, seemingly unaware that the general wanted her to stop questioning him.

My body tensed. Would he strike out at his warrior for speaking out? The queen would.

Soren simply snorted. "The queen expects me to torture her, humiliate her, and torment her *before* I kill her."

"Sounds like a fun afternoon," Gray said dryly.

"An afternoon? Soren promised to drag out the humiliation and torture for longer than an afternoon, Gray. Isn't she expecting more like a month?" Raya asked.

"At least two months," Soren corrected.

I hated being talked about and not able to contribute. But my lips still felt glued together. That stupid spell the queen had put on the collar apparently didn't let me do anything my owner hadn't granted. The slaves in the castle weren't treated this way. I suspected she'd added this extra bit of magic just to add to my torment. It wasn't enough that I was to be executed by one of the deadliest warriors in all the four kingdoms. I had to remain silent and at his mercy, while he tortured and killed me.

Oh, goddess. Oh, goddess. There had to be a way out of here. There had to be an escape.

My heart started panicking again. My breath was all over the place. I couldn't control it. I couldn't control myself. I needed to escape. I needed to get away from these killers. Sure, they had saved the little princes when the Tiburnians had breached the wall. But they'd done it by brutally slaying an army. And now they were going to turn that killing power on me?

A fast death.

That was the best fate I was going to be able to hope for. A fast end to my existence.

I don't know how I managed it. Perhaps it was a visceral survival reaction that pushed through the magic. One moment I was following like a puppet a few steps behind the warriors. The next moment I was running like a rabbit fleeing a fox.

I had no idea where I was headed. I shoved my way past surprised warriors lounging next to their tents. I tripped over ropes tying down those same tents. But I didn't let anything stop me. I simply kept running and running.

A shout sounded behind me, but it was nothing more than a bit of noise. The magic trapped in the collar buzzed in my ears. It was much too loud for me to hear anything else.

The buzzing grew louder the further I ran from the Beast. The sound was joined by a tightening around my neck. And then…and then…I tried to fight it…but the buzzing and strangling suddenly merged with an insane need to get back to Soren. I needed to get back to him. I needed to be by his side and listen to what he wanted me to do. I couldn't exist without him.

My feet stopped.

I couldn't exist without Soren.

Where was he?

Why had I run from him?

He plans to kill you!

It didn't matter. I needed him. I lived for him.

He's going to torture and humiliate and kill you!

But my legs wouldn't move.

I could hear the pounding of feet growing louder behind me.

Still, my legs refused to move.

You have to get away from him!

I can't!

Oh goddess, I couldn't breathe. The collar had tightened so much, no air could get in or out of my lungs. Ripping at my throat, I stumbled forward and then started to run again. I ran from the pain and fear and away from the world closing in all around me. Away from the world turning black. I needed to get the queen's collar off. I needed… I needed…

In my delirium, I thought I heard the sharp cry of a dragon. But the dragons had left the valley, hadn't they? I couldn't remember. I couldn't think.

A bull tackled me from behind. I landed on the dusty ground with a heavy body on top of me. It had to be a bull. It sure felt as big as one.

"Foolish," the bull on top of me grumbled. The weight pressing me down lifted and I was tossed onto my back. "Shit."

"Why is her face blue?" Gray asked.

"That damned collar is too tight, nimrod," Raya said. "She can't breathe."

"Magic," the bull, still hovering over me, growled. "Dammit, let her breathe."

"Are you shouting at the collar?" Gray asked.

"It's enchanted," Soren, who obviously wasn't a bull, gritted out. "If you feel your life is in peril, Celestina, you have my permission to run from me. I'll fetch you. Now breathe, dammit."

My fingertips tingled. I couldn't really feel my legs anymore. And the world was still nothing but a black shroud, and his voice. I started floating in a sea of nothingness.

A fast death. This was what I wanted.

It wasn't so bad…

Powerful fingers tugged at the collar. "Breathe!"

A jolt of air burned my lungs as the collar loosened. I sucked in a deep breath of air that burned deep in my lungs. My next breath came with a fit of uncontrollable coughing that had me folding myself up into a ball.

"*Thank the goddess*," I thought I heard Soren whisper.

"She still sounds like she's dying," Gray said. And he wasn't wrong. I couldn't catch my breath. I remained curled with my legs tucked against my chest, still coughing as if my lungs were trying to find a way out of my body.

"She's breathing, nimrod," Raya snapped. "The goddess Perth won't be coming for her today. The girl will survive."

"She's going to survive," Soren repeated as he scooped me into his arms. He sounded angry. Had he suddenly realized that if I was dead, I'd no longer be the problem he needed to deal with after the queen's ball?

His chest felt warm. I don't know if it was because of the compulsion part of the magic the queen had placed on the collar making me crave my master or because exhaustion was taking over, but pressing my cheek against the strong plains of his chest made me relax.

"Do you know anything about the slave collar the queen used?" Raya asked Soren. She'd taken her position beside him again.

"Not a thing," Soren answered. "I've never seen the likes before."

But that wasn't quite the truth. He must have known something about the collar. He had enough knowledge of it to reset the parameters of the commands. He understood that the collar was choking me because I'd run from him. That was why he told me that I had his permission to run away if I felt my life was in danger. He was making it so I hadn't broken the collar's rules. He was taking away the death sentence the collar had imposed.

"The queen was whispering an incantation when she put it on the girl," Gray said.

"There's no seam." Raya reached over and traced her fingers around the full length of the collar. "None at all."

"It's a powerful spell," Soren said. He shifted me in his arms. "I can feel it like an electrical current on Lady Celestina's skin."

"Maybe you can learn more about it while you're flattering the gentry at tonight's party," Gray suggested.

Soren snarled. The sound that threatened imminent violence wasn't human.

Gray laughed.

"Raya," Soren said, apparently willing to ignore his warrior's insolence in a way the queen never would, "go fetch some appropriate clothes for Celestina. We can't leave her half-naked in the middle of an army encampment. Nothing good would come of that."

"Right." She hurried off in a different direction.

"Do *you* know how the damned collar works?" Gray asked me.

I tried to answer, but the blond-haired warrior wasn't my master. I couldn't answer without Soren's permission. I couldn't do anything without his permission.

"Why doesn't she say something? Anything? Why doesn't she curse you? That's what I'd be doing," Gray asked. "Did the collar make her mute?"

Soren shrugged. "Still don't know."

"Bringing a slave into our camp is going to cause a hell of a lot of trouble. Bringing her back with us to the capital will cause even more trouble," Gray cautioned. "Especially considering how you promised Queen Beatrice that you'd torture and kill her. She might want to know the details. She might try to glean those details through magic."

"I know," Soren said. "We'll figure it out." He stopped in front of a moderately-sized tent.

"Home sweet home, at least for a while," Gray said with a smile for me as he lifted the flap.

The inside of the tent was illuminated by a small oil lamp that was hanging from the center post. Instead of sweat or blood, the space smelled of cinnamon. There was a pile of furs on the floor that I guessed served as Soren's bed. There was a chair set up at a small wooden table that had papers spread across its top, which was the only sign of untidiness in the place. His leathers were hanging from a hook on one of the tent posts. A small mirror hung from another tent post. A large chest that probably held his clothes and other personal items sat near it. Next to the chest was an assortment of weapons. The metal on them had been so carefully polished that they gleamed despite the dim lamplight.

Soren walked over toward the weapons before lowering me to my feet.

He'd been fighting the Tiburnians in the bailey with that broadsword that lay near my foot. How much blood had stained that blade? How many Tiburnians had it killed? He also had an axe, daggers, crossbow, longbow, several quivers of black-tipped arrows, and an exotic-looking curved sword with a blue jewel on the handle. So many weapons, and yet I suspected he could just as easily kill a man—or a slave—with his bare hands.

I kept looking at those weapons and thinking of the dead that must haunt this tent. My thoughts then wandered to the world of the living and to those poor souls who would soon be dead because of those blades, blades created for no other purpose other than to kill. I couldn't stop looking at them. My body started to tremble.

What would it feel like to have one of those sharp blades cut into an arm or leg or plunged into my gut? That was a question I would soon know the answer to, wasn't it?

By this time every muscle in my body was trembling. *Be brave.* I bet he knew how to injure a body without killing it, at least not immediately. *No. Stop thinking that way.* But I couldn't stop.

I'd been raised in the castle and warned to stay away from the warriors, warned that they were like wild animals that couldn't be trusted if they'd been taken by bloodlust.

Heck, I knew from firsthand experience that they couldn't be trusted. I'd fought off the advances of that horrible royal guard more than once. That was why I'd started to carry a sharpened hairpin. Even with the hairpin, I'd been lucky to escape each time he'd cornered me. I suppose my luck had finally run out.

Gah! This tent wasn't where I belonged. I was a lady of the court. *Not any longer.*

As much as I tried to stop, I couldn't keep myself from picturing the many ways Soren and his warriors might abuse and finally kill me. My legs collapsed. With a strangled whimper that made me cringe, I fell on the rug covering the hard ground.

Get hold of yourself.

But I couldn't. I couldn't. I buried my head in my shaking hands and kept trembling.

Soren crouched down beside me. He placed his callused hands on either side of my face and lifted my head, forcing me to peer into those intense green eyes, eyes that reminded me of my green dragon. It hurt to look at him and be reminded of my beloved missing dragon. "No one is going to hurt you here."

His words should have calmed me. But I was too far gone in my current state of panic. My body felt like it was trying to tear itself apart from the inside as it attempted to break away from the horrors that were surely going to happen to me inside this tent.

"Should we tie her up?" Gray asked. He sounded worried.

"Maybe." Soren's grip tightened as he kept looking at me with those dragon-colored eyes. "I can't leave her alone like this. Celestina, can you even hear me?"

"What did that witch of a queen do to her?" Raya asked. She'd returned with a pile of clothes.

"I don't think this is the spell," Soren said. "I think she's having a mental breakdown."

Goddess, no. I was stronger than that. Wasn't I?

"Celestina, you're going to hurt yourself. You need to calm down. You need to stop fighting me." *I was fighting him?* "You need to stop fighting the spell the queen put on you." The command snapped through my body so forcefully my muscles burned.

Against my will, my muscles stopped trembling.

"Good." Soren sounded relieved. "Now, take a few deep breaths."

Again, the command slammed into me. A heartbeat later I was sucking in so much air my lungs felt like they might burst.

"That's right," he said. "Keep doing that."

Ugh! His commands physically hurt.

Once I'd settled down, he let his hands slip from my face. "Good. Just be calm now." He wrapped one of his furs over my shoulders and then stood. "I need to get cleaned up for the damned ball." He made a shooing motion with his hands toward his warriors.

Neither moved.

"We can't leave her alone with you in your tent," Gray said. "It'll make the men—"

"And women," Raya interjected.

"And women," Gray repeated with a nod. "It'll make them question what you're doing with a slave."

"They are all unrepentant gossips," Raya agreed.

"I don't have time for this. I have less than an hour to make myself look like a damned popinjay for that damned ball."

"You're going to have to make time." Raya folded her arms stubbornly over her chest. How could General Kitmun be an effective leader of his army when he let his warriors talk to him like this?

"Fine. I'll send her to Mary," Soren said with a slash of his hand.

"Mary?" Gray asked with a shuddering breath. His eyes had gone wide. "You-you plan to torture the poor girl after all? And in the worst way possible?"

"Mary will help straighten things out," Soren said before crouching down beside me again. "You will do what Mary tells you to do, do you understand?"

The command didn't hit me as hard as the last one. Even so, I winced before I nodded my understanding. I would obey this terrible Mary. I wasn't a fool. I didn't need magic to know I needed to listen to a woman who could have a hulking warrior like Gray quaking in his boots.

"Raya, see that Celestina is properly dressed and then escort her to Mary," Soren said as he lifted the flap of his tent. "I suppose I should go explain the situation to my officers. I'll be back in twenty minutes. I expect you'll be gone by then."

"Ladies cannot be rushed," Raya said sassily. She winked at me. "Give us at least a half hour to primp."

"Very well." He grabbed Gray's arm and pulled the big warrior out of the tent with him.

Chapter 5

Queen Beatrice once told her boys that she had to be ruthless. That was the only way she could protect the kingdom from the vampires and the other frightful beasts that roamed through the night in the kingdom. That little tidbit had added extra fuel to the young boys' fascination with vampires. According to the royal storytellers, the first queen of Earst had been the first to have conquered the vampires after those evil beasts had destroyed the dragon's fifth kingdom.

The old songs celebrated how the ancient queen had driven all the vampires out of the Kingdom of Earst. But Queen Beatrice insisted the bloodsucking beasts still existed in pockets throughout her kingdom. They lived hidden in nests, waiting and watching for the ruler to reveal a weakness.

One weakness…and then they'd strike.

Honestly, I'd never believed in vampires. The creatures sounded more like a fantasy the royals had invented to make their subjects fall in line, like the tales of boogeymen parents would weave for their children to trick them into behaving.

I much preferred the beautiful tales of the dragons, especially the tale of the moonlight dragon that glowed in the night as it flew large loops in the dark sky. The dragons were purported to be peaceful creatures. Unless threatened, they tended to keep to themselves, unlike the vampires who lurked in the shadows while stalking their human prey.

But the boys rarely wanted to listen to my stories about the dragons. They were much more interested in tales that offered gore and death instead of soft glow and magic. It was probably a good thing they didn't quail away from the violent tales. Their mother had committed countless acts of brutality under the guise of protecting her people from the vampires. And if anyone dared complain, she'd have them killed. It was the way of the kingdom. It was the life the princes were born into.

Historically, the sons of the queen became generals and assassins. They would be as violent as their mother, if not more so. And perhaps one day the princes would be called upon to hunt a vicious, bloodhungry vampire.

Maybe the vampires were real. And maybe I was looking at one now.

For if a vampire had ever existed in the four kingdoms of the Jayden Continent, the creature would look and act like the old, wizened Mary. Raya had led me to her after helping me wash up and change into black leggings and a black tunic that looked very similar to hers, all the way down to the Fein crest stitched on the tunic in gold thread. I'd never worn men's leggings before. Or sturdy boots. The outfit was…comfortable.

I was busy enjoying not having to worry about ruining my shoes from walking on muddy ground when we reached a large tent with a blazing fire outside it. That was where we found Mary.

The terrifying woman wasn't very tall. And her hunched back made her look even smaller. Her skin was the color of moonlight, pale and sickly gray. And it overflowed with wrinkles as if she'd lived more than a dozen lifetimes. It looked as if her outer covering was starting to wear thin. Her white hair was stiff and poked out at all angles. And when she sneered, for that's what she did when she looked at me, she showed off yellowed teeth that seemed to end in points.

Gah! Perhaps this was where the bloodsucking vampires had gone—hidden in the cooking areas of army encampments. Maybe she fed off the blood of the slain.

She had a large spoon clutched in her crooked fingers. Behind her hung a cauldron from a wooden structure that had been erected over a blazing fire. The cauldron bubbled with a fragrant soup. My stomach growled, reminding me that I hadn't eaten since yesterday.

"Don't you dare, Raya." Mary wielded her spoon as if it were a sword. "Don't you dare hand General Kitmun's troubles over to me."

"Sorry, Mary." Raya held up both hands in surrender. "I'm only following orders. Soren said you'd be able to get her sorted."

Mary pointed her huge spoon at my neck. "That's a slave collar. I won't have anything to do with slaves. He should know that."

"Consider her a political prisoner," Raya suggested as she skidded out of range of the spoon.

"Doesn't change that she's wearing the collar!" Mary shouted.

Raya started to run. "Sorry! General's orders. She's yours until he says otherwise!"

Mary huffed and seethed and hissed as she watched Raya dart like a deer through the encampment and disappear behind a series of tents.

"You!" Mary rounded on me with that spoon held at the ready. Her voice crackled like boots crossing dry leaves. "I imagine you have a name. Tell it to me."

The command zapped me. It wasn't nearly as strong as Soren's commands. Those still lingered like a dull pain through my shoulders and down my spine.

"I'm Celestina," I said.

"Celestina, huh." She raised a bushy brow. "Is that a common name in Earst?"

This time the question barely caused a ripple of pain. And I didn't feel compelled to answer. Instead, it felt as if I'd simply been given permission to talk. "No, ma'am. I've never met another by that name. I'm told it's unique. I once asked my mother about my name, but she couldn't tell me why she or my father would have picked it. She can be flighty sometimes. Perhaps she truly didn't recall." But then I remembered the soldiers dragging off my parents. "I think they're dead now," I said softly. "So, I suppose I'll never learn my name's origin."

Mary's stern face softened just a bit. Not enough to make her look friendly. "Next time I ask you a question, I'll make sure it's when I actually have time to listen to all that. I'm in the middle of making soup for the troop's dinner. You can peel and chop those carrots."

The zap of her command had my feet moving toward a worktable set up next to the tent's opening. Beside the table sat two baskets. One was empty, the other overflowed with carrots.

I brushed a couple of lizards from the worktable and then plucked a carrot from the basket. With a sniff, I picked up the sharp knife sitting on the table and then stared at the carrot.

How did one peel a carrot? Did carrots even need to be peeled? It didn't look like it had an outer skin that needed to be removed like a banana or a pineapple.

The longer I stood there not working, the stronger I felt Mary's command to peel the carrots. It burned like a brand against the palms of my hands. No one had ever taught me how to peel anything with a knife. I'd never even held a knife other than to cut my food with a small, not overly sharp dinner knife. But if I didn't get started working on the carrots, the collar would continue to punish me and punish me until I wouldn't be able to bear it.

"*Mary.*" I had to force her name from behind my sealed lips. "*Please.*" And that was all I had been able to manage.

"Speak up, child. You don't need permission to speak around me. Just talk if you need to talk." The zap of the command was a welcome one.

"I don't know how to peel a carrot. I've never—"

"Because you were pampered in the castle. Never did a moment's worth of work, eh? Then this new situation of yours must come as a shock to you." She put her hands on her hips as if waiting for me to throw a hissy fit or refuse to work.

"It is a shock," I admitted. "But that doesn't mean I mind working. I honestly don't know how."

"For goodness sake," Mary grumbled. She stomped over to the table. She picked up the knife and showed me how to peel and chop a carrot. "I'll go fetch Patty to help you. If you've never done this before, you won't be able to get through the carrots before I need to add them to the stew."

I made a mess of the carrot in my hand as I tried to mimic what Mary had done. By the time I started to hack away at the outer coating of my second carrot Patty arrived.

Patty was a teenager. Her long black hair had been tied up into pigtails. She wore a delicate blue dress with flowers embroidered over its entirety, which was quite a contrast to the heavy black boots on her feet.

"Nana said you need my help." Patty looked at the mangled carrot in my hand. "I see she wasn't exaggerating." She pulled a knife from a sheath at her waist. "Let me show you how to do that."

She talked nonstop while we worked. She'd never met anyone who was a slave before. Was it simply terrible? Mary was her nana, which in the Kingdom of Fein meant her grandmother. She had volunteered to come with Nana on this campaign because she was old enough to work. Her parents hadn't been happy about the decision. They wanted her to take an apprenticeship with a healer. But Patty wasn't interested in becoming a healer. She liked hanging out with the warriors. Weren't they all so strong and dreamy? And she was a good cook. She knew that because Nana had told her she was a good cook, and her nana didn't hand out praises easily. Patty liked to cook more than anything else. She figured she inherited that from her nana. Neither of her parents cared to do anything in the kitchen. But wasn't this the best adventure?

I couldn't answer or contribute since the collar kept me from talking. Patty didn't notice. She kept talking and talking while correcting my knife skills. By the time we'd finished peeling and chopping the basket of carrots, I was working nearly as efficiently as

Patty. And my carrots looked, well, they weren't perfect. But they no longer looked as if they'd been gutted by an angry beaver.

"Nana! Where do you want us to put the carrots?" Patty called out.

"In the pot!" Mary shouted back. But she hobbled over to inspect our work as we lugged the basket over to the large cauldron. "Not bad. Not bad."

"I'm so excited to have another girl around to keep me company," Patty said as she shook her skirt to chase away a pair of lizards that were climbing her dress. "I know Celestina and I are going to be the best of friends. Aren't we, Celestina? Do your friends call you something shorter, like by a nickname? Celest? Tina, perhaps?"

I wanted to answer, but since it wasn't Mary who had asked the question, the collar kept my lips closed.

"Go on. Don't be shy," Mary said, causing the collar to zap me. "Talk to Patty. It'll be easier on you if you put in the effort to make friends in the camp."

"I would like that," I said. "Friendships do seem to make even the most dreadful situations bearable."

Patty nodded enthusiastically, making her pigtails dance. "Friends are the best. And I hope we can be friends. There aren't many women in this troop. And they don't really want to hang around with me. They think I'm silly."

"I think you're smart and confident and wicked good with a knife," I said.

Patty squealed and threw her arms around me. "I knew I'd like you! Do you have a nickname?" she asked again.

"Not really." My friends used to call me by a pet name, but it hurt to remember how Rechel and Everly had looked through me after the queen had put the collar on my neck. They'd acted as if I no longer existed. "I'm not sure I've ever had a true friend."

"Well, you do now!" Patty hugged me tighter. "And I'll come up with something fun to call you."

"I'd like that."

Mary cleared her throat. "There are potatoes that need to be cleaned and chopped." She dropped a burlap sack on the ground next to the table. "Get back to work."

"On it, Nana," Patty said with a salute.

I smiled and saluted as well. Mary grumbled something about being plagued by too many cheery girls, and that we were almost as bad as those blasted lizards. As she hobbled back over to her large cauldron, I thought I saw a half-smile play on the old woman's lips.

Perhaps life as a slave with General Kitmun's army wouldn't be as bad as I initially worried it would be. Perhaps it would even be better than court life.

I grinned as Patty taught me how to chop the potatoes until the memory of the promise Soren had made to Queen Beatrice struck like a death knell.

She would not die tonight, or for many moon cycles, he had said, leaving out exactly how he intended the execution to happen. But he had made his intention absolutely clear.

I *would* die.

And *he* would be the one to kill me.

Chapter 6

"Hey, Sky Girl," Raya called out. She carried a bowl of stew in each hand. "Looks like you survived your first day with Mary, which must mean you're made of sterner stuff than most of the warriors here."

"Sky Girl?" Patty came running up with a bowl of stew of her own. We'd just finished helping Mary serve the warriors their dinner. Mary had dismissed Patty and me and told me to go be friendly, which the collar seemed to take as an order since it gave me a jolt of pain that made me rush away from the serving area. The compulsion to go 'be friendly' was why I'd left the cauldron without getting any stew for my dinner. But this time, I didn't mind since Mary's order had seemed to loosen my restriction on who I could talk to. "Why do you call her Sky Girl, Captain Raya?"

"Well, Squirt," the warrior said playfully bumping the teen with her hip, "her name is Celestina. 'Celeste' means 'the sky' if I remember my ancient Eirid language correctly. And the 'ina' at the end of her name makes 'the sky' a girl."

"Ohh!" Patty cried. "I love that! I'm going to call you Sky Girl, too."

"What's ancient Eirid?" I asked, still feeling kind of giddy to have the ability to talk with whoever I wanted to. "I've never heard of it, and I didn't know my name came from some ancient language."

"It's a language the scholars teach at our schools to torture the children with," Patty grumbled as she led the way to a table located just outside the cooking tent.

"It's the language that was purportedly spoken by the lost kingdom," Raya corrected. She handed me one of the bowls of stew.

"The lost kingdom?" I felt woefully stupid. Why hadn't I been taught any of this?

"The story is all very romantic," Patty gushed.

I slid onto one of the benches at the table and brushed away the troublesome lizards. Raya settled next to me. Patty took a place on the bench opposite us.

"It's a legend with an archaic language attached to it," Raya corrected. "We don't know much about the lost kingdom or if it truly existed. We don't even know where it might have existed."

"We know the lost kingdom is where the magic comes from!" Patty said. "Tell her that part!"

"You mean the fifth kingdom?" I asked. *The dragon's kingdom.*

Raya smiled indulgently. "Some say that all the magic and magical creatures in our world are remnants of the fallen fifth kingdom. But again, that's simply one of the many legends. No one knows if it's true."

"And that's where my name comes from? From the fifth kingdom?"

"There are books at home about it," Patty said. "I can take you to the Palladian Central Library when we get there."

"Let's not make too many plans for what you'll do with our Sky Girl when we reach the capital," Raya cautioned.

My stomach churned with that reminder. Patty fell silent. We all ate our stew without saying another word while everything between us turned awkward. I hated the awkwardness.

Even if I didn't have a future, I didn't want the time I had left to be uneasy between my new friends. Grabbing onto the small, shiny baubles of happiness today seemed more important now that I knew there wasn't going to be a tomorrow.

"Patty taught me how to use a knife today," I said, with more cheerfulness than I felt. "I feel rather fierce now."

"Is that so?" Raya asked, giving Patty a sidelong look.

"Oh, it is!" Patty shouted. "No carrot—"

"Or potato—" I added.

"Will be safe in our presence!" Patty finished.

And we all laughed while Patty described in gruesome detail how we managed to slay so many vegetables.

A few tears leaked out of my eyes as my emotions bubbled over, but thankfully night had fallen, and it was too dark by now for anyone to see them.

We ate and talked and laughed for what felt like hours. As the night wore on, the temperature dropped. I started to shiver. What I needed to do was to run up to my room in the tower and fetch my warm rabbit-lined cloak. It wasn't the fanciest cloak I owned, but it was comfortable and what I liked to wear up in my drafty tower. Actually, I needed to get that cloak and some winter wear if I was going to spend time with the army living in a tent and working in this outside kitchen. Winter had just entered its longest and coldest part of the season, and the mornings and evenings were already painfully icy.

And, worse, the Kingdom of Fein was located north of Earst, which had to mean it would be even colder there.

"Raya." I set down my spoon. "Do you think someone could take me up to my room in the tower so I could fetch a few items of clothing, like my cloak and gloves, and I have a lovely sable hat and there's also a small wooden dragon that has been with me since I was a baby. I'd hate to leave it behind." And my collection of found baubles stashed in a hidden cubby under a floorboard. I didn't add that last part. But I ached to get them in a way I didn't even begin to understand.

"I've been told that here in Earst slaves aren't allowed to have belongings," Raya said without looking up from the stew she was eating.

"That's terrible," Patty said with a gasp. "Can't you break the rules, Raya, and get her a few of those things?"

"Nope. It's not up to me. Sorry, Squirt."

"Who do I need to complain to?" Patty demanded. She'd jumped up from the bench looking ready to storm onto a field of battle. She waved her spoon like her nana would.

"Those kinds of decisions would be up to General Kitmun," Raya said. "And he's up at the castle enjoying the queen's victory ball."

"Oh." Patty flopped back down onto the bench. "It's so not fair."

"Rarely anything in life is fair." Raya looked up from her stew. "I am sorry, Sky Girl. I'm pretty sure your personal belongings in the castle will be off-limits to you."

"She needs warm clothes. We can't let her freeze!" Patty cried.

"Who can't we let freeze, Patty?" Gray asked as he came up to our table.

"Captain Gray!" Patty squealed. She jumped up and launched herself at the large blond-haired warrior, wrapping her legs around his waist and her arms around his neck. "You never come by to visit us."

"I wanted to see how Celestina fared against the terrifying Mary," he said with a dramatic shudder.

"I showed her what to do! We had a grand time of it! Didn't we, Sky Girl?" Patty yelled.

"Not so loud. You're going to break my eardrum." Gray shook his head as he set Patty back on her feet and tugged on one of her pigtails. "And maybe you can let Celestina talk for a moment. She has spoken, hasn't she?"

"Of course she's spoken to us, silly!" Patty answered before anyone else had a chance to say anything. "She's my friend. We've been talking all afternoon!"

He seemed relieved to hear it. But then he turned to me and waited.

"Staring at her like that isn't awkward at all," Raya said.

"I still haven't heard Celestina speak a word since we brought her to camp," he replied as he continued to stare at me in a way that no longer felt friendly. "If I were in your position, Celestina, I'd be angry and"—he flicked a glance at Patty—"on the verge of doing something stupid and perhaps even lethal."

I tilted my head. He was worried I might hurt Patty? I picked up my spoon and pointed it at him. "I must warn you. Mary and Patty taught me how to carve things up with a knife today," I said in my most fearsome voice—the raspy, monster voice I'd invented to make the princes giggle with delighted horror. "So, I suppose everyone should sleep with one eye open in case I decide to practice my newfound skills on human flesh."

His jaw dropped open.

Raya turned her head to regard me with a raised eyebrow. "*Sky Girl*," she hissed.

I held Gray's gaze as the tension built around us.

The collar around my neck sizzled. I gritted my teeth against the pain.

Patty clapped her hands and giggled and danced around the table. "Oh, that was good! Your voice gave me shivers. Look!" She shoved up her dress's sleeve. "Goosebumps all over my arm!"

I leaned back and chuckled. "The little princes always enjoy when I'd play with them like that. It's great fun." The stinging punishment from the collar dimmed but didn't fully go away. Apparently, I wasn't allowed to entertain others with my scary voice and shivery tales anymore.

Gray's eyes narrowed as if he wasn't sure whether to believe that I'd been playing around or not. Raya seemed still on edge as well.

"It was a joke," I told them, which did help settle the stinging collar. "And this is a spoon. A wooden spoon at that."

"She's the best!" Patty threw her arms around my neck. "And we need to take good care of her, so she doesn't freeze!"

"We do need to get you some warmer clothes for tomorrow," Raya agreed.

"And what about tonight?" Gray asked Raya. "Where is she sleeping?"

"With me! Please say she'll be staying with Nana and me! We can have girl talk all night!" Patty tugged on Gray's arm. "Tell her she'll be staying with me!"

"I don't think—" Gray started to say.

"How about I take her to my tent for the night?" Raya said brightly, cutting off whatever Gray was going to say. "I can get her kitted out for the trip and make sure our new friend has enough winter outerwear to keep from freezing."

"Thank you," I said embarrassed I came to them with nothing. No toothbrush or brush or clothes or money. I hated it. But I supposed that was part of what it meant to be owned by another. "I do appreciate your kindness."

"But you'll bring her back to me in the morning!" Patty insisted. "I cannot wait to show her how we manage breakfast. And we'll be packing up to leave tomorrow, won't we? That's always an exciting time! You have to bring her back to me so she can ride with me on the cart!"

The army was leaving in the morning?

So soon?

I schooled my features to keep the shock from showing. This news shouldn't have come as a surprise. I'd been handed over to a foreign army, which meant I was going to have to leave my home. *Be brave. Be brave.*

It could be an adventure. I could pretend I was going on a quest to find the dragons, maybe even a quest to find the mythical moonlight dragon. The last moonlight dragon that could unite the four kingdoms.

"Have you seen the dragons?" I asked them. Perhaps they spotted the missing dragons as they traveled through Earst's countryside to reach the castle. Wouldn't it be wonderful to find out where they went?

"Dragons?" Gray chuckled.

"You know, scaly things with wings that breathe fire." I wiggled my fingers.

Patty laughed and wiggled her fingers mimicking my movements, only she wiggled her fingers directly in front of Gray's face.

The warrior gently pushed her away. "There are no dragons," he said.

"I know they stopped coming to the valley a few years ago," I said. "But I was hoping you might have seen where they went."

He looked to Raya for help.

"The dragons died out eons ago when the lost kingdom disappeared, that is if they ever really existed," Raya said as she brushed away a lizard that was standing on its hind legs to sniff her bowl of stew.

I shook my head. "No. They used to come to sun themselves in our valley. There used to be more than a doz—" The collar struck hard and fast. I gasped and reached for the collar. But there was nothing I could do to stop it from hurting me. It sent a fire blazing down my spine. I doubled over in pain.

Raya put her hand on my shoulder. "Are you okay?"

Unable to answer, the best I could do was groan.

"What's wrong with our Sky Girl?" Patty screamed.

"Maybe she's not allowed to lie," Gray said, frowning again. "That collar seems to have a built-in mechanism for doling out punishments."

"How awful!" Patty grabbed my hand. "You can tell me about the dragons tomorrow! I'll believe you!"

"I don't think that's wise." Raya put her arm around my shoulder. "I don't think we should do anything that risks activating the collar again. No more tales about mythical dragons, okay?"

How could the Fein Kingdom not know about the dragons? They were as real as the lizards that were crawling over the table and climbing on the evergreen trees above us.

The burning pain shooting through my body like a million daggers pulsed as if shouting at me *"No dragons!"* and then it started to ease up. I shuddered a shaky breath.

"I don't understand it," I gasped. "I don't understand any of this."

"Stick to the truth around us, and you'll be fine." Gray's voice softened a touch. "Good night."

"But wait!" Patty tugged on Gray's arm. "She was kidding about wanting to carve us up with the knife, and the collar didn't do anything to her then. Why would it attack her now?"

Gray went still for a moment. "Indeed," he said and looked thoughtfully at me. "That is a good question, Patty."

Shortly after Gray had left us at the dinner table, Mary showed up to tell us that Patty and I were on KP duty with six others. We washed the dinner cups and bowls and then packed the bowls and cups up in wooden crates for the night. Once we were done, Raya returned to take me to her tent. "If you need anything, let me know, and I will get it for you from our stores of supplies. I'm sorry you lost all your personal belongings. I can't imagine how that must hurt."

"Nearly everything about this situation hurts like a burr in my toe," I admitted as I followed her to her tent. "But you must know I'd never do anything to harm Patty. She's been nothing but kind to me. I don't want to harm anyone. It's not in my nature."

"I believe you," Raya said. "It's Gray you'll have to convince. Don't take his worrying about you personally. It's his job to fret about threats to the army. He's in charge of camp security when we're not swinging swords on the battlefield."

I stopped in the middle of the path and pointed to the collar chafing my neck. "Even if I wanted to be, this thing makes sure I'm not a threat to anyone."

Raya nodded. "It's late and cold. We can talk about this more in the morning."

We started walking again. The temperature was dropping quickly. The puddles on the trail had turned to an icy slush. I shivered and suddenly felt thankful Raya had given me sturdy boots. Even if the rest of me was shivering, at least my feet were warm and dry.

"There's something wrong about the girl, something unnatural," I heard Gray say to someone in the distance. As I followed Raya through the maze of tents, his voice grew louder. "Call it intuition or instinct or whatever. The back of my neck has been itchy ever since you brought her into the camp. And then at dinner, she did something with her voice. It didn't sound human."

I halted. Up ahead on the path, I spotted Gray with Soren. Soren was dressed in a white doublet with matching pants and boots. The outfit had silver braiding at the seams that shimmered with a rainbow of iridescence in the pale light of the moon. A silver dagger hung from a black leather belt that hugged his hips. The sight of him made my body feel too warm and sort of tingly. He looked like a king. A devastatingly handsome king.

Though it was late, the queen's balls often lasted until dawn. And none of the queen's studs would be permitted to leave her chambers before noon the next day. Seeing him here meant he'd slipped through the queen's clutches. I don't know why knowing that made me smile.

"I don't have the energy to figure out what to do about Celestina right now." Soren did sound weary.

I felt a tug to go to him, to be near him, to rub his shoulders and help him relax. Was that tug because of the collar's power of compulsion and the fact that he owned me? Or did I want to be near him because I couldn't stop thinking about the sharp edges of his jaw or his slashing brows or the ripple of his strong muscles under his clothes. His raven black hair looked mussed. I loved how it always looked slightly imperfect like that.

Raya took my hand. "Come on, Sky Girl. Our supply wagon is this way." She had to tug at me until my feet stumbled beneath me before I followed. "And over there is a conversation we don't need to overhear."

"Wait," Soren called out to us.

My feet stopped as the command slammed into me. Raya stopped beside me.

"Isn't it early to leave a victory ball held in your honor?" she asked him when he reached the slushy puddle in the trail where we were waiting.

"Possibly." He pulled a hand through his already unruly hair. "Probably. I hate the simpering fools and social landmines that are the mainstay of any royal court."

Raya tsked. "The king won't be pleased. He's been wanting you to take a more active—"

"If *the king* wanted a diplomat, he should have sent a diplomat. I'm simply his sword."

"You're much more than that to the king and the kingdom, and you know that," Gray said as he followed Soren. "Besides, the only reason you're awkward when it comes to court affairs is because you won't put in the effort to play the game."

"I hate the game." Soren reached out and touched one of the intricate looping braids Trisha had fashioned in my hair before I headed to court so many hours ago. He ran his thumb down the length of the braid. It seemed like such an automatic gesture I wasn't certain he'd realized he'd done it. "Are we getting you settled, Celestina?" he asked.

I nodded. It wasn't the collar that had kept me from talking, but the bundle of nerves that had exploded inside me. I felt shy and tense, which was not at all natural.

"Have you been given dinner?" His thumb kept rubbing my braid.

Every muscle in my body held still, savoring the light tug on my hair his caress caused. "I have."

"We dined with Patty. The two of them worked together all afternoon, helping Mary prepare a stew. Patty has taken our Sky Girl under her wing and has been watching out for her," Raya explained.

The corner of his mouth tilted up. "Sky Girl?" Just then a stiff breeze spiraled down the path. "Damn, it's freezing out. Celestina, you should have a cloak and gloves and a hat," he said even though all he had on was a thin pair of white leather gloves.

"I'm taking her to the supply wagon to get her all the essentials she'll need as we travel home," Raya was quick to tell him.

"Good. Good. And she will be sleeping tonight…?" he asked, his thumb stilled on my braid.

"In my tent," Raya said.

He dropped his hand from my hair and inclined his head. "Then I'll bid the two of you goodnight."

"Did you see what her eyes did just now?" I heard Gray whisper as they walked away.

"I saw them," Soren answered.

"And?" Gray pressed.

"They…" His voice grew fainter, and I couldn't hear what he thought of my eyes. The silly girl inside me who loved fluffy skirts and fairytales and tales of moonlight dragons and men who gently stroked my braids hoped Soren thought my eyes looked pretty.

Chapter 7

According to the storytellers, the moonlight dragon loved winter and the snow. Unlike most other dragons, this was a beast of the winter. With its pale scales, it'd often disappear in snowbanks. One of my favorite tales told of a maiden traveling from her grandmother's house to the village. The maid stumbled over the moonlight dragon's tail as the beast slumbered while hidden in a snowbank. The dragon opened a silver eye and glared at the startled maid. Instead of screaming or running, the maid straightened her spine. She must have been frightened. The moonlight dragon could have easily snapped her in half with its mouth full of razor-sharp teeth. But the girl had wisdom beyond her years and instinctively knew what needed to be done. She lowered her head and begged the dragon's forgiveness. The dragon had been so surprised by the quiet apology that it offered the maiden its heart.

A light snow drifted down as the Fein encampment came alive the next morning. Watching the dance of the iridescent flakes as they fell reminded me of the story of the moonlight dragon and its eternal devotion to the young maid who'd stumbled across its tail.

I once hoped I'd find that kind of endless love for myself. Foolish.

Foolish. Love like that seemed to exist only within the minds of storytellers.

Though Mary kept me busy serving the warriors their breakfast, I was glad for the ermine-lined cape, gloves, and knit hat Raya had found for me. I filled yet another bowl with porridge and handed it to a mountain of a man. Like last night, most of the warriors gave me curious looks, but a few of them growled and snarled at me like this one did.

"You'll never be welcome in Fein," he said before turning away.

Mary overheard him and chased the man, who had to be three times her size, hitting him on his backside with her spoon as he fled.

"Every group has its share of idiots," she grumbled when she'd returned. "Don't pay them any mind."

Before I knew it, the army had been fed, the bowls and cups washed and put away, and the camp packed up and stowed on the convoy of wagons now lining the bailey yard. Some of the warriors had horses. Most, however, were going to have to march on foot all the way back to Fein, which I'd heard someone say would take the better part of two weeks.

I stomped my own feet and clapped my gloved hands together hoping to chase away the cold. How would I survive living outside in this endless winter for the next two weeks? Would I be expected to walk to their capital?

I touched the collar at my neck that served as a grim reminder of my new lowly status. I'd be expected to walk.

For how far? That was up to Soren. Did he plan to take me all the way back to his capital? Was the warrior who'd snarled at me this morning speaking the truth? Would no one want me to enter their precious capital city? If that were the case, Soren would have to find a way to rid himself of me before then.

But in the meantime, I suspected I'd be walking at the end of the line. It didn't matter that Patty had said she wanted me to ride in a wagon with her. What happened to me wasn't her decision. It wasn't mine, either.

Figuring it'd be better to take my place in the back instead of facing the humiliation of being sent there, I wandered in that direction.

"Sky Girl!" Patty yelled. "Where are you going?"

I pointed to where the foot warriors were milling about.

"No, silly! You're in front with Nana and me! Come on!" She waved me toward a wagon that was near where the officers' horses were being lined up.

Ice crunched underneath my boots as I wove through the line of wagons toward where Patty was waiting. I kept my head down, afraid to look up at the castle, afraid of the emotions that might leak out when I took my last glimpse of the only home I'd ever known.

"Where are you heading?" a gruff voice asked.

I looked up and spotted Soren striding my way. A piece of me felt a wild need to run. Whenever I looked at him, I saw danger mixed with a confusing sizzle of desire. He was a warrior to his core. His muscles rippled with the promise of death.

I had his permission to run if I felt my life was in danger. And yet…

I'll fetch you, he'd also said.

Goddess! I was being silly. He wasn't going to strike me down where I stood. Not this morning. Not until at least a month or two had passed.

I battled the part of me that was apparently the biggest coward to walk the four kingdoms and tilted my head up so I'd meet his gaze with a determined one of my own.

"I will ride with Mary and Patty," I said, daring him to command me to do something different.

He took his time, taking in the sight of me from my heavy boots to the knit cap covering my brown hair. This morning he was wearing the same plain black leggings and tunic as nearly everyone else in the camp. His leather cape lacked any markings of rank. The cape Raya had provided for me was made from a thicker, finer material than his. Mine was fur-lined too. To look at him, he could be mistaken for any one of his foot soldiers.

"Good," he said. "We keep everything important up at the front where it can be more closely guarded."

Important.

I tried to chase the word from my head. I was just as important to him as the sack of potatoes in the wagon. Just as important as the crates of beans. Just as important as—

"It can be hard to leave your home," he said, softening his tone. "Stick close to Mary and Patty. They can help you adjust to the shock of living with my army."

Damn, that emotion I'd been running from all morning found its way to the surface. "I will," I said my eyes filling with tears. But he'd already moved on.

"There you are!" Patty reached down with her hand to help haul me onto the bench at the front of the wagon. She had me scoot over so I was sitting in the middle. "It took you ages to get here!" She tossed a heavy wool blanket over both our laps and placed a warm brick at our feet. It wasn't as warm as being inside the castle, but warmer than my icy room in the tower. "If we're lucky, Nana will let us drive for a while. I love driving the wagon! Have you ever driven a wagon?"

"I might let Celestina drive," Mary grumbled as she clamored up onto the wagon from the other side. "But not you, Patty-girl. I still have nightmares from the last time I handed the reins over to you."

"It wasn't my fault we ended up in the ditch!" Patty cried.

"It wasn't?" Mary leaned over me to peer into Patty's face. "You were talking so much you hadn't realized you'd drifted off the road until the horses were about to go into the trees. And then you pulled on the reins too hard, spooking poor Brian and Butters, sending them running."

"Which you slept through!" Patty shot back. "So it was hardly that traumatic for you."

"Having to repack our spilled food stores was what traumatized me. You're not driving." Mary clicked her tongue and twitched her wrists to snap the reins, urging the horses forward. And with that simple movement, the wagon jerked and started to roll. It took no time at all for the wagon to pass through the castle's portcullis. I finally turned and looked over my shoulder back at the castle. No one had come out to bid me goodbye. Not Rechel or Everly. And not even Trisha, the maid who had been looking after me my entire life. I supposed I shouldn't have been surprised. Still, it hurt to think my friends had let me go so easily.

Blinking away fresh tears, I turned back around and fixed my gaze on the road in front of us, a road that would take me beyond the hills. We were heading in the same direction the dragons would fly. My life so far had been safe, sheltered. But that hadn't stopped me from dreaming about the world beyond the gray castle walls and wondering.

Thanks to this collar around my neck, I wouldn't have to wonder anymore.

"Good morning, Patty, Sky Girl," Gray said as he steered his horse alongside the wagon a few hours into the travel.

"Don't you have a good morning for me, young man?" Mary growled.

"The last time I wished you a good morning, you threatened to disembowel me," Gray said. "So, no, ma'am. I do not."

"Good." She returned her attention back to the gravel road.

Patty flirted shamelessly with Gray as he continued to ride alongside us on a silver gelding. He had two swords strapped to his back, a longbow hanging from his saddle, and a dagger tucked in his tall leather boot. He smiled and laughed with Patty and teased her for talking so much.

"Gracious, Patty-girl, give someone else a chance to exercise their jawbones," Mary grumbled. "Our Celestina has been sitting here as mute as a stone for so long I'm starting to worry if she's still alive. And it would scare me out of my skin to have a dead body sitting next to me."

"I can't imagine anything that would scare you out of a glove, much less out of your skin, Mary," Gray said with a laugh.

"Don't you talk back to me, boy. I've got my spoon under my seat, you know. And we still haven't heard her talk. You are still with us, aren't you, girl?"

"I am," I said, shaking my head. "Don't worry about me."

"I didn't say I was worried." Even though she had. "Give us a break from Patty's prattling. What was your childhood like? Have you always lived in the castle?"

I opened and closed my mouth a couple of times, not sure if the collar would allow me to speak freely about court life. It hadn't liked when I'd talked about the dragons in the valley. "I—" I held my breath waiting to be punished. When nothing happened, I tried again. "I spent my childhood in my parents' set of apartments in the east wing of the castle. My father was an adviser first to Queen Freida and then to her daughter Queen Beatrice when she ascended to the throne. My mother supported my father by building social connections and holding parties and soirees and making calls on important members of the court."

"Oh! That must have been so exciting!" Patty exclaimed. "I've only been in the Fein palace once. And you lived your entire life in a castle?"

"In my experience, children are rarely invited to take part in those kinds of events," Soren said as he rode up on a large black and white speckled stallion beside Gray. "I'd be surprised if it'd been any different for Celestina. From what I saw of the Earst Court, their rules appeared even more stringent than those at Reinheart Palace. Court children are often forced to sneak away from their nannies and tutors to find their own entertainment. Is that how it was for you, Celestina?"

Soren had been raised in a royal court, too? That bit of information shouldn't have surprised me. He had the bearing of a king. Perhaps he was a king's bastard. I'd heard stories about foreign lands where royal bastards would be raised alongside the legitimate children and given important positions when they reached their majority.

In Earst, where there were no kings, only a succession of queens and their string of lovers, royal bastards had never been an issue needing to be diplomatically handled.

I could easily picture a young Soren sneaking away from his tutor like the young princes often did. However, instead of heading to the kitchens to steal sweets from the pantry, I imagined Soren would sneak into the bailey to spar with the warriors. "I'd sometimes get myself into situations that would lead to trouble," I said, smiling to myself. Whenever I found the opportunity, I'd take one of the royal horses and try to sneak out of the castle walls to get a closer look at the dragons. I didn't tell them that. I'd learned my lesson yesterday. The collar didn't want me to talk about the dragons. "I wasn't allowed to venture beyond the castle walls, and no matter how clever I believed myself to be," I confessed, "I always got caught before I could manage to slip through a gate."

"You weren't allowed to leave the castle walls without someone with you?" Patty asked.

"No. I was never given permission to set foot outside the walls," I said. "Not even with an escort. This is my first time outside the safety of the castle."

I shivered as I looked around me. The fields surrounding us seemed so open, so endless.

"Why the extreme caution?" Gray asked, his gaze now roaming over the landscape. "Are there fierce animals out here in the hills like a venomous bangeroo or the relict spiders?"

"Relict spiders." Patty shivered. "I hate those! They are as big as my hand!"

"Eww!" I shuddered at the thought. "There's nothing like that in these fields." *Only dragons, once.* "And the queen protects us from the vampires," I said as the thought came to me, "although there might be nests of them lurking in the far woods. But it's daylight, so I suppose we only need to worry about the bloodsucking vampire killers coming for us at night."

Soren, Gray, Mary, and Patty all looked at me for a startled moment and then broke out laughing.

My cheeks heated. "I know you're going to say that vampires don't exist. And I'll believe you. I've never seen one or heard of anyone who claims to have personally seen one. It's always someone who knows someone."

"Oh, vampires are real," Gray was quick to say, sounding terribly serious.

"But we don't have to worry about them!" Patty exclaimed. "Not with all these handsome warriors around us!"

"Is that why the children aren't allowed outside the castle walls?" Soren asked. "Because the people are frightened of vampires?"

"Oh, no. Other children were allowed to venture into the fields and villages outside the walls. My parents were terribly strict though. I think it might have been because I was their only child. I wasn't allowed to do anything like that."

"How did you go shopping for clothes and ribbons and presents if you couldn't go into the village?" Patty screamed.

"My parents shopped for me. It was fine." But after saying that aloud and seeing the shocked and pitying expressions on everyone's faces, I realized it wasn't fine. I had been jealous of my friends when they'd go on adventures beyond the thick stone walls, and I had to stay in the castle. "I spent much of my free time in the royal library reading." *And collecting my shiny treasures.*

"You should have spent some of that time in the royal kitchens learning how to cut vegetables," Mary grumbled.

"She's a quick learner!" Patty shouted. "A natural with a knife!"

Gray tensed at the reminder, likely worrying about how I'd teasingly threatened to carve all of them up like a carrot. But no one else seemed worried, so I settled back into the seat.

"How did you become one of the Queen's Ladies?" Soren asked.

"When I turned twelve, my parents gave me to Queen Frieda. She was Queen Beatrice's mother. Twelve is the age noble girls can begin service as a Queen's Lady. I loved serving Queen Frieda. She doted on me as if I'd been her own child. She gave me pretty dresses to wear, toys to play with, and sweets to eat." I wondered if the extra attention I received from Queen Frieda was one of the reasons Queen Beatrice hated me. Was she jealous? "It was the best four years of my life."

And then one morning Queen Frieda didn't wake up. The royal physician had called it an unfortunate, but natural, death. The whispers in the halls told a different story. The courtiers believed the queen had been poisoned.

The thought of telling the Fein warriors this part of the story felt like I was being disloyal to my kingdom. So instead of explaining what had happened to Queen Frieda, I simply said, "I was sixteen when Queen Beatrice took the throne."

Over time, as Queen Beatrice's cruel ruling style emerged, more and more of the court believed the earlier rumors. Soon, the entire court started to wonder—only in whispers—if Beatrice had killed her own mother. "Queen Beatrice was only twenty at the time of her ascension." She'd recently given birth to Prince Ronald and had been furious he wasn't the daughter she'd wanted. Her rage only grew over the years as she gave birth to three more sons.

She needed a daughter to continue her line. In Earst, royal sons were useless.

"The queen is only twenty-six now," Soren said. "It's a shame she had to take the mantle of power at such a young age. It might have been better if she'd been given time to gain experience and grow into the position."

"She's kept the kingdom safe." I'd heard the queen tell us that so many times, the words came without having to think about them.

Soren tipped his head as if to say *I stand corrected.* He rode off toward a group of officers on horseback several yards ahead of us.

I watched him go, feeling sorry that I'd chased him away. But really, what had he expected? Despite its flaws, Earst was my home. I wasn't sorry I'd spoken up to defend it. All the four kingdoms must struggle with some form of internal troubles. I witnessed enough court life to know that the biggest problems came from what had to be the pettiest—but most natural—of human desires: jealousy.

Gracious, I was currently feeling my fair share of jealousy. And I wasn't sure where it had come from or why. But I had trouble taking my eyes off Soren as he laughed and talked with his men. They clearly enjoyed his company. Everyone in the Fein army seemed to love him. And he was generous giving out his attention.

"Sky Girl?" Patty waved her hand in front of my face. "Did you fall asleep with your eyes open? My cousin Starla does that sometimes. It's freaky!"

"What? I'm awake."

"No, you weren't." Patty nudged my shoulder. "You were totally sleeping!"

"Or distracted by the view," Gray said, following my gaze to where Soren was still riding with the group of officers at the front of the troops. Soren's black cape fluttered in the late morning breeze. It made him look as if he had a predator's wings.

"What view?" Patty shouted. "It's nothing but fields and more…oh…Oh! Sky Girl!"

"I was sleeping. Totally sound asleep with my eyes open like you said. I do that all the time."

"Right," Gray drawled. "Patty was asking you about Queen Beatrice's magic."

"What about it?" I wasn't sure how much the other kingdoms knew about the royal's powers and how much information about Earst I should share.

"I heard that only members of Earst's royal family had magic," Patty said. "But you're practically a royal, right?"

"She was a member of the court's nobility," Gray corrected, "which isn't technically a member of the royal family."

"Whatever." Patty shrugged. "Do you have magic?"

Gray looked at me and lifted a brow.

"Me?" I laughed. "That would be something, wouldn't it? Only the female line of the royal family can channel magic." Should I have said that? I flinched, expecting to be punished. But the collar didn't seem to mind that I was talking about Queen Beatrice's magic. At least not enough to make me writhe in pain. "That is part of the reason Queen Beatrice is so valuable to the Kingdom of Earst. From the farm fields to the battlefields, her magic protects us."

"That sounds like a propaganda slogan," Gray said.

"Perhaps, but it's also the truth." While I might not like how Queen Beatrice ruled her kingdom with cruelty and death, the alternative—living as a conquered nation under the thumb of a foreign kingdom—would be far worse.

And that alone was enough of a reminder to speak with better care around the Fein warriors. While they claimed to be allies of the Earst Kingdom, I couldn't forget the determined look on Soren's face when he looked up at the queen's throne.

The Fein were not my friends; they were my jailors.

Chapter 8

The next several days passed quickly. We traveled during the daylight hours, following gravel roads through the countryside. Every time we neared a village, Soren would lead us off the road to travel across the surrounding fields so the army would bypass the inhabited area.

I asked Mary about this. She explained he did it to avoid running into trouble with the local population. We were, after all, a foreign army in a foreign country. One could never be too careful.

When the sun started to set, Soren would hold up a fist. That was the sign that the army would stop for the night. Setting up camp involved quite a bit of work for everyone. It was chaotic and…well, fascinating.

While the army didn't carry any shiny objects that might be dropped or discarded, I did find a few stones here and there that looked like gems. I scooped up any I'd find when helping the camp get settled. Not that they were real gems. I'd lived in the castle long enough to know the difference between real gemstones and sparkly stones. Still, the way these stones glinted in the sunlight—some red and some blue—made me want to keep the few I found.

That was why I stole a small pouch from Raya's pack. I'm not proud that I did it. But I needed a place to store my new bauble collection. I tied the pouch to a loop on my leggings. The tunic hung low enough that it kept my treasures hidden from view. Since according to Raya slaves weren't allowed to have possessions, I didn't want anyone to know about the stones. I didn't want anyone to take them away from me.

I don't know why I felt so strongly about this. Perhaps it was because those silly shiny stones were the only things that were mine and mine alone. Or perhaps it was because I longed for a piece of what I'd left behind in the castle. But over time, my growing collection of stones in the small pouch at my hip felt more precious to me than a sack of gold.

I often ran my hand across the bag, reminding myself that it was there as I labored at the food preparation table. Although the work was hard, I enjoyed making meals with Mary and Patty. After the bowls and cups were cleaned and put away—often quite late at night—Raya would show up to lead me to her tent.

"I don't see why she can't stay in Mary's tent with me," Patty would complain every night.

"Sorry, kid. Soren's orders," Raya would always answer.

No matter how late the hour, Raya always had warm water and rose-scented soap ready in her tent for me to use to wash myself, a clean tunic for sleeping, and fresh clothes for the morning. She never gave me orders or treated me like I was her servant.

These are not my friends, I had to constantly tell myself. But the more time I spent with them, the more those repeated words lost their power.

How could I not be won over by someone as open and sunny as Patty? How could I not appreciate how attentive Raya was to my needs? Even cranky Mary had a hidden soft side to her. One sunny day, she'd patiently taught me how to drive the horses pulling our wagon.

Something else was happening as we traveled further and further away from the castle. It felt like my spirit was expanding. The winter wind no longer held the sting of cold, but instead felt cool and exhilarating. As we rode in the wagon, I would sometimes close my eyes, lean forward, and pretend I was flying with my beloved green dragon. With my eyes closed like that, I could feel my leathery wings stretching and sailing on the eddies and currents. It seemed so real that when I opened my eyes it would be a shock that I wasn't actually soaring through the clouds.

"Are you dreaming again, Sky Girl," Gray asked one afternoon as he rode alongside the wagon. We'd been on the move for a week now and the silences between the conversations had grown longer. The snow was falling in earnest today, slowing our progress. "It looked like you were dreaming. Were you?"

I was flying. "Maybe," I said, not wanting to share my fantasy of flying with the dragons with anyone who doubted they existed. Not that the damn slave collar would let me say anything anyhow. And now I felt as cranky as Mary thanks to being rudely pulled from my airborne fantasy. I drew a shuddering breath, leaned forward, and added in the fearsome voice I had developed for teasing the princes, "Maybe I was dreaming about crunching on the meaty bones of my captors."

Gray's complexion went white.

At the same time, Patty squealed and shouted, "I love it when you do that! You'll have to teach me how to have such a growly voice like that! Look!" She held out her arm. "Goosebumps!"

"What's going on?" Soren asked with a chuckle as he rode up on his black and white dappled horse. But then he took one look at his warrior and stiffened. "What's wrong?"

"Sky Girl scared the shit out of Gray with her funny voice!" Patty kicked her feet as she hooted.

"Watch your language." Mary reached around me to swat Patty in the back of the head. "And apologize to the general for sounding like a gutter rat.”

“Yes ma’am,” Patty said, no longer shouting. “Sorry, General Kitmun.”

Soren seemed less concerned about Patty’s language and more concerned about Gray’s reaction to my teasing.

They aren’t your friends. This time the whispery reminder felt real.

“She—” Gray started to say and then shook his head.

“Gray woke Sky Girl up from what had to be a lovely dream,” Patty said, not letting Gray explain. “You should have seen how she was smiling.”

Soren turned to me and gave a look that seemed to say, “I wish I had.” Tiny dragons fluttered in my belly as the tension eased from the corners of his mouth.

“Our girl then teased Gray that she was dreaming about chomping on our bones in a deliciously evil-sounding voice,” Patty continued.

“Is that so?” Soren said, one eyebrow rose.

I held my breath, expecting to see the same wariness crawl across Soren’s expression that had struck Gray’s.

“That’s exactly so,” Mary grumbled. “The girl was teasing the boy. You need to teach your warriors to develop a sense of humor. The way he reached for his sword was ridiculous.”

Gray had reached for his sword? I hadn’t noticed that.

“Gray,” was all Soren said. But it was enough. His voice carried enough warning that the slave collar gave me a jolt.

Gray slowed his gelding, putting considerable space between him and the wagon.

“I didn’t mean to cause trouble for him,” I said. I’d lived my entire life in a court where such a misunderstanding would surely result in turning a friend into a lifelong enemy.

“He’s not in trouble,” Soren assured. “And Celestina”—he flashed a wolfish grin that made my heart stutter—“you’re more than welcome to do anything you want to my bones whenever you wish.”

My face heated.

Mary slapped her leg and gave a rusty laugh. “If you ask her nicely,

I'm sure Sky Girl would gladly climb up on your horse for a ride."

"No, don't tell General Kitmun to do that. I like having her ride in our wagon," Patty cried.

"I'm not going anywhere." My face heated even more. I didn't have the courage to look at any of them.

Mary laughed again.

When I finally forced myself to stop staring at my hands, which weren't doing anything interesting, I noticed that Soren had dropped back and was now riding alongside Gray, who still looked furious.

"Don't fret. You're good for the general," Mary said softly. "The boy has been far too serious lately. I cannot remember the last time he let himself have a little fun like that. Keep doing what you're doing, and I'd wager you won't be wearing that slave collar come the full moon."

Would Soren do that? Would he remove my collar?

That hadn't been a possibility I'd even considered. But now that Mary had put the idea in my head, I couldn't stop thinking about it.

The whispery voice shifted as seeds of hope started to grow. *Maybe the Fein could be my friends.*

Two more days passed. I'd added one more shiny stone to my collection. A round one that was the color of the sun. As the wagon rocked and rolled, I spent more and more time imagining myself soaring with the clouds over our heads. The snow had stopped. It now lay in delicate mounds that somewhat resembled puffy clouds, which only made me think about the dragons and where they might have gone.

Ever since Gray had overreacted to my joke, he'd stayed away from the wagon, making Patty nearly as grumpy as her nana.

Yesterday, Soren rode alongside us for several hours. He kept sliding me a look as if he wanted to say something. But while he spoke with us, he never did direct any specific questions my way. Still, my mind kept circling back to the idea that if I could charm him, he would free me from this horrible collar.

That night, as I snuggled into the furs in Raya's tent, the thought that had been building and building in my head all evening popped out of my mouth without my permission. "What if I wanted to stay in Soren's tent?"

Oh, my goddess. I slapped my hand over my mouth. I didn't really just say that, did I?

I had. And now that it was out there, the silence in the tent felt like it needed to be filled. "Not that I'm saying I wanted to, just that maybe if he…if I…if it seemed like a good idea." Gracious, I seriously needed to stop thinking about how he'd teased that I could do anything to his bones and imagining and wondering what it would be like to be intimate with him like that.

Raya sat up and, despite the darkness, stared in my direction for several awkward moments before saying, "I don't think you and Soren together would be a good idea."

"Why not?" What if becoming Soren's lover was what I needed to do to convince him to get rid of this slave collar?

"It's natural that you'd be attracted to the general. He doesn't look like a troll."

"Not at all," I agreed.

"And he does have a commanding personality women can't seem to resist."

"Like the way he looks at me and I forget to breathe," I confessed.

Raya snorted softly. "Don't let him know that. It would only make him that much more insufferable. I'm sorry, Sky Girl. But Soren isn't someone you want to get involved with unless you're looking to have your heart not just broken but crushed, absolutely crushed."

"Did he break your heart?" Say no. Say no. Say no.

"No. It's never been like that between us," Raya said. "But there are too many differences between you and Soren. I just—" She shook her head. "I just don't see how it could work."

"Because I'm a slave and he's a general? He could free me, couldn't he?"

"I suppose... But there are other differences too. You're from Earst. He's Fein." She said it as if being Fein was like being an entirely different creature. "Look. I can tell you're already falling for him. But if you let this go further, when it's over, you're going to end up falling even harder. Trust me, Celestina. Do whatever it takes to stop feeling what you're feeling for him. Do it now."

Chapter 9

The next day the landscape changed from endless fields to rolling hills and then to taller peaks with rocky outcroppings. The road took us past frozen lakes and across stone bridges that traversed tumbling streams. Alongside the road I spotted stone pillars, many had fallen over or had crumbled. All of them looked weathered and beaten. They appeared at regular intervals, too regular to be natural to the landscape. Ages ago someone must have put those pillars along the road. I wondered what they once represented.

I asked Mary about them, but she just shrugged. "Maybe they're old property markers," she said.

That seemed like the most reasonable explanation. And I'd stopped thinking and wondering about them until I saw Soren stop at one. He jumped down from his horse and wiped away the snow covering its surface. He frowned at whatever he saw etched into the stone.

The next time he rode alongside us, I asked him the same question I'd asked Mary about the pillars. He also shrugged. "They're nothing more than piles of old stones."

His words seemed to hum under my skin. He was lying. I don't know why I knew this. I simply did.

As the afternoon dragged on, the snow started to fall again and the wind grew stronger, but everyone seemed to be in a better mood as the horses plodded their way deeper into the rocky hills.

The sun was still high in the sky when Soren held up his fist, signaling for the troop to stop for the day.

"What's going on?" Mary asked him as she slowed the wagon.

"There's something I need to look at," Soren answered before riding away toward one of the hills with Gray and Raya following not that far behind. They all were wearing their double swords and battle axes and were more than capable of taking care of themselves. Even so, I felt a tremor of unease as I watched them disappear over a ridge.

"What would he need to look at here, in the middle of nowhere?" I asked.

"How should I know?" Mary grumbled. She climbed down from the wagon. "Better get some food prepared. We'll have hungry mouths in search of an early meal now that we're done riding for the day."

After stretching out my stiff back, I followed Mary to help unpack supplies from the wagon. We set up the cauldron and got the fire going not far from where a massive tree was growing along the side of the road.

"That girl has to be as old as time," Mary had said as she took a moment to admire the towering evergreen giant.

"Nah, it's got to be older than that," Patty said with a smirk. "I'd wager it's nearly as old as you, Nana." She giggled as Mary growled and chased the girl around with her oversized spoon.

But after the initial playfulness, Mary put us all to work preparing the meal. Patty went off to fetch water from a nearby stream while I chopped dried meat into small chunks. Mary had set up a workstation nearby and was busy with the vegetables.

"You're going to have to forgive me, Mary," Soren called over to the old cook as he came up behind me. He placed his hand on top of mine, stilling my chopping action. "I'm going to steal Celestina away from you for a while."

"You'd better bring her back quickly. She's the best worker in the camp," Mary shouted the same time that I asked, "Where are we going?"

"Into the hills." He looked so serious my heart did a little flip-flop. He still hadn't lifted his hand from mine.

"Did I do something wrong?" I asked quietly.

When he didn't answer right away, my flip-flopping heart dropped into the pit of my stomach. What did I do wrong? And what did he plan to do to me in retribution?

His brows furrowed. "We need to talk."

Okay. Talk.

His hand still pinned the hand holding my knife to the worktable. Did he think I would stab him? Had Gray finally convinced Soren that I was a threat to them all?

"Find someone else to finish chopping the meat and vegetables," he called to Mary. "We'll be gone a while."

We would be?

Before my panic grew into something noticeable, Soren wrapped his hand around mine and led the way out of the camp. We walked toward a long-forgotten trail that led into one of the nearby hills.

My heart thundered in my chest. I searched for something to say, anything to say. But my tongue felt as if it had tied itself into knots. He kept a brisk pace as we climbed up the hill. His gaze remained focused forward. His lips were closed in a tight line.

He still wore his swords at his back and a dagger in his boot.

Don't be such a ninny. He's not going to kill you. He told Mary that we'd be a while, not that I was never *coming back.*

"What are we doing up here?" I finally managed to ask.

"Sightseeing," he said and pointed to a distant waterfall. "That's Sour Milk Falls. And that,"—he nodded to the top of the hill—"is Cat's Bells."

"Cat's Bells? I didn't know cats had bells." Having never traveled beyond the castle walls, I knew nothing about the country I lived in, which was kind of embarrassing. And it was also kind of amazing to finally get to see some of it. I never imagined there was a landscape that looked so rugged within the kingdom's borders.

Soren knew the names of the streams we were passing and the names of the hills. I supposed as a general for the Fein army, he'd have to learn the landscape he was passing through.

"Bells is an old way of saying home," he said. "There used to be wild cats the size of horses living up in these hills. Mammoth cats, they called them."

My eyes grew wide as I looked around me. "Really?" I'd never heard of wild cats that could get that big.

"Really. Farmers around here have found bones of them. Their teeth are…" He held his fingers to his mouth miming how large the cat's teeth must have been.

Again, I was amazed at how much more he knew about my homeland than I did. Cats the size of horses? I would have never guessed it. "What happened to them?" Did they go to wherever the dragons had gone? I knew well enough not to wonder that aloud.

"No one knows. Perhaps they disappeared along with the fallen kingdom, supposedly most of the world's magic and magical creatures left when the fifth kingdom collapsed. Not that I'm saying the cats were magical. No one knows that for sure. Come, look at this." We had reached the top of the hill where there was a large expanse of tumbled-down stones. It took me only a moment to realize what I was looking at.

"It's a ruin." The outline of what appeared to be foundation walls was still visible in the landscape. "The building had to have been huge."

"It was a palace, one with elegant soaring columns and tall archways and grand halls," he said looking at the ruin as if he could see it when it was still intact and in use. "It was once the center of a large capital city."

"The legendary fallen kingdom?" I asked, intrigued by this mysterious realm that no longer existed.

"No. But wouldn't it be something if we found that?" He looked younger and happier as he walked through the ruins, picking up stones here and there and turning them in his hands before returning them to where he'd found them.

"You're a closet scholar, aren't you?" I couldn't help but smile as I watched him. "I bet all this chest-beating and sword-swinging is just a cover for your real passion."

He looked at me. A corner of his mouth curled up. "But I'm fantastic at sword swinging. And my chest is large enough to make quite an impressive sound if I ever were to beat at it."

"So it is," I murmured. My cheeks heated when I realized that I had been staring at his chest as if it were a piece of honey cake. I quickly turned away and pretended to be extremely interested in a broken design etched on one of the fallen stones.

The design looked familiar. It was nearly identical to the crest that had been stitched on my tunic—the Fein Kingdom crest.

I looked up suddenly. "How far are we from the Fein border?" I asked.

"About a four-day journey."

That far.

And this land used to belong to the Fein? It was once the center of the kingdom? Oh, gracious. Did the Fein once hold claim to this land? Did they now want their land back?

"Why did your king send you to defend our kingdom?" I asked. Why would a kingdom that had been closed to outsiders for as long as anyone could remember and had a history of ignoring the affairs of other kingdoms suddenly become interested in helping the Kingdom of Earst? Had Soren's king sent his general and warriors to fight for a foreign court as a means to assess the enemy and prepare for an assault of their own?

Did the Fein help stop the Tiburnians from taking Earst because they wanted to take the land for themselves?

"It was a diplomatic mission," Soren answered. A muscle in his jaw jumped.

"I see." I took a step away from the etched stone. I hoped he didn't notice I'd been studying it. "Thank you for showing me these ruins. I...I'm embarrassed to be so ignorant about my own kingdom's landscape and of its past."

He stepped over to me. "Don't be embarrassed, Celestina. That's not why I brought you here. I thought you might enjoy seeing some of the countryside and have a look at a piece of the past." He shrugged.

Our eyes met. He was big. A brutish warrior with the power to kill with a swipe of his sword. And yet, and yet, he had this other side to him. He had learned all about the lands he traveled through. He knew the history.

I envied him.

And the foolish wanton girl that lived in me wanted to run my hands over his broad chest and feel the power of his corded muscles underneath my fingertips.

It was insanity, I know. But anyhow, I took a step toward him.

He took a step toward me.

"*Celestina*," he whispered.

"Yes?" My voice sounded odd. Husky.

He blinked.

"Raya told me that you wanted to move into my tent." He stepped away and spread his arms wide. "I…I…don't…"

"She already told me it was a terrible idea," I quickly cleared my throat and said before he could explain why he couldn't…why he wouldn't…why we shouldn't.

"She told me the same thing. But"—he put his hands on his head and looked at me again—"I don't hate the idea."

"Really? You don't?"

He nodded. "I like the idea of keeping you close by."

"You do?"

He moved toward me again. "You are"—he frowned—"unique."

"Unique." My shoulders dropped. He thought I was unique, as in an oddity, as in the girl with the nose that was too large and body that was too gangly, as in that peculiar friend who really didn't fit in with the rest of the group, as in an enemy who might strike when everyone is sleeping?

He swore. "I'm not explaining myself well."

"No. I understand." Where was a hole for me to dive into when I needed one? "No need to explain yourself. You want to keep an eye on me because I don't fit."

He hooked his thumb under my chin. "No, Sky Girl. I want to keep you close because I think you and I might fit."

His lips hovered so close to mine that his warm breath felt like a caress. He smelled of pine and snow and caramel. I trembled, waiting.

But before anything happened, he dropped his hand and turned away. "Raya is right. We should not. At least not until we reach the capital and figure out what to do about that damned collar around your neck."

"Are you going to free me?" I don't know what was making my heart pound faster—the thought of him wanting to kiss me or the thought of him granting me a reprieve from the queen's death sentence and her slave collar.

"It's not really up to me to decide, but I will tell the king about your bravery." He shook his head. "I believe Queen Beatrice acted in haste when she punished you for your parents' actions. You acted with honor that day you saved the—"

He moved quicker than my eyes could follow. He roughly shoved me behind him and drew one of his large swords.

"What?" I gasped.

"I don't believe it," he said while backing up, pushing me to retreat with him. "They-they aren't supposed to be around anymore."

I peeked around him. My heart froze.

Standing on one of the tumbled-down fluted columns was a cat. It had sleek, golden-colored fur and bright green eyes. And it was the size of a horse.

"*It's beautiful*," I whispered.

"Don't make any sudden movements," he warned as he kept backing us away from the beast.

I tried to sidestep him. "I don't think it wants to hurt us."

"I don't think we should stick around to find out what that monster wants to do." He kept backing us away from the cat and around the outside of the ruins toward a path that would take us down the hill to where the warriors were setting up camp.

The large cat stretched its back and then leaped, not toward us, but toward the path. It then turned around and sat down in the middle of our escape route. It seemed like it wanted to trap us within the ruins.

"What do we do now?" I asked Soren.

He glanced around. Anywhere else on the hillside was too steep and littered with too many loose stones to try to climb down. We could possibly climb down the far side of the hill, but that would take us further away from his army. Unfortunately, with the cat sitting where it was, the long route might be our only escape. We started to move in that direction.

The cat moved again to block our path.

"It's playing with us like a house cat plays with a mouse," Soren said.

"I don't think it wants to eat us, do you?" The cat sat back on its haunches and lifted a paw and started to clean itself. All the while, it kept its emerald gaze locked on us.

"I don't know." The muscles in Soren's back tensed under my fingertips.

"I think it's curious." I stepped out from behind Soren and then took another step toward the cat. I held my hand out as if trying to let it know that I meant it no harm.

"Celestina, no." He grabbed my shoulder. "I cannot let you risk yourself like that."

His command zapped through me like a burst of lightning.

The cat hissed.

"I…" How did I explain to him that it didn't feel like a risk? "The cat wants me to go to it." I looked up at Soren. "Please. It feels like something I need to do."

He shook his head. "I don't like it."

"The cat won't let us leave. It's waiting. I think it's waiting for me."

"That doesn't make sense."

"No," I agreed. "It doesn't. I can't tell you why, but I think it's true though."

And since he still hadn't given me permission to get near the cat, the collar kept me rooted to the spot where I was standing.

"We should wait here. It'll either get bored and leave or attack." He tightened his grip on his sword as if expecting the second option to happen any moment.

After the cat had finished cleaning its paw, it stood up. Keeping its intelligent eyes trained on us, it made a soft chuffing sound as it closed the distance.

I reached my hand out to it.

"Celestina…" Soren warned. But he didn't order me to lower my hand or to get behind him.

Ever so slowly, the cat stepped closer and closer. I could feel Soren growing tauter and tauter beside me. I could also feel a ripple in the air. It reminded me of tasting something sweet, as wild as childhood laughter, and as alluring as one of Soren's near kisses.

"Don't strike out at it," I whispered. *"It's magical."*

"It is." Soren lowered his sword just a little. "The magic feels like warm raindrops against my arm."

The cat lowered its head and pressed its wide jaw to my hand. A low rumble came from its throat.

"Is it *purring* for you?" Soren asked while holding as still as a statue.

"I think so," I breathed. Its fur felt like silk. I wanted to pet it like I would one of the castle cats, but I didn't think that would be appropriate, considering how it was a magical being, and perhaps treating it like a pet would be offensive.

It sniffed and nudged my hand. I held my breath as it then sniffed my arm and moved closer and closer to my face. The cat's long fang-like teeth extended out of its mouth by at least an inch. The tips looked as sharp as a knife's edge.

The part of me that had been pampered and locked away in the castle my entire life screamed at me to run. *Run as fast as you can move!*

Which was ridiculous. No matter how fast I ran, that cat could catch me with one pounce.

But there was another part of me, one I really didn't know all that well. It was the part of me that enjoyed pretending I had wings and could fly with the dragons above the clouds. That part of me smiled.

"*You are utterly amazing,*" I whispered to the cat as it sniffed my cheek. Its magic bubbled around me like bubbly wine.

It sniffed my chin, my neck, and then its velvety black nose touched the gold slave collar.

With a jerk, it peeled back its lips, revealing a mouth filled with knife-sharp teeth. The gentle purr turned into a low, unfriendly growl. Its emerald gaze seemed to harden as it turned its massive head from me and toward Soren. Its muscles tightened. Its ears flattened onto its head. And there was an almost musical zing as its claws extended from its front paws. The cat was going to strike!

Soren started to swing his sword.

"No!" I shouted. It came out in that growly voice that I used to scare and thrill the princes.

Both Soren and the cat froze.

Their surprised gazes shot toward me.

"No!" I repeated, still in that unsettling growly voice that seemed to come naturally from the base of my throat.

The cat lowered its head and stepped back. It remained just out of range of Soren's sword for several minutes. It simply stood there watching us before it finally turned. It then shivered and jumped. As if leaping through an invisible doorway, the majestic cat disappeared before it landed.

"What just happened?" Soren asked as he turned around full circle with his sword still held at the ready.

"I don't know." I put my hand on Soren's arm. It seemed natural to reach for him, especially since I needed to touch something real to ground me. My nerves seemed to be firing all over the place from the aftereffects of the magic that had ripped through the ruin. "I don't know."

"I think you do know." He covered my hand with his. "Because you, Celestina, have magic."

Chapter 10

"No." I shook my head. "No." I didn't have magic. Only the royal family possessed magical powers. "My parents weren't magical, and neither am I."

Soren raised a brow. "What you did with your voice, that wasn't natural. You commanded a giant cat to leave us alone. With the power of your voice. And it obeyed you."

I slapped his shoulder. "No, I didn't."

"I felt the magic. It was like pinpricks against my arm. It made me want to obey you. That was you. That was your magic."

"No," I repeated.

"And your eyes. They sometimes glow."

"I—I don't have magic." But what if I did?

Only the royals had magic. That was why we were so dependent on the queen. Only she and her family had the power to protect us from outside forces like mammoth cats or vampires or whatever other bloodthirsty creatures might lurk in these hills. I hugged myself as I looked around, half-expecting something else to jump out at us.

"No one has seen a wild cat like that in centuries, and then you come up here and there's one waiting for us? You can't tell me you didn't notice how it seemed interested in you."

I had noticed. But that didn't mean I was ready to admit I was magical, so instead I said, "It could have showed up because of you, because you are Fein. And then it smelled me and got distracted since I haven't had a full bath in days, and I'd been cutting meat before coming up here. I'm sure that's it. I'm sure the cat had gotten distracted by my meaty scent."

"Yeah, that makes sense. A creature that can jump through portals wanted to sniff you because you smelled of dried venison." He rolled his eyes. "Come on. We should head back if we want to return to camp before sun fall."

At the camp, everyone was busy setting up the tents, preparing the meal, and caring for the horses. Very few paid any attention to our return.

"What can I do to help out?" I asked Mary, ready to be put back to work.

"Take the night off, Sky Girl." Mary pushed me back toward Soren and winked. "I've wrangled up enough hands to get the dinner prepared. I don't need you stepping and mucking things up."

That was how I ended up following Soren around as he checked in with his officers and visited and joked with his warriors. Everyone seemed to love and respect their general.

The same couldn't be said for how the warriors viewed me. I was the outsider, the one who they looked at with wary side glances, the one who couldn't be trusted. I understood that. Of course, I did. Still, still, their cold reception stung when compared to how closely they embraced Soren.

Soren had done his part to try and include me in his dealings with his officers. He kept his hand on my lower back as if signaling to the others that he claimed me. He took the time to introduce me to the men he met. And he'd asked my opinion about various matters several times during his conversations.

None of that seemed to matter. Most of his men couldn't stop scowling at the slave collar. It hurt that they couldn't see there was a person attached to the collar.

Not that I let the hurt show. I held my head high and met their disdainful looks with an air of confidence. I had nothing to be ashamed of. I wasn't guilty of my parents' crimes. Plus, I was doing my best to help feed these warriors. They should appreciate the work I did for them. Maybe the only way I could win Soren's warriors over was to hit them with Mary's giant spoon.

"Hey, Sky Girl!" Raya came running up to us. She was wearing a strange smile. "I went looking for you, color me surprised when Patty told me you weren't there to help with dinner prep." She shot a glance in Soren's direction.

"I wanted to talk with Celestina in private," Soren said.

"And?" Raya nudged his arm while making her eyebrows dance.

"And before we had a chance to say much of anything, a supposedly extinct mammoth cat came out of nowhere to sniff at our Celestina," he said, sounding as if he still couldn't believe it. "The creature was taller than me."

Raya just stood there and stared at him.

"You're joking," Gray said as he joined us.

"Wish I could say I was." Soren went on to recount how it had happened, only leaving out the part where he suspected I had somehow called the cat to me because I possessed some kind of magic.

I was glad he'd left that part out. Gray already acted wary around me. And Raya treated me like her friend. I wouldn't want anything to happen to ruin that.

"The cat jumped and disappeared through a portal? You're serious?" Gray glanced at me as he asked that.

"That's what happened," I confirmed.

Gray shook his head, sending his shaggy dark blond hair flying about his head. "You could have been killed, Soren."

"I would like to think I'd have put up a bit of a fight before that happened," Soren countered with a half-smirk.

"Still, you left without any of us and put yourself at risk," Gray growled. "You shouldn't have done that."

Soren, who had ignored or laughed off pretty much every bit of disrespect both Gray and Raya tossed at him since I'd joined them, went tense. "I am the general of the entire fucking army of Fein. I don't answer to you."

"You are also—" Gray started.

"Done here," Soren finished with an angry slash of his hand. "Unless you want to start something between us. We are done here."

He stalked off, leaving me behind.

I knew I shouldn't feel upset about it. It wasn't as if I expected him to invite me into his tent that night. Well, actually, that wasn't true. I had wound myself up all evening. With each brush of his hand and each time he touched my back, my arm, my face, my body grew tauter. So, when he left abruptly like that, like he'd forgotten I was there, the cold he left behind prickled my skin.

"It's late," I said, hugging myself. "I'm going to go find my bed."

"I'll show you where my tent is set up," Raya offered, for which I was grateful. I wouldn't have known where to go if she hadn't.

Later that night, as I snuggled into the warm furs, my thoughts drifted back to the idea that I might have some hidden magic. Gah! I could make a growly voice only because I'd invented the voice to scare and entertain the princes, not because of some secret power lurking deep within me. Sure, it would be nice to think there was something about me that was special, that I had powers like the queen. Who wouldn't want that to be true?

But honestly, other than becoming the former queen's pet, there wasn't anything about me that made me stand out. I wasn't pretty. I didn't possess any amazing physical skills. And even though I enjoyed reading, my mind wasn't nearly as sharp as many in the court. I had trouble remembering facts and figures.

I was simply me. Normal me.

Not that I had anything to be ashamed of. There were advantages to being average. No one expected too much. No one pestered me to do things for them. And on most days, I could skate by without being picked on by the queen. I truly believed my averageness was the reason I'd survived this long in Queen Beatrice's court. She would have surely struck me down ages ago if there'd been something, *anything* about me that made me stand out.

"Out with it, Sky Girl," Raya said from her pile of furs on the other side of the tent.

"Out with what?" I asked as we lay there in the dark.

"Neither of us will get any sleep if you keep tossing and turning like that. Are you fretting because Soren pulled you aside to let you down easily? Because if you are, don't take it personally."

"What?" Now she got me thinking about *that* too! "No, I'm…"

"It's for the best that the two of you keep your distance."

"He didn't… I mean…" I sighed. "He told me he didn't hate the idea of sharing his tent with me."

"That nimrod." Raya groaned. "He shouldn't have said that."

"But he did. And then we didn't get to finish talking about it because that mammoth cat showed up. And afterward he stalked off when Gray insulted him about needing to have minders follow him around."

"We're not minders," Raya corrected. "And Gray was right. Soren shouldn't go wandering off alone, putting his life at risk like that. Who knows what kind of trouble he might have encountered."

"It was a mammoth cat. That was the trouble he encountered. And it turned out fine." Except that Gray's overreaction had ruined my chance to move into Soren's tent and perhaps even convince the general to release me from the slave collar. Or had something else changed Soren's mind about sharing his furs with me? He believed I had magic, and even if that was bonkers, people often became wary around magic. The unpredictable nature of supernatural powers seemed to make everyone edgy. Even me.

Especially me.

I wasn't magic.

Queen Beatrice was magic.

She'd put this damned collar on me with those powers of hers. That alone was reason enough to not want to have anything to do with those kinds of powers.

If the cat sensed any kind of magic on me, it had to be from the collar and the queen's spell that stripped away my free will.

Did I even like Soren? Or was my attraction a product of the collar?

"Go to sleep, Sky Girl," Raya said with a yawn. "I'll help you face your relationship troubles with our cranky general tomorrow."

I tried to close my eyes and drift off. I truly did. But sleep refused to come. Every time I closed my eyes, the mammoth cat's wide golden head appeared. I could still smell its warm breath on my face. I could still feel its silky fur as it brushed against me. It had sniffed the magic on my slave collar and then hissed at Soren as if the collar had been his doing.

Whether I liked it or not, Queen Beatrice had made certain Soren and I were irrevocably linked together. The more I thought about what the queen had done, the more I realized my body liked the idea of being linked with Soren.

It liked it a lot.

Chapter 11

The next day we rode further into the jagged mountains. By the time we stopped for the night, we were surrounded by boulders the size of the wagons and rocky crags loomed in the distance. While the army rushed about to set up tents, a cold breeze rushed down from those crags and cut through my clothes. Something tinged the air in this rugged part of the countryside. It smelled metallic and unfriendly. Not that I recognized the scent. I didn't. But it triggered an instinctual part of me that made me uneasy.

Everyone else in the camp seemed to be reacting the same way. Tempers were short. Voices sharp. At least a half dozen fights had broken out in the past half hour.

"It's going to be a long night," Mary cautioned. She scanned the surrounding hillsides that looked as if they'd been soaked in blood as the sun dropped lower and lower on the horizon. "Keep close to the kitchen area and keep your head down. I don't need either you or Patty getting yourselves in trouble, you hear me?"

"Yes, ma'am," I said as the collar gave me a little jolt. "Do you know what's going on?"

"Just a bad feeling," Mary answered. "Something's not right out there." She looked over her shoulder at me for a moment and then nodded as if satisfied by what she saw in my expression. "I wish I could trust Patty to be as sensible as you seem to be, Sky Girl. You're always doing as you're told."

"I'm sure she'll be careful tonight." At least I hoped that was the truth. Patty was taking her time fetching water from a nearby stream, which clearly had Mary worried.

Mary ordered me to start chopping onions. Patty still hadn't returned by the time I'd finished the task. Granted, I'm a quick learner and with Patty's help, was now quite skilled with the knife. Mary, I noticed, kept looking toward the stream.

As I started working on peeling potatoes, I spotted Raya. Without missing a beat with my peeling, I called out to her.

"What's up, Sky Girl?" she asked after she'd joined me at the prep table.

I tossed a large, cleanly peeled potato into a basket. *"It's Patty,"* I whispered. *"She's not returned from the stream."*

"I'll tan that girl's hide when I see her," Mary grumbled as if she'd heard me, which I knew she hadn't. Mary was over near the iron kettle, mixing herbs for a concoction that she said should keep the demons at bay. And her hearing couldn't possibly be keen enough to hear what I was whispering.

"Mary's worried," I added.

"I can imagine." Raya clasped my shoulder. "I'll go see if I can't find her."

"Thank you," I said, my hands not slowing as I peeled the next potato in the sack. "I hope everything is okay."

"I do, too." Raya looked concerned. She hadn't gotten far from the kitchen area when she started rubbing the back of her neck as if trying to calm the tiny hairs there that had suddenly decided to stand up.

I was just finishing up with the potatoes when Raya returned with her arm slung over Patty's shoulder. Patty kept her gaze trained down on the ground.

"And where have you been, missy?" Mary rounded on her

granddaughter with such ferocity that I felt an urge to run over to step between them. But the collar wouldn't allow it.

"I-I—" Patty stammered.

"Gray waylaid her," Raya said. "He needed an extra hand with some of the tents."

"Is that so?" Mary lifted her oversized spoon and made an aggressive move toward Raya. "You let that simpering warrior know he can't have my staff. Not if he wants to eat."

Raya threw her hands in the air and danced out of hitting range. "It won't happen again." She shared a look with Patty who nodded sadly. "I promise."

Patty set down the bucket of water, ducked under her grandmother's raised arm and spoon, and hurried over to my side. She pulled her knife from the sheath at her belt and got right to work on a potato.

Mary watched for a bit as we worked in silence. I could feel the nervous energy coming off Patty as if it were heat from the sun. After a bit, Mary shook her head. "Girls!" she scoffed and got back to work on her foul-smelling concoction.

"*What happened?*" I whispered to Patty.

"I don't want to talk about it."

I nudged her arm. "This is me. A slave who's drooling after the general of your army. Clearly, this is a no-judgement zone."

Patty turned and looked me up and down. "You're more than a slave. And you, at least, have a shot with General Kitmun." She blew out a frustrated breath. "I'm just a mewling kid, apparently."

"Did Gray say that?" My fingers tightened on the hilt of my knife. I'd watched Patty flirt and flash Gray sunny smiles day after day. The warrior sometimes encouraged her, sometimes laughed with her, and sometimes ignored her. It had to be like getting stuck in an emotional cyclone for Patty.

"He—" She sniffled.

"Is a brainless jerk," I finished for her.

The collar gave me a light jolt of warning. Insulting others must not be proper slave behavior. Well, I didn't care. Patty was my friend. And I'd stand up for her every chance I got.

Patty blinked away the tears that were swimming in her eyes. "He is, isn't he?" She tried out a weak smile.

"And blind," I added. Another jolt. "And he smells. Haven't you noticed how bad he smells? Like a sweaty horse?" And yet another jolt. My spine jerked.

Patty giggled.

After we finished peeling the huge sack of potatoes, Patty said, "Thank you, Sky Girl." She squeezed my hand. The warmth that filled me from her friendship made any amount of punishment worth it.

Tensions remained high throughout the evening, especially after the meal. Though the sun had set hours ago, the moon refused to rise and the stars kept their distance. The night pressed down on everyone like a scratchy blanket.

Mary grumbled and swung her spoon around with added fierceness. She put extra warriors to work alongside Patty and me washing the bowls and cups. I didn't mind. More hands would mean the work would get done quicker.

I'd only seen Soren from a distance today. And I itched to go searching for him. It wasn't only because the collar fueled a constant need to be at his side. I wanted to be near him, to find out if he still welcomed the idea of me moving into his tent. I wondered what it would be like to sleep next to someone so large and muscular. I wondered what it would be like to kiss him.

Would he be gentle? Or would his kisses feel like attacks against my virginity? Would I prefer slow and careful or wild and overwhelming?

Would his lips even feel soft against mine? Every other piece of him seemed so hard and unyielding. How could there be a part of him that was soft? Oh, I'd never been kissed. Only groped by that idiot royal guard who seemed to think I'd like that kind of thing. I imagined that Soren's hands would glide over my body as if he knew what he was doing when he touched a woman. I would like that. I would welcome that. It would be like—

A shout startled me. It was followed by a sharp cry of pain.

Were the warriors fighting again?

"Run!" someone yelled off to my left. "It's a swarm of chort!"

"Chort?" Patty cried. She dropped the bowl she'd been washing. It splashed into the washbasin as she ran to find Mary.

I looked around. The other warriors helping with the dishes had already fled, charging toward the fighting.

Chort? I hadn't really believed they existed, not outside the realm of the storytellers who visited the castle. Chorts were supposedly mindless beasts who roamed through the countryside in large swarms, eating their way through herds of deer and sometimes even attacking small villages. And they were notoriously difficult to kill.

Their thick gray fur was purportedly as strong as steel. They ran faster than the eye could see. They could stand on their long, powerful hind legs, but when they ran, they would get down on all fours and run as fast as a jackrabbit. A long-toothed, bloodthirsty jackrabbit. And they possessed magic. They could jump through time and space with deadly precision. At least that was what the last storyteller who visited the castle had told us.

I supposed I would soon find out which parts of the tales were true.

A group of warriors rushed past me, some gathering up weapons, others securing stores of food. I remained at the water basin, scrubbing a particularly crusty bowl. Mary had told me—and the other warriors helping with the washing—to not move until the dishes were clean. Soren had told me I could run if I felt my life was in danger.

Was my life in danger?

I paused long enough to survey the area around me. No chorts. No warriors, either. Everyone had run off to other parts of the camp, presumably to where the chorts were attacking. My life must not have been in imminent peril since the collar seemed determined to make me stay until I finished my task.

That was why I remained glued to my spot at the washtub, scrubbing dishes. I moved like an automaton. Scrub a bowl, set it aside, pick up another bowl. There were shouts in the other parts of the camp. A distant cry of pain. Scrub out a cup, set it aside, pick up another. The battle for the camp wasn't happening here. I wasn't in danger, and Mary had given me this task, a task that seemed impossible now that I was the only one left to wash the army's endless stack of dirty dishes. This was going to take forever.

The collar sent a shock of pain down my back, urging me to work faster. I dipped the crusty bowl into the water again and started to scrub harder.

The sounds of fighting seemed to grow louder, but there was no sign that it was coming close to me. I wondered how many chorts arrived in a swarm. One storyteller had recounted how a chort attack had completely wiped out an entire herd of deer in less than an hour, leaving only clean bones in their wake. Storytellers often embellished their tales. I knew that. But still…how many chorts had to be out there to keep the warriors fighting them for this long?

A shiver tiptoed down my spine as I started to work on yet another crusty bowl. What did the warriors do to these bowls to make them so hard to clean? Were they storing them in their packs for the day?

A hot breath curled around my neck. I dropped the bowl in the water, splashing myself as I spun around and came face to face with a chort.

It stood on its hind legs and towered nearly a full foot over me. It had a long snout and so many sharp teeth that its mouth could barely contain them all. The silvery fur covering its entire body clumped into sharp points. Not something I'd want to pet.

Its yellow eyes stared at me, pinning me in place, as the beast continued to stand there sniffing me. My heart knew what to do. It started beating at double speed like it wanted to burst through my chest and escape the danger.

The creature lifted its paw. The claws on that thing looked like a series of curving knife blades.

I was so, so dead.

"*Help!*" I tried to call. But it only came out as a whimper. "*Help!*" Came another strangled whimper. Something inside me knew instinctually that making any loud sounds or sudden movements would end badly for me.

And yet, dead was dead.

The chort bent toward me and sniffed my hair. Its breath smelled like rotten meat. If I hadn't been so frightened, I would have gagged. It lowered its head and continued sniffing my face and down my neck. It was just about at the slave collar when I couldn't take it any longer. I swatted at the muzzle, hoping to push it away.

Big. Mistake.

The chort snarled and snapped at my hand. Damn, that hurt! I cradled my stinging fingers against my chest. Ow! Ow! Ow!

Still growling, it drew back its lips to show more of its wickedly long teeth.

"No!" I instinctively growled in that scary voice the princes loved but had worked to startle the giant mammoth cat.

The chort's yellow eyes widened.

"Get away from me!" I ordered, still using my silly growly voice.

The beast jerked its huge body back, knocking over the neat stacks of cleaned bowls and cups, sending them tumbling onto the slushy ground.

Dammit! It was going to take me forever to gather those up and clean them again. "You heard me! Get out of here!" I growled.

The chort shook its head and then, much like the mammoth cat had, disappeared into nothingness.

My shoulders sagged with the sudden weight of relief. It was gone. But it had left me with a huge mess. Still holding my stinging hand to my chest. I went about collecting the spilled bowls and cups. I'd be lucky to get them all cleaned by morning.

Chapter 12

"What are you doing?" Mary shouted when she returned to the kitchen area. She'd been gone forever. The sky had already started to turn gray in advance of the sun's rise.

"I-I'm working as quickly as I can." The collar kept a dull ache shooting down my neck and shoulders, reminding me the pain would increase if I let myself collapse before the job was completed. "The chort knocked the bowls and cups to the ground, so I had to start over. And it's just me. No one came back to help."

Mary grunted before turning around and leaving.

When she returned, she'd brought Soren with her.

"I swear," I cried. The collar seemed to pump up the pain level as Soren got closer. "I'm working as fast as possible."

"At first I thought our Sky Girl was simply a conscientious worker," Mary grumbled. "Which shocked me, since none of the louts in this camp know what that means."

Soren crossed his arms and watched as I washed and rinsed bowl after bowl. The pile of dirty bowls and cups had been enormous. I'd worked on cleaning them all night, and I still had a small mountain of them to get through.

"I'm sure she's working hard because she's grateful for the rescue. It couldn't have been easy living with that nest of vipers Queen Beatrice has gathered around her," Soren said.

Mary spat on the ground. "Gratitude has nothing to do with what's happening over there. She'd work herself into the grave if I didn't stop her."

"I know it may seem—" he started.

"Celestina, stop," Mary said.

The command zapped through me. I set down the cup I'd been scrubbing and stood with my arms at my side waiting to be told what to do next. And I hated every moment of it.

Soren shook his head. "She's good at following orders. I wish all my warriors were as well trained."

"That's the thing, isn't it?" Mary said. "None of your highly trained warriors act this way. They don't, General Kitmun, because how she's acting isn't natural. The collar's controlling her and having her follow orders like a robot. If one of your warriors was tired from doing their chores for me, they'd sit down. There's a chair right there for breaks. She hasn't used it once. Last night I asked her to wash the dishes. I meant to come back with the team of warriors who had run off to fight the chort. You and I both know the job is too big for one person and besides which your warriors are pigs. But what with the attack, your warriors were otherwise occupied. Even I couldn't get back until a few moments ago. Look at her hands."

"They're bleeding," Soren said as he approached me.

He carefully lifted my water-soaked hands and studied them. The skin had torn on my fingertips from scrubbing the dishes for hours and hours without stopping. And the skin on my right hand where I'd tried to push the chort away was—

"Oh, goddess! Is that…bone?" I cried. The flesh on two of my fingers looked as if it had been ripped off down to the white of my bone. That chort. It had bitten me. I'd forgotten. I'd been too busy scrubbing those stupid bowls to pay much attention to the harm the chort had done when it had snapped at me. But now that I saw my fingers. Goddess. It looked bad. My head started to spin. I was-I was going to faint.

Soren looked at me with those compelling green eyes. I could lose myself in his eyes. "Oh, it's not that bad," he said. His voice seemed to rumble through my body. The pain throbbing in my hands eased up. And I no longer felt like I was going to pass out. He smiled gently at me. "It's barely a scratch."

"Is it?" My voice trembled.

He nodded as he pressed a clean dishcloth to the injured fingers. It stung, but not as badly as I'd expected it to. When he lifted the washcloth, I saw he was right. The cuts really weren't that deep. The skin had been worn off a bit, which made my fingertips bloody. I must have imagined that the flesh had been torn or that I could see the bones where the chort had bitten my fingers. "I bet it barely hurts anymore." Again, his voice felt strange. It seemed to push through my body. But he was right. I barely noticed the pain.

"The collar uses compulsion," Mary said.

His eyes flashed surprise. "Impossible," he said as he lightly ran his callus thumb over a shallow sore on my forefinger. I shivered. "Only vamp—" He stopped whatever he was going to say and frowned at me. His frown deepened as he used clean dishcloths as makeshift dressings to bandage my sore hands. He worked with the skill of a man who clearly had a great deal of experience tending injuries. "No magic can create a compulsion like a vampire."

"Test it," Mary said.

He continued to frown at me. "It's impossible. And she needs a healer."

"Fine. I'll show you," Mary grumbled. "Celestina, dance a jig."

Goddess, no. I hated—

My body jerked into action. I grimaced and pulled away from Soren. My feet moved to the beat of a silent song as I started to dance in tight circles away from the piles of bowls and cups. My boots stomped through the muddy ground to a one-two-three beat. My feet, which were already throbbing from standing on them all night, screamed in pain.

"Girl, smile as you dance," Mary said.

Dammit, though I fought it, a grin pulled at my unhappy lips. I hoped Mary could see the promise of violence burning in my eyes. I hated being moved about like a puppet.

"Just because she does as you say, doesn't mean she's been compelled. She might simply be terrified at what you might do to her if she doesn't obey. We're all terrified of you, Mary," Soren said, although his frown had deepened.

"Celestina, would you like to stop dancing?" Mary asked me.

"Yes, please. I'm exhausted. And I really don't like the jig. It's a common dance. And—"

"Stop talking," Mary barked.

My lips closed.

"She's really a chatterbox if you let her talk," Mary said. She then called over young Patty. "Tell Celestina to stop dancing, dear."

"Stop dancing, Celestina," Patty shouted.

Nothing happened. My feet kept spinning. Tears sprang to my eyes.

"Stop!" Soren shouted.

The command slammed into me with such force I collapsed to the ground. Panting, I tried to drag myself back to my feet, but my body refused to cooperate. It wasn't the collar's compulsion that kept me from doing what I wanted to do. It was exhaustion.

"You told her to obey me, didn't you, General Kitmun?" Mary said. "That's why she follows my commands as quickly as she follows yours, but Patty's command meant nothing. No one else can compel her unless you tell Celestina to obey them."

Soren dragged a hand through his hair, tugging at the ends in frustration. "Thank you for pointing this out to me, Mary," he said, he sounded defeated. "Please, send a healer to my tent." He scooped me up into his arms. I didn't mind. I liked it there. He was strong and warm, and my body ached so wretchedly. "We could probably use some of your healing tea as well," he called over his shoulder to Mary as he carried me away from the basin of soapy water and those never-ending piles of bowls and cups.

After we'd gone several yards, he looked down at me. "You're a chatterbox?"

I nodded. I wanted to tell him how my incessant talking used to try my nanny's patience and how my love of talking would be a way for me to entertain the princes. They so enjoyed hearing my stories. I wanted to tell him how my friends used to tease me and call me Swift Tongue because when I got excited I talked so fast that they had trouble understanding what I was saying. I wanted to tell him all those things, but I couldn't because the collar didn't allow me to talk.

Was it because I was still under Mary's command to "stop talking"?

I hated this. It grated being completely at the mercy of another. But there was nothing I could do. So instead of fighting against a force I could never defeat, I leaned my head against his chest and closed my eyes and enjoyed how he smelled of pine and snow and caramel.

I hadn't realized I'd fallen asleep until I woke up in a pile of furs in his tent.

"We were supposed to be rescuing her from that hellish place, not making her life more miserable," I heard Soren whisper harshly to someone.

"She would be dead right now if you hadn't stepped forward and volunteered to take her. Don't forget that," Raya said. She wasn't whispering.

I decided to stay nestled in the furs with my eyes closed and pretend to be asleep. For one thing, I wanted to listen to what they had to say about me. And also, I was comfortable.

"It's just…do you think I walked into a trap?" Soren said. "Did Queen Beatrice play me for a fool? If I'd been in the queen's place and I wanted to torture someone, I would have gone with Prince Dimitri. What he planned to do to Celestina was ghastly. And what had I proposed? That I would do…something? Why in all the kingdoms would Queen Beatrice hand Celestina over to me unless…?"

"Unless what?" Raya asked.

"You don't think the queen suspects the reason we came to Earst's aid, do you?" Soren had whispered this so softly I could barely hear the words.

"Impossible," Raya said. "Impossible."

"The collar has the power of compulsion," he said.

"Which means the queen could still have power over her? Damn." Raya stomped noisily around the tent. "I was starting to like her, too."

"Now, that's not to say we have a spy in our midst or that we need to make any hasty moves yet," Soren cautioned.

"But it does mean I need to be careful about who I befriend. And the same goes for you." Raya picked something up and tossed it down again, making it clatter.

I decided that there was no way anyone could believe I would sleep through that ruckus. Perhaps all of this was a test to see if I would listen in on conversations I shouldn't be hearing while pretending to be asleep.

What if I am unwittingly a spy for Queen Beatrice? I touched the golden collar circling my neck. *Could she somehow listen in on what is happening to me?*

Gah!

"I'm awake," I said to Raya as I slowly sat up. My muscles ached.

"Good," Soren said stiffly. "The healer will be here soon. You will cooperate with her and answer her questions. Excuse me." He glanced only briefly in my direction before ducking through the tent's opening.

Raya watched the flap fall closed. She shrugged and then plopped down on the furs beside me. She sat cross-legged and nudged my leg with her toe.

"I bet you heard more than you wanted to," she said.

I let my head drop.

She nudged me with her toe again. "Come on, Sky Girl. Talk to me."

"I'm not a spy," I grumbled. "At least I don't think I am. I mean, I hope I'm not."

She nudged my leg with her toe again. "I know. I know. You're too…good. I mean honestly good. Like sugar dipped and make my teeth rot level good.”

“I’m not that good,” I protested. “I have *thoughts*.”

Raya tilted her head back and laughed “Now I’m dying to hear some of those *thoughts* of yours. Are they about Soren? I bet they are. We already know you want to move into his tent. Plus, I’ve seen the way you look at him.”

“I don’t look at him.”

“And now you’re blushing. Those *thoughts* about Soren must be pretty saucy.” She laughed again.

Thankfully, before Raya could say something to embarrass me more, the healer came in. I was surprised the healer was a woman. But the woman had donned the long blue robes of a healer. She had a leather rucksack slung over one shoulder. But, unlike the healers in Easrt, she didn’t keep the hood over her head or wear a mask covering her face.

“I heard that someone worked their fingers to the bone,” the healer said. Her voice was calming. “Let me see what I can do.”

She came and sat down next to Raya. I was glad my friend remained with me as I held out my hands. The healer unwound the dishcloths that Soren had used as bandages. My fingers didn’t look too bad. When Soren had first held my sore hands in his, I could have sworn I’d seen the bones on my right hand. But looking at my hands now, they only looked slightly bloody and raw.

Raya hissed when she saw them.

“Squeamish, Raya? That’s not something I’d expect from a battle-hardened warrior,” I teased.

“Yeah. Yeah. That’s me, weak stomach Raya. Excuse me.” She jumped up and hurried out of the tent.

“How did this happen?” the healer asked. Her hands were so tender on my sore fingers.

“I think the chort bit me. I was washing the dinner bowls and cups at the time and not paying too much attention to anything else.”

The healer nodded as if hearing that I would be more interested in washing dishes than protecting myself from a chort made perfect sense. “It might burn a bit when I put a salve on the wounds.” She rummaged around in her bag and pulled out a purple canister. She unscrewed the lid and dipped her fingers into the canister, covering them in a sweet-smelling paste. "I'll need to put this on thick to protect from infection. It's going to hurt. I am sorry."

I nodded. How bad could it hurt? The cuts weren't that deep.

She pressed the salve to the first finger.

Goddess, that burned.

I screamed.

And passed out.

Chapter 13

"Now who's the squeamish one?" Raya's smug face was the first thing I saw when I opened my eyes again. She was back in the tent, bending over me where I'd collapsed on the furs. Her long braid fell over her shoulder.

"Many a warrior has passed out when I applied the salve to a deep wound like that," the healer said as she calmly finished wrapping my hands in thick, clean gauze. She patted the back of my left hand. "No washing dishes for a while, okay?"

"That'll be up to Mary and Soren." My heart squeezed. My life was no longer my own. If they wanted me to work until my fingers fell off, I would have no way to stop it. *Soren wouldn't do that*, I reminded myself. Still, if he wanted to…

"I'll talk to them," Raya said to the healer. "I'll make sure they understand our Sky Girl needs time for her hands to mend."

The healer bowed her head before leaving the tent.

I sat up as Raya dropped down onto the furs next to me. She lifted my right hand into hers. "Does it hurt?" she asked.

"Not too bad," I lied. It felt as if the healer had wrapped a horde of stinging bees in the gauze. "That healing salve must be pretty powerful stuff."

"It's what we use in the field to keep a wound clean until we can get back to where we can use more effective healing techniques."

"Like what?" Healing salves were all that was available for injuries back at the castle.

Instead of answering that, Raya shook her head. "You're lucky you're not going to lose those two fingers."

"What? Those little scratches?" I felt a pinch of sadness. Raya no longer trusted me, at least not enough to share Fein's most basic healing techniques. "I've had worse bites from the princes back at the castle. They could be like little chorts sometimes."

"Did you have to take care of them all the time?"

"Only after their lessons and until dinner when I handed them back over to their nurses. They liked to—"

What I was going to say about the princes died on my tongue as the flap to the tent lifted. Soren ducked as he entered. Gracious, my stomach flipped. He was so big. It wasn't just his physical size. His presence seemed to fill the tent, taking up all the air.

"I hope you're doing well," he said to me. He looked worried. Was that because he thought I'd been sent to spy on them?

"The healer must have gotten carried away. She wrapped my right hand in so much gauze I feel like I have clubs at the ends of my arms." I held my hand up.

"One can never be too careful," he said. He'd brought a carafe into the tent with him. He pushed aside some of the papers on the table to make a place for it.

"Seems like a bit much for those minor cuts on my hand," I said with a laugh. "Is everyone in the entire Kingdom of Fein so squeamish? Raya has been going on and on about how I was lucky that I didn't lose a finger."

"Yes, my mistake," Raya said dryly. She looked over to Soren and raised her brows.

He shrugged. "I need to find a cup." He pulled open his chest and started to dig around. "I had Mary make her healing tea for you. It'll make your hands feel better right away."

Raya made a face. "That stuff tastes like swamp water."

"But it's very effective," Soren said.

Raya snorted. "So she says."

"Here's what I'm looking for." He pulled a wooden cup from the chest and held it up like he'd just found a treasure. "Mary has been giving me this tea to treat my injuries since I was a lad." He carried the cup over to the table. With his back to us, he started to prepare the drink, which seemed to involve more than simply pouring the potion from the carafe into a cup. "For a while there, my brother and I were drinking it almost daily. You get used to the strong flavor."

"No, you don't." Raya made another ugly face and stuck out her tongue.

"That's because, Raya, unlike me, you were too swift to ever get hurt," Soren said with his back to us.

"Well, that's true." Raya's eyes glittered with pride.

"The tea's ready." When Soren turned around with the cup in his hand, I spotted a fresh cut on his forearm. It looked as if someone had slashed him with a dagger.

"What happened to you?" I asked. That hadn't been there earlier. I would have noticed.

He looked down at his arm as if he'd forgotten it was there. "An accident, I suppose."

"Is that so?" Raya raised an eyebrow at him.

"If I say it is, it must be," Soren answered with a hint of warning. He handed me a mug of strongly spiced tea. "Here. Drink this. It'll take away the pain."

The command zapped through me. I drank the tea, which tasted bitter and metallic, until the mug was empty. "Yuck." I wrinkled my nose. "What was in that? And why was it so thick?"

"Yes, Soren. Why would the healing tea be thick?" Raya asked.

"Don't you have somewhere to be?" he asked his warrior.

"Not really." Raya smiled as she crossed her arms over her chest.

She turned to watch me with a little too much interest.

"What?" I asked her.

"Just waiting to see what the tea will do," she said with a great deal of amusement.

"Will it work that fast?" I asked.

"Oh, it'll do something," she said. "Won't it, Soren?"

He grunted. "You might be interested to know, Celestina, I've told the warriors that from now on they'll be washing their own dishes and cups after meals."

"That's a relief." My skin started to feel warm. No, not my skin. The blood running in the veins under my skin seemed to be heating up. I pushed off the fur that someone had draped over my legs after I'd passed out.

"Soren," Raya said.

"Hm?" He was busy rinsing out his wooden cup in a ceramic washbasin that he'd fetched out of his trunk.

My heart started to beat faster. And my skin felt sensitive. Too sensitive. Like I could feel the smallest brush of the air against my arms. It felt like a caress. I closed my eyes. A mistake. My imagination took over. I could picture and feel things in my head as clearly as if they were actually happening. In my mind's eye, I imagined Soren had knelt next to me. He was caressing my arms, and his warm breath teased my neck's tender skin. My entire body shivered with delight.

"Soren," Raya said a little louder. "You might want to handle this."

I opened my eyes. Soren had turned around and was looking at me. I loved how he looked at me with his beautiful green eyes. Whenever I was the object of his intense scrutiny, it made me feel both vulnerable and strong. And incredibly needy.

He crossed the room to me. I lifted my arms to welcome him. I needed to taste his lips. I needed to feel his body pressed against mine. Skin to skin. I didn't even care that Raya was there to watch. I needed him.

He leaned over and gently pushed me back into the pile of furs. *Yes,* my body cried out. *Yes, touch me.*

"Sleep," he commanded in that all-encompassing deep voice that filled every part of me and at the same time didn't make the collar hurt me. His strong hands held my shoulders down as I struggled to pull him down onto the furs with me. "Sleep until you feel rested."

No, that wasn't what I wanted. I needed *him*, not sleep. How could he not understand that? I tried to fight against his command. But my eyes closed before I could even complete a protest. My muscles relaxed as I sank deeper into the furs.

Someone—Soren, probably—draped the fur I'd kicked off back over me.

"*Sleep well*," he whispered. I jerked as the command hit me and then I was gone, floating alone in a dark, silent sea.

When I opened my eyes, I was no longer in Soren's tent. I was back in my tower at the castle. How could this be? I tossed off the rough wool blanket, climbed out of the bed, and crossed the room to the arched opening. It was morning. The golden sun shone down in the valley far below me. And—my breath caught in my throat—the dragons had returned!

They were rolling around in the meadow. A few had their wings stretched out to warm themselves in the early morning sun.

The large green one with the golden sheen on its scales was sprawled on its side. It lifted its head as if it sensed me peering at it from the narrow window opening. The pupils of its yellow eyes constricted as it watched me.

I looked down at myself to see what it saw. I was wearing nothing over my thin shift, the same thin shift the queen had stripped me down to in front of everyone. In the hall, I had felt naked in the nearly transparent shift. Under the scrutiny of my green dragon, I felt…wanted.

It pushed up onto its massive legs and shook, shedding the morning dew from its scales in a burst of tiny rainbows. It then snapped its leathery wings out. With its powerful gaze still locked on mine, it took a graceful leap. The wings beat slowly, lifting the heavy dragon higher and higher into the air.

Instead of flying off toward the hills beyond the castle like it always would, the green dragon plotted a course toward the tower. It came closer and closer. The movement of its huge wings created a gale that riveled the strongest windstorm. I had to clutch the stone windowsill to keep from being blown off my feet.

It hovered at my window, with its wings moving in a steady rhythm, and stared at me with those intelligent eyes. I felt like it was trying to ask me a question.

"Yes," I said, my heart thrilling. "Yes."

With a jerk of its head, as if it understood me, it reached out its large foreleg and wrapped its claws around my body. I grabbed hold of the top claw and held on for dear life as it pulled me through the window and into the sky.

With a deafening roar, it flew as it clutched me close to its soft light green chest. We flew over the far hills and toward a mountain range with four jagged peaks. On the highest peak, it landed in a tall cave that was deep enough to hold all the dragons that liked to warm themselves in the valley.

But at the moment, I was alone with the green dragon in the cave. It gently carried me deep inside the earth where very little sunlight could penetrate. There, it circled around three times like a cat finding the perfect spot to settle down, and then it lowered itself, curling around me like a serpent. It kept its claws wrapped protectively around me. So warm. So safe. So right.

I had found Home.

Chapter 14

"Tell us about how vampires make more vampires," little Ryan squealed. The princes' obsession with vampires never seemed to wane. They would pester me for story after story. The more vicious the tale, the happier they were.

"Wellllll," I'd drawn out the word while tapping my chin as if trying to remember. I'd told them this story so many times, I could practically tell it without listening to myself. "The evil vampire"—I held my arms up and wiggled my fingers as if they were claws at the ends of long wings—"stalks its victims in the night. Always in the night. That's why you need to stay in bed after Nurse tucks you in. No sneaking out to put lizards in my bed, understood?"

The boys nodded. But I could see that Ronald had his fingers crossed behind his back.

"Most of the time, the vampire stalks its prey because it's hungry. They are always so hungry. Endlessly hungry for human blood." I whispered that last part. The boys shook with delighted fear. "But sometimes, very occasionally, a vampire becomes lonely. That's when it goes out into the world—in the dark of the night—in search of a companion. The vampire will stalk the unaware human, learning her ways, maybe befriending her, tricking her with its charming manner. For a vampire can be charming when it puts its mind to it. It can seem like the most charming human one could hope to meet."

"Does that charm come from drinking all that human blood?" Ronald asked.

"I believe it must. The vampire gets more than just nourishment from the blood it takes, it also steals bits and pieces of its victims' souls."

"But how does it make a companion?" little Rupert asked.

"It tricks the human, that's how. Once she thinks she's made a new friend, it tricks her into drinking its blood. And when she does, a piece of the vampire's demon soul infects her pure human soul. And she turns into…" I drew in a deep breath and then jumped up from my chair as I shouted, "A VAMPIRE!"

The boys all screamed and laughed and rolled on the unadorned stone floor in my chilly tower room.

While I might not miss the castle or the court or the tower with no glass in the windows, I did miss the princes and their endless supply of happy energy.

But at the same time, it felt so nice sleeping next to my warm green dragon.

I rolled over in my sleep. My memories had merged with my dreams in such a delightful way. I snuggled against the green dragon and sighed.

I rubbed my cheek against the chest that I had been using as a pillow like a contented cat. I would have purred if I could have. The delicious scent of pine and snow and caramel wrapped around me like a comforting embrace. The feel of his soft chest hair against my cheek tempted me to want things that made a tantalizing heat pool low in my belly and swirl like the promise of new beginnings between my legs. I shifted against him feeling desperate to rub that heat onto his body.

Everything in me stilled.

It felt as if even my heart had stopped beating.

This wasn't the green dragon. And I was no longer asleep.

I drew a fortifying breath before daring to open my eyes. His green eyes with gold flecks were open and watching me. His expression, which almost always looked severe, lightened.

"I hope you slept well," Soren's deep voice rumbled under me.

I nodded like a ninny.

My gaze strayed to where my heavily bandaged hand rested on his chest. His bare chest. Was-was the rest of him bare too? I mean, surely Soren didn't sleep in the nude.

I'd been sleeping in his pallet of furs. Of course, he would have joined me in the pallet at some time during the night. Where else could he have gone on such a frigid winter night? There was plenty of room on the large pallet for two people to sleep without disturbing the other. And yet. And yet, I had rolled over toward him, as if seeking him out. Half my body was wantonly sprawled over his.

What he must be thinking about me! I needed to get off him. I needed to put some distance between our bodies.

His arm tightened around my shoulders. "It's okay," he said softly. "I like where you are. It's comfortable."

"Really?" Tears flooded my eyes as a sea of emotions hit me. My parents' defection, the queen's punishment, and then having to live like a slave among strangers. I hadn't realized how out of place I'd felt until he spoke the exact words I'd needed to hear. *I like where you are.*

I liked where I was, too. Being close to Soren like this, despite that I'd been given to him as his slave to kill, made me feel protected.

"I—I've never been kissed." I don't know why I confessed that. My cheeks certainly didn't approve. They burned with embarrassment at my revealing too much of myself.

A corner of his mouth tipped up. "Is that so? The Queen's Ladies are that protected?"

"No, we aren't protected in that way. It was the queen's disapproval of me that kept the courtiers away." How pathetic that must have sounded. I cringed as I hid my face against his chest. "No one wanted to risk suffering the queen's wrath. Not for someone like me."

"Someone like you?"

My cheeks burned even hotter. Certainly, he wasn't going to make me say it aloud. That would be too cruel.

"Someone like you?" he repeated. "Celestina?"

"I'm not…I'm not…" I swallowed, and then said in a rush, "I'm not as pretty as some of the other ladies."

"Well, I don't give a flip about the queen's wrath. And you're pretty enough to my eyes. Would you like me to remedy your predicament and kiss you?"

Would I ever!

Soren hooked a finger under my chin and lifted until we were looking at each other again. He raised a brow.

"Yes." The admission came easily now that I was gazing into his warm green eyes. "I would like that very—"

He closed the distance between us. His lips gently brushed mine, tasting, tempting. And then he deepened the kiss. Mating his mouth with mine until I found it hard to catch my breath. Our tongues played a game I instinctively understood. Kissing Soren felt natural and oh, so right.

Without lifting his lips, he managed to roll our bodies so he was leveraged on top of me. His knee pressed my legs apart in a way my body welcomed. Our kisses deepened as I welcomed the pressure of his leg against my core. My hips instinctually moved against his legs.

"Celestina," he breathed into my mouth. His fingers loosened the ties on my leggings. "I need you more than I need air to breathe."

"Goddess, I feel the same way," I answered like a plea for him to keep doing what he was doing to me. He started to push my leggings down over my hips. I reached down to help him.

That was when someone in the tent cleared their throat.

Soren stilled on top of me.

"I brought breakfast," Gray said with a smile. He sat cross-legged on the floor near the tent's entrance. I had to wonder how long he'd been sitting there. He had a bowl in his hand. Two more bowls sat beside his boot. "The tents are being broken down, and we're packing the wagons for that early start you wanted, Soren."

Soren dropped his forehead to mine. *"My friends are pests,"* he whispered.

"I heard that," Gray said as he scooped a large spoonful of porridge into his mouth.

Soren rolled off me and then pulled himself off the pallet of furs. I was relieved to see he was wearing pants, wasn't I?

As I sat up, Soren handed me one of the bowls of porridge.

"Do your fingers hurt this morning?" he asked, eyeing the ridiculously large bandages the healer had wrapped them in yesterday. The bandages made it difficult to hold either the bowl or the spoon. But I was so hungry. I couldn't remember the last time I'd eaten. It took some work, but I managed to wrap my thickly bandaged hand around the spoon…just barely. I wasn't sure if I would have enough control over it to actually get any food to my mouth. If I did somehow manage it, it would be messy.

"May I help?" Soren asked. He sat down next to me on the pallet and held out his hand. "I'm not sure we'll still need these bandages. That healing tea should have done its job overnight."

"Raya told me about the tea you gave her," Gray said.

"It wouldn't be right to leave her with just field dressing and antiseptic salves when the…uh…tea is available." Soren's hands, so strong and so used to wielding a sword, worked with delicate precision as he unwound the bandage on my right hand.

"I didn't like the taste," I admitted.

Gray choked on his porridge. "That's got to sting, Soren."

"What?" I asked.

"Nothing," Soren said. "Celestina, I told you that you could run if you felt your life was in danger. You remember that?"

I nodded.

He unwrapped layer after layer of the gauze on my right hand. "Why didn't you run when the chorts came into the camp?"

"There were so many bowls left to clean," I said. The bandages fell away. The gashes had knitted together, leaving only a red line marking where the injuries had been. "And I didn't feel like my life was in danger."

"I heard a chort nearly bit your fingers off," Gray said. "It could have done much worse. It could have cleaved you in two with its claws." He finished his porridge and reached out to grab Soren's.

Soren, moving preternaturally fast, slapped his friend's hand away from his bowl. "I'm going to eat that." He went back to unwrapping the bandages from my left hand. "Gray's right, though. The chort could have killed you."

"Did you at least try it hit it with that makeshift mace you've been carrying around?" Gray asked.

"My what?"

Gray pointed to my bag of shiny treasures that had slipped off my leggings sometime during the night.

"That's not—" I felt my cheeks heat. I tried to tuck the bag under my leg out of sight. "Those aren't for—"

"Uh, huh." Gray shook his head.

Soren reached over me to lift the small bag into his hand. "Rocks," he said, frowning as he swung the bag on the string like he would a weapon.

"I told you about it," Gray said.

"It's not a weapon. They're just my…my…things." I snatched the small sack from Soren and quickly tied it back to the loop on my leggings. I held my breath, fully expecting one of them to take it away from me. I'd fight them for it. I don't know why, but I felt it in my bones that I'd fight them for the right to keep my treasures.

"Look, the chort merely nipped me," I said, hoping to distract them. "The bites weren't that bad. Just scratches really." I looked down at the red slashes that remained on my right hand. Herbal teas and salves couldn't have healed anything deeper than a scratch overnight. Nothing was that powerful. "And the creature didn't seem too interested in me. Besides, Mary had told me not to move from my spot until all the bowls were clean."

Soren nodded as if he understood why I hadn't run from the chort when everyone else had. "Mary's order to stay put must have superseded my giving you permission to protect yourself." He sighed. "May I give you a command to try and fix that in the future?"

"They do hurt," I confessed. "But if you think it's necessary…" I nodded my consent.

"What hurts?" Soren asked.

"Your orders. They batter me like fists. Some hit stronger than others. Mary's commands aren't so bad. But yours are…" I winced. "They hurt for a long time."

Soren closed his eyes.

"Shit," Gray said. "Can we command the collar not to hurt her?"

"I don't know." Soren pulled his hands through his black hair. "Do you know, Celestina?"

I shook my head. "Although there were slaves in the castle, I didn't have much interaction with them. They did menial work and generally stayed out of everyone's way. But from what I saw, I feel as if the magic my collar contains makes mine more restrictive than theirs."

"Your queen is a bitch," he said.

Part of me wanted to defend her. She was my queen, after all. She protected the kingdom from chorts and vampires and the vile Tiburnians. But really, Soren wasn't wrong. Queen Beatrice had never been kind to me.

"Gray has had a good idea there, even if he is a food thief. I think we should try and get the collar to stop hurting you. Are you willing to try that?" Soren asked.

I braced myself for the bolt of pain his commands would cause before giving a nod that I was ready.

Soren seemed to brace himself for my pain, too. It took a moment before he said softly, "Celestina, my orders, commands, and requests will not cause you physical pain."

The command slugged me in the side. I jerked.

"Did that hurt?" he asked.

"No," I said when I really wanted to groan "yes." Yes, it hurt and would likely hurt for the rest of the day. The collar hadn't allowed his command to take away the pain. Instead, it had stolen my ability to admit to it.

"She's lying," Gray said.

Soren leaned forward, resting his elbows on his knees. "Are you lying?"

Yes! "No." The damned collar wanted Soren to hurt me.

He studied me for several uncomfortable moments before saying tightly, "I see."

I had no idea what he saw. Things were better when we were still half asleep and kissing. I enjoyed kissing Soren more than I should admit.

"The collar seems to have less control over me when I'm first waking up," I said, trying to explain to him that I wasn't deliberately lying to him. "My thoughts and words feel like they are my own in that short time before I'm fully awake. Like this morning," I quickly added that last part. I wanted to say more, but the collar stopped the words before they could form in my mouth.

I growled with frustration. I needed him to understand that what happened between us this morning wasn't about me responding to a compulsion to kiss him. I had wanted his lips on mine. I had wanted that *and more*. But the collar wouldn't let me tell him any of that.

"This isn't something we're going to solve right now. And I don't want to hurt you any more than I already have," Soren said as he set aside his half-eaten porridge and rose from the furs. "We'll come back to this. But, for now, we do need to get on the road if we're going to make it back to the capital before the next winter storm hits." He pulled on a fresh shirt and tugged on his tall leather boots. "In the meantime, I want you to stay away from me—that way I can't accidentally give you a command—and stick close to either Gray or Raya since neither of them have been given control over you, and I trust them with my life."

The command struck me in the jaw this time. I winced.

"Dude, you really should have just told me all of that," Gray said as he scooped up Soren's bowl of porridge and shoveled a spoonful in his mouth.

"I gave her a command, didn't I?" Soren said. "And it hurt her."

"No," I said.

"Yes," Gray said at the same time, his mouth full of porridge.

"Goddess, help me," Soren said, looking as if he hurt as much as I did.

"It's not as if you can help yourself. You are a general of an entire fucking army." Gray put his hand on his friend's shoulder. "Come on, Sky Girl," he then said to me. "Let's go see if we can find you a horse to ride. Do you ride?"

"I do," I said jumping up. I jerked up my leggings and hastily knotted the ties. Gray turned his head away and pretended not to notice, which was decent of him.

I would enjoy riding on horseback through the countryside for a change.

Soren paused at the tent's flap and turned back to me. I felt captured in the heated look that made me remember his kisses and how they'd made my entire body tremble.

"Bring Celestina back to my tent tonight," he said right before stepping through the opening.

Gray's jaw tightened. He turned away from where his general had been standing to stare back toward me. But he didn't say anything other than, "Let's finish up with breakfast and get moving. We've already lost a day of travel thanks to those damn chorts. Unless we want to risk another round with them, we need to get on the road and moving."

Chapter 15

"Where are you going?" Patty grabbed my arm as I followed Gray toward the horses.

"She's riding with me today," Gray called over his shoulder before I could answer.

"What?" Patty's eyes grew wide with hurt as she looked at me. "Why?"

"Soren's orders," Gray answered.

"Are you okay?" Patty whispered to me. "You disappeared into Soren's tent for an entire day, and now you're being kept under Gray's thumb? What's going on?"

"I'm okay." The collar wanted me to keep following Gray, but when I tried to go with him, Patty tightened her grip on my arm. While I could have twisted away from her, I could see by the vulnerable quiver of her lips that she needed to talk, she needed a friend. I stiffened my spine against the pain radiating down it and said, "Are *you* okay?"

Tears sprang to her eyes. "I don't know, Sky Girl. I don't know."

"Celestina!" Gray called to me. "The horses."

He hadn't used my nickname, which was telling. Thankfully, Soren hadn't put me under Gray's power, so his calling to me didn't cause any additional pain.

"Just a minute!" I pulled Patty into my arms. "What happened?"

"Those-those chorts. They were everywhere. I grabbed a sword to help fight them, and Gray took one look at me, threw me over his shoulder, and tossed me onto one of the supplies carts. The one with the clothes. He looked at me like I was a child and told me to stay out of trouble. He told me others would get hurt if I tried to help because I didn't know what I was doing."

"Do you know how to swing a sword?" I sure didn't.

"No, but that's not the point." She sniffled. "He thinks I'm a baby. I'm not."

I put my hand on her wet cheek. "He cares about your safety. That's something."

"Celestina!" Gray called again. "We need to get riding. Patty, where is Mary? Why isn't she watching you?"

Patty pulled out of my embrace. She fisted her hands at her sides as she turned to face the hulking warrior. "I'm a grown woman. I don't need a minder."

He snorted. "Come on, Sky Girl. Our horses are ready."

He walked away without a backward glance.

"He's the worst," Patty growled. "I hate him."

My heart ached for my friend. "I'll try to get Gray to ride alongside Mary's wagon," I said. "That way you can keep hating on him all day."

"I'm glad you finally decided to join us," Gray snapped. "I thought you might hold us up from traveling for yet another day."

I quailed at the thought that my little injuries had caused the entire army to miss a day of travel. The warriors had to be anxious to get home to their families. And because of me, they had to sit around all day waiting for me to wake up. Gah!

"Don't let him intimidate you, Sky Girl." Raya swaggered up and punched Gray in the arm. "You didn't delay anything. We had to take the day to repair tents and tend to the half dozen warriors who suffered severe injuries. Those chorts are tough bastards to kill. Heard you're riding with us today." She grabbed my hands and looked at my fingers. "Those look good."

"They feel good." I smiled. "Just a little redness left."

"I have some healing cream in my pack that will take care of that. You can use it on your fingers tonight after we get settled in our tent," Raya said as she mounted her horse, a compact dapple brown horse that looked too tame and dainty for someone as fierce as Raya.

"Soren intends to keep Celestina in his tent tonight," Gray grumbled.

"Is that so, Sky Girl?" Raya asked me with raised eyebrows.

"Apparently." A shiver of anticipation surged through me at the thought. The corner of my mouth hitched up despite my attempt to hide my feelings.

Raya shook her head.

Were the Fein all a bunch of prudes? I'd heard stories of other kingdoms, like the evil Tiburnians, who viewed sexual activities as being something shameful unless the couple who intended to have relations received permission from their religious leaders. Having to get permission from a third party like that seemed rather embarrassing. But I supposed it would also make the pair slow down and really think about what they were doing. In Earst, many of the Queen's Ladies jumped into bed with anyone who showed the least bit of interest in them. Occasionally, trouble followed. Like the time the head cook tried to stab my friend Everly after she came home to find Everly in bed being serviced by the cook's favorite "assistant." Perhaps some religion would help curb that.

And yet the Fein didn't strike me as religious. I hadn't seen them break for prayers to higher deities, and they didn't travel with a holy man. But that didn't mean they weren't religious. They were, after all, extremely private.

It might not be religion, though. Perhaps there was another reason Raya and Gray didn't want me with Soren.

He was a general, and I was a slave.

Did they think I wasn't good enough for him? I hadn't forgotten how some of the warriors in the army had openly expressed their hatred because of my slave status.

"Stop thinking so hard," Gray said as he walked a compact black horse over toward me and tossed the reins in my direction. "Show me that you weren't lying when you told me you knew how to ride."

I greeted the small mare by letting her sniff my hand, which she then nudged playfully with her velvety nose. "What's her name?" I asked.

"That's Posey," Raya said as she rode past on her brown gelding. "She's as friendly as a puppy."

"I hope we'll be good friends, Posey."

Because we weren't in a stable and there weren't any mounting blocks in sight, Gray had to help me climb up into the saddle. But once I was properly seated, I was able to show I wasn't without skills.

Riding Posey felt like freedom. I hadn't had the opportunity to ride since Queen Beatrice had decided to punish me three years ago for looking at Her Majesty the wrong way. She'd taken away my stable privileges, which had been one of her worst punishments. Although I hadn't gone riding in a long time, my body instantly remembered how to move.

Posey's rhythmic sway as she walked down the gravelly road lulled me into a meditative frame of mind. My thoughts kept turning back to this morning and the thrill of Soren's mouth on mine. Would he do that again tonight? Would he do more? I couldn't forget the way his eyes had darkened when he'd ordered Gray to bring me to him. He wanted me in his tent. I wanted to be in his tent. He was the general. His commands were second only to the royals. His warriors should accept that.

Why didn't they?

Because they thought I was Queen Beatrice's spy?

Because they were worried I would somehow hurt Soren?

How could I harm him? The collar would kill me before I could raise a hand against him…wouldn't it?

"You're doing it again," Gray grumbled as he rode alongside me.

"What?" I asked without turning my head.

"Thinking too hard."

I slid a glance in his direction. "Maybe you don't think hard enough." I countered, remembering Patty's hurt feelings.

"Ignorance can be a happy existence."

"And an empty one." Where did that thought come from? I'd lived most of my life not thinking too hard about what Queen Beatrice was doing to her kingdom, to her court, to me.

"Are you speaking from experience?" Gray asked, sounding a bit more serious.

Had my life been empty?

"Yes." It had been.

I should have pushed harder after the dragons had disappeared. Queen Beatrice should have tried everything in her power to get them back. She'd left us vulnerable. And because of that, the Tiburnians attacked.

A lizard dropped from a tree and skittered across my lap. I flicked it away. It flew through the air and landed on Gray's lap.

"Where do these creatures keep coming from?" Gray muttered as he picked the lizard up by the tail and dropped it to the ground.

"They're everywhere," I said.

"Not everywhere," Gray said. "We didn't come across the lizards until we reached Earst's capital. I fear we're bringing a plague of them home with us. Shouldn't it be too cold for these cold-blooded buggers?"

I hadn't thought of that.

"I never knew there might be a place without them," I said. The lizards had survived in the castle because they could seek shelter inside its walls. But out here, in the rocky hills, how were they surviving?

"Apparently, Reinheart Palace is going to be overrun with them, thanks to us bringing them home."

"I'm sorry."

"Not your fault." But still, it felt like he thought it was.

We were riding near the middle of the army but slightly removed from the rest of the mounted warriors and behind the line of supply carts. Not far behind us were the warriors who were on foot. They jogged, keeping pace even when Gray and the other warriors that rode with him spurred their mounts to move faster.

Other than Raya and Gray, no other warrior tried to speak to me or even glance in my direction in a friendly manner. All I got from them were silent glares.

Their disdain made me feel sick to my stomach. I nudged Posey with my knees, prodding her to trot ahead of all of them. The collar sent shards of pain through my shoulders as I moved away from Gray. Soren had ordered me to stay near him or Raya, and apparently the collar thought I was disobeying his order by riding ahead of them. I glanced around, hoping to spot Raya.

I'm riding toward Raya, not away from Gray. My silently stating my intention didn't stop the collar from punishing me. I gritted my teeth and kept riding.

"I'm riding toward Raya," I ground out. "I'm supposed to stay near Raya."

"Or me," Gray said as he rode up alongside me.

The pain immediately dissipated. I slumped in the saddle.

"If you know it'll hurt, why do it?"

Did he really need to ask? "Because I don't want to be around people who hate me because of this." I tugged at the collar that was half embedded in my skin.

He shook his head. "You picked one hell of a time to start fighting for yourself, Sky Girl. Things would be easier—and less painful—if you just went with the flow for a while."

"I can't. I won't." He didn't understand. I couldn't ride silently with him and his warrior friends feeling their hate beating against me like tiny fists simply because I was from Earst, because I'd been made a slave, because I might be their enemy. I'd lived that way for too long, and *this* was where my silence and complacency had gotten me.

If I wanted a different outcome, I was going to have to be a different person. I was going to have to become a person who forged her own future.

Chapter 16

We'd moved deep into the mountains by the time Soren called the army to stop for the night. The ruins of pillars lining the road continued at their regular intervals. I'd tried counting them for a while but lost interest after reaching one hundred and twenty-eight.

Although I'd enjoyed the freedom of riding astride a horse instead of sitting squished between Mary and Patty on the narrow wagon seat, I missed their easy conversation. And my rear and legs ached like the devil when I finally managed to get myself out of Posey's saddle. As I stretched and walked off the soreness, I could feel a hum of anticipation in the air all around me.

"Are we getting close to the Fein border?" I asked Patty, feeling it must be true. Hoping it was true.

"It's just a few days away," Patty answered while we unpacked the supply wagon.

"Patty, fill the buckets. There's a stream over there. But be careful, it's near a waterfall and a steep ravine," Mary called as she came by. "Sky Girl, there's meat to be chopped. I'll need you working at the prep table."

While I'd slept the day away yesterday, a herd of deer had been spotted near the camp. Soren and Gray had led a small team of warriors on a hunt and managed to bring back fresh meat for dinner. Mary had reserved part of the deer carcass for today's stew. She'd also salted and dried strips into jerky.

The army got to work setting up camp near the edge of the deep ravine. I did my part by unloading the heavy wooden kitchen prep table and started screwing in its legs.

Gray jogged over to help.

"You don't have to do that," I told him.

"Until Soren releases you from your command, either Raya or I have to stay near you. And since I'm stuck over here in the kitchen area, I'd better make myself useful."

"Because you'd be bored otherwise?" I asked.

"Because I'm terrified of Mary and her spoon!"

I chuckled. "I'm sure if I'm working under Mary's compulsion, the collar will be happy. You don't need to stay here."

"Let's not test that by putting you in a damned if you do, damned if you don't position, okay? Soren would have my head if I caused you to turn blue again."

Not long afterward, Soren came striding up with Raya beside him. He looked so serious, as if he was wearing all the problems of the four kingdoms like a heavy cloak. But when his gaze met mine, his stride stuttered. The tension in his jaw loosened.

Just looking at him made me start to think about tonight and spending it with him in his tent. How would his strong hands feel as he touched my body? Would he be gentle? Would he be rough? Did I care which way it went? My breath caught in my throat.

Time couldn't move fast enough for me.

"Celestina," he breathed my name, deep, seductive as he closed the distance between us. His voice was almost like a command, but without the collar's accompanying punishment. The corner of his mouth had tipped up into a half-smile. "You don't have to stay close to either Raya or Gray," he said. It was the release of his previous command.

I felt a small jolt of pain, but I worked hard to not let it show.

His eyes narrow anyway. "Sorry about that," he said softly.

I nodded. *It's okay. It really doesn't hurt.*

I kept my lies silent.

"Mary has already put Sky Girl to work." Gray gave Soren a hard look as if warning him to tread with care.

"There's venison to be chopped for the stew," I said brightly as I screwed in the last leg of the prep table. The collar made sure I didn't stop working. "At least I won't be washing bowls and cups for half the night, thanks to you."

"It's a change I should have made years ago. I didn't realize how much we were asking of Mary and her helpers," Soren said.

"Maybe that's why the old girl is always so cranky," Gray added. "You're overworking her."

"Maybe it's your lazy attitude that puts me in a sour mood," Mary countered as she came up behind him. She raised the spoon she carried with her everywhere.

Gray threw his hands in the air. "I'm on your side, Mary. I promise."

Mary took a menacing step toward Gray. "Isn't there someplace you sorry warriors need to be? A camp to be erected? Or anything that doesn't involve bothering my hardworking helpers?"

"We're leaving." Gray sidestepped Mary and her spoon.

"See you around, Sky Girl." Raya winked at me before chasing after Gray.

Soren pulled his fingers through his raven-black hair. "Do you have everything you need, Mary? Do you have enough hands for the dinner prep? I could send a few warriors—"

"We've got it covered, General Kitmun, as long as we're not troubled with interruptions." Her eyes twinkled with amusement. She pushed at the large warrior. "Get on with you, now. Sky Girl and I have work to do."

Soren lightly ran his hand across my shoulders as he let himself be shoved away. "I'll see you tonight, Celestina." His deep voice made my

skin shiver in a way that made me want to count the hours until sun
fall.

"Slave," one of the brutish warriors who'd been rude to me the
other day barked as he walked toward me. I'd only started chopping
the venison and still had a couple of huge slabs of meat to prepare.
"Get over here."

Only Soren and Mary had the power to order me around, and even
though Mary was off erecting the kitchen tent, I was under her
command so I couldn't do anything for him even if I'd wanted to.

And I certainly didn't want to.

"Slave, are you deaf?" He marched over to me. Gracious, he was a
mountain of a man. "I said get over here."

I continued to chop the meat.

He grabbed my arm and shook it. I did my best to keep chopping
the meat because that was what the collar had compelled me to do.
"What's wrong with you?"

"I'm carrying out Mary's orders," I said as I jerked my arm away
from him.

With a growl, he grabbed it back again, bruising me. "You won't be
welcome in Fein. We don't welcome outsiders, and we sure as hell
won't welcome the daughter of traitors. You'd do yourself and the rest
of us a favor if you'd take off while no one is watching."

"You're watching. Your friends are watching," I pointed out. A
group of warriors stood at the perimeter of the kitchen area, staring at
me with their arms crossed over their large chests.

"We won't stop you." He grabbed my arm again because I'd gone
back to chopping the meat.

Honestly, I couldn't stop myself from working. "It's not that simple.
The collar—"

"I could remove it." He drew out his sword. The way he was swinging it toward my neck, it looked like he planned to take my head off with the collar.

"Please don't!" I cried.

"Stop chopping that damned meat and get out of here," the warrior growled. "Run!"

"I can't!" I kept chopping.

He pried the knife from my fingers and tossed it on the ground. The collar sizzled its disapproval. I cried out in pain. But the warrior didn't seem to care. He wrapped a thick arm around my waist and tossed me over his shoulder like I was a deer carcass. My feet dangled several feet above the ground as he carried me toward the stream.

"What are you doing!" Patty, who had just returned from the stream with two filled buckets of water, screamed at him.

"What should have been done days ago. We can't let her cross the border," the warrior growled at Patty. "Get out of my way."

"Make me!" she shouted.

He shrugged and pushed her over, spilling her buckets.

The further he took me away from my work, the hotter the collar burned. It shot scorching heat through my body. I felt like I was being cooked from the inside out. I writhed against the pain.

"Stop struggling," he ordered. "I'm helping you escape."

"I can't escape," I wheezed. "There is no escape."

He marched me over to the stream. Was he planning on dropping me in? I hoped not. Thick sheets of ice floated on top of the fast-moving water. I struggled, pounding my arms against his back.

"*Please, please. Let me go back.*" I didn't think I could take the pain much longer.

He continued to walk along the stream. Hanging over his shoulder like I was, I couldn't see where we were heading, but I could hear the roar of the water. Why would he take me toward the waterfall? What did he plan to do?

"Stop!" Mary ordered. "Put her down!"

"Very well." The warrior took another step forward and then tossed me over the edge of the icy waterfall and into the ravine below.

I screamed as I fell. The collar cinched tighter and tighter. My skin felt like would start boiling at any minute. I hit the ground hard and then rolled over rocks and ice, scraping and bruising my arms and legs and sides as I continued to tumble.

"Get Soren and a healer!" I heard Mary scream from what sounded like a far, far distance.

I landed at the bottom of the ravine with my legs badly twisted and partially submerged in freezing water. The swift stream tugged at me. I tried to roll away from the stinging ice-infested water while fighting against the worst pain I'd ever felt. I needed to get back to the camp. I needed to get back to work with the meat. That was the only way I could stop the collar from killing me.

Mary, huffing and puffing, skidded to a stop where I'd landed. I looked up at her and tried to promise her with my eyes—since I couldn't breathe, much less talk—that I would go back to chopping the meat as soon as I managed to stand. The collar didn't care what I intended to do. It kept tightening and tightening.

"Shh," Mary said sternly. She hooked her hands under my armpits and dragged me out of the stream. "A healer is on the way. Don't move." Her order zinged through me. I stopped struggling to get back to the worktable and the slab of venison. Inch by inch the collar loosened its grip on my throat. The pain slowly started to clear, making room for the sharp pains from my fall to the bottom of the ravine.

"Why did he throw me away?" I managed to croak through a burst of coughing. My throat burned as if I'd swallowed hot ashes.

Mary looked away. I thought she might not answer me. But then she said, "The Fein are private people. Our borders are closed to outsiders. That one who took you was worried, like half the warriors traveling with us are worried, that bringing you to the capital will endanger Soren. I'm sure he thought he was protecting the general by trying to get rid of you."

"He tried to kill me." Gah! My side felt like it was on fire. I rolled into a ball and groaned.

"Stay with us, Sky Girl. Don't let the goddess Perth take you away from us." Mary grabbed my hand and held it so tightly that it hurt. Heck, everything hurt. "The healer is coming. Hold on for her."

I held on one breath at a time. But I could feel myself slipping. I was too broken. The thought of being carried out of the ravine with all the bruises and breaks made me want to give up and join my parents who were surely living the high life in the Great Beyond.

Was that the shadow of a dragon flying overhead?

A lizard dropped down on my head and licked some blood on my temple. That must have been what I saw. A lizard. Not one of my beloved dragons coming for me. Mary shooed the tiny creature away.

Queen Beatrice had wanted the Fein army to torment and kill me. She'd be happy to know she'd gotten her wish. Soren, Patty, Mary, Raya, and even Gray had made me feel hopeful, made me look forward to tomorrow. And now as I lay here staring up at the sky, I realized that the hope I'd felt had all been an illusion.

I was never going to leave Earst.

I was always going to die a slave.

That hope they made me feel had been the cruelest torment of all.

"She's slipping away." Mary's voice sounded gruffer than usual. "Her legs are broken. Ribs too. And it looks like there must be some organ damage and internal bleeding. It's too much."

"Move aside." That wasn't the healer's calm voice. "We need to save her," Soren growled. A moment later something thick and metallic filled my mouth. "Swallow." The dark command eased through me without a stitch of pain. I immediately swallowed. More liquid filled my mouth. "Again," he commanded in that velvety rich voice that made me ache to obey him. More metallic liquid and then a whispered, *"Again."*

"You won't be able to hide what you've done like you did last time," Mary warned.

I peeled open my eyes. Soren sucked in a breath and leaned down toward me. His lips nearly on mine. "I don't care," he growled but then he softened his tone after my mouth was flooded with more of that warm drink, "Again."

I don't know how long this cycle continued. I don't even know how they got me out of the ravine. The injuries I'd suffered were too severe, too deep. I shouldn't have survived them. As it was, it hurt to breathe. I couldn't keep my eyes open. I couldn't keep my mind clear.

I seemed to remember Soren lifting me at one point. And I don't think I dreamed that he'd kissed my brow or told me to sleep.

When I managed to open my eyes again, I found myself buried under a pile of furs in Soren's tent. Alone.

I took a shallow breath, expecting to be wracked with pain from my crushed ribs. No pain. I took a deeper breath. Again, my ribs didn't hurt me.

Had I dreamed that Mary had told Soren that my legs and ribs were broken?

I wiggled my toes. No pain.

Someone outside the tent shouted. A moment later the clang of sword against sword rang out. It sounded like…fighting. Had enemy forces attacked the camp?

I jumped up and hurried toward the tent flap. Suddenly, I remembered that I'd been at death's door, that I shouldn't be able to walk. That's when I froze. I looked down at my bare feet. My legs ached. My chest ached. My stomach ached. But not nearly as keenly as my body should have hurt after being hurled over a waterfall.

I'd fallen into a freaking ravine!

I'd hit boulders on the way down.

I had been bleeding.

I had been broken.

I shouldn't be standing.

I shouldn't be whole.

More shouts. More clanks of metal against metal.

Pushing the mystery of my miraculous recovery aside for a moment, I poked my head through the tent flap. All I could see was a crowd of warriors. They weren't in battle. They were standing around with their backs to me watching whatever fight was happening a few yards away.

I stepped outside. I had no hope of peering over the mountain of warriors, so I gently pushed my way toward the front. What I saw within the circle of the men was a two-man battle. Despite the icy winds blowing through the camp, Soren had removed his tunic. He wore no weapons and only wielded a short sword. The man he was battling was the same man who'd thrown me over the waterfall. He was much better armed with a large broadsword in one hand, a shorter sword in the other, and two daggers sticking out of his boots.

My breath caught in the back of my throat as the man slashed his long broadsword, nearly slicing into Soren's chest.

"This is your fault, you bloody girl," the man standing next to me grumbled. "You bring dishonor on all of us."

Though he shouldn't have been able to have heard the warrior's complaint, Soren flashed his eyes unerringly in our direction. He kept his gaze trained on me as he fended off a frenzy of parries.

"Queen Beatrice punished Celestina for the actions of her parents." Soren swung his sword. It clanged off the broadsword. "I volunteered to take her into our camp." He swung again. "I did it because she was being wrongfully persecuted." Another swing. "If anyone is to blame for the situation that exists in our camp today, it is both Queen Beatrice and me. Not Celestina." He then lunged toward the man who had tried to kill me. He swung his sword in a wide arc. I didn't realize what had happened until the man's head dropped to the ground and started to roll. A moment later his body collapsed in a bloody heap.

Soren, breathing hard, turned a full circle. "Does anyone else feel the need to question my authority?"

No one moved. It seemed as if no one in the circle even dared breathe. Raya was standing on the opposite side of the circle with her arms crossed over her chest. She looked furious. Gray, standing beside her, bit down on his bottom lip. His gaze met mine and all the color in his cheeks drained away.

"Good." Soren tossed his sword to the ground. The heat in his eyes felt like it could burn. He stalked toward me with such a look of violence, that it took all my courage not to turn and run.

He grabbed my arm and spun me around. The warriors opened a pathway to let Soren pass through the crowd. His grip on my arm wasn't bruising, but it also wasn't gentle. He made a straight path to his tent, pulling me along with him.

Once we were inside, he turned me until I was facing him. The tips of his rough fingers brushed against my face as his gaze ran up and down my body.

"Are you…?" he asked gruffly, still taking an assessment of my body.

"My muscles ache, but I seem to be fine." I shivered. The violence he'd unleashed on that warrior seemed to be still trapped inside his body. And I was now trapped inside the tent with Soren.

I eased away from him just in case he decided to take his anger out on the nearest object…me. Queen Beatrice had been known to strike out at innocents after one of her bloody spectacles. Violence that builds and builds like a storm cloud demands an outlet.

Soren took a step toward me. I raised my hands as if that simple act could keep him away. I couldn't protect myself. If he wanted to harm me, there was nothing I could do to stop him.

"Dammit. You're afraid of me." He raked his fingers through his dark hair. "You don't have to be frightened. I won't…I won't…I didn't intend for you to see what happened out there. You were gently raised and probably have never witnessed such a death."

Thanks to Queen Beatrice, I'd seen plenty of violent deaths. Still, my familiarity with it didn't stop my stomach from roiling or stop wave after wave of worry from bubbling up when I recognized the anger that still had the gold flecks in Soren's eyes sparking.

He didn't give me a chance to explain any of that. He swore just as violently as he'd swung his sword. "You have to realize, Celestina," he growled. "A man under my command tried to kill you. Hell, he nearly succeeded. I couldn't let that pass without severe consequences."

"I understand," I said quietly.

He closed the space between us. With the tip of his rough finger, he gently caressed the contour of my jaw. "Your face is still bruised. But you look so much better than when you were down in that ravine. When I saw you, I thought we'd failed you."

"Failed me?" I shook my head, not understanding what he could mean by that.

"Failed to protect you. What I said out there in front of my warriors was true. I took you from Queen Beatrice's court because you didn't deserve what was happening to you. You acted bravely, fought against your own father, and saved the lives of the queen's sons. And despite that, in her anger, Queen Beatrice wanted to see you tortured and killed." He shook his head. "But by trying to save you, I've created trouble within my army's ranks. And I'm sorry you've been put in the middle of all that."

"Why do they hate me?" I asked instinctively leaning into the battle-roughened fingers that continued to caress my face. "What threat do they think I pose?"

"The Kingdom of Fein is a closed society. We turn foreigners away at our borders. And because of our history"—a history Soren still hadn't elaborated upon—"slavery has been outlawed for many, many generations. The punishment for keeping a slave is death. My men are worried about what will happen when I bring you into Fein territory."

The punishment for keeping me was death?

I inhaled sharply and pulled away from him. "Will you…will you be put to death for bringing me into your country?"

He shook his head and smiled in that arrogant way he had about him. "No one would dare do that."

Because he was the Beast? Because he was so fearsome that even the royals in Fein let him do as he pleased with no consequence? He'd just taken off a man's head with hardly any effort. What kind of man did that?

"I fear you're jumping to the wrong conclusions." He wrapped his hands around my hips and pulled me closer to him. It was an intimate gesture that reminded me of the kisses he'd shared with me that morning. "Why don't you ask the question that is making you tremble like a frightened rabbit?"

"Maybe I don't want to know the answer."

His grip on my hips tightened. He leaned toward me and nipped the skin on my neck. A rush of heat passed over me. "Killing doesn't give me a sick sense of satisfaction. I hope you already know that."

"Then why?" I whispered. "Why aren't you afraid of the laws of your people? Why don't you think you'll be punished for bringing a slave into your kingdom?"

The gold in his eyes glittered as he stared intently at me. "Because, Celestina, I don't consider you to be my slave."

He didn't? I don't know why that surprised me. Of course, he didn't think of me as his slave. It was the collar that bound me, not him. Never once had he acted like I was below him or less important.

"Can you—?" I started to ask, but hesitated, afraid of the answer. But if my slave status caused trouble for his kingdom and if he didn't think of me as a slave, then why wouldn't he agree to it? "Can you remove the collar?"

"Goddess, I wish I could. But there's no seam. It appears to be magically bound to you," he said. "If I knew how to get rid of it, I would have cleaved it from your neck the moment we left Queen Beatrice's castle." He sighed. "And then there's also the political side of things. The king will need to decide what we're to do with you. But I promise you"—he brushed his lips over mine—"I won't let anyone harm you. Even if I have to take on an entire kingdom, I'll protect you."

Chapter 17

In the age of the fifth kingdom, some of the dragon lords fell in love and mated with a few of the primitive humans. Actually, the dragons fell in love and mated with many kinds of creatures. They were lusty creatures, those dragons.

The children produced from such matches were magical thanks to the dragon blood that ran through their veins. The magical humans took places of leadership in their tribes, eventually over generations becoming what we know as royalty today. The other magical creatures, such as the mammoth cats and the chorts, made places for themselves in the wilds of the Jayden Continent after the fifth kingdom fell.

Only the vampires weren't affected by the dragons, for the bloodthirsty beasts never loved. And the dragons felt no affection for creatures who fed on their human friends.

"We can make faster progress without having to travel with an entire army," Soren announced when he brought me a bowl of stew for dinner later that evening. "That's why I've decided you and I will ride out alone tomorrow."

Soren had instructed me to stay in the tent and rest while he left to speak with some of his captains. He'd also needed to fetch the sword he'd tossed away after executing that brutish warrior. I wasn't to help with kitchen duties. I suspected he'd wanted me to stay in his tent, not because he thought I needed more time to heal, but because he wanted me tucked away from his army for my own safety. While no one openly spoke out against Soren's decisions, I hadn't forgotten the warrior's friends who had watched him carry me to the ravine. They might seek to respond with violence in retribution for their friend's death.

"We will ride by ourselves? Is that wise?" I asked before eating a spoonful of the meaty stew. I recognized the taste of Mary's pungent healing tea mixed in with the venison and veggies.

"The sooner I get you to the capital, the sooner I can get on top of any rumors that are surely starting to simmer." Fast riders had been sent out every morning to carry news from the army to the capital, which no doubt included stories about me.

That realization made the food I'd just swallowed sit like a lump in my stomach. "I don't wish to be a burden."

Soren paused in packing his saddlebag and crouched down in front of me.

"Maybe you shouldn't even take me to Fein," I said in a rush.

He tilted his head to one side. "What do you suggest I do?"

I shrugged. "Take me to another kingdom, one that will give me refuge."

He drew in a long, steady breath. It looked as if he was seriously considering the idea. "The queen bound you to me. We don't know what punishment you'd suffer if I permanently left you on your own in some faraway kingdom."

He was right. "Even sleeping in Raya's tent, which really isn't that far away from this one, the collar emitted a faint burn that continued until I could get back to you."

"What?" His muscles tightened. "You should have told me, Celestina."

"Everyone seemed so adamant I keep away from you. And the pain wasn't as bad as other times."

"Like when I accidentally give you an order?"

"Yeah, then. But, you know, there are times when you give me an order and your voice sounds kind of weird."

"Weird how?"

"It kind of echoes."

"Ah. What happens when I sound like that?"

"It doesn't hurt. I feel the same amount of compulsion to do whatever you say, but there's no pain associated with it."

"Really? That's interesting." He returned to packing his saddlebag. "I'll be sure to use that voice with you more often. Now, eat your dinner. You'll need to regain your strength. We won't have the comforts of the camp for the next several days. It might be hard on you, especially after that fall you suffered."

"Why am I not more seriously hurt?" I asked him. "Didn't Mary say my legs were broken?"

"Hmm? She must have been wrong."

There were other things Mary had said as I lay barely conscious at the bottom of that ravine—hadn't I seen dragons flying overheard?— things about Soren not being able to hide what he'd done. What had she meant by that? And how could I have survived such a fall with only a few bruises?

Something wasn't quite right here.

"Are you like Queen Beatrice?" I asked him. "Are you magic?"

He laughed. "I'm nothing like your witch of a queen. Finish your stew and get some rest. I'll want to leave at daybreak."

Patty, Mary, and Raya came to check on me that evening. Patty burst into tears when she saw me, hugging me and sobbing about how she was sure I'd perished.

"Thank goodness Soren saved you!" Patty shrieked. "I don't know what I would have done if you had died! You're my best friend!"

"I love you, too," I said, hugging Patty just as tightly as she hugged me. She really was a good friend. But something she'd said tickled the back of my mind. "How did Soren save me?"

"He used his—" Patty started to say.

"Enough of that," Mary grumbled, pulling Patty away from me. "Give Sky Girl some room to breathe."

"We're all glad you're okay," Raya said, giving me a nudge with her shoulder. "You had us worried there for a bit. But you're better now, aren't you? Your face is a riot of bruises."

"I'm sore, but nothing seems broken."

Again, that tickling started up at the back of my mind. When I'd hurt my hands, the healer had tended to me. But this time, I hadn't seen the healer at all. Why was that?

I'd been thrown over a waterfall. A tall one. I'd crashed down on the rocks and had rolled to the bottom of that ravine. My legs had been broken. I was sure of it. And the pain in my chest had been excruciating. And yet, yet I woke up a few hours later feeling only a bit sore.

That couldn't be right.

Something else had happened.

You won't be able to hide what you've done, Mary had told Soren. But he'd said he didn't care.

What had they been talking about?

"How am I not hurt?" I asked the women in the tent with me. "How is this possible?"

"Soren broke the rules and—!" Patty started to shout excitedly.

"Hush now," Mary scolded.

"What?" I demanded. "What did Soren do?"

"It's not important," Raya said.

"He saved you," Patty said at the same time.

"Patty! It's not our place to talk about it," Mary said and cuffed Patty's head.

"But I want to know." I really did. "Why am I okay? And why hasn't the healer been here to take care of me? What's going on?"

"That's something you should ask Soren," Raya said in that calm way of hers.

"But—" I wanted them to tell me what they knew.

"Talk to Soren," Raya said. "If he thinks you need to know, he'll tell you."

"What if he doesn't think I need to know?" I felt like screaming my frustration.

"Then, I'm sorry," Raya said. "I really am."

"It's not fair," Patty cried. "She's one of us. And she's my friend. We shouldn't be keeping secrets from her."

"Thank you, Patty." At least one of them understood how I felt.

"I understand your frustration, Sky Girl," Raya said. "I do."

"We all do," Mary agreed gruffly. "But that doesn't change what we can't tell you."

"As much as we all love you, you aren't Fein. We've all taken an oath not to talk about Fein affairs to outsiders. Please, don't ask us to break that oath," Raya begged.

My shoulders sagged in defeat. "I wouldn't want you to do that."

Raya brightened. "We'll be in Fein soon, and out of these mountains."

"Hopefully, we'll find warmer weather on the other side of the border." Patty smiled at that.

It had been bitterly cold for the past several days. The wind had whipped relentlessly down from the mountains, making everyone miserable. I supposed I shouldn't have been surprised that more warriors hadn't snapped and tried to kill me.

"It'll be warmer in Fein," Mary said with a sage nod. "It always is."

"Is it? But it's to the north of Earst." I'd always heard that the northern parts of the Jayden Continent were perpetually cold.

"Fein isn't like other places," Mary said. "That's one reason we protect it so fiercely."

"I look forward to seeing it." A bit of hope bloomed in my chest. "Maybe I'll be able to make your country my home as well." If they accepted me.

Mary reached over Patty and gave my hand a squeeze. "I'm sure you'll be fine once you reach the palace. The general has many allies there who can help smooth the way for you."

I prayed she was right.

Chapter 18

My friends stayed with me in Soren's tent for several hours. We traded stories and laughed until my sides hurt. I appreciated their company. But as the night got later and later, my nerves revved up in anticipation of Soren's return. Mary, who must have noticed my agitation, stood up and announced it was time for everyone to find their beds. "The morning will be here sooner than we can realize."

Raya seemed uncomfortable about leaving me alone, but Mary grabbed her arm and pulled her out. "She's fine. She's fine."

"Soren has three guards standing outside the tent," Raya told me. She started to duck through the opening, but then paused. "Good night, Sky Girl. And"—her brows furrowed—"guard your heart, okay?"

"I will." There was no danger of me losing my heart to him. This desire I felt for Soren had nothing to do with my heart and everything to do with lust. My body craved his. I wanted to feel his muscles ripple as he pushed into me. I wanted to watch his expression change as he came apart inside me. Oh, goddess, how I wanted that.

For the next several hours I sat cross-legged on the piles of furs and waited for him to return, my body getting more and more keyed up as I thought about spending the night alone with him. Our first night alone. Soren had ordered Gray to bring me to his tent for the night. Because he'd wanted me.

But that had been before the warrior had tried to kill me.

Would he still be interested in finishing what we'd started this morning after all the drama I'd caused in his camp? A man—one of Soren's men—was dead because of who I was.

Gah! Despite all that had happened, all I'd witnessed, and all the unanswered questions surrounding why I wasn't dead, I wanted Soren. I wanted him more now than ever. It felt like that first kiss between us had happened a lifetime ago. I wanted to taste him again. My body ached for the feel of his hands on my body. And I wanted more. I wanted to give him every part of me. And at the same time, I wanted to take everything he had to give.

For too long I'd watched my friends and rivals at Queen Beatrice's court find partners to slake their lust. Occasionally, one of them would find love. Thanks to the young queen's dislike of me, members of the court didn't want my bad luck to rub off onto them. If I'd been in their shoes, I probably would have done the same. Being disliked by Queen Beatrice never ended well.

Unless, unless one considered that the queen's previous actions were the reason why I was now sitting in the middle of Soren's tent, shivering with anticipation for his return. In that case, I was grateful for Queen Beatrice's constant disdain.

I must have fallen asleep at some point because when I opened my eyes, I was tucked under the heavy furs with a warm, deliciously male body pressed against my backside. His arm was snug around my middle as he held me tight against him.

I shifted around to look at his face. It was dark inside the tent with only a small lantern still burning, making it hard to study his features, not that I needed to see him to know that it was Soren who was holding me so tenderly. Even if I lost my sight tomorrow, I would always know him by the way he moved and by the pine and snow scent that could only belong to him.

His eyes were closed, and his breathing had turned slow and deep. He'd had a long day, what with having to rescue me out of the ravine, using some sort of forbidden magic to save me, killing one of his own men, and then making sure no one else under his command tried to retaliate against me.

He'd been gone forever talking with his captains. If his army was anything like Queen Beatrice's court, he'd been using the time to soothe egos and make sure he held onto his position of power.

He had to be exhausted.

Because of me.

I ran my fingers along the side of his face. I may not have deserved Queen Beatrice's slave collar, but at the same time, Soren didn't deserve the trouble I'd brought to him.

I gently traced the square plane of his jaw with my fingertip. He sighed. He looked tamer, almost innocent as he slumbered. Raya had warned me to guard my heart. But that warning had come too late, hadn't it? I'd first started to slip when he'd protected the princes' lives at the castle. Even though he and Raya and Gray were grossly outnumbered by the enemy, they'd battled fiercely to save us. I'd slipped even more when he showed how troubled he was that his commands caused me pain. And I'd completely lost my footing after he kissed me.

"You're supposed to be sleeping," Soren grumbled without opening his eyes.

"I waited up for you." I kept touching his face. Gods, how I wanted this man. "I mean, I tried to."

"I know." His eyes still closed, he leaned his cheek into my hand and sighed again. "I waited until I knew you were asleep before I returned."

He'd waited? "How did you know I'd fallen asleep?"

"Superior warrior senses," he said sleepily. "Took you forever to drift off, which is a shame since we have an early start in the morning that is now probably less than a few hours away."

My fingers traced the outline of his lips. "But I was waiting up for you. I wanted—" How did I tell him that I wanted to pick up where we'd left off this morning without risking my tender heart?

His hand moved with blurring speed. His fingers latched onto my wrist, stilling my fingers' movements. "After what happened earlier, I wanted to give you space to rest."

"Thanks to whatever forbidden magic you did, I'm fine. Better than fine. And I still want—" I swallowed down a lump of fear. But I must not have managed to swallow it all the way, because my voice sounded gravelly when I said, "*You. I still want you.*"

His eyes had drifted open. The green orbs gazed at me through the darkness as if lit from within. The gold flecks in them sparkled.

He didn't say anything. And he still held onto my wrist, keeping it trapped within the cage of his strong grasp.

"Forget I said that." I tugged on my hand, desperate to get it back, desperate for a sudden case of amnesia so I could forget how I'd confessed that to him. "I know I'm not anything special. You don't have to let me down easy. I've seen myself in the mirror."

"Have you?" His hold tightened. "Are you sure?"

"Please." I tried again to free my hand. "Like you said, we should be sleeping."

He kissed the tips of my fingers. Slowly. One after the other, starting with the pinkie and working his way to my thumb. "But I'm awake now. And it seems like you need to know something."

"W-what's that?" I asked, my voice cracking a bit.

"You need to know that you are so fucking special, Celestina, that it hurts to be around you." He propped himself up on one elbow and turned his body toward mine. "When I watched you try to defend those boys against an army with only a toy wooden sword, you took my breath away. That night I ached every time I thought of you. I ached so badly, I wanted to tear down the doors to the castle keep and find you and bury myself inside you. And that was before I even knew you."

"I'm glad you didn't," I said with a nervous laugh. "The princes stayed in my room that night. They would have been terrified if you'd done that."

"You are"—he kissed the tip of my pinkie again—"a warrior in a siren's body." Fire flashed in his eyes. "And my wanting you hasn't diminished, not one tiny bit."

"Oh." I didn't, I didn't know what to say to that.

"And that is why I waited until I knew you were asleep before joining you. I didn't want to start something with you tonight. Not when it's only been a few hours since you'd fallen into the ravine. It wouldn't be right. You must still be sore."

"I'm not." Well, perhaps a little. But I should have been very sore. Worse, I should have been *dead*. But I wasn't. And while I knew I should ask him what he'd done to heal me, that wasn't the thought that kept pushing its way to the top of my mind. I was much more interested in discovering more about his strong body.

He let out a long, frustrated breath. "*We* should be sleeping."

"Probably," I agreed.

"Definitely." His voice turned rough. "The road ahead is not one we would want to take while drowsy."

"Is that so?" I asked. I wiggled even closer to him.

He nodded and then nipped the tip of my middle finger.

"You know I'm not going to fall back asleep anytime soon," I said, loving this feeling of intimacy between us. "Not while I feel like I do right now. And whatever it is you're doing"—with how he was looking at me and how his lips were nipping at me—"is only making me feel even more…restless."

"So, you're saying you need me to help you relax your body?" The corner of his mouth hitched up just a bit.

A shudder worked its way down my spine. "It's only fair since you're the reason I'm feeling all worked up."

He looked at me as if he was trying to figure out the mysteries of the universe and like maybe he could see the answers to those mysteries reflected in my eyes. He then shook his head. "Damn, but you make me want to make all the bad decisions." Still holding my wrist, he pushed it into the furs and rolled over on top of me. His lips crashed down onto mine. He made love to my mouth with a desperation that took my breath away.

I was glad I wasn't the only one feeling this way.

Even though I'd never been with a man like this before, my body seemed to know exactly what to do. I arched into him, pressing my chest against his hard plains, delighting in the friction of our bodies. And aching to feel skin against skin.

He gave me an arrogant look and whispered, "I don't know who is going to enjoy this more, you or me." He shifted down my body, kissing my neck, my chest, each of my breasts. Lingering on my breasts, suckling on them through my heavy tunic. The scrape of the damp material against my nipples combined with the pressure of his lips and teeth made me squirm. He paused and looked up at me. And smiled. "Oh, this is going to be fun."

He continued to tease my breasts with his mouth until I was instinctually spreading my legs, panting loudly, and digging my fingers into his hair with such determination, that I was surprised he didn't cry out.

He lifted his head. "And to think, Celestina, I haven't even gotten you out of your clothes yet."

He helped me lift my tunic off over my head. I held my breath, expecting a shock of embarrassment or awkwardness to hit. But the heated way Soren was looking at me, like I was the most beautiful sparkly stone he'd ever set eyes on, made me want to taste him. So much so, I reached up and pressed my lips to his.

He growled low in his throat and deepened the kiss I'd initiated. His lips pressed against mine as he licked and thrust his tongue, making me feel as if I were spinning out of control.

His fingers skirted down the column of my throat, over my collarbone, and then up the swell of my breast. He pinched a nipple, making me cry out in his mouth from the shock of it. The brief sting hadn't hurt exactly. The feeling had zinged through my body, settling in the damp heat pooling between my legs. My back arched up toward him as if my body was begging for him to do it again.

He made a sexy sound in the back of his throat before putting his mouth over one of my breasts and started to suck. Oh goddess, that felt good.

His hands moved to the ties on my leggings. I helped him loosen the knot and shove them off. Nestled between my legs, he sat up and pushed my legs wider apart.

"So beautiful," he said before dipping his head and placing his mouth where he was looking.

Oh, my goddess. My friends had talked about how having a man's head between their legs was like being drunk on candy. So dizzyingly sweet and delicious. But damn, they were downplaying the…the feelings…I couldn't even describe…I couldn't…couldn't catch my breath…

I stretched out, clutching the furs with a death grip. It was too much. Too much. I couldn't…couldn't…

I tried to wiggle away from his questing tongue before I exploded. But his mouth followed me. And his hand landed on my hip, holding me in place. He started sucking on my sensitive clit in a way that made my entire body tremble. He pressed a finger inside me and then added another, pumping them in and out in a rhythm I never realized my body craved as desperately as it craved air.

"*Soren*," I moaned.

"*Celestina*," his deep rumbly voice answered, and I came apart.

He continued to lick me as tremors continued to pulse through my body. Finally, he lifted his head and smiled at me. He crawled back up my body, pressing the hardness between his legs against my still throbbing center.

He kissed me deeply. I sucked on his tongue. I wanted…more…needed…more…

I rubbed against him like a house cat. He peeled his lips from mine and watched me.

He was breathing hard. "Celestina, tell me to stop. Tell me not to take your virginity on the ground in the middle of fucking nowhere."

"I…can't. I want you. We could be trapped in a nest of vampires, and I'd still want you."

He stilled. His pupils were large and dark as they searched my face. "I—" He started to roll away. I wrapped my legs around his hips, stopping him.

"*Please, Soren.*"

"Gods." He closed his eyes and let out a long breath. "There's too much you don't know about me."

"Then tell me, and I'll still want you." I tightened my legs around him and rubbed my body against the hard ridge pressing against his pants. "I'll still want us."

He kissed my forehead. "I want to believe that's true, but—" He shook his head and then placed a sad, gentle kiss on my lips.

I tried rubbing against him again. But he stopped me with another kiss. "It must be morning. I can hear the camp starting to stir." Instead of pulling away from me, he kissed me some more. "And we have a long day of riding in front of us."

Cold air hit me as he suddenly pushed up to his knees, knocking the furs to the side. I grabbed ahold of the thickest one and snuggled down into it, curling into the heat he left behind in them. "I've never been a morning person."

"You can sleep until noon every day after we reach the capital." He gave my bottom a gentle swat. "But today, we need to get moving by sunrise."

Chapter 19

The frigid morning slapped my face as I stepped out of the tent. A few warriors turned to glare. Did they seriously begrudge their general a tumble with the camp slave?

Maybe. Maybe. While the Earst army traveled with whores to keep the men satisfied, the only civilians that traveled with the Fein troops were Mary and young Patty, and no one dared touch Patty for fear of feeling the sting of Mary's oversized spoon.

Perhaps the Fein military had taken a chastity vow to purify their minds, just like the mysterious fighting monks of Karraugh. A storyteller from the far south had once spun a rich tale about their commitment to keeping themselves pure in mind and body to achieve killing skills that rivaled the gods.

I felt a cold rush of dread, which only made me shiver that much harder in the biting morning air. No wonder the warriors hated me. I was the temptress who was ruining the fighting prowess of the best and most deadly among them. Hell, when I thought of it that way, I wasn't a fan of myself and how I'd been tempting Soren.

Why hadn't Raya been plainer about it?

Why hadn't Mary?

Or Soren. He could have told me he'd taken a vow of chastity.

It wasn't as if I had *known* that I shouldn't want him. Or that he shouldn't want me.

Even so, I couldn't stop the pang of guilt from twisting in my gut. My lips, lips that still were swollen and slightly bruised from his kisses felt like a damning brand as I passed even more frowning warriors, no longer sure about where I was supposed to be heading.

Heck, my body was still tingling, and my legs felt like loose noodles after the attention Soren had spent between my thighs. I tried not to let any of that show as I hurried toward where Mary had set up the outdoor kitchen. I didn't want anyone in the camp guessing what I'd done with Soren last night. I didn't want them to guess how I'd already corrupted him. I figured I'd been successful in my ruse until my gaze met Raya's. She lifted a brow and mouthed, *"Oh, Sky Girl."*

I tilted my chin up and pretended I didn't see her.

A heartbeat later, Soren put his hand on the small of my back and tugged me slightly toward him. He smiled as he leaned even closer to me. "Hungry?" he asked.

I welcomed the heat of his body even while thinking I should insist we put some distance between us if only to preserve peace among his warriors. But, dammit, he didn't seem to mind the glares coming from all corners. And it was bitterly cold out this morning.

"How about we go see what Mary is cooking up for us this morning," he said, sounding awfully pleased with himself. "And then we can go get the horses ready."

The gentle way he spoke to me didn't zing through me like a command. His words were an invitation, an offering of himself, of his company. It felt…nice.

And yet, at the same time, I couldn't stop worrying that our slave/master connection was somehow destroying his command over his men and whatever else it might mean for him after he broke his vow to remain celibate.

That had to be the reason why the others desperately wanted to keep me away from Soren. They loved him and wanted to protect him.

For the future safety of their kingdom, they needed their leader to remain strong and pure. And untouched.

I could respect that.

What if that mysterious magic of his, magic that he refused to acknowledge, had been born from his self-imposed purity?

I would really need to practice keeping my hands to myself.

We approached the open fire where Mary was serving a savory porridge from her enormous kettle. Soren had us walk past the line of hungry warriors because he was the leader and never stood in a line, apparently.

Mary took one look at the two of us and glowered. "I see I've lost my best helper. First, you saddled me with this girl who didn't know how to even hold a knife, and then after I went through all the effort of training her, you yank her away from me. I'll never forgive you, you inconsiderate beast."

Soren held a fist over his heart and bowed his head. "Then I must beg a thousand pardons, Lady Mary," he said softly.

A huge smile shattered her scowl. She barked a laugh and thrust a bowl filled with porridge into Soren's hand and a second bowl into mine.

"We'll miss having you travel with us, Sky Girl," Mary said in that gruff manner of hers. "Don't let this big oaf monopolize all your time after you reach the capital. Patty is going to want to show you around. She won't shut up about how she's going to take you to the library."

"Where is she?" I asked, looking around. She usually helped serve breakfast.

"She's taking down the tent. But I'm sure you'll see her before you leave."

And I did. She came running up and gave me a huge hug while I was in the middle of eating my porridge. She squeezed me so hard that the air in my lungs came out in a loud swoosh.

"Don't strangle her," Soren said, with an indulgent grin for the young woman.

"I'm going to miss the stuffing out of you!" Patty cried.

"Not if you squeeze it all out of me here," I said with a laugh.

"You'll only be a few days behind us. And I'll make sure you get a chance to spend time with her—"

Patty squealed in ear-splitting delight.

"After," Soren continued sharply, "you spend time with your parents, Patty. You know they must be missing you fiercely."

"I know. And I will. Nana will make sure of that." Patty's scowl looked nearly identical to her grandmother's.

Soren chuckled as he finished up his porridge. "I look forward to seeing you around the palace then." He looked over at me. "Are you ready? We have a long day of riding ahead of us."

I quickly finished my porridge and gave Patty a hug that made her squeal again. After she left, I took Soren's bowl from him, intending to wash them both.

He resisted. "We all now do our own washing in this camp. Even me."

He then did something completely unexpected. He took my dirty bowl and washed it for me.

We had two saddlebags filled with provisions and one change of clothes, two horses, and that was pretty much it. Soren, naturally, was wearing his broadsword on his back, two daggers tucked into his boots, and a crossbow tied to his horse's saddle.

I patted my little pouch of treasures tied to my leggings to make sure it was still secured in place. It was.

Soren gave me a quick smile as we led our horses through a snow-covered field that took us around the camp and back to the road.

"If you get tired or need a break, please let me know. Otherwise, I'll keep us moving until sun fall," he said. "We've got about three days of hard travel in front of us. But I think you can manage it."

"I hope so." I hadn't worried about being able to keep up with him…until he'd said that. "Yesterday's travel wasn't that bad."

"We'll be going quite a bit faster today. But you should be fine."

His reassurances were having the opposite effect. I gulped down a lump of worry.

Posey, the friendly mare I'd ridden the other day, seemed happy to be setting out on our adventure. She kept nudging my shoulder with her broad nose as if telling me not to worry.

Sheesh! I wasn't worried until everyone around me seemed intent on telling me to stop worrying.

Stop it. Just stop worrying. It wasn't as if I was being asked to run to the border. All I had to do was sit atop this charming horse while she did all the work. How hard could that be?

I was still arguing with myself by the time we'd led our horses to the road, which was why I'd failed to notice Soren's abrupt halt. Or that his good mood had vanished.

His sudden, harsh curse startled me.

I glanced up to find both Raya and Gray waiting for us. They both had their horses saddled and ready for travel.

"No." Soren slashed a hand through the air. "Absolutely no. I don't need you following along like a pair of fucking nannies."

"You don't?" Gray shot back with a smirk. "And how long did it take you to notice that I'd come into your tent the other morning? You remember the morning? The one when you were distracted learning the curve of—"

"I don't need it spelled out," Soren gritted out. "And that was different. You were in my tent, where you shouldn't have been entering unannounced."

"Please, don't fight us on this, Soren," Raya said as she guided her gelding toward us. "We're only doing our duty to the king."

"And you have been distracted, my friend," Gray said quietly. He placed his hand on Soren's shoulder. "We'll watch your back while you watch Sky Girl's—" He cleared his throat. "Okay?"

Soren glanced at me. His cheeks reddened with embarrassment.

"No," he said as he turned back to Gray. "I'm more than capable of taking care of myself and Celestina."

"I know you are," Gray was quick to agree. "And yet, I also know that the king would have our heads if we didn't follow his orders. You want Raya and I to lose our heads for dereliction of duty? Will you be okay with that?"

"What's going on?" I asked. Weren't Gray and Raya under Soren's command? The way they were talking sounded as if they were royal guards instead of part of Soren's army. But why would they have been fighting alongside Soren? Royal guards didn't fight battles. In Earst, they had one job and one job only—to protect the royal family.

And if that were the case, what were they doing here?

"You're royal guards?" I asked Raya.

"We have many roles, but yes, we answer to the king first," she said. "We're part of the King's Guard."

"But then why—?" I started to ask.

"Don't slow me down," Soren cautioned Gray and Raya, speaking at the same time as I had. He then turned back to me. "Celestina, I'm sorry. This is part of that situation I was telling you about this morning, the one that's complicated and..." He rubbed his jaw. "And might change how you feel about me."

"So you didn't pull back this morning because I was about to make you break your warrior's vow of chastity?"

"That's what you told her?" Gray snorted. "Damn."

"I didn't tell her that." Soren spun to me. "I didn't take a vow of chastity. Why would you think that?"

"What else was I to think?" I demanded. Tears sprang to my eyes. I hated them because they put a spotlight on how vulnerable I'd let myself become around him. "Why else would you push a willing woman away?"

He pulled me close to him and wrapped his arms around me and just held me. "Because, Celestina, you aren't simply a willing body to me. I want you to come to me when you understand who I am...*what* I am. And after that, if you still want me, I want your first time to be perfect."

He tightened his hold for a moment before letting me go. The cold air rushed between us as he stepped back. I started to reach out to him because nothing he could say to me would make me change my mind about him. But I stopped myself when I remembered the number of questions that still existed between us. Like the grim-faced King's Guards standing a few feet away.

"Then tell me this," I said. "Why do you have guards? You're not a prince, are you?" Certainly, that couldn't be the case. He would have announced the fact that he was royalty back at court. In fact, he'd said just the opposite when trying to get out of going to Queen Beatrice's ball. And he'd called himself his king's sword.

But…but I'd forgotten about the second role the royal guards would sometimes play back at Queen Beatrice's court. They'd sometimes escort royal prisoners.

"You're not a prisoner?" I felt stupid even asking the question.

"I'm not." He lightly stroked my jaw. I instinctively leaned into his touch.

"Is it the magic that you weren't supposed to use? Did that cause trouble for you?"

"No," he whispered against my temple. "Not that. And it's too complicated to get into right now. May I help you onto your horse?"

I nodded, still uncomfortable with this secret he thought would make me hate him.

His large hands felt warm at my waist as he lifted me into Posey's saddle.

Gray and Raya looked relieved as they mounted their horses. But Soren, I could tell, was still feeling irritated by their presence. The muscles in his jaw kept tightening as he mounted his horse and led our small group away from the camp.

Chapter 20

Instead of avoiding towns and villages like the army had been doing, the four of us rode our horses straight through the center of towns whenever that meant we were on the fastest route. Soren hadn't been kidding about the quick pace. Raya and Gray seemed unaffected by how hard he pushed the horses. My back, on the other hand, was screaming in pain as we rode into a small village with tidy slate-roofed houses and a marketplace at its center.

Soren, who had kept to my side for most of the day, would pull ahead to the front as soon as we entered the village. Gray would fall back to the rear. And Raya would ride next to me. In this village, she seemed to tense up as people came out of their homes to watch us. Her right hand moved toward the hilt of the broadsword strapped to her back.

"Are you expecting trouble?" I asked. She hadn't acted this way when we rode through the last village.

"Not really. Just good to be prepared. The villages on the border have a reputation of being hostile to the Fein."

"Why?" That didn't make sense. "The Fein are our ally. I mean, allies with the Kingdom of Earst." Was Earst still a home I could claim?

"The queen considers these towns along the border as her first line of defense against attack, even from those she believes are her friends. She has filled the towns with rogues, killers, and criminals."

"And slaves," I said, with a nod to several collared women who were scurrying away from us. I felt an instant connection to them. And not in a good way. I ached to save them, to free them.

Raya bared her teeth. "I hate this place."

"If the Fein and Earst kingdoms are so different, why did your king make an alliance with Queen Beatrice?" I asked.

"Politics," Raya said, urging her horse to speed up. "It's all above my paygrade to question it."

I clicked my tongue behind my teeth and gave Posey a nudge with my thigh. She nodded her understanding and kept pace with Raya's mount.

Thankfully, it didn't take long to leave the small town. I wasn't sure why riding through it bothered me so much. The place really wasn't much different from Queen Beatrice's court. Slaves were everywhere, doing drudgery jobs or dangerous jobs others didn't care to perform, just like at the castle. The slaves, while not mute, had always acted like their spirits had been beaten down, squashed. That was their lot in life.

But seeing the slaves here and knowing I was now one of them changed everything, a knot coiled tight in my gut. How had I not noticed the injustice of their lives before now? How had I blindly accepted that slaves were beneath me and somehow deserving of the treatment they received? How could I have been so blind and self-centered?

Oh gracious, I felt sick.

I lifted my head to the sky. It had been snowing on and off all day and had recently started to come down in heavy flakes again. The chilly flakes stung as they melted against my face.

"Celestina?" Soren had slowed his horse until he was riding next to me again. "What's wrong?"

"I…" I blinked several times. I don't know when I'd started crying. Tears weren't going to help anyone. They showed how callous I'd been and what a spoiled brat I was now. Crying simply because I was now part of the lowest level of society which I used to (at best) ignore and (at worst) look down upon. "I'm—"

"We're stopping," he called to the others.

"I'm fine," I said, not wanting to be seen as the weak link in our small traveling party. "I'm fine. We don't need to stop."

"You might not need to." He was already directing his horse and mine off the road and toward a tight copse of trees. "But if we don't stop, I won't be able to put my arms around you. And I need to hold you in my arms more than anything else right now."

Gray, who had caught up to us, heard this and sighed deeply. "I'll go scout out the area," he said before urging his horse into a run.

Raya remained mounted on her horse a few yards behind from where we'd stopped under the canopy and pretended not to be watching us. But I could tell she was totally watching. Not that I was surprised. She was, after all, doing her duty.

Soren jumped down from his horse and was at my side before I even saw him move. He reached up and gently guided me off Posey. I was glad his hands were around me since my legs had given up remembering how to work properly a few miles back.

He tightened his arms around me and held me as if I was the most important thing in his life.

I knew I wasn't. And knowing that only made the tears fall harder.

Gracious, I hated this feeling. I hated that I was slipping deeper and deeper into whatever this was between us. He had a secret, a complicated secret he believed would make me hate him. And he planned to reveal this devastating secret once we reached the capital.

Why did he have to hold me like I was precious to him?

Why did he have to be so, so easy to love?

He pulled back and wiped the tears from my cheek with his gloved thumb. "We'll figure out how to get that collar off you and break the spell." His voice sounded rough. He pressed a soft kiss to my lips. "I promise, Celestina. We'll figure it out."

We rode for a few more hours. Soren kept right at my side, his worried gaze turned toward me so often I was glad we had Gray and Raya around to keep an eye out for dangers on the road. A few times, they spotted someone far ahead on the road and had us pull off into the trees to avoid a confrontation.

We passed vast hillside fields where collared slaves shivered in inadequate outerwear as they tended large flocks of sheep. Every time we passed a slave, Soren would reach over and take my hand. "*I promise*," his touch seemed to say each time he gave my hand a squeeze. "*Not just you. I promise.*"

Chapter 21

Even after the darkness of night blanketed the sky, we kept riding. I'd begun to think we'd never stop riding, not even to sleep, when Soren led his horse off the road. "I was hoping to reach the border today," he admitted. "But we'll lose even more time if we push too hard and end up laming our horses.

"We'll cross the border in the morning," Gray said with his gaze off to the north.

"And we'll sleep uneasily tonight," Soren said.

"We'll take turns keeping watch," Raya offered as she led her horse to join us. "Gods it's going to be a cold night."

The icy winds blew down from the northern mountains like an endlessly flowing river. We'd been riding directly into it all day. I'd wrapped a thick wool cloth over my face, but now that the sun had left us, the bitter winds managed to work their way through the heavy cloth to sting my cheeks.

"Let's get the horses settled and then catch some rest for ourselves," Soren said.

He had to help me slide down from Posey. And even after my feet had hit the ground, it took several moments before my sore muscles managed to support me. He handed me our bedrolls and pointed to a mossy spot beyond some bushes. "Get our bedding set up over there and see to your needs. I'll join you after I tend to the horses."

The collar gave me a jolt that nearly knocked me off my tired feet. With my head down, I shuffled over to where he'd pointed and got to work.

I was just settling down onto my bedroll when Raya dropped hers next to mine. "We can't risk a fire this close to the border. It wouldn't be safe. We'll be huddled for warmth." She wasn't much more than a dark shadow in the starless night. But I could hear a touch of humor in her voice as she dropped down next to me. "It'll be cozy, like a girl's sleepover. We can braid each other's hair."

"But who will do Gray and Soren's?"

She chuckled and then slipped a cloth bag into my hand. "You'll want to start drinking this tea every morning."

I opened the bag and sniffed the pungent herbs. "What is it?"

"It'll keep your womb empty. You'll want that."

Did I? I stared at the bag of herbs as if it contained poison.

"I don't need it yet," I whispered. I tried to hand the bag back to her. "We haven't…"

"But you will." Raya closed my hand over the bag.

"I don't know. With you and Gray acting like the world's best chaperones, I doubt I'll get any time alone with Soren…ever."

Raya laughed. "It's our finest talent."

Gray whistled over at us. "Could use some help putting up the tarp, Raya. Unless you'd rather wake up buried under a couple of feet of snow."

I didn't think I'd be able to sleep on the cold ground with nothing more than a thin wool blanket tucked around me. My shivering alone would surely wake up the dead. And yet once everything had been settled and Soren tucked his body around mine, and then Raya pushed her backside up against my other side, warmth slowly seeped into my skin. Still, I lay at the center of our little huddle wondering about my three traveling companions who didn't seem bothered by the harsh weather. Did the Fein train their warriors from childhood to be like this? Did they not know the pleasures of sleeping inside a warm room with silken sheets? No, no, that couldn't be the case. Soren had said he'd been raised in a castle much like I had. And both Raya and Gray had obviously received an education that extended to more than the swiftest ways to kill an enemy.

Which begged the question, how in the world could anyone sleep on the ground in the middle of a snowstorm? With no fire. And with Gray keeping the first watch.

Fires attract attention, Raya had explained. And this close to the border, the less attention attracted the better. But even though we were supposed to be resting, the cold and my tumbling thoughts wouldn't let sleep come.

I doubted I needed that tea Raya had handed me. Soren seemed convinced that once I knew the truth about him, I wouldn't welcome him into my bed. Yeah, that had me worried.

Why couldn't he simply tell me about himself now? The wondering and worrying had to be worse than the truth, didn't it?

The Fein should practice talking about themselves. Honesty wasn't a weakness. Keeping secrets was. How could they not understand that?

And if Soren cared for me even just a little bit, shouldn't he trust me with a few of his secrets? It wasn't as if I could run home and tell anyone. I was bound to him. I would die if I left him. My life was so tied up with his, I wasn't even sure I could trust that the feelings I felt for him were real or if they were what the collar wanted me to feel.

But oh, the things I felt for him. The sight of his toned body alone made my thoughts stutter. The way he commanded his army with kindness instead of brutality made me want to stay up late watching him joke around with his warriors as if they were all his dearest friends. And the slip of vulnerability he'd shown when faced with having to attend to Queen Beatrice made me want to hug him.

Gah! Were those even my feelings? Was what I saw in him even real? Or did the spell Queen Beatrice cast on me cause me to see things to make me play the role of a fool?

Soren was the Beast.

He had a reputation for brutality. For killing.

He'd separated that warrior's head from his body as if slicing off a pat of butter from a block. But he'd done it for me. To protect me. Because he cherished me.

He cherished me?

"*Celestina*," Soren's voice sounded groggy from sleep, but there was a power in that deep sleep-rumpled voice that tingled all the way down to my toes, "*stop fretting and rest.*"

Instead of a jerk of pain, the command spread over me like a warm blanket.

Still, I didn't think I could manage to obey the command. How could anyone sleep on the ground in the freezing…

"Celestina." A hand on my shoulder caused me to jerk awake. Soren's smiling face was inches from mine. The sky was gaining light. "It's time to get moving again."

"We should make it to the border by midday," Raya said as she shook snow from the tarp that had kept us from being buried in the night.

"Won't be soon enough for me," Gray said, stomping his feet as he headed over toward the horses.

"What can I do to help?" I asked as I struggled to move my stiff muscles so I could sit up.

Soren started to answer, but then he stopped himself from saying anything that the collar might view as a command. He shrugged. "Raya?"

"You can help me roll up the tarp."

The three of them moved in tandem without even needing to talk as they packed up the gear and prepared the horses. I felt so out of place.

And stiff.

And hungry.

And grumpy.

Gray kept sending wary glances in my direction. I barely managed to suppress an urge to growl at him.

Thankfully, we set off before I actually did growl. As we were riding, Soren passed me a hunk of cheese and a flagon of water he'd retrieved from his saddlebag.

"When we're trying to make good time, we eat while we ride," he explained.

The road took us high into the mountains where the wind felt even sharper and the air that much colder. I was shivering and hoping the tips of my fingers weren't going to fall off by the time we reached what looked like a military outpost. As we approached, three guards dressed in heavy furs and carrying pikes emerged from a stone tower.

"In the name of the Kingdom of Fein, I command you halt!" one of the guards shouted when we were still a good distance away.

Soren raised his fist, signaling us to stop. "Must have some new recruits on duty today," he muttered.

"This is going to be fun," Gray said stonily.

"I think I should handle this," Raya offered. "I know how to talk to the newbies without coming down on them like a battering ram." She shot Gray a pointed look.

"Sometimes lessons need to be learned," he said with a shrug.

"And you think you're the one who needs to teach it?" she asked.

"Go talk with them, Raya," Soren said just as Gray started to argue. "Make sure they understand we're in a hurry."

She gave a brisk nod and rode off toward the guards, calling to them in a language I didn't understand. The guards swiftly lowered their weapons.

"Do the Fein speak a different language from the other kingdoms?" I asked. Was I entering a world where I wouldn't be able to communicate?

"For security purposes, our guards and troops will sometimes speak

Eirid," Soren explained.

"Raya had said that my name has roots in that language."

Soren gave a thoughtful look. "I hadn't thought about that. But it might…"

"No one in Earst speaks Eirid," I said. "At least, no one I know of."

"Very few in the other kingdoms are taught the ancient words," Soren said. "That's one reason why we rely on it for our communication."

Raya looked back at us and waved to us to join her.

"By the horns of Galbraith, safe travels," the lead guard said as the three of them stood aside so we could ride past. The horses moved forward at a sedate rate. I was just about past the guard tower when one of the other guards cried, "Hold there!" He grabbed hold of Posey's reins, jerking her to a sudden halt.

The two other guards lowered their pikes, blocking my path.

"She's not Fein," the guard said.

"And she's a slave," the guard to my right cried. "She can't cross this border. You should know that. You're a King's Guard."

"And I'm General Kitmun." Soren stared down at the guards as if they were unpleasant insects. "I grew up with the laws of the kingdom being recited to me as bedtime stories. Stand down. This woman is not a slave."

I shifted nervously in my saddle. I didn't want these men to come to harm because of me.

"She wears a slave collar," the first guard said, still holding onto Posey's reins. "And she's not Fein. I know my orders." He added a belated "Sir" as tensions rose. The guards adjusted their stance and tightened their grip on their weapons.

A lizard crawled up my arm. I brushed it away. I didn't want anyone to fight or get hurt because of me. Who was I anyhow? Just a run-of-the-mill Queen's Lady, one the queen never particularly liked.

If I could slink off into the mountains unnoticed, I would have.

But where would I go? I didn't have much in the way of survival skills. And besides, the collar would never let me leave Soren's side.

Raya must have sensed my discomfort. She caught my gaze and mouthed, "*This isn't your fault.*"

"And you said we wouldn't need a battering ram, eh, Raya?" Gray said, speaking up for the first time. He huffed a breath. "We ride for the king. We ride with the general. If you have ambitions to ever be moved from this frozen outpost and if you value living"—his sword zinged as he pulled it from its scabbard—"I suggest you stand down and stop threatening the woman the general has been working quite hard to protect."

Raya rolled her eyes but unsheathed her sword as well.

The two guards exchanged nervous looks. But their leader remained determined.

"Stand down, boy," Soren said to the resisting guard, sounding tired.

I'd seen him take the head off the hulking warrior without any effort. I'd seen him with Raya and Gray take on dozens of enraged enemy soldiers and survive without any visible signs of injury. These three scrawny border guards would be no match for them.

Still, the head guard stood his ground.

Soren's jaw tightened. I had a feeling that while he wouldn't hesitate to swing his sword, this wasn't a fight he wanted. Those three guards were sons of his people.

"Wait," I said. I straightened in my saddle.

Everyone turned to me.

I drew a deep breath. It wasn't as if I'd expected to leave Earst alive. The queen had put this collar on me to make sure I died for my parents' crimes.

"I will not allow a battle to be waged over me." I couldn't bring myself to look at Soren as I spoke, my only hint of cowardice. I directed my words to the guards. "If anyone here swings their weapons, I will fall on the nearest blade and end myself. General Kitmun is taking me to your king to plead for my life after my own queen has placed a death warrant on my head for a crime I have not committed. It's compassion and a sense of justice, which he assures me is ingrained in the Fein society, that drives him in bringing me to your king. But that said, I'll not allow my life to outweigh the lives of others. We are all, are we not, merely sons and daughters of our respected lands doing our best to survive?"

The silence that followed my speech made my heart thud even harder. I still couldn't bring myself to look over at Soren. Was he angry? Would he seek to punish me for usurping his authority by speaking up?

"Well," Gray said with a dry laugh.

"Our lady guest has certainly made herself clear," Soren said. Did he—? Did he sound amused?

I jerked my gaze in his direction.

He smirked as he looked down, studying his nails. "I wonder if you're prepared to allow an innocent lady, a refugee at that, to fall upon your pike. Or will you stand aside and allow us to ride to the capital and allow the king himself to decide the lady's fate?"

Two of the guards lowered their pikes and stepped aside, leaving their leader standing alone in the middle of the road. After a few moments, his hold on Posey's reins slipped away. "By the horns of Galbraith, safe travels, my lady," he said quietly and stepped to the side of the road.

"Thank you," I rasped. Posey followed Soren's mount. I held my breath as we crossed the border into the Kingdom of Fein. The collar buzzed slightly as I left my homeland, likely for good.

Surprisingly, the air smelled the same. The land felt just as firm. The only difference between the two kingdoms was that I was a slave who had entered a land where slavery was outlawed.

My life was not going to get any easier.

Chapter 22

"Do you want to talk about what happened back there?" Soren asked when we stopped at a snowy overlook a few hours after the border crossing.

"Not particularly." I slid off Posey's back and turned away from the general, stretching this way and that.

"I'd like to talk about it." He took hold of my hand and tugged me toward him. "Celestina, you didn't need to threaten your own life to get those guards to back down. They would have let us through without anyone having to shed a drop of blood. I don't want you to ever feel like you have to do that again. You're a guest in my land. I'll do my duty to keep you safe."

"We all will," Raya said as she walked by. She nudged Gray in the side. "Won't we?"

Gray grunted.

I felt like Gray. This wasn't something I wanted to talk about. I tried to pull away. But Soren tightened his grip.

"Even if it meant bleeding those guards dry, I would do it a hundred times over to protect you."

I shook my head. "No. Don't."

"Celestina. You're important."

"Because of this magic you think I have?"

"No. You're important because you worry about foolish guards who dare question their general. You're important because you'd rather fall on a sword than cause anyone around you a lick of trouble. You're important because you pick up pretty rocks alongside the road when you think no one is watching. Gods, Celestina you're important simply because you are who you are. And the more time I spend with you, the more I want to tear out the throats of anyone who looks at you wrong."

I shook my head. "You're ridiculous."

"Just when I'm around you." He brushed a quick kiss on my lips.

"That's the truth," Raya called out.

I could no longer look at Soren and imagine the man everyone called the Beast of Fein. While he was large and strong, he continually proved himself to be the kindest man I'd ever met. And no matter how I tried to protect myself I kept falling. And falling. And falling for him.

This is going to end badly, Raya had warned.

Goddess, she wasn't wrong.

As soon as we passed over the mountain's ridge, the punishing winter winds stopped. Even though we were still heading north, the sun felt warmer. Blessedly warmer. I gazed out over the landscape reaching beyond the mountain that we were now riding down and gasped.

Baked red earth.

For as far as I could see.

The land in Fein appeared to be dead.

Barren.

A vast ocean of desert.

Why would the Fein work so hard to keep other kingdoms from coming into this…this wasteland?

The landscape reminded me of a tale about the vampires the princes liked to hear. The vampires, as they traveled from kingdom to kingdom, scrabbling to put in a foothold and build a kingdom of their own, would use their horrible magic to strip the land of vegetation, water, of anything that was good and life-sustaining. Because vampires didn't need these things. They fed off the blood of humans. Blood from a half-starved human tasted just as good to a vampire as blood from a well-fed human. And the half-starved humans rarely managed to fight back. That was why the vampires liked to ruin the lands they wished to claim.

"Breathtaking, isn't it?" Soren asked as he rode past me.

Was he serious? I jerked my gaze away from the lifeless land we were entering and gaped at him. He was smiling at me. And not in an "I'm joking around with you" kind of smile. That bright look on his face as he watched me was the same look the young princes would get whenever they'd bring me one of their best treasures—like the time they found a green, many-legged creepy-crawly creature under Ronald's bed.

Soren's smile faded when he noticed the look of horror that had to be present on my face.

This was a vampire's wasteland.

"How?" I asked, feeling a little breathless. "How does the Fein Kingdom support itself on such lands? How do you grow crops? Keep livestock? How does anything…any*one* survive?"

Maybe the Fein kept their borders closed to hide that their lands were infested with vampire nests. Maybe they'd given up on ever routing the vile creatures and this was why the Fein had come to Queen Beatrice's aid. They were planning to expand their kingdom into healthy neighboring kingdoms.

"We don't grow food here," he said as if it were obvious. "This is the Rainbow Desert, one of our most revered places. It would be sacrilegious to use this land.”

I nodded. And honestly, I tried to understand. But all I could see was a wasteland that seemed to go on forever. A vampire’s dead land. The lush Earst countryside had so many shades of green during its short summer season that centuries ago scholars invented hundreds of new words to describe them all.

“How long will it take for us to reach the capital?” I asked, worried about how many nests of vampires had to be lurking out in such a desolate place.

“Two days if we push ourselves.” And with that, he urged his horse to pick up the pace.

Two days?

I found that impossible to believe.

I clicked my tongue, urging Posey to keep up with Soren. My mind replayed the many tales where hapless travelers were set upon by vampires. The slowest of the group in such tales would always be the first to die.

I might have managed to survive long enough to leave Earst, but I was starting to doubt that I’d make it to the capital city alive.

This was not going to end well.

The pillars I’d noticed along the Earst road leading to the border also lined the desert road we were riding down. But instead of being smashed and pushed over, these pillars still stood upright. On top of nearly every pillar sat a bust of a stern-faced man with a bald head and pointed beard.

“Who is that man?” I asked Raya who’d been riding alongside me for a while. Soren and Gray had forged ahead to check out the road and to talk. Were they searching for signs of vampire nests? I didn’t ask because I honestly didn’t want to know.

"Frendrick the First," Raya answered, nodding to the pillar to the right of us. "He was one of the original leaders of the Fein. Many of the roads were built and towns settled because of him. Every summer there's a three-day celebration in his name."

"And the pillars were placed here to remind the people about his works?" I asked.

"Raya makes it sound so noble. It's not. Those pillars were put alongside all the kingdom's major roadways because the Fein royal family have a long tradition of vanity and seem to think the people want to see their faces everywhere," Soren called over his shoulder.

Gray chuckled. Raya smiled and shook her head.

I didn't join in. A vain and capricious ruler was not going to look kindly on me and my situation. I wasn't a great beauty that could be shown off. I couldn't sing or play a musical instrument. I wasn't even that smart.

I had as much to offer a kingdom as those pesky tiny lizards that had seemed to follow us from Queen Beatrice's court. What king would risk war to save someone as plain and uninteresting as me?

Not a vain king, I knew that for sure.

This was not going to end well.

Night fell quickly in the desert. The warmth I'd enjoyed during the day disappeared nearly as swiftly as the sun. Gray, who'd been riding next to me for the past half hour, tossed a wool blanket he'd tied to the side of his horse onto my lap. "You'll fall off Posey and scare Thunder here if you shiver any harder," he said.

"Thank you." I wrapped the heavy wool blanket over my shoulders. "Will we ride through the night?"

"No. There's a traveler's hut just over the ridge. With beds. And running hot water."

A bed? A chance to wash with hot water instead of frigid stream water? "That sounds heavenly."

"If there happens to be other travelers staying in the hut, I suggest you wrap yourself up in that blanket and not let anyone see your slave collar. It would save us from having to handle extra trouble that seems to erupt whenever anyone notices that damned thing."

"Yes," I said, glad the darkness hid how hotly my face burned from embarrassment. "I suppose I should keep it hidden when we reach the capital, too."

"No, that won't work," Soren said as he rode up alongside us. "We'll have to face the consequences of your slave collar head-on as soon as we reach the capital city."

"We can't have anyone thinking we're trying to hide what you are," Gray added.

What I was? Did the two of them understand how their words crushed me? "I thought… I thought…" I couldn't finish what I'd really wanted to say. Soren had told me that he didn't think of me as a slave. Had he changed his mind? "What am I?" I managed to ask, pleased my voice didn't sound too strangled.

"I'm going to tell the king you're a political refugee," Soren said. "And that you're requesting sanctuary."

But what am I to you? I wanted to scream.

He reached over the distance between our horses and gave my hand a squeeze. "No threatening to fall on any more sharp blades, okay?"

"I'll…try." I couldn't promise him any more than that.

"Do more than try, Celestina," he said softly. "Don't let Queen Beatrice win."

I swallowed over a lump and shook my head while one thought kept circling round and round in my head in time with the rhythmic clop-clop-clop of the horses' hooves.

This was not going to end well. This was not going to end well. This was not going to end well. This was not going to end well. This was not going to end well.

Chapter 23

It was midday the next day when the gateway to the capital city finally came into view. The Rainbow Desert had gradually given way to fields and farmland and finally to forests.

Men and women worked side by side in the fields. All the workers appeared to be well-fed and in much better health than the slave farm workers we'd passed in the Earst countryside.

Even in the forest, cottages dotted the landscape here and there. All of them appeared to be in good repair. Instead of weathered wood, the cottages were constructed from mud and straw. Each had been painted bright colors. One was pale blue. Another was a shockingly bright green. There were three purple cottages. And a lemon yellow one. Many had flowers growing in the shaded front yards.

Unlike the desert, the memory of which still chilled my bones, the forest felt warm and friendly.

"How is it warm here?" I asked. We'd been traveling further and further north, and yet the endless winter we experienced in Earst had given way to spring.

"The Faraday Sea not far to our west pulls warm air up from the tropics," Soren explained. "It's still icy up in the mountains this time of year. I can take you up there whenever you miss the cold weather."

Soren planned to take me on trips with him? My heart skipped a beat. "I'll let you know when that happens." I peeled off the heavy wool gloves Raya had given me. "It'll probably take a hundred years or so before I tire of not shivering all the time."

In the distance, I spotted the snow-topped mountains he would take me to if I ever felt too warm. They weren't as steep or jagged as the ones that formed the border between the Fein and Earst kingdoms. And while I'd never seen anything like them before, their rounded peaks felt familiar. I squinted at them.

There you are. There you are. There you are. They seemed to call to me, which had to be a product of my sleep-deprived mind. Mountains were nothing more than piles of rocks. They didn't have the power to speak to people. And even if they did, such a magical rock wouldn't waste its time speaking to me.

Still, the mountains held my attention. *There you are. There you are. There you are.*

"What are they called, those mountains?" I asked Soren.

A corner of his mouth tilted up. "They're the Yurdu Mountains. In the summer they can be quite pleasant. When I was a young lad, my family would summer in a cabin up there. There's a lake right about…there." He pointed to a tall mountain peak. "The water is spring-fed and cool in the heat of the summer and is the most brilliant shade of blue I've ever seen."

Though I tried, I had trouble picturing Soren as a young boy enjoying a frolic in a mountain lake. In my mind, he came into being as a fully-grown, terrifyingly strong warrior.

"We would float in the icy water until our fingertips were puckered like prunes. We wouldn't have gotten out even then, but our mother would finally come down to the lake and order us out. She'd go on and on about how the three of us always made the adults wait too long for dinner to be served."

"You have siblings?"

"Two. A younger brother and sister. I was always leading them into mischief. Still am, if truth be told. My parents don't know what to do with us."

"It sounds as if your parents love the three of you very much."

"Too much," he said, with a rueful shake of his head, but he was smiling full-on now. Until he glanced over at me. "We need to talk." He led our horses off to the side of the road. Raya, who'd been riding at the lead, halted her horse and waited for us while Gray pulled up alongside me.

"We're nearly at the capital," Soren said. "I'm sure I don't have to tell you that there will be a fuss made. Don't panic. Don't fall on anyone's sword. Just trust that I'll stay by your side the entire time. I'll protect you."

I swallowed down a lump of nervousness before nodding. "I'll try."

It wasn't as if I'd expected my introduction to the royal court to be an easy one, not after the cold reception I'd gotten from Soren's own army and the fight that had nearly broken out when I'd tried to even enter his country. Knowing Soren would stand up for me did nothing to settle my nerves. But I appreciated that he'd taken the time to reassure me.

"That's my brave warrior." He leaned toward me and pressed a quick kiss to my lips before turning to Gray. "There are some things you might feel you need to report to the court about Celestina. I'm asking you don't."

"But we can't just—" Gray started to object.

"I'm asking as your friend to let us deal with one crisis at a time," Soren said, his brows raised. "Please."

Gray glanced at me, then back at Soren. "I don't think it's wise not to warn—"

"This is Sky Girl we're talking about," Raya called back to us. "She's your friend, Gray. Or she would be your friend if you'd give her the chance."

Gray turned his head away. "I can't ignore—"

"You can," Raya said. "Sky Girl isn't a threat."

"I'm not even sure what any of you are talking about," I said. *A lie.* I knew Gray (and Soren) believed I possessed magic. Soren seemed to be impressed with the idea, while Gray acted alarmed. "You do remember that the collar won't let me do anything that could hurt anyone?" I asked him.

"That damn thing is part of the threat," Gray complained. "You're here, in our land, because that's what your queen wanted. Even if you aren't in on the plan, Sky Girl, you can't guarantee you'll be able to control your magic or even your own actions."

"I don't have magic."

"Maybe you didn't," Gray said in such a patronizing manner I gritted my teeth and snarled at him. He held up a placating hand. "Maybe it's the collar that's the source of the powers we've been seeing. And if that's the case, that only increases the threat your presence in the capital poses."

I closed my eyes. "What do you want me to do?"

Did Gray wish Soren had followed the queen's orders to kill me? Was that what they'd been talking about during their long, private conversations? Had Gray been pleading with Soren to slice his sword through my neck like he had with his warrior?

"Gray is being overly cautious," Raya said, sounding irritated. "Like always."

"If you're uncomfortable with Celestina, watch her, guard her," Soren said. "Just don't say something that might convince someone to hurt her. Keep quiet about your…concerns until we can pull our allies to her side and keep her protected."

"Very well," Gray said with a sigh. "I'll keep my mouth shut for a week because I don't want anyone to harm Sky Girl. She's had a rough enough time of it already. And a week should give you enough time to get ahead of the narrative. But don't be surprised if some of the advanced riders haven't already told the court that there's something different about her."

"I'm expecting it." Soren gave his reins a quick flick. "Let's get moving. The watchers at the gates have surely spotted us by now. I'll stay at Celestina's side as we move through the city. I want Raya on point and Gray guarding our flank. Keep things tight. Understood?"

The two guards nodded. "We've got her," Raya said.

"And you," Gray added. "Always you, my friend."

Chapter 24

The walled city of Sukoon was like nothing I'd ever seen. It had been built on a hill with a fairytale palace at its highest level. Slender glass turrets twisted and sparkled as they seemed to reach for the sky. When we rode up to the intricately decorated bronze city gates, five guards emerged from a rugged tower. I held my breath, expecting the guards to protest my presence like the ones at the border had. But as we passed through them, the guards at the gates bowed low with their arms crossed over their chests. Soren nodded in acknowledgment and continued without pause into the city.

Carts, carriages of all shapes, horse riders, and foot traffic crowded the road inside the gate, which slowed our pace considerably. Buildings as tall as five stories high lined the road. Businesses with glass fronts displaying all manner of goods occupied the ground level of most of the buildings. My entire body trembled at the sight of a jewelry shop and its front window filled with the most deliciously colorful sparkling gems. I *needed* those stones.

"Stick with me," Soren cautioned when I'd inadvertently veered Posey toward the shop.

Along the way, I noticed several of the city dwellers bowing low like the gate guards had. Their arms crossed over their chests.

"Why are they doing that?" I asked.

"I'm a popular guy," Soren said with a shrug.

"So popular that they bow to you like you're a god…or…or…*no*."

Soren looked over at me and frowned. "I'm not a god."

"But you have King's Guards. And…and…" I shook my hand toward a small group of older women who were lowering themselves to their knees. How had I not seen it before? Because I hadn't wanted to see it? "Oh, my goodness. You're part of the royal family."

"Yeah," he said, wincing. "There are a few things I need to tell you about that."

"Why didn't you use your title in Queen Beatrice's court? The captain of the Asterian forces had called himself a prince even though it's his uncle that's the king, and there are like twenty people between him and the crown."

"I didn't use a title because I'm a warrior, not a courtier. Marching out some silly royal title when acting as my king's sword causes too great of a distraction. It's bad enough my parents insist on these guards shadowing me wherever I go."

"It's no picnic for us either," Gray said.

Raya nodded her agreement. "Always fun to be somewhere you're not wanted."

"But…but the people…they're bowing to *you*," I pointed out. If any of Queen Beatrice's subjects bowed like that to one of her sons or to any of her siblings, she'd have both the citizen and the royal executed in a public and bloody way. She was vain like that.

And Soren had said the royals in Fein were vain.

"You should have told her sooner," Raya said, clucking her tongue.

"It's not like it's a carefully guarded secret," Gray agreed.

Soren shifted uneasily in his saddle. "It's not who I am when I'm leading the troops."

My eyes grew wide. "Who are you?"

"I'm the—" Soren started to say but a commotion on the road up ahead interrupted him.

"What have you done!" an old woman screeched. Dressed in a dove-gray gown, she ran around in the middle of the road with her arms stretched out to the sky. Twigs hung in knots throughout her long, white hair. And there was a smudge of dirt on one cheek.

She appeared to be looking directly at Soren. Pointing at him. But that couldn't be true. Her eyes were nothing more than large milky globes.

"The monster of Dunhirve has landed in our kingdom!" she shouted as a crowd gathered around. "It will destroy some and enslave the rest of us! It will be the end of Fein! The eeeennnnddddd!"

"She's stark raving mad," Raya said. Both Gray and Raya kept their hands on their swords.

"She's upset," I said as I climbed off Posey. The woman was moving so erratically, no one could ride past her without risking harming her. The traffic on the road had come to a complete standstill. But no one seemed to be inclined to help her.

"What are you doing?" Soren asked.

"I'm going to try and calm her."

The onlookers circled around her but kept out of reach of the raging woman.

"What? Wait! You can't do that. She might hurt you."

"She's upset," I repeated.

Soren swore. His boots thudded against the pavement behind me. That didn't slow me. I felt this poor woman's panic as if it were my own. She needed help.

"Honored madam," I said calmly as I approached her. "No one wants to harm you. Let us help you find your way home."

"Ahhhh!" she screamed, spinning away from me. "Don't touch me! Monster! Monster!"

"I believe that was the opposite of helping the troubled lady," Soren said with a chuckle as his arms curled around my waist, pulling me out of the woman's reach.

The woman screamed even louder, pointing at me and Soren, and stomping her feet.

"Please, Grandmother." A young woman about my age rushed onto the street. She was dressed plainly, like her grandmother. An old shawl, worn through to bare threads in several places, was wrapped tightly around her shoulder. "Please, Grandmother," she repeated, her voice soft but pleading. "Come with me. I have soup on the stove."

She tugged at the old woman with both her hands.

The old woman resisted. "I must warn the good people of Sukoon. They can't see like we can. They don't know."

"I'll take the news to the palace tonight. Please, come with me now." The young woman tugged even harder.

Others on the street, I noticed, kept their distance. No one stepped up to assist the woman in guiding her grandmother home. Just like when she'd been ranting on the street, the onlookers had made sure to stay far enough away to avoid letting the woman touch them.

The young woman, with much tugging and pleading, finally managed to move the old, confused woman out of the road. "I have soup on the stove. You like soup," she repeated over and over. And then she added, "I'll tell the palace about the monster. You can trust that I will, Grandmother. You can trust me."

"The monster has already breached the walls! It is right there!" the old woman screeched, but it was with much less force than before. She seemed to give up the fight and go with her granddaughter.

"That poor woman," I said. "I hope her granddaughter can help settle her nerves."

"Don't feel sorry for her," Gray said as he rode up leading the horses Soren and I had abandoned. He handed Soren both reins. "She's a seer. Granddaughter likely is one too." He shook his head. "They're all off their rockers."

"The seers used to have power in the kingdom." Soren helped me climb back onto Posey's back. "But that power died out ages ago. They generally keep to themselves. People around here don't trust them."

"She seemed so upset." My body started to shake as her angry words repeated over and over in my head. "She called me a monster."

"Don't take it personally," Soren said. "I'm sure you're not the first person she accused of being from Dunhirve this week. Gray is right. The seers are an unstable lot. Let's get into the palace before another one stumbles out into our path."

Chapter 25

"Vampires are great deceivers," the princes loved for me to tell them this tale. "They can pass as humans if they try hard enough. You can tell a vampire from a human by their thin frame and pale skin. And the fact that they can't be outside in daylight. But they'll make you think otherwise. They'll make you believe you've seen them basking in the sunlight. They'll make you believe they can feel compassion and love for you. That's part of their allure, part of their magic. That's what makes them so terribly dangerous."

The crowds grew thicker as we approached the palace gates. People knelt. Some cried out greetings. Everyone seemed thrilled to see their general had returned. He'd clearly won over the common man just as surely as he had his warriors.

And yet, there was something about him that he hadn't told me, something about him being part of the royal family. I leaned toward him and tried to ask him to finish telling me whatever he needed to tell me before that seer had burst into the middle of the street. But the noise of the crowds had grown so loud, that Soren and I had trouble hearing each other.

"Don't worry," he shouted. "I won't leave your side."

The palace gates opened just as we rode up to them. We passed through without having to alter our horses' strides at all, which was incredibly lucky on our part. For the foot traffic, there was a long line of people waiting to get in.

The palace looked so sleek and modern compared with Earst's stone castle.

"Is it polished marble?" I shouted the question, staring up at a wall that seemed to reach into the clouds.

"What?" Soren shouted back.

As the gates closed behind us, the noise of the city seemed to fade away.

"The walls? Are they polished marble?" I shouted in the sudden quiet. My voice upset a flock of ravens, sending them winging off the trees and into the sky.

"They're onyx," Soren answered while watching the ravens flee the palace walls.

"Blissful silence," I whispered in the sudden peace. I turned to Soren, who was still staring after the ravens and frowning. I brushed a lizard off my arm. I hoped they wouldn't plague this palace like they had in Queen Beatrice's castle. "What were you trying to tell me earlier?"

"Oh, you need to understand that I'm not simply the general," he started to explain. "I'm also—"

"General!" Four warriors ran up and caught the reins of our horses. "The king and queen are anxious to meet with you. They're waiting in the throne room."

"Certainly, we'll have time to wash up," Soren said as he dismounted. He came over and helped me slide off Posey. We'd been riding hard for the past couple of days, and I stumbled a bit.

"They were most adamant, General," a large warrior who looked as powerful as an oak tree rumbled. "They've been hearing…er…alarming stories from the advanced riders and want an accounting of your activities post-haste."

Soren sighed. "I hope they realize the throne room will smell like sweaty horses for weeks. And my news won't change in the hour that it would take to bathe and change."

A man with a shaggy black beard dressed in long black robes hurried up to us from a side passage.

"Redfern." Soren shook the man's hand heartily. "Tell the king we're going to clean up before giving him an audience. I'm not going to make an appearance in the throne room wearing a day's worth of road dust."

I agreed with Soren. The courtiers in Earst would never take a dirty messenger seriously, not even the general of an army. Looks mattered. Perhaps more than it should, but that was simply the reality of royal courts.

Redfern, whoever he was, glanced over at me and then latched onto Soren's arm. "I'm afraid if you don't attend the king immediately, he'll send armed guards to deliver you to him…even if that means pulling you and this foreigner from the bathing chambers naked. He's that serious."

Soren rolled his eyes. "Very well."

"Captain Gray and Captain Raya," Redfern said. "You two are dismissed."

"No, they are not." Soren took my hand as he held his ground against this Redfern. "They stay at my side."

Raya and Gray both nodded. "Of course, we will," Raya said, her gaze narrowing as she stared down Redfern.

What was going on here? Was Soren planning to overthrow the king? Or was he worried the king might try and attack us?

The dark onyx walls that had initially looked beautiful now gleamed ominously on both sides of us as we worked our way through the palace, down one hallway and another. Finally, we reached a set of golden double doors that held Fein's royal seal. Four guards pushed the doors open.

"The Crown Prince of Fein," the herald announced in loud, round tones as we stepped into a gilded hall. The crowd of courtiers all turned and stared at us.

I looked behind me, expecting a prince to walk through the archway and march past us. But it was empty. Soren's hold on my hand tightened.

"*Don't fall on any swords*," he whispered.

And then he stepped forward.

He wasn't—?

I tried to wiggle my hand out of his grasp. But he wouldn't let me budge from his side.

He took another step toward the twin thrones and the grim-faced monarchs who sat on them, pulling me along with him. When he reached the base of the dais, he went down on one knee. He tugged my hand. With a start, I dropped down on one knee beside him.

Holy crap, of course he was. No wonder I'd thought he looked like a king. He had the bearing of a king because Soren was the king's eldest son, which made him not simply a prince but the bachelor *crown* prince of Fein.

Raya had tried to warn me. But I hadn't listened. I'd fallen for the man who had to be the most unattainable in all the four kingdoms.

"Mother. Father. I have returned." Soren turned his bowed head toward me and winked.

"Prince Soren, my boy," the king said, his voice stern. "You have returned sooner than expected."

Soren lifted his head. "The Tiburnians were no match for our forces. It was a quick war."

"I sent you to do more than fight," the king said with a sigh. "You were supposed to—"

"And who is this woman you have brought home with you?" the queen asked at the same time. "We have been hearing disturbing tales."

Soren rose, guiding me to stand with him. "This, Mother, is Lady Celestina of Earst. She used to be one of the Queen's Ladies."

"And now she is with you instead, dressed not as a lady but in your army's tunic and leggings? You have brought her—an outsider—here to Fein?" The queen surely knew everything about me from the information that had been provided by the army's advance riders. But apparently, she wanted to hear the tale from her son.

"I have brought Lady Celestina here. It's true," he answered, clearly not at all intimidated by his parents who I, quite frankly, found completely terrifying. They were the freaking king and queen of Fein, after all. Both had long straight dark hair. Their skin was so pale it looked as if it would glow in the dark. Their large black eyes looked cold enough to freeze a fire.

"And what is that strange gold collar around her neck?" the queen leaned forward to ask.

Soren gave my hand a squeeze. "It's a slave collar, ma'am."

The entire court gasped.

"What have you done?" the queen demanded.

"You know the penalty for keeping slaves? And yet you choose to flout it?" the king said with a raised brow.

"Well, that is a story that needs to be told," Soren said, still acting not at all worried that both his parents now looked like they'd breathe fire if they could.

"Then I believe you should start telling us right now, son," the king said, his voice hard.

"I'm not sure it's a tale for the court's ears," Soren shot back. "May we adjourn to the family sitting room? We've been riding all day and haven't eaten or had barely anything to drink since the sun's rise. And I'm sure Lady Celestina would appreciate being able to sit a soft armchair instead of standing in front of my parents as if she were on trial."

The king's nostrils flared. "It's not only her who is on trial. You flout the law and bring an outsider who's also a slave into this court, a court who has been hearing disturbing news about her and about your questionable decisions regarding her from your runners. You, Soren Kitmun, will stand here like a man stripped of his king's favor and explain yourself."

The queen's hand flew to her mouth to cover a gasp.

Others in the court weren't as discreet. Murmurs grew into a low roar.

"You really stepped in it this time," a young man with raven black hair said. He bumped Soren's shoulder as he passed him to stand directly in front of me.

"That rude welp is my younger brother, Prince Cullen." Soren gave my hand a gentle squeeze as the well-dressed man continued to stare at me. There was a family resemblance in his features. Both men had the same dark hair. And both had the same strong chin as their father. But while Soren towered over most and had muscles on muscles, Cullen wasn't quite as tall. And he had a more delicate structure that resembled the queen's birdlike features. Gold-rimmed glasses sat perched on his narrow nose.

"Back off, Cull," Soren warned.

Cullen's eyes were as black as the midnight sky as he leaned forward slightly to peer at me even closer.

I felt a zing of power.

The collar reacted with a burn of power of its own. I hissed a breath.

Soren's attention shot to me. "What's wrong?" he demanded.

"Your brother has magic," I said, not sure why I should have been surprised. I was alive thanks to Soren's strange healing magic. And Queen Beatrice had magic of her own. Why shouldn't this bookish-looking prince possess magic too? "My collar didn't like whatever he did to me."

Prince Cullen lifted a dark brow as he continued to study me. "Interesting."

"His power is the ability to peer through artifices and see the true person beneath our layers, or some such nonsense," Soren explained. "And he knows it's rude to go peering into someone's hidden depths without their consent, especially someone who is a guest of the court."

Cullen's gaze shifted from peering at me to examining his brother. His raised eyebrow inched up a bit more. "Even more interesting."

"Leave us alone, Cull," Soren grumbled. "Don't you have another history book to write?"

"I do." He crossed his arms over his chest and remained standing directly in front of me. "But I suspect this will be more entertaining."

Soren grimaced and then gave his brother a not-so-friendly shove. With my hand still firmly clasped in his, he moved closer to his parents' twin thrones. Cullen trailed behind us like a sentient shadow. I could still feel his sticky power coming off him in sheets. It made my skin crawl.

"Priscilla will be interested in meeting your new pet," Cullen said.

"Shut up," Soren grumbled.

"Who's Priscilla?" I asked at the same time Soren asked, "Where is Pris?"

"Who knows?" Cullen answered his brother. "Last I heard she was heading toward some remote village to provide medical supplies to a clinic she'd opened. Was the battle in Earst not bloody enough for you? Is that why you decided you needed to start a battle at home?"

"I did what any honorable man would do in the same situation." Soren looked behind him and motioned for Raya and Gray to stick close behind us.

As if moving pieces in a game of chess, his father waved for a couple of guards to stand closer to the throne. "You had better hope, son, that this tale of yours adequately explains the outrage that you have brought to our kingdom."

Soren closed his eyes for a moment. His shoulders drooped just a bit.

His reaction to his father's warning worried me. This was exactly what I feared would happen. Well, I didn't know Soren was a prince and that this confrontation would have the added family drama of a father's disapproval of his son attached to it. But I had worried that my presence in his court would cause Soren trouble. This was why so many in his army hated me. This was why Raya and Gray had worked so hard to keep me away from their general. No, not just their general, he was first and foremost their crown prince. And they were the King's Guards tasked to protect him.

That wasn't simply the king and queen. That was also Soren's mother and father sitting up on those thrones. He'd spoken so fondly of how close he was with his family. Fearing I'd damaged that relationship hurt like a knife in my chest.

Soren glanced over at me and scowled at whatever he saw in my expression. "I forbid you to fall on a sword for me."

"That's not a promise I can make, Your Highness."

He flinched when I'd used his title. At the same time, the collar gave me a jolt of pain. That awful piece of enchanted metal would make sure I obeyed Soren's order.

"Well?" the king prompted curtly. "Our patience runs thin."

Instead of bristling with anger, which I'd expected, Soren lowered his head. "Father," he said quietly. "I apologize for failing you with the larger matter concerning Queen Beatrice. I'm not cut out for diplomatic missions." He looked up and smiled wanly. "When I see a problem, my instinct is to attack it with a sword. Perhaps you should be grateful I didn't do that this time." He then launched into the telling of how he met me in the castle bailey yard, how I'd protected the queen's sons from the Tiburnians, and how the queen had then punished me for my parents' acts of treason. He went on to explain what happened as we traveled to Fein and the troubles we encountered along the way. He explained how he thought the collar worked and the concerns he and his King's Guards shared that Queen Beatrice might be using the collar (and me) in a game against the Fein. I was grateful that he left out the part about the mammoth cat and how he thought I had used magic to scare it away. And I was also grateful that he left out how close we'd grown. Although, I supposed he didn't need to say that. His fingers, which had remained twined through mine ever since we'd walked into the throne room, said that for him.

"Lady Celestina may have been gifted to me—and I do believe the queen's plan all along was to lure me into taking her—but I don't consider the lady a slave. She's a pawn in a game Queen Beatrice insists on playing with us. I have broken no laws by bringing her here," he concluded.

Prince Cullen took a step forward to speak, but the king raised his hand.

"You accepted this gift and made a promise to Queen Beatrice, even knowing you weren't going to carry out that promise?" the king asked.

"I was never going to torture and kill Lady Celestina, no," Soren answered without hesitation.

"Then you should have never accepted the gift," the king said.

"Lady Celestina isn't a trinket that could be given away, but a human. And may I remind you, she acted against her parents' will and had defended the queen's sons with her life. She didn't deserve the punishment the queen had decreed," Soren shot back.

"It was not your place to interfere with the sovereign whims of another kingdom. We are trying to build ties with Earst. Thwarting the kingdom's queen does the opposite," the king explained.

"What would you have asked me to do? Allow the queen to hand Celestina over to a man who'd promised to allow his army to rape her before feeding her to his dogs? That would not be honorable."

"You should have never lied to Earst's queen! You should have never promised you'd carry out her wishes. What will happen when she sends missives demanding to know if you've carried out that promise? What will happen when she realizes through the bond you worry exists between this magical collar and the queen that her slave still lives?"

"Celestina is not a slave," Soren corrected.

The king didn't seem to hear him. "We'll send her back. Wars have been waged for less. And a war with Earst is not one I want to fight right now, especially not over the life of some inconsequential Earstian slave."

"She. Is. Not. A. Slave!" Soren shouted. After several seconds—in which the stunned court seemed to hold their breath—he added, "Sir."

"And yet the woman is bound to you by a magical slave collar the queen has placed on her neck?" the king asked.

Soren gave a tight nod. "Yes."

"Can the collar be removed?" the queen asked.

"That's something I hope to find out," Soren said. "With your leave, I hope to enlist the help of Redfern and the other royal mages.

Celestina is not a slave. I've never meant to keep her as one."

"And yet, you said the collar has the power to compel her actions?" The queen sat forward and looked at me with what felt like kindness. "Does everyone have power over her?"

"No. Not everyone. I suspect Queen Beatrice still retains power over her. She granted power to me. And I seem to have the ability to grant that power to others, although she does not seem to be as bound to others as she is to me."

"How do you mean?" the queen pressed her gaze locking on to our clasped hands.

"Celestina feels compelled to stay near me. It causes her physical pain if we're apart. She doesn't feel that compulsion toward others."

The queen sat back and pinched her lips together with displeasure.

"Show us," the king barked. I felt the back of my neck prickle with alarm.

"I beg your pardon, sir," Soren said, tensing beside me.

Cullen's brows flattened as he watched me.

"Show us how she can be compelled," the king said. He'd barely looked at me once. Even now, his gaze was locked on his son's.

"No."

"It wasn't a request." The king sounded as if he was losing his patience. "Show us how the collar works."

"I understand you've given this order. And yet, I can't be forced to do this," Soren replied, seemingly unconcerned that his father—the king—could lose his patience and…and I shuddered to think what this sovereign would do if he lost his patience. He seemed even more dangerous than Queen Beatrice. "I won't compel her. Doing so causes her pain and takes away her freedom to choose how to act. I won't treat her as if she were a slave because she's not one."

The king stood. "You dare defy me in front of the court?"

"I requested a private audience, Your Majesty," Soren reminded him.

Raya and Gray moved to stand on either side of us in a show of support.

But it didn't matter. The king descended the raised dais and marched toward his son. Alarmed at what might happen next, everything in me screamed that I needed to run. I remembered only too vividly how Queen Beatrice reacted whenever someone in her court dared to defy her. No one, not even her relatives, was immune. She'd once sliced off her sister's arm for daring to question the queen's decision to go riding one afternoon. It had looked like rain, and her sister had worried that they would get caught out in it and ruin their new feathered riding hats.

And for that minor quibble, the queen had chopped off her arm. Her arm!

This was Soren refusing a direct order from his king. In Queen Beatrice's court, that would be an immediate death sentence. It wouldn't matter who you were in the hierarchy. You didn't refuse the queen anything. And she liked to turn her punishments into spectacles. After surviving one, I certainly didn't want to be part of another royal spectacle.

Soren tightened his grip on my hand, refusing to let me leave his side even when I tried to jump in front of him. And he made sure I couldn't get anywhere near his sword.

Well, if he was going to foolishly put his head on the chopping block for me, the least I could do was to speak up for him.

"You act as if your son has failed you, which is ridiculous," I spat.

Soren looked at me with surprise, his eyes going wide.

"Your son is the most honorable man I've ever had the pleasure of knowing. He not only saved my life…more than once, mind you…he's loved by his warriors, he's loyal to a fault, and he would never ask a child of his to do the things you're asking of him."

The king's face had turned red by the time I'd ended my explosion.

Oh gods, oh gods, what had I done? I wasn't this king's first-born son. Nothing would keep this man from chopping off my head. Hell, that would solve all his troubles, wouldn't it? Kill me, and the trouble with his son, with Queen Beatrice, with having an outsider and a slave in in kingdom, it would all go away.

I lowered my head and belatedly muttered a respectful, "Your Majesty."

The king continued to stare at me. I could feel the heat of his anger thrumming against my skin. What had I done? What would Soren do? Would he try to protect me? Would he fight his own father? Would a bloody coup follow?

Soren's fingers remained twined with mine. His muscles hadn't even flinched as I railed at the man who'd sired him.

I knew better. I hadn't survived for so long in Queen Beatrice's court by spouting off every time I'd witnessed an injustice. Why in the hell did I decide to start now? Because I treated Soren like he was one of my precious baubles? Because I've always had some insane impulse to protect my baubles with no regard for my life?

"She's got a fire in her," the king said after several tense moments. He put his hand on his son's shoulder. "I can see why you wanted to bring her home, and why you're so adamant about defending her. Now, get out of here and get washed up. You reek of sweaty horse."

"Yes, sir," Soren said with a smirk. He gave my hand a gentle tug when I didn't immediately follow him as he turned to leave.

We were nearly at the door when the king called out to him, "I'm not saying this matter is settled or that she'll be allowed to stay in the kingdom. We still have the matter with Queen Beatrice and to figure out how to clean up the diplomatic mess you've made, but I'm glad you've returned safely to us, son. We'll have a feast tonight at eight. Be on time."

As we left, I heard the queen give a royal shriek before demanding, "Is that…is that a *lizard?*"

Gray chuckled. "I warned you they would follow us here, didn't I?"

Chapter 26

"Vampires lived in nests that were hidden in brambles, and altogether uncomfortable," I'd told the boys as part of a tale that recounted the history of vampires.

"Why would they choose to live like that?" Roland had asked squinching his face as if he'd bitten into a sour apple.

"Comforts like warmth and soft beds aren't what they seek. Their main desire is to feast on human blood. Thornes and beetles and worms mean nothing to them."

The boys had crooned with happy chills at the thought of such beasts.

Soren's royal apartment reminded me of that tale. I hadn't expected the space to be so spartan.

"You're the crown prince?" I asked as I turned a full circle in the anteroom that also served as a small windowless parlor.

"I am." He frowned.

There were a few hardback chairs, a desk tucked into a corner, and a small side table that looked as if it had been salvaged from a garbage heap. No artwork or heavy woven tapestries hung on the walls.

"And your father recognizes you as such?"

"He does." Soren's frown deepened.

I wandered through a rounded doorway and into the room the antechamber led into. This one at least had a large glass window that overlooked the rocky cliffs that protected the palace from the north. This had to be his bedroom. There was an old bed covered with several blankets pushed against one wall, a wardrobe against another, and a rack for hanging weapons on the third wall. But again, the furniture was battered and lacking any kind of decoration that would let me know that I was in a royal bedchamber instead of a servant's quarter, a lowly one at that.

"I understand you must be upset that I didn't tell you about my…status." He opened and closed his fist. "But you need to understand the Fein have enemies outside our borders who would be only too thrilled to get their hands on me. By traveling as simply General Kitmun, I'm protecting my warriors and myself from unnecessary ambushes."

I nodded. "But—"

"I know you must feel betrayed I didn't trust you with this information earlier. But hurting you was never my intention."

"Yes, I…" I couldn't tear my eyes from the bed. The top blanket had a hole in it. I swung to face him. "Is the Fein Kingdom poor?"

"What?" He jerked, clearly taken aback by the question. And I supposed I understood why. The palace was lovely. The furnishings in the public areas were gilded and looked quite exquisite. But those items were for others to see. This room, this sparse, tattered room was where the royalty actually lived. It was a room that should have been even more comfortable than the other spaces. And since Soren was the crown prince, his rooms should be nearly equal to a king's…unless the kingdom was hurting for funds, and they were hiding this sad truth from their people.

I spread out my hands. "This is not the room of a crown prince."

"Oh." He looked around as if seeing it for the first time. "I see."

Did he? "You're either living like this because your father is punishing you—perhaps he sends you to fight wars hoping you'll get yourself killed?—or because your kingdom lacks the funds to properly furnish the castle's private rooms. Which is it? Does he favor Cullen for the throne?"

He chuckled. "My father would be most angry if I managed to get myself killed on the battlefield. He'd likely bring me back to life just so he could scold me for neglecting my left side. He says it's a weakness I keep ignoring. And there's nothing sparse about our kingdom's coffers."

"Then why?" I asked. "Why is the crown prince living in a room not fit for a royal scullery maid? My room in the tower, even with the glass missing from the windows, was more luxurious than this."

"It's not that bad. I mean, it could—Wait," he said, raising a hand. "Your room didn't have glass in the windows? How did you not freeze to death in Earst's endless winter?"

"Extra blankets." Certainly, he'd survived colder situations. And the tower wasn't as bad as this room. Only occasionally did I wake up to find the water basin frozen completely solid. "This isn't about me. We're talking about your room and why it looks so…so…*like this*."

"Whenever I'd leave on a campaign, my brother and sister would raid my room, stealing the best furniture for themselves, leaving me with pieces like these. They think they're hilarious. Honestly, I grew tired of fighting with them to get my property back, so I decided to leave the room as it was. It's good enough for a warrior. And with my rooms lacking comfortable furniture, my siblings no longer steal from me every time I venture out the city walls."

That made sense. But still, it felt as if there was still something Soren was hiding from me.

He looked around the room and grimaced.

"You really should get some nicer pieces," I told him. "Not just for your own comfort. The servants will see this and think you're weak."

He turned toward me. "Is that what you think?" He stalked toward me. "Do you think I'm weak?"

My heart stuttered in my chest at the heated look he was giving me. I took a step back, not because I was afraid of him, but because I was afraid of my reaction to him. I felt too much, too quickly.

"There's no one in this room but the two of us, Celestina." His voice was a low purr. "You can tell me what you really think of me."

"I think…" *you make me feel like my skin is too tight when you look at me like that.*

I didn't dare tell him that. It would give him too much power over me. As it was, he held too much power already.

"I think…" *you make me want to scrape my nails down your chest like a wild animal.*

Also, not something I'd dare tell him.

"Yes?" he prompted. He crossed his arms over his chest and looked amused.

I glanced around the room again as the last important thing he said to me sunk in.

"We're alone?" I could hardly believe it. Every time we'd been together, there was always someone with us, or someone—or some magical creature—interrupting us. We'd never really had a chance to be completely alone.

"The door is locked." He took another step toward me. His hands cupped my face. "Do you think I'm weak, Celestina?"

I closed my eyes. "You stood up to a king for me. That's not the actions of a weak man."

"Celestina, look at me."

I opened my eyes. His lips hovered a breath over mine. "You stood up to a king for me, too."

His delicious lips descended over mine. They played against mine, stealing the strength in my legs. And then his tongue pushed into my mouth tasting me deeply, urging me to join him. Yes, I wanted to join him in everything this amazing man had to offer.

One hand moved to the back of my neck, holding me in place as he continued to make love to my mouth. His other hand moved down the side of my body. My back arched in response, molding myself against the hard planes of his body. His hand landed on my hip. He lifted me so my center pressed tightly against the thick ridge of his erection.

With a low groan, he wrapped my legs around his body and rocked his hips against mine. I gasped as pleasure rippled through me. I wanted to press him even closer to me. The clothes between us became a source of frustration.

I tugged at his tunic. Finally, he got the message and ripped it off over his head and tossed it to the floor.

My hands roamed over his chest's rippling muscles. My lips followed my hands. I rained kisses on his warm skin until he groaned and grabbed my hands, prying me off him.

Breathing hard, he pressed his forehead against mine.

"*Celestina*," he exhaled my name like it was a prayer. Or a wish.

"We're alone," I reminded him. And the secret he'd been keeping didn't feel all that great. Sure, I could never expect to marry the crown prince of a foreign country. But we had right now. Right here.

With a groan, his mouth went back to mine with an intensity that left me breathless. "Goddess," he panted when he pulled away again.

I whimpered.

"We should clean up and rest. The last couple of days have been hard on you. I don't…" He drew a long, deep breath as if trying to settle himself. "I want our first time to be special."

"Against the wall in your chambers can be special." My body was begging for him not to stop, not that I'd actually beg. "Being with you will be special."

He nodded. I felt the movement of his head against my neck. And when he pulled back, his green eyes searched mine as if trying to find the permission he refused to give himself. Something flickered in his gaze.

Regret?

Guilt?

There was something in the way the skin around his eyes tightened that worried me.

"What?" I asked him.

"Why don't you take the first bath?" He pointed toward a door on the far side of the bedchamber.

"We could bathe together," I said, still not ready to step away from the attraction burning between us.

He placed a gentle kiss on the top of my head. "Not today. The bath is through there. I imagine the servants have already filled the tub with piping-hot water. If not, just turn the knob on the left, and the hot water will flow."

The thought of lounging in a hot bath almost made my knees buckle. I'd been bathing with wet washcloths since being fit with the collar. I'd nearly given up hope of ever experiencing the luxury of a bath again.

And I supposed a little time away from Soren would give me the chance to sort through everything that had happened these past couple of weeks. I hadn't really had many moments alone. And none where I hadn't been under a command that had taken control of my thoughts.

"If that's what you want," I said, still not completely ready to give up.

He gave me another heart-meltingly gentle kiss. This time on my lips. "We'll have a lifetime of getting to know each other. There's no need to rush."

A lifetime?

He was expecting to keep me around forever?

I'm sure my expression showed how his words stunned me. His lips curled into a smug grin. He gave me a slight nudge toward the door that led to the bath.

Chapter 27

The warm water did wonders for my stiff muscles. I emerged from the bathing room wrapped in a fluffy robe that felt like a cloud against my skin that now smelled like lemons and roses. My damp hair was clean and pulled into a simple braid.

I emerged into the bedchamber to find three women standing around chatting. I froze. The oldest woman, a large silver-haired woman with a broad smile, hurried over to me.

"You must be Lady Celestina," she boomed. "I'm Morgana Goldfinch. But you can call me Goldie. Everyone does."

"Where's Soren?" I asked. Had I taken too long? Had he grown frustrated with waiting? He was the crown prince, and I'd made him wait to wash the dirt of the road and the smell of the horses from his royal body? How rude of me.

"Captain Gray needed to talk with him. I'm sure the prince will be back soon." Her eyes glittered with mirth. "He hadn't wanted to leave you. Gave me all sorts of orders to make sure you were well cared for before he left. Acted as if I didn't know how to tend to a lady. I've been a lady's maid for more years than that boy has been alive, I'll have him know."

"I am glad to have your assistance then." I frowned as I looked around the room. My dirty tunic and leggings were nowhere to be seen. Not that I'd really looked forward to putting them back on. But I needed something to wear. "The king and queen had mentioned a feast tonight. I don't suppose you'll be able to find something suitable for me to wear." My hand brushed against the collar at my neck. How could I have forgotten? Slaves weren't invited to feasts. It would be awkward for everyone in the kingdom if I'd tried to take a place at a table. A blaze of embarrassment stung my face. "I mean…I need some clean clothes to wear while I wait here for His Highness's return from the feast. I wasn't…I wasn't suggesting I'd been invited."

Goldie chuckled. "I don't know if the king and queen invited you. But I do know that Prince Soren expects you to stay by his side tonight. That's why I'm here to see to fixing your hair and your makeup. A dressmaker will be along shortly to alter a gown to fit you. A cobbler should already be here to fit you with a pair of slippers. But Horace, he's always running late. Please, sit, my lady." She gestured to an old wooden bench that had been pulled away from the wall and closer to the fire that was blazing in the fireplace. "I'd like to get started."

By the time Soren returned, my hair had been styled into a series of tiny braids that had been looped around to make an intricate crown around my head. My lips looked as if I'd been kissing berries. And my cheeks had a gentle blush. I was standing in the middle of the room with my arms outstretched while the dressmaker, a woman nearly as old and frightening as Mary, stitched a lightweight lavender-colored gown with a skirt that hung like clouds to my ankles and a bodice that fit like a glove.

When our eyes met, Soren stumbled over his own feet. "How is it that you're even more beautiful now than when I left here?"

"That wasn't a great feat. I was covered with road dust, my hair was tangled, and I was wearing the same shapeless tunic and leggings every man or woman in your army wears."

"They weren't shapeless on you," he muttered. "But now…" He

gave his head a shake. "Do we really have to go to my parents' fete?"

While his wide-eyed gaze was still fixed on me, the royal mage, who'd entered the chamber behind Soren, answered the question. "Your parents are holding the feast in your honor, Your Highness. They'd send guards to drag you there if you failed to show up."

"You know how much I loathe those crowded events, Redfern. I much prefer more intimate dinners." Soren took a step toward me. "I have half a mind to clear everyone from this room right now."

Even so, it was Goldie who answered, "If you touch her before the feast and ruin all the hard work we've put into making your Celestina look like this, I will hurt you in places that will render you forever childless. Now, stop being a pest and clean yourself up, so you don't embarrass your lady here."

Soren held up his hands and backed away. Redfern caught Soren's escape into the bathing room. He placed his hand on the prince's shoulder. "Your Highness, you're not seriously planning on bringing your slave, are you?"

"First off, Celestina is not my or anyone's slave." Soren bit off the words. "And secondly, where I go, she goes."

Redfern's hand tightened on Soren's shoulder. "No disrespect, but do you think that is wise?"

"To do otherwise will make the court believe I'm trying to hide her away," Soren answered without hesitation.

"And to parade her around on your arm will raise speculations about her position that might in the long run harm her," Redfern was quick to point out. "Even if you tell everyone she's not a slave, she's still a foreigner wearing a slave collar. You can't seriously believe you can get away with housing her in your chambers and attending events with her on your arm. What's your end game here?"

Soren flicked a meaningful glance in my direction. "For Celestina's safety, she stays with me, even if that means she lives in my chambers and attends royal events. If my father objects to this, tell him to stop inviting me to damned court affairs that I have no patience with in the first place. Now, take your arm off my shoulder before I seriously lose my temper with you."

Redfern lifted his hands and took a step back. Soren gave the older man a sharp nod before heading into the bathing chamber. Before leaving, Redfern turned in my direction and scowled deeply.

Goldie tossed a brush at him.

Chapter 28

Soren escorted me to the feast, only because Goldie (who had to be related to Mary) stood at the door and made sure we both made it out of his chamber with our clothes on. Gracious, the Beast of Fein looked dashing with his black hair tied back, a crisply pressed linen white shirt, and black leather pants. He wore a simple golden circlet in his hair signifying his status as crown prince.

While he didn't wear any weapons on his hip, I noticed a dagger tucked discretely into his right boot. As we made our way to the palace's grand dining hall, Raya and Gray fell in step with us. They had bathed and were wearing fresh tunics and leggings and also had daggers tucked into their boots.

"Stay close by," Soren told them right before we entered the hall. "I'm worried about some of the court misunderstanding Celestina's presence and overreacting."

"Understood," Gray said.

"We've got both your backs," Raya said with a wink in my direction.

Soren gave me a look that was filled with worry before he threaded his fingers through mine.

"Do you really believe someone will attack me?" My heart started pounding.

"No. I just…" He shook his head.

"Court events make Soren squirm," Raya stepped up to explain.

"He'd rather be cleaning out the stables than sitting on display before all those jackals," Gray added. "And I don't blame him."

"At least the food will be good," Soren muttered and, with his hand still tightly wrapped around mine, made his way toward the head of the single long table that ran the length of the room.

Nearly every chair had already been taken. There was one place setting open next to Soren's brother near the head of the table and two grand chairs at the head of the table I assumed were waiting for the king and queen.

I glanced around.

Fein didn't have slaves, but there were servants standing behind the chairs of some of the court members with their gazes lowered and their hands clasped in front of them. Was I going to be expected to stand like that behind Soren?

I couldn't.

I wouldn't.

Not unless he ordered me to, and then I'd have no other choice. But he wouldn't do that to me, would he?

He walked up to the empty chair, the chair that was directly to the right of the king, and pulled it out. But he didn't sit. Instead, he turned to his brother.

"Move." He kicked the leg of his brother's chair.

"What?" His brother grumbled.

"I need your chair."

Prince Cullen turned and slowly looked up at his brother. "I think everyone hoped you would leave her locked away so they wouldn't have to think about the troubles you've brought back with you."

"Everyone should have known better." Soren kicked the leg of his brother's chair again. "Move."

"Will you never learn to play the game, brother of mine?" With a sigh, Prince Cullen pushed his chair back. He slowly rose and gave me a courtly bow as he offered his chair to me. "My lady."

But then his body shook as if he'd been struck by lightning. His head jerked in my direction. "Goddess help us, Soren." His penetrating gaze seemed to burn my skin. "I don't think you realize the extent of trouble you've brought to the kingdom when you decided to champion this one."

"I know better than you might think," Soren said. His jaw tightened when he noticed everyone in the room was watching and listening.

Cullen put his hand on his brother's shoulder. "I hope you do."

"Where will you sit?" I asked the younger prince when he started to move away from the table. There were no other places available.

"Don't worry about me. I'll take my meal in my room. I have some ancient texts I suddenly want to look through." He gave another bow. "Good evening, my lady."

The room fell silent as the people at the table watched as Cullen left the hall. Soren offered his seat of honor to me. I tried to object, but he was insistent. After I sat in his chair, he plopped down into the chair Cullen had vacated and glowered at everyone who dared stare in our direction, especially at Redfern who was seated directly across the table from us.

Luckily, the uncomfortable stare-down didn't last too long. A gong sounded and everyone rose as the king and queen entered the hall from a separate golden doorway. They walked arm in arm, smiling at each other as if they truly liked each other. Until they looked in our direction.

Their smiles faded. The king's face turned slightly red.

So, the lack of seating wasn't simply the king's advisors acting on their own to discourage my attendance at their celebration feast. From the looks of things, the king knew I wouldn't be made welcome and was unhappy to see me.

The royal pair didn't say anything until they were seated on their thrones at the head of the table. The king kissed his wife's knuckle before turning to Soren.

"What game are you playing, son?" he demanded.

Soren stared mutely at his father and acted as if he had no idea what the intimidating man was talking about.

The king gestured, not toward me, but toward Raya and Gray who were standing directly behind us with their arms crossed over their chests.

"You bring your King's Guards to the feast being held in your honor? And you have them stand behind your chair as if expecting someone to stab you in the back?"

"I have no worries about my ability to protect myself, Your Majesty." Soren sat back in his seat as if his father's anger didn't concern him at all. But his grip on my hand tightened, letting me know that he wasn't as chill about this as he was letting on. "My guards are here to ensure that Celestina remains safe throughout the meal."

"You dare suggest—?" the king started to shout.

"I'm not suggesting, I'm saying I know she isn't safe in this hall." His gaze flicked to Redfern. "She wasn't even provided a seat at the table." Soren's voice softened. "I can imagine how eager your advisors are for me to rid myself of her. But know this, Father, Celestina is here, sitting at my side, in my place of honor for a reason. As long as she is under the thrall of Queen Beatrice's magical collar, she stays with me. Under my protection. And if we do manage to break the spell and get rid of the collar"—He broke eye contact with his father and turned toward me. The look in his eyes made me feel as if I suddenly couldn't quite catch my breath— "when that moment comes, she'll still be welcome to stay with me, or I'll take her wherever she wishes to go."

Soren's mother leaned forward. "You can't mean that. She's not even Fein."

He kept his gaze locked with mine. "I mean every word I say. Shall we have the servants bring in the meal? Celestina hasn't had much to eat since breakfast."

The food, as Soren had predicted, was excellent. The Fein used spices I'd never tasted. The meat was tender. The vegetables were fresh despite the fact that it was winter. And the cake at the end of the meal was so moist it tasted like pudding. I had to stop myself from rudely scraping every last crumb from the plate with the side of my fork.

Throughout the meal, the king and queen asked me polite questions about my family, and my former role in the Earst court. I told them about my adventures with the royal sons. The queen seemed to enjoy my tales of their naughty antics so much so that I continued to tell her about what they did and how they'd pester me to tell them stories about magical beasts.

"Their favorite tales are those about the terrible blood-thirsty vampires Queen Beatrice works so hard to protect us from," I told her with a laugh.

The queen's smile faded. "You speak as if you believe vampires are mindless, vicious creatures."

"Aren't they?"

The queen's eyebrows lowered. "Soren? You haven't—?"

"No, I haven't," he said sharply. His entire body seemed to stiffen next to me. "But I will."

The queen sat back and shook her head in a way that suggested her son had sorely disappointed her. I didn't understand the exchange. Perhaps talking about vampires in Fein was a taboo topic. In Earst, the stories of vampires and other magical creatures came up at nearly every meal. It was a national obsession Queen Beatrice encouraged. She liked that the people talked about the dangers in the kingdom because it gave her an opportunity to remind her people how she is the only one who can keep the kingdom safe.

Perhaps the Fein weren't as adept at protecting their own. Perhaps talking about vampires opens a national wound that no one really wanted to face. Considering the vast wasteland we'd traveled through, the country must have suffered terrible losses from vampire attacks.

"It's a blessing we don't have to worry about vampire attacks during the daylight hours since even the weakest rays of sunlight would burn the skin off their body," I said, hoping to soften any fears and sadness I might have stirred up by mentioning vampires. "After all, the creatures can only walk in moonlight."

Redfern, who was seated directly across from me, coughed loudly.

That wasn't the reaction I'd hoped for. I pressed on, desperate to ease the fears of vampires in those around me. "In Earst, only warriors travel outside city walls at night. And as a result, we haven't lost anyone to vampire attacks in modern recorded history."

Soren bent down and whispered in my ear, "You do realize that moonlight is actually reflected sunlight."

Of course, I knew that. But what would that have to do with—?

Oh. My. Goddess.

I.

Did.

Know.

That.

How had I never thought about the source of moonlight before? I could have smacked myself in the head. If vampires couldn't survive even a whisp of sunlight, then moonlight would have to be just as deadly.

I turned toward Soren as my mind put the pieces together. "The stories aren't true?"

He shook his head.

"She's a vampire hater?" someone further down the table said.

"Why did he bring her here?" someone else asked.

"He should send her home." The rumbles along the table grew louder and more aggressive.

Soren wrapped his hand around my arm. "I think it's time we leave."

With a graceful move, he pushed back from the table and had me on my feet before I realized what was happening. Gray and Raya flanked us as Soren rushed me toward the exit.

"But I didn't get to apologize to the queen for sounding so ignorant or to thank your parents for the lovely feast." The king and queen were going to think the people of Earst had no manners at all. "I'm sorry I made such a humiliating mistake, Soren. I'll watch what I say more closely. I promise."

We'd made it out into the hallway by the time I'd finished apologizing. My entire head felt as if it had caught on fire from the heat of my embarrassment.

Soren had to regret his decision to bring me to the feast. Perhaps he even regretted saving my life. I knew very little about the land in my own country. I was ignorant about my kingdom's history. And clearly, my knowledge of vampires was vastly different from everyone in Fein.

"I feel like such a stupid daughter of the soil," I grumbled.

The collar seemed to agree. It buzzed, sending a constant low-level pain spiraling down my back.

Soren spun me toward him and pressed his forehead to mine. His body was shaking.

Was he so angry that he was trembling with rage? Was he fighting an urge to choke the life out of me?

I opened my mouth to cry out in fear.

But then Soren started laughing aloud.

"Thank the goddess for you, Celestina. This has to be the first official meal where I wasn't the one who caused the table to erupt in outrage like that."

I groaned and buried my face in his shirt. "I can't believe I never thought about where moonlight comes from. How is it that no one in Earst ever thought about the relationship between sunlight and moonlight?"

"I'm glad they didn't." He grabbed my shoulders and pulled me away from him. His green gaze sought mine. He stopped laughing. "I swear, Celestina. I'm relieved. If the worst thing that happened tonight was that you left the hall feeling embarrassed, then the feast was a huge success for us. No one tried to kill you. No one tried to overthrow the kingdom because they were upset that I brought an outsider into Fein. We didn't have to use our daggers and kill anyone. And…" He gave me a wide, toothy smile. "And for once I wasn't the one putting my foot in my mouth."

"He's so bad," Raya confirmed.

"The worst," Gray agreed. "It's incredibly embarrassing."

Chapter 29

Gray and Raya invited themselves into Soren's chambers that night. The three of them sat in the sparsely furnished anteroom joking with each other and drinking directly out of a blue bottle Gray had snatched from the dining hall on our way out.

I refused to drink the foul-smelling alcohol and felt left out of their jokes that seemed to involve people I didn't know. That was why I ended up sitting cross-legged on the floor near Soren's chair with my arms folded over my chest while feeding the grumpy emotions that kept burbling up from my stomach like acid from a rotten apple. Why would Soren be more interested in playing with his King's Guards when he could be spending time alone with me? Alone where we could be *doing things*?

Dammit. I knew I shouldn't take his behavior personally. It wasn't as if we'd already become lovers. Sure, we'd kissed. And sure, he'd done things to my body that made me feel as if I could soar into the clouds. But that didn't mean *feelings* had been involved. At least not on his part.

Goddess, my heart couldn't be more in love with the big, stupid warrior.

"What's wrong with her?" Gray asked. He took another swig from the blue bottle and swiped the back of his hand across his mouth. "She's not about to go all monster-y on us, is she?"

He'd chuckled when he'd said it, but the narrowed gaze he kept locked on me held no humor.

"She's thinking this room is too crowded," Raya said.

"No one asked her to sit on the floor." Gray gestured toward an old wooden chair next to the small, battered table.

Raya swatted her friend's chest. "That's not what I'm talking about, nimrod."

Gray protested when she snatched the bottle away from him. She laughed before lifting the bottle to her lips. "God, that's awful. Couldn't you have swiped the good stuff?"

Soren leaned forward with his elbows on his knees as he peered at me. "You're upset?"

"Got nothing to be upset about." I turned to stare at the wall.

Even here, away from the court and in his chambers, I was an embarrassment. I needed to stop imagining what it would be like to be alone with him with no threat of interruption. Where would he put his callused hands first? Would he let me taste every inch of his body? Because I couldn't stop wondering what he tasted like. Would he want to do the same to me?

Or had I been a convenient diversion when he'd been traveling? And why wouldn't he have taken an interest in me? I'd practically jumped into his furs while screaming "Take me! Take me!"

Raya had warned me he'd break my heart. She sure nailed that prediction. My heart stung from the broken shards.

He hadn't been back at his palace for more than an hour before he'd started asking about another woman. *His* other woman.

"Who's Pris?" Her name had been one of the first words to come out of Soren's mouth at the sight of his brother. Goddess, if I could, I would have stuffed those words back into my mouth. I didn't want to know. Hearing him talk about someone who was so important to him that his first concern back at court was of her would only cause more of those painful shards to tear away from my heart.

Someone snorted. I shouldn't have put my back to them. Keeping my head turned away was a coward's way out. And I hated anyone thinking I was a coward. Turning back, though, would reveal the jealousy ripping through my body with such force I was surprised it wasn't shooting out my ears with a bright green glow.

I had no hold on Soren. The collar bound me to him, not the other way around.

Then why did he make those promises? Why would he make it sound as if he cared if he had someone else? He shouldn't have been playing with my emotions like that. It's not like I could run away from him. The collar keeps me bound to him like a dog on a chain.

Maybe he likes that. Maybe he likes how I fawn stupidly over him. Like a pet.

He was such a jerk. A stupid, inconsiderate jerk. I hoped his precious Pris saw through his charming, handsome façade and into his rotted, deceitful core.

But maybe precious Pris didn't care. Maybe she was with him, the crown prince, because who wouldn't want to be with a crown prince?

Gah! The more I tried to talk myself out of feeling jealous of that stupid, stupid warrior, the sharper the sting of jealousy stabbed at me.

The rough pad of Soren's fingers traced a line down the back of my neck. I shivered.

"Celestina," his deep voice rumbled in a way that I felt it all the way to my core. I had a sudden urge to press my legs tightly together. "Look at me."

The collar sent a shock of pain down my back, and I was forced to turn my gaze to meet his.

His elbows were still resting on his knees. There was humor in his expression…until he realized what he'd done.

"I'm sorry," he said. "I didn't mean to make that an order."

Raya and Gray were no longer in the room. The blue bottle was gone, too.

Soren cupped my cheeks in his rough hands and leaned closer to me. I tried and lost the fight against the thrill of his touch. It had to be the collar. This was just another way Queen Beatrice had set me up to suffer.

Fall in love with the prince.

"You're crying," he said.

"No, I'm not." I blinked hard several times, which only made those absurd tears spill out onto my cheeks. Soren caught one with the pad of his thumb. He lifted his hand and brought his thumb to his lips. His tongue, the same tongue that had done such wicked things to my body, snaked out and licked away the tear.

"Priscilla is my sister," he said. "Not a lover. I don't play those kinds of games. Not to you. Not to anyone. That's not who I am."

His sister. Gah! I'd gotten myself all wound up over his sister. Of course, he'd ask his brother about the whereabouts of his sister.

But…

"That doesn't explain why you're hanging out with your King's Guards and ignoring me the first chance that we get to be alone while clean and with little chance of being disturbed all night."

His cupped palm slipped away from my face as he sat back. "Because Gray and Raya are King's Guards. Not *my* King's Guards. The two of them answer to my father. And yet tonight, they put their careers and their lives at risk by standing with me and you in a direct insult to their ruler. They did it because they're my friends. And friends thank each other by spending time together blowing off the nervous energy that is left over after taking such a risk. Will they suffer for what they did for us? Probably. Will they take that risk again? Goddess, I know they would even if I told them not to, because that's who they are. And so, yeah, I wanted to spend some time tonight with them."

I jerked my head sharply to the left to study the plaster wall again. I did it mainly to hide the stain of mortification stinging my face. "I'm such a bitch."

Soren chuckled.

How dare he laugh at me when I'm wallowing in self-recriminations? I growled.

He laughed even harder.

"No one blames you for being horny for me. I mean, you should look at me."

No, I refused to look.

That didn't stop him. "I'm a wet-dream kind of gorgeous. I'm sure even the men in my command get boners whenever they think about the perfection that is my body. It's only natural you'd get all frustrated whenever you're near me and you can't act on those desires. I bet your lady bits are throbbing with unfulfilled—"

"Stop. Please, just stop." I pressed my hands to my ears.

He trailed his finger down the back of my neck again.

Again, I shivered.

"Celestina." His deep voice rumbled through my most intimate parts like a rough caress. "We're alone now."

Chapter 30

Soren pried my hand from where I'd tucked it under my opposite arm and gave a gentle tug. I looked up at him.

"Come on, Celestina," he said with a chuckle that made me want to smack him. "Don't let your emotions ruin our fun."

I looked back at the wall. There was a crack in the plaster that ran from the floor to the ceiling. "You mean you simply want to fuck me?" That's what the ladies and gentlemen in Earst's court did. And everyone had fun…until emotions got involved and ruined everything. "I'm sorry to tell you, but my messy emotions are splattered all over everything we do together."

"Good." He gave my hand another, slightly harder tug.

I refused to budge. Perhaps I'd sleep on the threadbare rug underneath me. I'm sure I'd already ruined this beautiful diaphanous dress by sitting cross-legged in it on the floor.

But he hadn't said he didn't want my emotions. He'd said…

"Good? I thought you didn't want my emotions to ruin our fun."

"I meant I didn't want you to feel embarrassed because you're feeling jealous. And I know I shouldn't, but I'm soaking up your jealousy like a conceited sponge." He dropped down on the floor behind me. He sat with his legs splayed around mine. The warmth of his chest seeped through the thin layers of my dress. "Don't let your embarrassment stop you from"—he pressed a kiss on my bare shoulder—"seeking what you really want from me."

I buried my face in my hands and groaned softly. Gah, I wanted him. I wanted his hands on me. I wanted him to bury himself so deep in me that it felt like our souls had merged. But could I do it like my friends in Earst did? Could I chase my physical needs and pretend it wasn't the most intimate I've ever been with someone?

"It won't be meaningless for me," I said to the palms of my hands.

He shifted slightly.

Was he about to pull away? Would he leave me aching, wanting?

One more kiss and I'd give him all of me. Hell, he already owned my battered heart. It was his to crush. His to destroy.

"Celestina." My name this time sounded like a quiet plea. His hands closed over my shoulders. He guided me to turn until we were sitting on the floor face-to-face. He'd bunched up the hem of the dress, pushing it higher and higher until I could drape my bare legs over his warm thighs. He then moved my hands away from my face. "I want all of your emotions, Celestina, especially the messy ones."

He dipped his head and pressed his lips to mine.

Goddess, he tasted like that foul alcohol and pine trees and snow and caramel. His tongue pressed into my mouth as he lifted my bottom and repositioned me on his lap. The ridge of his arousal pressed against my core. I groaned and rubbed against him, wishing there were no barriers between us. His fingers tightened against my bottom, pressing me even tighter against him as he moaned in my mouth.

"Sky Girl, what you do to me," he whispered. "You unhinge me."

He nudged my neck to one side and, just below the collar, sucked at the tender skin between my neck and my shoulder. It felt as if sparks were dancing on the surface of my skin. His teeth scraped against that spot. Oh, so sharp. The sudden jolt of pain surprised me. I sucked in a breath. But then he kissed the pain away. And sucked. And the room started to spin.

"We…we would be more comfortable on a bed," he panted. "The floor is no place for you to lose your virginity."

I nodded in agreement, although I would have agreed to anything at that point. He could have me on the floor, in his arms, or on a bed. I didn't care as long as he took care of the heat that kept building and building inside of me.

"Don't worry, my beautiful Sky Girl," he said between kisses as he somehow managed to get to his feet with my legs still wrapped around him. Had I spoken those last thoughts aloud? "I'll take care of you."

He carried me into his bedroom and gently lowered me onto the threadbare quilt covering his old bed. With a smile, he joined me on the lumpy bed. His battle-hardened fingers traced the length of my neck. I shivered.

"We won't need this anymore," his deep voice grumbled as he reached for the front of my gown. The muscles in his hands flexed. A loud rip filled the bedchamber. And suddenly, I was surrounded by a silky puddle that used to be my dress.

"Goldie is going to flay you alive," I warned.

"Probably," he agreed. "But I needed to get you out of that dress, and I don't have the patience to mess with all those tiny buttons running down your back." He drew a deep breath. "Beautiful," he murmured. "So damned beautiful."

I swallowed down a lump of nervousness, especially since he was looking at me with no fabric to hide the parts I wasn't that comfortable sharing with the world. "You're the masterpiece." I reached up and dragged the tips of my fingers down the length of his solid chest. "Can I see all of you, too?"

"Sky Girl, I'm hurting so bad for you, you can have anything you want right now." The seam of his shirt ripped loudly as he pulled it off over his head. A couple of tugs had his boots clattering to the floor. And then he shed his pants.

Goddess above. His thick cock jutted out at me. And…I swallowed hard. This wasn't going to work.

"Trust me," he whispered, lying down alongside me. He pressed gentle kisses to my neck while his hands explored my body. He cupped my breast before his questing fingers squeezed and turned the nipple.

I hissed a breath.

While it pinched, the pressure there also sent an electric zing straight down to my core. I stretched my legs and arched my back as my body chased the sensation. A low moan rumbled in the back of my throat.

Soren took control of my lips with a kiss that felt like it might consume me. At the same time, his hands had made it down to my core. He caressed the length of my opening. My hips lifted from the bed as my body reached for more.

My hands weren't idle at my side. No, I'd wanted to touch him like this for days now. And I wasn't going to pass up the chance at unrestricted access to his body. The corded muscles in his arms flexed as he moved. Feeling the strength in them made dragons flutter in my belly. His broad chest was as smooth as iron, save for the arrow of curly, brown chest hairs that pointed down to his erection.

He hissed when I wrapped my hands around him there. He was so thick, I couldn't close my hand around him. His tip felt velvety soft. And there was a drop of pre-cum begging me to taste it. I started to move down to lick it off when his hands folded over my shoulders and pressed me back into the mattress.

"As much as I'd love to have your lips on me right now, I think we shouldn't go down that path. Not this time. I'm struggling with control enough as it is. I—" He pressed a passionate kiss to my lips. With his knee, he nudged my legs to open for him.

He pressed a callused finger into me. I sucked in a sharp breath as he pumped the digit in a prelude to what he planned to do with that monster of a cock. I cried in his mouth as my body shook with need.

"That's right," he praised. "Feel what I can do to you."

He swirled his finger in a way that had me crashing into an orgasm. While I was still riding the sensation, he pressed his thick tip against my opening.

His green eyes deepened in color as his gaze caught mine like a rabbit in a snare. He linked his fingers with mine and moved slowly, giving my body time to adjust to his size. I winced. I so wanted us to fit, but heavens, this wasn't going to work.

"If it hurts too much, we can stop." By the way his voice strained, it sounded as if stopping might kill him.

"Why?" While his body in mine was uncomfortable, I wanted this. I wanted *him*. Even if it wasn't going to work, I wanted this. But what if he didn't think it would work? "Why would you stop?"

"You look…" He grimaced as he pulled out. "I don't want to hurt you."

Blinking against the sudden moisture in my eyes, I turned away from him. "I don't want you to stop. I…" I couldn't trust my voice not to break against the sudden flood of emotion. Goddess, he must be regretting getting saddled with a virgin slave. "It's embarrassing. I feel like I should have something to offer you other than my unskilled body." None of the ladies in Queen Beatrice's court were still virgins at my age. I was an oddity. A misfit. An undesirable.

"Hey. Hey. Hey." He rolled, taking me with him so we were both lying on our sides looking at each other. He brushed a kiss against my lips that was so gentle I started to cry even more. "It's okay. Let's just try this a different way." He kissed me again, deeper this time. "I have to confess I've never been anyone's first time before. The thought of doing this wrong for you terrifies me."

"Don't be nice about this." I tried to roll away from him. But he tightened his fingers in mine and wouldn't let me escape. "Your niceness is only making me feel worse. I wish I could be an experienced lover for you."

"You will be." He kissed me again. "Believe me. You'll be more than experienced before this night is through." He untangled his fingers from mine. "Now, where were we?" He settled his hands on my hips. "Right. We were in the process of trying something different." He rolled again. His hands on my hips guided me to roll with him. When we settled, he was lying on his back, and I was straddling his hips. My wet center pressed against his ridge.

He smiled up at me. "You're in charge, my lady. You can do or touch whatever you want, however you want."

I bit my lower lip. While I knew in theory how all this worked, "I don't know where to start."

His grin warmed. "Why don't you guide my hands on you?"

I nodded. I could do that. I placed my hands over his and brought them up to my breasts. I did like it when he'd touched me there earlier.

"Good choice," he said, his green eyes glittering with pleasure. He took over, stroking and touching me until I was crying out and arching my back to press my breasts tighter into his hands. He groaned and lifted his head to put his mouth on one nipple. He sucked hard, sending a dizzying ripple of pleasure down to my already wet core that wanted…needed…

I started to rub myself against his shaft.

"Yeesss, do that," he purred and lifted his hips.

I rubbed myself shamelessly against him, thrilling at how good it felt. But then my body wanted more. "Please," I whispered.

Thank goodness he understood what I was asking. He helped line up his shaft. I took a deep, shuddering breath before impaling myself on him.

It hurt. I pinched my eyes closed and panted as I sat with him fully embedded in me.

"It gets better." He put his hands on my hips, holding me steady as he started to move slowly. In and out. The lazy friction did feel good. His mouth was on my breast again and sweet goddess, *I…I…yes.*

I started to take control, moving my hips so that he hit all the right spots. My body felt like it was getting tauter and tauter. He put his hand on my center and rubbed. His rough thumb pushed me over the edge, and I came shuddering apart.

With a shout, he followed. His shaft jerked inside me, setting off another trembling orgasm in my already overstimulated body.

Afterward, he wrapped his arms around me and held me as if he would never let me go. Still joined, we lay on our sides. "What am I going to do with you?" He caressed the side of my face. "You leave me breathless, Celestina."

Chapter 31

"Vampires can't control their cravings. Once they start in on their prey, they don't stop until their victim is drained dry," Queen Beatrice liked to tell her people. Without her, we would all be husks of ourselves. And dead. "Nothing survives a vampire."

I wasn't sure why her words kept echoing through my head when I woke up the next morning. Wanting to wash them away, I reached out to pull Soren to me. I needed his arms around me so I could feel safe. He'd protect me from the vampires I suspected infested every corner of the Fein Kingdom. Soren could fight any beast and win.

I ran my hand along the lumpy bed. The space next to me was empty. The sheets were still warm though. I cradled the pillow he'd used against my chest and inhaled his spicy scent.

As much as I wanted to stay in his bed all day getting drunk on his intoxicating aroma, the collar bucked against my desire to bask in the memory of our lovemaking. The cursed thing gave me a constant low-level shock until I pushed out of bed. Oh! Parts of me that I really hadn't ever taken notice of before ached. I headed straight for the bathing chamber and turned on the hot water in the bath. I peered at myself in the chamber's mirror. A small bruise marred the soft skin on my neck.

He'd scraped his teeth against my skin there. Goddess, just thinking about his mouth on my body made me long for him. It was a good thing he wasn't in the room, or else we'd be tumbling back into the bed. I couldn't seem to get enough of him. I doubt I ever would.

After washing up in the bath and braiding my damp hair, I dressed in a pair of black leggings and a green tunic that someone (*Soren?*) had left on a chair in the bedchamber.

A tray piled with fruits, cheeses, and pastries waited for me on the table in the outer chamber. I went straight for the strawberries and sighed as the sweet juice teased my senses. How did Fein grow them in the middle of winter? I was going after another strawberry when I noticed a piece of paper, neatly folded in half, peeking out from beneath the tray.

It was a handwritten note.

The army arrived late last night. I will be busy putting out fires in the court until late afternoon. (Hopefully no later!) You are welcome to stay in my room. I'll have lunch delivered to you. I'm also sending Patty to you. If you'd like, the two of you are welcome to visit the city library. I know she's anxious to take you there. If you do leave, please have Raya and Gray serve as your escorts.

He'd worded the note with care to make sure the collar wouldn't take anything he'd written as a direct order. We didn't even know if written notes would be considered orders, and still he he'd taken that precaution. If I didn't already love him, I would have fallen in love with him in that moment.

I was finishing up my second sticky pastry when there was an excited knock at the door. Smiling, I ran to swing it open.

Patty pulled me into a big hug. "I missed you, Sky Girl! Are those sugar rolls?"

"I-I think so."

She pulled me back into Soren's poorly furnished rooms and started stuffing small, sweet buns into her mouth. She leaned her head back and moaned. "They're so good!"

"Give the rest of us a chance to have some," Gray said as he came into the room without waiting for an invitation. He snatched a bun from Patty's hand and, with a playful smile, tossed it into his mouth.

"You beast!" Patty launched herself at Gray.

The two tussled like children. Since Patty seemed to be enjoying getting her hands on Gray, I decided against trying to stop them.

Raya stepped into the doorway. "Already, Gray?" She shook her head.

Gray looked up. He had Patty tucked under one arm while he tickled the back of her knees. "What? She was eating all the sugar rolls." He jostled Patty, causing the giggling girl to squeal. "She deserves this, don't you, brat?"

"What happened to taking Sky Girl to the library?" Raya sidestepped Gray and Patty to get to the platter. She snagged the last two sugar rolls, popping an entire one in her mouth.

"We're going! We're going!" Patty smacked Gray's arm. "Put me down, you big oaf!"

And that was how I ended up leaving the palace gates with my new friends and heading into the city toward the largest, towering structure I'd ever seen.

"I promise you!" Patty linked her arm with mine. "The building is filled with books!"

"I don't see how that could be possible. There can't be that many books in the entire Jayden Continent."

"There are! There are! You'll see!"

Gray tugged Patty's ponytail as he sauntered past us. Patty hooted and ran after him. She jumped on his back and tugged at his short brown hair. Many in the street shook their heads.

But I laughed.

Raya tossed her arm over my shoulder. "You have an extra glow to your cheeks today."

"Do I?"

"I hope you're drinking that tea I gave you. Every morning. It'll keep you from getting pregnant."

"I...I'm drinking it." I was, even though a piece of me didn't want to. But the irritatingly rational part of me knew better than to add any more complications to my already troubled life. I needed to get that collar off my neck and myself out from underneath Queen Beatrice's influence before I could even begin thinking about the possibility of building a future with Soren.

"While he's an excellent general, Soren refuses to put the time needed into learning how to play the games at court. He blasts through protocol as if attacking a foreign line." She grimaced. "It's never been a huge issue for him since everyone in the court loves him. But that was before he brought home an Earstian slave and set her up as his mistress in his personal chambers. The Fein can be forward-thinking and forgiving, but not when foreigners are involved with their beloved crown prince, I'm afraid. Complaints are already swirling through the court that you—with the help of Queen Beatrice—have bespelled their precious prince. I don't think Soren understands that the more he ignores the court whispers, the more power he gives them. Many see his actions, including how he defended you last night, as proof of how deeply you've imbedded those talons of yours."

"What do you suggest we do?" I prayed Raya wouldn't suggest I break things off with Soren. I didn't think my body would be able to survive the withdrawal. Not when everything with him was so new and exciting and so intoxicating.

"I think he needs to go to the court advisors and ask for their advice…and then follow it. Even if that means separating the two of you."

I let out a squeak of distress.

"I know. I know. I see how besotted you are. And I'm sorry for it. I've been there. Not with Soren, but with another. I know how it feels in the early days of a relationship. You can't get enough of the other. But think of the long-term, Sky Girl. The separation doesn't need to be forever."

While I grudgingly agreed that she might be right, I didn't like it. Not. One. Bit.

"We're here!" Patty shouted.

I looked up and up and up to take in the sight of a building that seemed to occupy the entire street.

This was the library?

Oh.

My.

Goddess.

"I promised to show her around." Patty pulled me away from Raya. "You're going to love it in there, Sky Girl! Whatever you can think of, there's a book about it."

"How about a book on how to get rid of a slave collar?" I asked.

"I…I…maybe?" Patty looked troubled at the idea.

"I'm only joking." Sort of.

"We could ask the librarian," Patty suggested as she hurried up the grand stairs, tugging me along with her. "Is there anything else you want to look up? The librarians are the most helpful ladies in the world. They can find just about anything for you. Anything!"

Anything?

If not the collar, then perhaps I could learn more about the dragons, their history and where they might have gone after they left the valley. I knew the collar wouldn't let me mention dragons without suffering a severe punishment, so instead I said, "I'd be interested in the section on mythical and magical creatures of the kingdom. Like—I don't know—vampires."

"Vampires?" Patty giggled. "You don't need to read about—"

"He's not told her?" Gray grumbled. "How could he not have told her?"

"Told me what?" I looked from Gray to Patty to Raya. They all were frowning at me as if I'd said the wrong thing.

"You should talk to Soren about vampires," Raya said after a long, awkward silence. "It seems as if you might still have several…um…facts about them wrong."

"And Soren is some kind of expert?" Was that because he traveled a great deal in his role as general? "I suppose he must be tasked with sending out warriors to destroy nests within the kingdom. The vampires are a large problem here, aren't they?"

"Talk to Soren," Raya said before nudging Patty to lead the way into the library.

The Palladian Central Library proved to be as amazing as Patty had promised. After signing me up for membership as Soren's guest, the librarian at the front desk then led us to the section of the library that housed their mystical beasts' collection. It took up an entire floor! I spent most of my time browsing the stacks, pulling books out, and reading sections.

"I could live my entire life here and never get bored." This library had to be Fein's most precious resource, most valuable treasure, a gem worth more than all the other gems combined. And it was a tragedy that the kingdom kept their borders closed. A place like this should be shared. The kingdom should be inviting scholars from the other kingdoms to come and study here, not keeping their library locked up for only their own people.

My membership allowed me to check out three books at a time to take back to the palace. It took nearly four hours to select an encyclopedia of mythical creatures, a crumbling tome that claimed to hold the complete history of dragons, and a small pamphlet on the magic of Earst. About an hour into my search, Patty had groaned that all the books were starting to look the same to her. She then claimed to have forgotten about an errand she had to run for her grandmother. While dashing off, she promised to come back and visit me again tomorrow.

Raya and Gray, on the other hand, had followed me through the stacks without complaint. I supposed as King's Guards they were used to standing around with not much to do but wait.

But as soon as I started down the stairs to the ground level, the two of them each breathed a sigh of relief.

"When you said you could live here, I was starting to believe you meant to move in," Gray teased on our way to the librarian's desk.

"Oh, I still might do that. This place is— Amazing is too weak of a word." Being at the library filled me with the same bubbling happiness that I experienced whenever I was around Soren. Like I'd found home. But I didn't think admitting that aloud would be wise.

Sure, Soren had brought me into his chambers and had made love to me as if he never wanted to let me go. But that didn't change the fact that he was the crown prince, and I was an outcast and a slave from a foreign kingdom. I wasn't so gullible that I believed we had any chance for a future.

Enjoy the now, my mind reminded me. No one's life came with a guarantee. I'd seen fortunes won and lost quickly enough in Queen Beatrice's court.

I hugged the books to my chest and battled back a moment of panic. Although I knew I shouldn't wish for a storybook happy ending, I also knew that giving this up, giving Soren up, would destroy me.

So, I closed my eyes and wished.

Chapter 32

After checking out the books and heading toward the exit, the librarian who'd given me the library card chased after me. At first, I was worried that the library had changed their minds about letting me check out the books. But when she caught up to us, she was smiling. "I haven't been able to find any sources about your slave collar, but I'll continue to look. There are some old foreign texts in the basement that might prove useful."

I thanked her and asked her to send a note to the palace if she located anything, anything at all. No matter how small, I wanted to learn all I could about the collar and how it worked.

Apparently, Soren had been doing something similar. When we returned to his palace chambers, we found a note on his small table from Soren asking me to join him in the king's formal chambers to discuss the collar. I considered ignoring the request. To show up wearing leggings and a green tunic for an audience with a king would be the height of disrespect.

I needed a formal court dress like Queen Beatrice had stripped off me in front of her court. Back in my drafty tower in Earst, I had enough court dresses to wear a fresh one every day for two weeks.

Here, I had this outfit and nothing else. The lovely dress I'd worn to dinner hadn't survived Soren's impatience to get me out of it.

"I need court clothes," I told Gray and Raya. "I can't go to a king's chamber wearing this."

"What you have on is fine," Gray said.

Raya rolled her eyes at her partner. "Unfortunately, Sky Girl, what you're wearing is going to have to be suitable for today. We can't summon Goldie to come dress you. Only Soren can do that on your behalf."

"I could stay here and wait for Soren to return," I said, crossing my arms over my chest. "I won't be winning any allies by showing up to the king's chambers dressed so disrespectfully."

"You're dressed like us!" Gray complained.

"Exactly!" I shouted back. "I'm a guest, not a King's Guard."

"You're more than a mere guest when Soren has made it plain to everyone how you're under his protection," Gray pointed out. "And he clearly wants to show the other courtiers that he's actively working to free you from Queen Beatrice's influence. He probably wants to show them that you're working to free yourself from her influence as well."

"Gray has a point," Raya said quietly.

"But I'm wearing leggings and a plain tunic." Certainly, showing up dressed this way would cause more trouble than they realized.

But neither of them seemed to agree and had kept badgering me about it until I followed them out of Soren's chambers.

My cheeks burned as if I'd stuck my face into a fireplace as I entered the king's rooms. If Gray and Raya hadn't flanked me, I probably would have run the other way instead of walking through the door and facing a room filled with formally dressed advisors and courtiers.

Most of the ladies in the room wrinkled their noses when they looked at me. Some of their expressions turned to relief after raking me over with their unfriendly gazes. I lifted my chin and tried not to let them bother me.

I finally spotted Soren standing at the far end of the room. He was in deep conversation with Redfern, the court advisor who'd glared at me all through dinner last night. Soren looked my way and smiled. He placed his hand on Redfern's arm and said something to the man. I was too far away to hear them. The room was that large. And filled with dozens of people. Some were lounging on the ornate gold and black furniture. But most were standing around in groups. I knew from my own court experience that the courtiers would separate themselves in a hierarchy that only existed in their world. As an outsider wearing a slave collar, I figured I didn't qualify for any of their groups. I was sure I wouldn't even qualify as a servant bringing them a tray of food.

While Redfern scowled, Soren sauntered over to us. Goddess, he was a handsome man. And the things he knew to do with a woman's body…

My muscles trembled in anticipation of a repeat performance.

Soon.

I hoped.

"Celestina." He cupped my face with both of his hands and kissed me deeply.

Gray grumbled. Raya scoffed. And I blushed at Soren's blatant display of affection. If anyone in the room questioned our relationship, they wouldn't now.

The room seemed to tilt on its axis when he lifted his lips from mine. "Did you have fun with Patty today?"

I nodded dumbly before remembering how to form words with my mouth. "She showed me the library. I cannot believe how many books there are."

"She spent three and a half hours in one section." Gray rolled his eyes.

"Outlasted Patty by two hours," Raya supplied.

"I remember how you said you enjoyed reading back in Earst. I hope you'll be happy with the books we have available for you here."

"She told us she wants to live there," Raya said with a laugh.

"You can't do that, Celestina. I need you to keep my bed warm." His voice wasn't at all quiet. And he had to know the entire room was listening.

My cheeks blazed hot again. At least neither his mother nor father were in the room to hear him.

Was he really as clueless about court life as Raya had suggested? Or was he acting this way toward me in public for a reason?

Soren wrapped his hand around mine and led me over to where Redfern waited.

"Redfern, allow me to present to you again Lady Celestina from the Earst Kingdom. Celestina, let me formally introduce you to Redfern, my father's mage."

"It's nice to make your acquaintance." I held out my hand to shake his, a greeting common in Earst and one that I'd watched practiced here in Fein.

Redfern glared at my hand for a few moments before turning back to Soren. "I'll need to examine the collar. Order your slave to sit."

Soren's entire body tightened. He closed his eyes and drew and long slow breath. "She's not a slave," he said once he'd opened his eyes again. "We've already discussed this."

"Until that collar comes off, she's what Queen Beatrice created." Redfern's voice was crisp. "If you want my help, you'll have her sit down."

Soren narrowed his gaze at his father's mage. His lips pressed tightly together. At my sides, I could feel Raya and Gray tensing.

"Oh, for goddess sake." I dropped into a heavily padded armchair.

Redfern pulled a pair of glasses from his pocket and slipped them on. He then crouched down next to me and performed a thorough examination of the collar. Several of the courtiers came to stand around us, making me feel even more self-conscious than I had before, which was saying something considering my inappropriate clothing and how thoroughly Soren had kissed me in front of them.

"I can feel the queen's magic coursing through the collar," Redfern said.

"Do you think the queen can control Lady Celestina through the magical bond?" Gray asked as he shifted closer to me.

"It's impossible to say," Redfern answered.

"And how do we rid ourselves of the collar?" Soren demanded.

Redfern shook his head. "I don't know. There's no latch." He removed his glasses and stood. "She's a security risk."

Soren flicked his gaze over to Gray, who shrugged.

"My recommendation to the king will be that she shouldn't be allowed to stay in the palace," Redfern said. "She should be treated like we'd treat any suspected spy to the kingdom and keep her up in the Sunjin."

"No." Soren pulled me from the chair and, pressing my backside to his front, he wrapped his arm around my waist. "No. She stays with me where I can protect her."

Redfern shook his head and disappeared through a narrow door on one of the side walls.

"You know he's going straight to the king," Raya said.

"I know," Soren growled.

"What is the Sunjin?" Perhaps I should do as Raya suggested. Follow the advice of the royal advisors. I could stay where they wanted me to stay for a while to prevent Soren from going to battle with his father. I didn't want to be the cause of a rift between the royal family.

"It's the royal dungeons. Only, they aren't located in the palace. They're up at the top of the mountain." Soren pointed to a craggy peak outside the window. "Deep underground."

"You don't want to go there, Sky Girl." Raya shook her head emphatically as if she could read my thoughts. I suppose she realized that in a roundabout way, she'd put the idea in my head.

"Don't worry." Soren's hold tightened. "I'll tear down this palace before letting anyone send you there."

Chapter 33

When we returned to Soren's private chambers, I walked in, turned around, and then stepped out again.

This wasn't the right place. It couldn't be the right place.

I looked around. But this was the same door I'd gone through. The same hallway. Wasn't it?

"What's going on?" I asked.

Soren followed me back into the hall. "Did I surprise you?"

"She's surprised," Raya said as she pushed her way past me to get into the anteroom. I followed her back into the chambers.

Soren stayed by my side, wearing a pleased smirk. He crossed his arms over his chest.

The place had been transformed. Instead of the drab, battered furniture, the room had luxurious silk-covered sofas, a large ornate desk sat in the corner, and a table covered with a crisp white cloth off to another side that was surrounded with golden chairs. None of them broken. A rug woven to depict the mountains and ocean visible outside the window spanned the room.

"You told me that my chambers weren't fit for a servant, much less a prince, so I fixed it," Soren explained. "Does it meet your lavish standards now, my lady?"

Heavy tapestries covered the walls, blocking the drafts that had once made the place feel so unwelcoming.

"Does it meet my…?" I turned full circle. My gaze fell on a hand-carved dragon, a child's toy, that had been placed on a side table. It wasn't anything like the one I'd had to leave behind at the castle in Earst. This one was blue, twice the size, and much more intricately carved. But the fact that Soren remembered how I'd been forced to leave my childhood toy behind, and the fact that he thought to try and replace something that had been precious to me made my heart feel like it might burst. I picked up the dragon and clutched it tightly to my chest. "Oh, Soren…it's…it's…"

"Come back in a couple of hours," Soren said to Raya and Gray softly.

The door behind me opened and closed.

Soren wrapped his arms around me from behind. "There are no slaves in Fein. No laws barring you from owning possessions. You're allowed to have as many treasures as you want. So don't feel like you need to hide your collection from me." He lightly touched the small pouch hanging from my belt containing the sparkly rocks I'd gathered as we'd traveled. I tensed, prepared to defend my treasures. But he quickly moved his hand to rest on my hip. "Which reminds me. I got you something else."

He turned me toward a large chest on the far wall and released me. It had the crest of Fein carved into the deep red wood.

I frowned as I made my way to the chest. I feathered my fingers over a carving of flowers across the top of the beautifully crafted piece.

"It's yours. You can store anything you like in it." He pulled from his pocket a golden key hanging from a golden chain necklace. "This is the chest's only key." He placed it in the palm of my hand and closed my fingers around it.

"Thank you," I breathed the words.

Kneeling in front of the chest, I slipped the key into the lock, opened the chest, and carefully placed the toy dragon inside. After carefully closing and locking the chest, I drew a slow breath. A smile formed on my lips. Soren didn't have to do this. He didn't have to do any of this. But he had.

I turned around and tackled him. I kissed him and showed him exactly how grateful I was for his thoughtfulness.

Hours later, Raya and Gray returned with a tray of food. The four of us ate and teased each other. Goddess, I could see myself making my home here. No, that wasn't right. This place already felt like home.

I was in the process of stealing a piece of gooey cheese from Soren's plate when a knock sounded on the door. Gray had his hand on his sword as he went to open it, which reminded me that this place wasn't mine.

Not yet.

A tall, wiry footman stood on the other side. His gaze bounced from Gray to Gray's hand on the hit of his sword to me to Soren and then back to me. He cleared his throat a couple of times before saying, "The king and queen request your presence in the private quarters for dinner tonight."

"Whose presence?" Soren stood as he demanded of the poor nervous man.

"Um…the…um…slave's?" the man stammered.

Soren stepped to the door. His voice was surprisingly sweet as he said, "Go back to my beloved parents and inform them that Celestina is not a slave." He then slammed the door in his face.

"Was that wise?" I asked. Going against a monarch, in my experience, was never a good idea.

"I'll not have anyone think I'm weak or mistake you for a slave," Soren said, his jaw tight with tension. The way he was looking at me, the heat in his gaze, the anger in his expression, made me shiver. He wanted me. I knew that without a doubt. That man's sexual appetite was nearly unquenchable. And thinking of the forceful way he would take my body when the world upset him had my body pulsing with anticipation. "Raya. Gray. I think you should leave now."

"Is that wise?" Gray asked. His hand still rested on the hilt of his sword.

Soren took a predatory step toward me.

"Leave. Now," he growled.

Raya grabbed her plate and Gray's as she jumped up from her chair. "Come on, Gray. We can finish our dinner in the hall."

I didn't see our friends leave. Soren had taken me into his arms and had his mouth on mine before the door opened.

"We'll make sure you'll not be disturbed tonight," Raya promised from behind me.

"Thank you!" I yelled as Soren tossed me over his shoulder and carried me into his bedchamber where he planned to have his wicked way with me. I was thrilled.

Chapter 34

Soren kissed me awake early the next morning. They were drugging, slow kisses that made my chest feel all buzzy and happy.

"*Stay in bed if you want,*" he whispered as he bent over where I had been sleeping. "*You're welcome to stay in my bed all day. I like thinking of you all tousled and sleepy like this while I swing my sword on the practice field. I'll be back when I can.*"

His hair was damp, and he was already dressed in his warrior leggings and tunic like he was about to go out the door. With a sigh, he climbed onto the bed and stretched out next to me. His hands threading through my hair.

"*Goddess, Celestina, I don't want to leave you.*" I could feel the evidence of how much he wanted to stay pressing against my leg. He wrapped his arms around me tightly and held on as if he never wanted to let me go.

"Then don't leave." I liked the warmth of him. And his strength. Whenever he held me like this, I felt like I'd found home.

He stayed with me for longer than I'd expected. I was drifting back to sleep when his hold loosened. He kissed my forehead, murmured words I didn't understand, and eased himself from beside me.

The cool air that rushed into the space he'd left behind startled me awake. Even so, I lingered in the bed for a while longer, remembering the warmth of him on my skin.

I pressed the heels of my palms to my eyes. Goddess, I needed to protect my heart better than this. Despite how he acted toward me—perhaps especially *because* of how he acted toward me—I needed to remember Soren was a crown prince of a kingdom not of my birth. I had no future here.

Even if I accepted being nothing more than his mistress, he would eventually have to marry, and I'd be moved somewhere out of the way. Kept, but apart from the life he would be building with his future queen who would give him his future children.

A life like that would be akin to forever drowning in the shadow of sorrow.

Just thinking of such a future left me gasping for air.

I needed to think of something else. I crawled out of Soren's comfortable bed.

Like the day before, I took a bath, braided my wet hair, and then dressed in the leggings and blue tunic that had been left out for me. I made a mental note to ask Soren about getting me a full wardrobe when he returned.

Once dressed, I made my way to the antechamber. Once again, a tray waited for me on a table filled with fruit and pastries. And there was also a note tucked under one corner. While munching on a sugar roll—they were mouth-watering good—I unfolded the note.

Celestina,

Go to the market and pick up a package waiting for me at the codman's shop. Then meet me in the great hall for luncheon.

Soren

The collar reacted to the order even before I'd finished reading the note. I dropped the bun and headed toward the door. The collar was insistent. I needed to get to the leather-maker's shop. There was no time to find Raya or Gray. No time to even put on my boots. I needed to leave the palace and pick up Soren's package.

It was strange that Soren, who'd so carefully worded yesterday's letter, would write such a blunt one today. But the collar didn't give me the chance to stop and worry about what Soren had been thinking or why he would do this to me.

I had to complete the task. Without even having to think too hard about the palace's maze of hallways, my feet seemed to know the way to the exit. I shivered in the brisk weather as I walked through the bailey yard since I hadn't taken the time to don a jacket or a cloak. Though it wasn't as bone-chillingly cold as Earst, snow had fallen last night reminding me that Fein was still in the thick of winter. I should have put on my boots.

Ah, well, a little bit of cold wasn't going to kill me while not following Soren's orders just might. I continued to the gates that opened up into the city. I didn't know where I could find a codman's shop, but I figured someone on the street would be able to help me.

"I can't let you go out." The guard at the gate moved swiftly to block my exit. "I'm sorry, Lady Celestina. Those are my orders."

"And my orders are to fetch a package for Prince Soren. You'll have to let me pass." The longer I stood there, the sharper and hotter the pain the collar sent shooting through my body. I shook with it. "I. Have. To. Go," I gritted out.

He grabbed my arms when I tried to push past him.

"You. Don't. Understand." The pain had worked its way to a point where it felt like it might rip me in half.

"Is this the lady from Earst?" a soft voice inquired behind me.

"Yes, Princess Priscilla. She's attempting to leave the palace, but I have orders that she can't leave without a proper escort."

"Oh dear, she looks to be in considerable distress."

I would have been on my knees if the guard hadn't been gripping my arms so tightly. The pain had seized me so hard it had blinded me.

"I. Have. To. Follow. Orders," I managed to get out. My voice sounded raspy.

"Let me escort her." A warm arm slipped through mine.

"You're not a King's Guard."

"No," the princess agreed. "I'm better than a King's Guard. Stand aside."

The guard tried to protest a couple of more times before uttering, "Please, Your Highness, don't get me in trouble."

"It's all on me," the princess said brightly. The next thing I knew, I was being guided by that warm arm out through the gates. Once through, the collar immediately pulled back its assault.

"Take a few deep breaths," Princess Priscilla said once we were further away from the palace. "And then tell me where we're heading. And why you're not wearing anything on your feet."

My legs kept walking, but I did manage to breathe deeply now that my body no longer felt as if it was being torn in half. "The codman shop."

"Really?" She lifted a perfectly plucked brow. "You're in need of some leatherwork? He doesn't make shoes. That's the cobbler."

The princess had long, silky black hair that flowed about her face. She was dressed in a pale green gown with tiny golden dragons stitched in the hem. A simple gold chain encircled her neck. Her lips had been painted red, which suited her coloring perfectly. She was taller than me, nearly as tall as her brothers.

And she was smiling.

"Soren has a package waiting for him there," I said.

"And he sent you instead of one of the servants? How odd. Well, his behavior works to my advantage does it not, Lady Celestina?" She hugged my arm to her side and patted it. "I can't tell you how pleased I am to have some time with you. I've heard my brother keeps you locked up in his chambers and only lets you out with him by your side or one of his personal guards."

"Well, I've not been in Sukoon long." I blushed thinking of how Soren often kept me in his bed. "But I have been to the library. It was…more than I could have ever imagined in a hundred lifetimes."

"You should talk to my brother Cullen. He practically lives at the library."

"We've met. I don't believe he approves of me." I hadn't met many in Fein who did. It was refreshing to talk with someone who seemed genuinely interested in getting to know me, instead of wanting to see how an Earstian slave behaves. Most seemed to worry about how I might harm the kingdom, instead of wanting to get to know the person behind the slave collar.

"Talk about your interest in books with Cullen, and he'll fall in love." She laughed. It was a beautiful sound. "Speaking of brothers falling in love, you're not at all as I had expected."

"Is that a bad thing?" Who had she been expecting? A barbarian from the south?

Princess Priscilla laughed again. The sound made my insides flutter. "Not bad at all. You seem lovely. It's just that Soren has a type. The women he hooks up with are usually, um, flashier. And usually about as deep as that puddle over there." She patted my arm. "He's also never taken much of an interest in any of them, not like I've heard he has with you. Did he really threaten to attack my father over you?"

"Threaten seems like a harsh word," I said, my cheeks heating up.

"I wish I'd been in town to see that. I've only returned this morning. You can imagine my surprise when I discovered the court in an uproar over my brother's mistress. Some think you've bewitched him, or your queen has. And that you're a danger to us all. You haven't bewitched him, have you?"

"No. I'd never do that. Soren has been nothing but kind to me."

"And you love him. No, I won't let you deny it. I can tell by the way your eyes glitter when I speak of him. That means he's not the only one besotted, which is splendid. I look forward to seeing him with you, all goofy in love. He's so serious all the time, I thought this day would never come."

Soren lusted for me and cared about me, but love? I doubted he felt that much emotion for me. I'd become his burden, his responsibility. He acted toward me like any man with honor might.

There were so few men of honor in the world today. That was why his behavior stood out like a shining beacon. But that didn't mean he loved me like I loved him.

"He is kind to me," I repeated.

"Kind." The princess rolled her eyes. "That's how everyone describes the Beast of Fein," she said with a laugh. We walked for another half-block before either of us spoke again. "Why was the collar punishing you at the gate back there?"

"Soren had left a note telling me to go fetch a package for him. The collar, it makes sure I follow his wishes."

"The collar was truly punishing you because you'd been delayed?"

I nodded.

"I heard a bit about how the collar works." No doubt, my situation was the talk of the palace. She shook her head. "But it is something else to see it in action. And my brother, he knows about this?"

"Probably better than anyone."

She made a rude sound. "Then my thick-headed brother shouldn't have tasked you to run errands for him. I heard he doesn't consider you to be his slave."

"He's usually more careful." The terse note still perplexed me, not that I had the freedom to stop and wonder about it, because I didn't. Not until I delivered that package to him.

"It's market day. That's why the main roads are so crowded." Priscilla tugged on my arm. "It'll be faster if we get over to one of the minor roads."

She ducked into a shadowy alleyway. The back of my neck prickled.

"Are you sure this is safe?" I thought I saw the old blind woman who had accused me of being a beast going down the same alleyway.

"You're as safe with me as you are with my beastly brother." I couldn't see how that could be true. But since it'd be rude to point that out, I kept my mouth shut.

"Is it far?" I asked instead. We'd rounded a corner. The old woman was nowhere to be seen. I must have been mistaken when I thought I saw her.

"Just a few more blocks this way." The alleyway grew even narrower. So narrow, we could no longer walk side-by-side. "I think it's rather inconsiderate of my brother to keep you locked away in his room and away from the rest of us. You should stay with me. I have an extra bedroom in my chambers you could use. And it has its own bathing chamber. We'll have girl time. I can introduce you to my friends in the palace. I'm sure they'll fall in love with you once they're allowed to get to know you. I'm sure I'll fall in love with you myself. What do you think?"

"I—um—the collar doesn't like me to stray too far from Soren." It wasn't just the collar that kept me tied to his side. The thought of staying away from his bed set off an ache in my chest.

She slid a glance over her shoulder at me. "I see."

"It's not that I don't want to meet your friends," I rushed on to say. "It's just I don't—"

"How about I don't take you from his bed at night? But can I get you during the daylight hours for a while? Would that suit?"

I opened and closed my mouth a couple of times before admitting, "It's…it's up to Soren."

She frowned at that. "You are your own person. But I'll talk to my brother. He can't be so oblivious to the politics of court that he doesn't see the need."

"I'm sure you're right." Trouble prickled at the back of my neck. I would have demanded we stop and make sure we weren't walking toward danger if not for the compulsion that I make haste to the leatherworks shop. "Princess," I grabbed her hand. "We should walk faster, there's—"

The attack came from behind. There were four of them. Big. Burly. Men. Their faces twisted with an expression of hate. One of them grabbed me, spun me around to face them, before slamming me against the brick wall.

"You are a stain on our land," the biggest, ugliest one spat at me.

"Run!" I pushed the princess away from me. "Get help!"

"You have bewitched our prince," the smallest one, who wasn't really that small, growled as he cracked his knuckles. "We'll do what your magic has stopped him from doing."

"We're going to kill her, right?" the third asked.

The big one punched his arm. "Yeah. That's what we were told to do, wasn't it?" He grabbed my arm with such force, I felt the bone snap. "Our prince killed my brother because of you."

This all happened in a matter of a few heartbeats. The men nearly speaking over themselves.

The princess had stumbled when I'd pushed her, but stubbornly she refused to run. With a shout, she leaped onto the biggest man's back. "Let her go or I'll end you!"

Princess Priscilla moved with lightning speed. While still holding onto my attacker, she struck her foot out at one of the other men who'd charged her, slamming her booted heel into his middle. He grunted. She then boxed the side of the big man's head several times. He staggered and released me. Clutching my broken arm to my chest, I whirled away from him.

Giving me a wink, Priscilla clasped both fists together and slammed them on top of the man's head. She leaped off his back as he started to go down to his knees. In a blur of motion, she whirled to face off with one of the other men.

"Stop!" I growled at the men. "Stop!"

Unlike with the magical beasts, the men kept coming.

There were too many of them for us to hold off, especially since I'd never been taught how to fight. My broken arm screamed in pain. Still, I wasn't going to give up. Not while Priscilla continued to fight. I wouldn't have her get hurt in my place.

I kicked the men and hit them with my left arm. Tears sprang to my eyes as the tearing pain in my arm joined forces with the collar's punishments for acting in violence. But I kept going. A fist came out of nowhere and slammed into my ribs with crushing power, knocking me to the ground. At the same time, I watched in horror as one of the men slammed the princess's head against the brick wall. She fell like a sack of rocks.

No!

I struggled to get back to my feet.

The horrible man picked the princess back up and started to slam her against the wall again.

"*NO!*" I jumped on his back. He easily shrugged me off.

But my actions bought us enough time. Just enough.

Someone shouted from down the alleyway, "Oi! What's going on down here!"

Heavy footsteps followed.

The four men dragged themselves up. One kicked me in the chest before fleeing. Another stomped on my already injured arm as he made his escape.

I don't know how I managed to get myself over to where Princess Priscilla lay frighteningly motionless against the hard stone ground. The collar around my neck was still pulsing angrily.

I still needed to get that package for Soren.

But, oh, Princess Priscilla. Oh no. Blood pooled around her head. The puddle growing larger and larger. I couldn't leave her. I couldn't.

"Hel—!" I started to shout.

"What have you done to our princess?" a King's Guard grabbed both my arms as he pulled me away from her. His rough handling jostled my broken arm, sending pain even sharper than the punishing burn my collar was giving me. I whimpered.

"Keep that filthy foreigner away from our princess!" another guard shouted.

"It's that slave! The bitch who bewitched Prince Soren. I heard she couldn't be trusted!" The guard holding my arms slammed me against the wall. "It's to the Sunjin for you, may you never see the light of day again." He spat in my face.

The cobbles paving the alleyway seemed to rush up toward me as darkness closed in. My gaze drifted to the sliver of sky above me. In my delirium, I imagined I saw my dragon, my beautiful green dragon that was the same color as Soren's eyes, circling overhead. Too late. Too late. I was beyond rescue now.

I need to get to the codman's shop.

I need to get Soren's package.

I need to—

As I hit the ground, I spotted the old, blind woman—*the seer*—standing in the middle of the alleyway. She wore a smile that made my insides crawl. A moment later, a fist smashed into the side of my head with an explosion of pain.

And then, nothing.

Chapter 35

"Vampires, you have to watch out for them." The little princes would hang my every word whenever I told them this story. "They can sense a drop of blood from miles away. The scent gets their hunger pumping. They are animals. They can't help themselves. When they're around blood, they rush in and feast. They feast, feast, feast on their poor, helpless human until there's nothing left but an empty husk. Not even the victim's closest kin would recognize their dried-up skin and bones. That's why you must be careful when you run around with scissors. If you cut yourself, the vampire will sniff you out and the next thing you know, you'd be dead."

The princes would both laugh and scream in delight when I'd jump at them and start tickling their sweet necks.

"Blah!"

The princes screamed even louder.

A sharp bump jolted my arm. I groaned from the pain of it as awareness seeped back into my body. The princes? No. Wait. Not the princes. I'd been with Princess Priscilla. And we'd been attacked. She was hurt. Where was the princess? She had been bleeding from a head wound. So much blood. I could still smell it.

"*Please,*" I wheezed. "*Please, help Princess Priscilla.*"

Or was that the scent of *my* blood?

But, but I hadn't been bleeding.

"*You need to stop,*" a gruff voice whispered. "*You're going to kill her.*"

There was a growl.

My body was jolted again. Pain pierced my neck and seared its way down my arm.

Another growl.

"I'm serious. I won't let you do this. Prince Soren will have both our heads if you kill her."

"She's dead anyway. You and I both know she won't last two hours below the ground in Sunjin. Hand her back."

"No, I'm not going to let you get me killed."

I struggled against the arms that held me.

I need to get that package for Soren.

But I couldn't even open my eyes. And I felt like I was swimming in a muddy puddle of pain. I wasn't even sure the man holding me realized I'd been struggling to get away.

A screech tore through the air high above us.

Wake, a voice in my head demanded. It wasn't my voice. It wasn't any voice I'd ever heard.

The men who'd been arguing over whether to kill me or not both cried out, "What—? They don't—! That can't be—!"

"Holy shit on a sugar roll! Is that a dragon?"

Wake, the foreign voice demanded again.

The men screamed. I hit the ground hard. The sharp jolt of pain managed to rouse me enough that I opened my eyes. What I saw made the air in my lungs seize up.

I was on a narrow pathway leading up the side of a mountain. And the green dragon—*my* green dragon—had its wings tucked beside its body. It was shooting out of the sky like a falcon diving for its prey. Fire roared from its mouth, incinerating every bit of the ground below it. And it was heading for me! I curled up into a tight ball, fully expecting to be reduced to ashes.

The men running away from the dragon screamed again.

And then…

Silence.

When I lifted my head, a strong wind pushed at me.

Two powerful, leathery wings flapped as the dragon gracefully lowered to the ground next to me. I held my breath as its long, horned snout came near me. Its hot breath surrounded me, making everything inside me, even my bones, shiver.

You're still bound, the voice in my head said.

The dragon nudged my side with its snout. In reaction, the collar shot burning pain down my spine. I cried out. And the dragon wrenched away from me as if it had been stung.

"Soren's package." It couldn't wait. Not even for a dragon. Not even for *my* dragon.

I pushed to my feet. Stumbling, my vision blurred in and out of focus (but mostly out of focus), I trundled my way down the steep path. I had to get back to the city and to the leatherworker's shop. It was down there, somewhere, at the bottom of the mountain.

Let the dragon follow me. I didn't care. I needed to get to the shop.

"Fuck!" someone shouted. Arms wrapped around me, stopping me.

No. No. No. "Let me go." I kicked and punched and fought as hard as I could to get away. "Help the princess."

Arms around me tightened. "Pris is okay. You're the one that's covered in blood. Did, did someone feed off you?"

"Soren?" I blinked through a haze of blurriness. Was I dreaming? Or had the Beast of Fein really found me?

"I'm real," he said. "I've got you."

"I…" *need to get to the shop.*

"I…" *am so happy to see you.*

"I…I don't feel so good."

"No, fuck. Looks like some bastard has drained you nearly dry. I'll kill him." Soren shifted me in his arms.

"Vampire," I breathed. "Must have stumbled into a nest." But that didn't make sense. I'd heard the two men arguing about feeding from me. They had sounded as if they were the guards who were taking me to the Sunjin dungeons. Had the vampires infiltrated Soren's army?

"I'm going to fix this."

"No. No. I need to get to the shop," I said, struggling to get out of his arms, my voice raspy. "I haven't picked up your package." My body ached everywhere, especially my broken arm and ribs. And my head spun as a dark haze descended.

"There is no package, dammit. All you need to do right now is let me take care of you." He gave me a shake as the world started to drift into nothingness. "Hey. Hey! Stay with me, Celestina. Don't slip away from me now."

The next thing I knew I was on the ground. Soren was kneeling beside me with his wrist pressed to my mouth.

"*Drink,*" he commanded in that velvety voice that made my body want to obey him. "*Drink some more.*"

I looked up at him and, watching him through my blurry gaze, saw what I'd refused to see before now. The evidence had been there all along. Raya and Gray had nearly blurted out the truth every chance they'd gotten. And Soren really hadn't tried that hard to hide himself from me, had he?

He was a vampire.

But, I'm guessing, you already knew that.

Should have…should have…warned me…

Chapter 36

"Don't." I managed with a weak movement to push Soren's arm away after swallowing a mouthful of his blood. How much had I already been forced to drink? How much did it take to turn a human into one of them? *"Don't turn me."*

The warrior sighed deeply. "You know what I am." Not a question. Simply a grim acknowledgment that his secret was out.

I might have known many times before. Vampires can alter memories. They can make the unreal feel real. *"Don't. Vampire. Don't make me forget."*

"Celestina, darling, very few of those stories you like to tell are true. *Keep drinking,*" he commanded in that velvety tone. While I wanted to resist him, I had no choice but to obey. My hands wrapped tightly around his wrist, I pulled the vein that had been cut open on his wrist to my mouth and suckled like a hungry lamb.

"Vampires aren't ageless, soulless creatures that are created. We're magical beings that live, love, and die much like any other creature in the four kingdoms." Soren's voice flowed over me like a calming balm. Was this part of his magic? Part of his glamour over me? "Unlike mammoth cats, chorts, and even your queen's magics, our powers aren't remnants from the lost fifth kingdom. Our kind can trace our lineage back before the rise of the dragons. In that respect, vampires are ageless. But individually, our natural lifespans are only slightly longer than yours.

"And we can walk in the sun. We live in towns and cities alongside humans, not in nests. Contrary to how my chambers looked when you first saw them, we do like comfort. I miss my hot baths when I'm out in the field like you cannot imagine. And we have feelings. We—"

"You fed off me," I mumbled, remembering finding the sore, red mark on my neck the morning after our first time together.

"Um…" Soren grimaced. "I shouldn't have. Not when you didn't know. But in the heat of the moment, I did take a sip. I'm…it shouldn't have happened."

"You feed off humans," I accused between gulps of blood, *his* blood, that I was feeding from. Oh goddess, his blood was tainting mine, wasn't it? I struggled to pull away from his open vein, but I couldn't, not with the press of his compulsion forcing me to drink.

"We gain power from blood. It doesn't have to be human blood. Any living creature can provide us with the necessary sustenance. And we still need to eat food just like you do. Blood feeds our power. Food feeds our bodies. There are humans who willingly offer their blood to us. We take what we need, leaving the human alive. If there are no humans around, we can feed off any creature. Deer. Squirrels. Even those awful lizards that followed us from Queen Beatrice's court have proved useful in that manner. But understand this—just because we feed on blood, that doesn't make us mindless killers."

I touched one hand to my ruined neck. "Tried…to…kill…me."

Soren swore. "Yes. Yes. There are killers in every community that need to be rooted out and removed. Even humans have this problem. *Keep drinking.*

"The power in our blood can also strengthen and heal humans, which I'm sure you're now realizing. We're forbidden from healing anyone who isn't a Fein citizen. It's not because we're selfish. It's because we don't want humans to hunt us for our blood. Or kill us for our blood. It's happened before. This is why the Fein now have closed borders. This is why we keep our secrets. Even within our lands, there aren't enough vampires to help every human who falls ill, but we…we…do our best."

He weaved. His arm twitched. "*Keep feeding.* You lost a substantial amount of blood. Too much."

I nodded. His blood was life. *His* life.

"While I can alter your memories, I've never done it. I have used compulsion on you. I am now. To…*ah*…save…"

He weaved again, nearly falling over from where he was kneeling next to me. That guard had drained my blood like I was now draining his. This wasn't right. I needed to stop. I shook my head, fighting against the compulsion. I'd taken too much. I was hurting Soren.

"Stop this," I begged between swallows. "Stop this."

His gold-flecked dragon-green gaze had turned black. He wrapped a hand around the back of my head and held my mouth firmly against his wrist. "*Keep feeding.*"

My body started to feel heated. My hips rocked against the air as more blood flowed into my mouth. It came nearly faster than I could swallow.

"Yes, Celestina, keep doing that," Soren moaned.

A shout came from down the trail. Heavy footfalls pounded on the packed earth. My ears, which felt more attuned to the world around me than ever before, heard even the rustle of birds in the trees. But it was the boot falls that worried me.

"Soren!" That was Gray's voice. He skidded to a halt beside us. "I heard about the attack in the capital. What's going on?"

"She's hurt." Soren's hand slipped from my head. He leaned forward, pressing his elbows to the ground. "Give me a moment." His skin looked deathly pale.

"You gave her too much." Gray ripped Soren's wrist away from my mouth. "She's done. You're—"

"I'll…be fine." Soren paused to catch his breath. "I haven't given her…enough. Look at her neck. It's still…in ribbons. When I found her, she'd been…nearly drained dry."

"Must have been the palace guards taking her to Sunjin who attacked her." Gray cursed. "I'll kill them."

"They're dead," I rasped. The dragon had seen to their end in a most violent way. Not that the collar would let me tell them that part.

"What's that, Sky Girl?" Raya asked as she ran up with her sword drawn. She slid her sword into the scabbard on her back before kneeling next to me. Her long braid slipped over her shoulder as she leaned forward.

"Dead," I repeated. My blood started to feel heated again. My skin felt too tight. I remembered this from before. "All dead."

I wanted.

Ached.

Needed.

"Soren?" I needed Soren.

I reached out for him only to find empty air where he'd been a moment ago. I searched frantically around for him to find he'd collapsed on the hard-packed ground.

When I couldn't have him, I reached for Raya.

The beautiful warrior bent over me like she was going to kiss me. I would like that. I'd like to have her lips on mine. I wondered if they'd taste like berries. Her hand pressed down on my shoulder, forcing me back to the ground. *"Sleep, Sky Girl, sleep while your hero recovers."*

Chapter 37

I woke up feeling groggy and disoriented in a bed I didn't recognize, and in a room I didn't recognize. A silky sheet covered me as I lay on a mattress that could have passed as a cloud. I stretched out the arm that had been broken, turning it this way and that. It only felt slightly stiff.

I touched my neck, expecting to feel the gaping wound that had been there. The skin was smooth.

It shouldn't be smooth. And my arm should be wracked with pain. This wasn't right. This wasn't natural.

And this wasn't the first time he'd done this to me. I shouldn't have woken up healthy in Soren's tent after being thrown into that ravine. It was his vampire's blood. Something in the blood had healed me then. Goddess, his blood had healed my hands after the chort's attack, not Mary's tea. And Soren's blood had healed me now.

"Soren?" He'd given me too much blood this time. That was what Gray had said. The crown prince had given too much and then had collapsed.

The crown prince who was also a vampire.

A vampire.

A blood-sucking, soul-stealing, untrustworthy vampire.

Who'd saved my life.

With his blood.

More than once.

My head dropped back to my pillow as I pressed my fists to my eyes and groaned.

Did his blood change me?

Did his blood give me his poisoned magic?

That must be the reason he thinks he senses magic in me. He gave me his blood. And now I'm cursed.

For.

All.

Time.

That was what the storytellers had taught us.

He'd infected me.

Perhaps even turned me?

Goddess, and I still worried about his health? I still wondered why I was in this strange room instead of with him?

I should be with him.

The collar sent a searing pain down my spine. I needed to get to him. Now.

I jolted up in the bed. The sheet covering my body slipped down. The cold air in the room brushed against me. I'd been stripped bare! Of course, I had. I'd been covered in the princess's blood and my own. Whoever tended to me must have stripped those bloodstained clothes off me. Perhaps even now, whoever had looked after me—Raya?—was off searching for a new outfit I could wear.

I jerked the sheet back up, clutching it to my front.

Where was I? This room, with the large arched windows, looked out over the same ocean as Soren's room had. Did that mean I was still in Reinheart Palace?

Probably, I answered my own question since no one else was in the room to do it for me.

The pale wood dresser and wardrobe had gentle curves and flowers carved into their legs. So did a cushioned chair that was sitting next to the canopy bed. The room was decorated in soft shades of blue. A tapestry hanging on the wall depicted a young woman with a unicorn sleeping on her lap. The soft rug on the floor was a carpet of blue wildflowers.

I swung my feet over the edge of the bed and, after wrapping the sheet around me, padded across the plush wildflower carpet to the wardrobe. With one hand still holding the sheet to my chest, I opened the wardrobe to find something to put on.

The shelves and pegs inside sat empty.

I don't know how long I stood there, staring into the dark interior, wishing for clothes to appear, when the door beside me opened.

"Oh! You're up. Wasn't expecting that."

I spun around to find Princess Priscilla hurrying through the doorway with three court ladies following in her wake. They were all peering at me with wrinkled noses, like I was an exhibit at a traveling menagerie. My grip on the sheet tightened.

"Go fetch the tray, and put it over there," Priscilla told one of the court ladies, indicating a small table surrounded by a few chairs in the corner. The princess then smiled at me. "I had the kitchen bring up a late lunch in case you woke up."

I gaped at the princess while the lady, a petite woman with a tight expression left and returned with the tray. "You were badly injured," I finally said. "How are you…here?"

Priscilla's smile widened. "Superior healing abilities." She swept into the room and lifted the lid to peer at the food underneath the tray. "Let's eat."

"I need clothes first," I said, not willing to eat with one hand clutching the sheet to my chest. My hair had to be a mess too. Oh, I could only imagine the horrid things the ladies would say about me to the rest of the court the minute I was out of earshot!

Princess Priscilla looked momentarily nonplussed by my demand. But then her expression softened again. "Of course. Lady Sela, please find Goldie for me. Tell her to bring something comfortable for

Celestina to wear." After the lady left, Priscilla watched me for a moment. I felt like a mouse being stalked by a snake. "I imagine you're still terribly sore."

"Not too bad. Where is Soren?" Vampire or not, the collar was still demanding I get to him.

"My brother's in his chambers with a healer, the royal mage, and a bevy of advisors. I believe Mary's tea has been fetched." Priscilla made a face. "Nasty stuff. Serves him right, though. He was close to death by the time Raya had carried him back to the palace. And that was even after Gray and Raya had given him their blood. Which is troubling. Raya's blood is extra powerful, you must know. Her feeding him alone should have revived him."

"What?" I shook my head. "Why is Raya's blood more powerful than Gray's?"

"Because she's one of us, of course." Priscilla smiled that sly smile again.

Raya was a…a… "She's a vampire?"

Priscilla nodded.

But-but that couldn't be right. Raya was my friend. "And Gray?"

"Oh, he's human, but we don't hold that against him." She winked.

Gray, I would have expected to be all fangy and evil. I shuddered, realizing how wrong I'd been about everything.

"I need to go to Soren. He's sick because of me." I rushed to the door, but then remembered the sheet. The nakedness. And the twittering court ladies. The small lady who'd brought in the lunch tray muttered something I couldn't hear.

"Behave, Lady Ginger," the princess said. Suddenly, she was at my side faster than humanly possible. She placed a hand on my shoulder. "My brother is sick because of his own actions. You didn't force him to feed you until he had nothing left. That's on him. He's not supposed to be healing anyone in the first place. For many, many reasons. Daddy is furious."

That was just what I needed. More reasons for the king to dislike me.

A vampire king?

Oh goddess, save me.

"Come on." She hooked her arm with mine. "Sit down with us. Have some lunch. Even though Soren filled your belly with his lifeblood, you still need to eat."

"After I'm dressed." And after I figured out how to make things right with Soren and his father. My heart pounded nearly out of my chest at the thought of seeing Soren again.

Goddess, he was a vampire.

A monster.

Literally, the Beast of Fein.

What was I going to say to him?

How was I supposed to act?

Priscilla frowned. She looked ready to argue that I should follow her orders when a lady knocked on the door. "Princess?" came the shy voice.

"Yes, Lady Rose," Priscilla said.

"The queen requests your presence in her private chambers."

"I suppose she wants a personal accounting for what happened this morning. I'm sorry, Celestina. I'm going to have to leave you here. But my friends, Lady Sela, Lady Quell, and Lady Ginger will keep you company, won't you ladies?"

"I could think of nothing better to do," Lady Sela said dryly. She settled down on a chair located next to the lunch tray.

"We'll do our best," Lady Quell said.

"We've all been anxious to talk with her," Lady Ginger said and giggled.

Priscilla hesitated at the door for a moment before saying seemingly to herself, "It should be fine. I'll be back as soon as I can." And then she left.

I paced the princess's beautiful guest room. This had to be her guest room, the same guest room the princess had invited me to stay in not that long ago. But no matter how lovely the room, the walls seemed to be pushing in on me. I felt trapped. The court ladies had started to eat my lunch like a trio of ravenous rats. When they finished with that, would they mistake me for their next snack?

Were they all vampires?

My stomach complained as I watched the pile of delicious-smelling food being devoured. But I wasn't going to sit down with a bevy of vampires wrapped only in a sheet.

"Celestina," Lady Quell said as she chewed on a piece of brown bread. "I heard your chamber at Queen Beatrice's court didn't have glass in the windows."

"I heard it's because Earst doesn't possess the knowledge to make their own glass," Lady Ginger giggled as she spoke. She reached across Lady Quell to pick out a few choice pieces of cheese.

"We have glass in Earst," I corrected.

"Oh! But not in your chambers?" Lady Quell asked. "So, even before your queen made you a slave, you didn't have enough status for glassed windows?" She lowered her voice. "Were you a castle servant?"

"Isn't it perpetual winter in Earst?" Lady Sela shivered dramatically.

"It does have a long cold season," I admitted, looking directly into the young lady's big, beautiful eyes. Were those the eyes of a vampire? Was that a vampire glamour making her look extra lovely to us mortals? I gave myself a mental shake. "I-I'm grateful to Prince Soren for rescuing me from the situation I'd found myself in. I don't wish to do anything that will harm him."

"Is that so?" Lady Sela asked.

"I said it, and you can trust my word. Prince Soren has been nothing but kind to me. He's protected me in more ways than I could ever repay." He might be a vampire and that truth might scare the living breath out of my lungs. But my fear of him didn't stop my body from yearning for the touch of his body against mine. It didn't stop my eyes from longing to watch his face light up with a playful grin. And it didn't stop my heart from aching at the thought of him taking a lady from this court, perhaps one of these ladies, as his partner, as his princess.

"You can prove your gratitude to *our prince* by staying as far away as possible from him," Lady Sela said as she rose from her dainty chair.

The skirt of her lovely blue cloud-like dress swished around her legs as she advanced on me. "You can prove your gratitude by taking yourself off to Tiburnia—isn't that the kingdom your parents aligned themselves with when they'd betrayed your queen? Go there instead of staying here where you're not wanted. You can prove yourself by leaving the palace. Now. Today. Your absence is the only way you'll stop tearing apart the royal family."

My hand went to the damning collar around my neck. "I would if I could." This kingdom was nothing more than a huge nest of vampires. I needed to find a way to escape.

But where could I go? How would I get there? And how would I survive leaving Soren with this horrible collar demanding I stay as close to him as possible?

"Good afternoon, ladies!" Goldie, thank goodness, blasted through the door like a cheerful tornado. Certainly, Goldie—sunny, smiling Goldie—wasn't a vampire. She couldn't be.

The older woman had a white frock draped over her arm that looked as if it would weigh nothing. She took one look at me and tut-tutted. "You need a full wardrobe. I'll speak to that prince of yours before the day is through about it."

"He's not my—" I started to say, the last thing I needed was for these judgmental ladies to go back to the court and report how I've been claiming Soren as my own.

Goldie didn't let me finish. Instead, she grabbed ahold of one end of the sheet and with a mighty tug, unwrapped it from my body.

I squeaked. My hands flew up to cover myself from the court ladies' calculating glares.

Goldie simply tut-tutted again. She thrust a pair of white lace panties into my hands. I had barely finished pulling them up when she tossed a silky slip over my head. She then followed with the lightweight dress. Finally, she spun me around to tie a large silk peach ribbon around my waist.

"Now that that's done, my lady, have a strawberry and sit down so I can work on getting rid of those tangles in your hair," Goldie said just as Lady Sela leaned forward and took the last strawberry from the nearly empty tray. All that was left really were crumbs and a half-eaten sandwich.

The court lady smirked in my direction as she tossed the strawberry into her mouth. I felt like snarling at her. But I had enough experience with court life to know when to pick my battles. Instead, I sat primly in the bedside chair Goldie had pointed to. Kept my chin up, even while fighting back a wave of tears.

"I'm not really hungry," I lied.

My stomach chose that moment to disagree.

"Girl! Have you eaten at all today?" Goldie asked.

A blush stung my cheeks. "I—"

"I'll go fetch another tray," Lady Quell offered. She jumped to her feet.

"Thank you, Quellie," Goldie said. "I'm embarrassed your new friends didn't leave you anything to eat on this tray, Celestina. After spending weeks with my brother and his army and now this, you must think the Fein have no manners at all."

"I would never think that."

Lady Ginger rolled her eyes. "She was telling us about the harsh conditions at Queen Beatrice's castle. No glass in her windows. The poor dove must think she's hit the jackpot when she saw Reinheart Palace."

"No glass in the windows? That must be rough in the winter." Goldie shivered. But then she gave me a kind smile. "Most of the other kingdoms don't have ready access to hot water. It's quite a luxury, indeed, to live in the palace."

While we waited for Lady Quell's return with a second lunch tray, Goldie started chatting with Lady Sela and Lady Ginger about their parents and some other courtiers. She tried to draw me into the conversations, but the other two ladies would either talk over me or change the subject to some member of the court I would have no way of knowing anything about.

I could only imagine how these ladies, along with many of the others in court, hoped to one day become the crown prince's mate. My presence in his bed must threaten them to no end.

Lady Sela leaned forward toward Goldie. *"Could you talk to the princess about this? About her?"* she whispered, but not nearly quietly enough that I wouldn't hear. *"We all know how the princess likes to take in strays, but expecting us to befriend a whore stretches the limit of propriety, don't you agree? I am certain my parents would not approve, especially considering how the king and queen are unhappy."*

"She's not—" Goldie flashed a nervous glance at me. "I'll let the princess know how you feel."

"Thank you, Goldie. She listens to you. Ah, here's the new tray. Let's see what you brought for us, Lady Quell."

"The tray is for Lady Celestina." Lady Quell swatted Lady Sela's delicate hand away from the pile of plump strawberries. "Especially the strawberries. I heard from the kitchen staff that they are your favorite, Lady Celestina?"

"I do love them. We don't have winter strawberries in Earst. I never even knew such a thing could exist. These are certainly a treat."

"My father grows them," Lady Quell said, smiling as she talked about her family. "He has greenhouses that are heated from the hot springs that run under the capital. If you'd like, I could show them to you some time."

"Really? I would enjoy that." I took a plump strawberry from the tray. The collar gave me a sharp jolt. "As long as Soren approves," I amended.

"Since this lunch isn't for us,"—Lady Sela frowned at me as if I were the one who had told her she couldn't eat any of it—"Lady Cris had invited us to go horseback riding through the Whispering Trails. And I don't want to disappoint her. Are you coming with me?" She gave a meaningful look to ladies Ginger and Quell.

Lady Ginger hurried to her feet. "Yes, that does sound delightful."

"Lady Quell? You are coming too?" Lady Sela pressed.

"Um, I think I'll stay and keep Lady Celestina company until the princess returns."

Lady Sela rolled her eyes. "Goldie, you will remember to discuss that matter with the princess that we'd talked about?"

Goldie bowed slightly. "I'll tell her what you said. Now, run along, girls. Lady Celestina needs to eat, and I still need to style her hair."

While Goldie worked her magic, Lady Quell told me all about the winter gardens her father had developed. Apparently, he was a gentleman scientist who dabbled in all sorts of projects around the capital.

An hour later, my hair was styled into a crisscross of braids that complemented the lightweight gown. And there still was no sign of Princess Priscilla or word from Prince Soren.

I hoped he was recovering.

I hoped he would call for me soon.

I needed to see him. And not just because of the collar.

I simply needed *him*.

Chapter 38

"He's still unwell," was the best I could get out of the princess when she'd finally returned from her meeting with her mother, the queen.

The collar burned. It wanted me to find Soren. It didn't matter that he was a vampire and that terrified me. It didn't matter that I felt a rational urge to run out of the palace and never look back. The collar wouldn't allow it. The collar didn't care that Soren was a blood-eating vampire. I was bound tightly to him. And I needed to get to him. But no matter how I explained this, the princess refused to tell me how to get to Soren's chambers or offer to guide me there.

"Give him time to heal," she told me over and over.

I'd been away from him for an entire day, and the collar was none too happy about that. Tears sprang to my eyes when it struck. Pain rippled in waves through my shoulders and down my back.

"You don't understand, Princess," I gasped. "I *need* to be with him."

"I understand that my parents and the healer both told me that my brother needs to rest." She chewed her bottom lip and frowned. "When he wakes up, I'm sure they'll let you go to him."

She didn't sound at all sure about that.

"Can you go to him?" Perhaps I could tag along with her.

Priscilla shook her head. "They told me that he needs rest, which really means they want absolute silence in his room." She made a face. "I'm banned as well."

"I need air." I shot up from my chair and made straight for the door.

"Wait!" The princess moved again with preternatural speed and caught me before I could get through the doorway.

My gaze cut to her hand that had curled around my wrist like a manacle. "Am I a prisoner here?"

She stayed silent for far too long. "No," she finally said with a sigh. "You're my guest." But her hand remained locked around my wrist.

"Then I'm free to leave this room."

Her grip tightened. "*I'd rather you stayed.*"

She'd used a velvety voice that buzzed in my head and made me want to do as she wished. Made even my atoms yearn to follow her every desire.

"*We should sit back down,*" she said.

"Yes." I couldn't remember why I would want to leave her. She was my everything. She held the keys to my happiness. What a beautiful princess. How could anyone deny her anything? I started to glide back to the chair. She'd like that. She wanted to sit with me. What an honor it was to have someone like her interested in spending time with me. "Yes, we should sit."

But that wasn't right. Being with her was making me forget something. No, not something, some*one.*

The collar sent such a blistering pain through my body, that it left me bending over and clutching myself.

"What's wrong?" she demanded.

It hurt too much to answer.

"Do you need a healer?"

I shook my head. A healer couldn't help me.

"I-I'm going to go get a healer." In a blur of motion, she was gone.

A healer couldn't help me. No one could stop the collar from punishing me for failing...failing...

Soren.

I had to fight against the princess's compulsion to remember his name. To remember what he meant to me. To remember why being away from him caused me physical pain.

Soren.

I had to get to Soren.

But I couldn't leave this room. I needed to stay sitting in this room because that was what the princess wanted. And my life was all about pleasing the princess.

Pain from the collar twisted every muscle in my body into unnatural positions. I had to fight to get moving. I had to—

Give up.

Give up.

Give up.

Die already.

That pinched, angry voice in my head sounded like Queen Beatrice's.

No!

I refused to let her win.

Soren.

He had the power to stop the collar from hurting me. All I had to do was get to him. One step at a time. I could do this.

I don't know how I managed it. The collar had left me barely able to walk, barely able to breathe. And yet, it also demanded I go, demanded I get myself to Soren. Even if it meant I'd probably run into deadly vampire guards. Even if I was taking myself deeper into the lair of my kingdom's greatest enemy, I didn't care. Despite Soren's command that I run if I felt my life was in danger, my desire to get to him—a vampire—to make sure he wasn't dying overruled any self-preservation instincts. I stumbled down one hallway, turning only to go down another. I went upstairs and downstairs until finally, finally, my hand landed on the knob to a familiar door.

Not that this particular door looked much different from the hundreds of others I'd passed. Don't ask me how I knew I'd find Soren inside this chamber. But I knew he'd be on the other side of the door better than I knew my own name.

"Sky Girl!" Raya jumped to her feet when I stumbled into the room.

Gray moved just as quickly. He caught my arm. "What is she doing here?"

"Is Soren—?" I couldn't get any more words out. Thankfully, I didn't need to.

"He's sleeping," Raya answered. "He's going to live."

"No thanks to you." Gray steered me back out the door. "You can't be here."

"I can't leave." I clutched my middle. My insides were boiling with pain, and it felt like they were going to burst through my belly. "Please. I must go to him."

"It's the collar," Raya said. "For whatever reason, it's punishing her."

"Our orders—" Gray started.

"Don't come from Soren," Raya finished. "He wouldn't thank us for turning her away."

"He nearly died because of her," Gray shouted. "And you're okay with leaving her in a room with him?"

"Soren nearly died saving her," Raya corrected. "And he'd not thank us if that damned collar kills her because we wouldn't let her in the bedroom with him."

Thankfully, there weren't any healers or advisors in the room with us. If there had been, I doubted I would have had any chance of getting close to Soren. But because they'd left the King's Guards in charge, Raya had the authority to push open Soren's bedchamber door.

"There's someone dying to see you," Raya said to her prince. Gray grunted.

Soren was laid out on his back in the middle of his bed. He didn't move. He barely opened his eyes as I approached the massive bed.

"Celestina." His voice sounded like footsteps through a pile of dried leaves in the fall. "Am I dreaming?"

Tears filled my eyes. I'd never seen Soren look so pale, so weak. I grabbed his hand and pressed it to my chest. As soon as I'd touched him, the collar loosened its grip, letting me breathe. The pain started to slip away. "I'm here."

"Good." The tension in his mouth softened. "Need you."

A tear tumbled down my cheek. I nodded because I felt the same way. "I'm here." And I planned to stay at his side until the king's advisors returned. (Even then, they'd have to drag me away.) I rubbed my thumb over the back of his hand. "I'm here."

He frowned. "You need to rest."

"I'm not leaving you. Not until you're well."

Moving slowly, he lifted the heavy blanket someone had draped over him.

I shot a worried glance over my shoulder to Raya and Gray who were watching from the doorway. Would they drag me from the room if I tried to get into Soren's bed with him?

"Come," Soren's voice rasped.

The command burned through my hesitation.

As soon as I slipped into the bed with him, he wrapped his arms around me. The blanket fell, enfolding us in a cocoon of warmth.

"Leave," he demanded of his friends.

Raya shook her head, but she smiled before ducking out of the doorway. Gray looked less than thrilled with the situation. But after a few scowling moments he backed out and closed the door behind him. He left me alone with Soren.

Alone and unprotected with a wounded, blood-hungry vampire.

Chapter 39

"I'm the only one with the power to protect you against those deceitful, deadly vampires," Queen Beatrice liked to tell us. "Step outside the borders of our kingdom, and you'll see how the vampires torment the humans. You'd see how unsafe the other kingdoms are. If not for me, you—every single one of you—would be dead."

My heart should have been pounding in my chest like a frightened rabbit's. I should have been trembling. I should have been *running away*.

Instead, I snuggled into Soren's warmth.

Goddess, help me. I love a vampire.

Was it the collar that compelled me? The glamour of his twisted vampiric magic that lured me? Or was this me?

He could kill me, and I'd still love him. How ridiculous was that?

Back in Earst, others might have considered me fanciful, living with my gaze turned out the window so focused on my dragons, but no one had ever accused me of being foolish.

A Queen's Lady had to keep her head on her shoulders if she had any hope of keeping her *actual* head attached to her shoulders. And yet with Soren, despite having spent years honing those survival instincts, instead of running, I'd snuggled in bed with danger because being with him felt right. Somewhere along the way, he'd become as essential to me as the air I breathed.

I sighed happily as he nuzzled the side of my neck, kissing, licking.

"*Celestina*," he whispered. "*My Celestina.*"

This was where I belonged. This was—

Soren struck. It'd been quick. His fangs pierced my neck. I jerked from the sudden shock of pain. And then his mouth was on my wound. Sucking. I felt my blood leaving my body. Not just my blood. He took something else with it. Part of my essence flowed out of me, feeding him.

An injured vampire is even more dangerous than a healthy one. I had warned the young princes of this often enough. The drive to survive overrides any other thought. Even love.

Soren's hands shifted to hold my hips tight against him as he drank. I felt pinned in place. My breath came in short bursts. He continued taking. I was his vessel. His to empty. The realization both terrified and thrilled.

He wouldn't be able to stop himself. Not when he was so weak. No vampire could.

Goddess, I'd have to fight him.

But I couldn't…I couldn't…

I didn't want him to stop. Having his mouth on my neck sent a fluttering zing of pleasure that made my nipples tingle and my womb clench.

"*Soren*," I groaned and rubbed against him.

He lifted his lips from my neck. His warm tongue lapped lightly over the wound. And he sighed. Every muscle in his body seemed to loosen with that sigh.

I shuddered, still needing him. Wanting him to take more, to take all of me. As my heart thundered wildly, I sucked the lobe of his ear into my mouth and gave it a small nip.

"I—I'm not—" He breathed out sharply. "I'm not strong enough to be able to love you as thoroughly as you deserve."

"Whatever you can give me." I placed my hand on his cheek, needing to touch him and to have him touch me. "It'll be enough."

With a nod, he eased my dress up until the skirt was bunched up around my waist. His rough hands caressed my hip, my thigh. A thick finger pushed aside my panties and delved into the center of my damp heat. I gasped at the suddenness of the intrusion.

"You are ready for me." His eyes darkened.

"I seem to always be ready when you're around." I drew my hand over his chest and down to where his erection jutted between us. "And I see you're ready too."

I pushed his drawstring pants down enough to free him, and so I could better caress the full length of him. Like hot silk over steel, I couldn't get enough of it. While I rubbed him, his fingers brought me to the edge of orgasm.

I was still facing him, still snuggled around him, but my left leg was now up over his hip. His beautiful green eyes met mine. He withdrew his fingers but kept the panel of my panties pushed to one side. Together we guided his cock to my center. With a swift movement, he pushed his way in. Gracious, he was big. Every time we had sex, his size surprised me. He held himself there, buried to the hilt. Not moving. A sheen of sweat glistened on his brow.

He was probably too weak to do more than to be there with me. While he generally took charge, I moved against the hard length of him inside me. I pressed my mouth to his, gripped his shoulders and, pistoning on his cock, chased my own release. My breathing stuttered. I...I... It didn't take long before my body throbbed around the length of him.

"*Goddess,*" he cried and joined me as I tipped over the edge.

The next time I opened my eyes, sunlight streamed in through the partially opened window. An icy breeze made the tapestries on the walls flutter.

I was still warm inside the cocoon of Soren's arms. His eyes were open. Soft, and friendly as he watched me. They were eyes that reminded me of my green dragon.

Memories came flooding back…

The green dragon.

Yesterday.

It had rescued—

Ummnnnmnhhn! That cursed collar snapped to action, using the sharpest pain to snuff out any thoughts of my brave protector.

"Breathe through it." Soren caressed the side of my face. "Dammit, I hate this collar. I hate what it does to you." His voice remained carefully gentle despite his words, as if he worried the collar might feed off any anger he might show. "Your thoughts should be your own, Celestina."

"They…usually are." Especially in the morning.

Something had changed. The dragon had touched the collar. It had—

I curled in on myself and moaned as a fresh wave of agony coursed through me. Whatever had happened yesterday, the collar didn't want me to puzzle it out.

When this current attack started to subside, I drew a deep breath and blurted out two words without allowing myself to think about what might happen. I hoped Soren had heard me. Goddess, I hoped he would understand their meaning. I doubted I'd be given a chance to repeat myself. As it was, those two words had cost me dearly. The pain that hit as I spoke them blurred my vision, muffled my hearing, and made me wonder if my head might explode.

"Fuck, your nose is bleeding." Soren pressed a corner of my blanket to try and staunch the flow. His eyes grew even more worried as he watched me. "Fuck. Fuck. Fuck. Your eyes."

Tears streamed from them from the pain, soaking my face.

"Your eyes and your ears are bleeding too."

I pulled my hand away from my face and saw that my fingers were drenched, not in tears, but in blood. Goddess. My head spun. Goddess. I wouldn't survive this.

"Dammit, collar, you will not kill her." He hauled me into his arms and held me tightly against his chest. "You cannot kill her. Queen Beatrice gifted her death to me. I'm the only one with the power to take it. You understand me, you shit piece of metal? You won't steal her death from me. I won't allow it." He rocked as he held me. "I won't allow the collar to take you, Celestina. I won't allow it. I can't."

Slowly. Slowly. The pain started to ebb. Or perhaps I'd passed out. I drifted somewhere on a cloud. I didn't think I was dead. But if I were, I wouldn't mind staying here. I liked this place. It was calm here. Safe.

The two words that had caused all the pain, I didn't dare think them. All I could do was hope that my uttering them was enough to get Soren thinking in the right direction. I hoped they were enough to save me. Goddess, I prayed those two words—whispered in a distant, blurry memory—held the promise of a better future, a future where I could be set free.

Dragon. Mine.

Chapter 40

A cool cloth moved like a cloud across my face. A voice, whispering and gruff, accompanied the movement.

"You're not giving her your vein." Raya's voice.

"She's coming around." That was Gray.

After the cool, wet cloth wiped away the crust that coated my eyelids, they felt lighter. Light enough to pry them open. I found myself in Soren's lap, cradled in his arms. He had his back to the headboard. His legs spread out on the bed. He looked down at me and smiled.

"Hello there." His voice was like a balm to my stiff muscles.

"How did you stop the collar?" My voice sounded raspy as if I'd been screaming. Had I been screaming?

"Superior power of persuasion," he said with a cocky grin. His eyes were red. And he looked as if he needed to sleep for the next week, if not longer.

"You didn't feed me more of your blood, did you?" Because, besides a few aches and pains, I felt fine.

"Didn't need to," he said, pulling me closer to his chest.

Then perhaps he'd stopped the collar before it had done too much damage. All I could remember was the blood. There'd been so much blood. And the cloth he was using to wash my face came away stained red.

But I felt fine. My body molded to his, like we'd been made for one another, like we were meant to be pressed together like two halves of a more powerful whole.

I rubbed against him and sighed. "I like being here."

"We're still in the room," Gray reminded.

"Sorry." I blushed and pushed the skirt of my dress back down over my legs. It had still been hiked up around my waist from earlier. It was stained with my blood. Yet another piece of clothing ruined.

"We need to discuss what happened out there," Soren said just as the door to his bedchamber slammed open.

"Why aren't the King's Guards—?" Redfern demand halted as he took in the scene before him. His angry gaze traveling from me, to Raya, to Gray, and back to me. His jaw tightened.

Redfern and three other court officials were coming into the bedchamber.

"What is *she* doing here?" Redfern demanded.

"Why have you failed in your duties?" A small, beady-eyed man with a pointed beard followed Redfern into the room and rounded on Raya and Gray. "Our orders were that no one be admitted. No one! What about that wasn't clear?"

Raya skittered a worrying glance in my direction before lowering her gaze to the floor.

Gray's scowl came nowhere near me, but it still felt as if his anger was meant for me. "The prince is healthy and safe, Healer Darius."

"The bed is covered in blood!" the small man shouted.

He was right. My eyes widened as I took in the scene around us. Soren's bed looked as if it had been the site of a fierce battle. The bed sheets were stained red. A puddle of blood next to his leg was slowly seeping into the mattress. Gracious. I swallowed down a thick lump of bile. *Gracious.*

"The blood isn't his, sir," Gray said.

That was mine? How was I still alive?

"It doesn't matter. This dereliction of duty can't be overlooked. I ordered him to be given time to heal. And you brought *this*. You are relieved of your posts." The healer spoke in a rapid staccato.

"I told you explicitly to keep *that human* away from our prince," Redfern added. "This will not go unpunished. Now, go. Leave us to pick up the pieces."

Raya and Gray started for the door.

"No." Everyone turned toward the man who uttered that one word. The muscles in Soren's arms tensed as if he was preparing for battle.

"No," he repeated. "My guards are not relieved of their duties. And no, Redfern, you will not punish them for following my orders. Celestina will never be kept away from me. That's a standing order. One that will never be breached. Is that understood?"

"You are ill." Redfern took a step toward the bed. "Weakened from blood loss and from the hold Queen Beatrice is exerting on you through her vassal. I had no choice but to step in. Your father—"

"Doesn't understand." Soren shifted me in his arms, turning me slightly away from the approaching Redfern as if he was worried the king's mage would snatch me away. "The king doesn't understand."

"*Don't*," I put my hand on Soren's chest and whispered. But I didn't have the kind of power over the crown prince as everyone seemed to believe I did. I couldn't stop Soren from playing into Redfern's plan to prove I was a threat, so he could sever our connection. I could see it in his raging eyes, Redfern wanted me gone in the most permanent of ways.

"Celestina is mine to protect. Because I've been listening to you and to the king instead of my own instincts, I did a piss-poor job of ensuring her safety yesterday. That stops now."

"See." Redfern looked almost triumphant as he moved toward the bed. "See, this further proves you are not yourself. You have always been loyal to the crown, to this country. But now—" He waggled his hand in my direction. "Now, the moment she shows up, you put her above all else. Your decisions are muddled because of her. You have been fooled, your highness, into thinking these thoughts are your own. We know that collar carries a whooper of a magical charge, most of which we don't understand. And I've also heard that the slave carries magical powers of her own."

"She's not a slave," Soren corrected.

Redfern continued as if he hadn't heard. "Is the slave also a witch, I wonder? A secret daughter?"

A secret daughter? Could that explain why Queen Frieda doted on me and why Queen Beatrice hated me?

No. I shook the thought away. Queen Beatrice has sisters. It's not as if the crown orders them killed. Besides which, their powers are weak compared to the queen's. A thimble's worth of magic to the queen's rushing waterfall of intensity.

"Is she even a slave at all?"

"Celestina's not a slave." Soren sounded angry. "And I'm not being influenced by a foreign bitch of a queen."

"No? Then why did you risk your life, and the future of this kingdom, by giving her so much blood that you nearly died? And why, when we did everything in our power to keep her away from you while you healed, do I find her here, in your arms?"

"With blood everywhere," Healer Darius chimed in.

"With blood everywhere," Redfern echoed, nodding.

"I wanted her here," Soren said. "The blood was the collar's fault."

"So, let me get this straight in my mind. For selfish reasons, you broke the king's command? For selfish reasons, you risked your life by bringing this foreigner into your bed when you were at your weakest? This reckless behavior is not how your father trained you. You must agree. You are not the crown prince I know."

"The Soren you know has always put duty above self!" the prince roared. "That is how I've been trained. That is what has always been expected of me."

"She is not Fein," Redfern was quick to counter. "You owe Queen Beatrice's slave nothing."

His jaw ticked at Redfern's persistent calling me a slave. But he managed to keep his voice steady. "The moment Queen Beatrice put her in my care, and I accepted, she became my responsibility."

I had to bite my tongue not to join in and defend Soren. But I knew enough about court intrigues to know that anything I said would be used against Soren. This was a battle he would have to fight for himself. But goddess, keeping quiet grated.

"I'm going to have to talk to the king," Redfern growled. "He won't stand for this." He whirled in a burst of fury and rushed toward the door.

"I command the army," Soren said. He didn't shout it. He didn't growl it. He simply stated it as a truth.

Redfern froze. The mage slowly turned around.

"You can tell the king that," Soren said and waved his hand in dismissal.

The two men glared at each other for several tense moments before Redfern stormed out. The healer followed.

"Soren," Raya admonished once the room had been emptied. "That wasn't wise."

"He kept our heads attached to our necks, Raya. Let's not berate the guy," Gray said. "But really, my friend, are you willing to go to war?"

Soren bared his teeth.

"That's not really an answer," I told him. "And you do realize, Soren, Redfern provoked you on purpose? He'll announce to the court how you've just threatened to overthrow your own father because of me."

He tightened his arms around me. "It's the truth. I would do anything to protect you."

That made no sense. Why would—?

He kissed me. It was so easy to sink into the warmth of his lips. But then I remembered. Redfern had clearly wanted Soren to make an outrageous declaration exactly like that. The provocation seemed obvious. And Soren walked right into his trap.

I pushed at his chest. "He—" I had to peel my lips from his. "Redfern will be using this outburst to remove me from your presence."

Gray nodded. "Likely in the most permanent manner possible."

"He does see Sky Girl as a threat. I wouldn't be surprised if he'd orchestrated the attack on her," Raya said.

"No." I shook my head. "No, he's not responsible." Memories of those men attacking the princess and me tumbled back to me. "It…it was the old woman, the blind seer, she was there. She…wanted me dead."

Soren grunted as he shifted toward the edge of the bed. "That doesn't mean Redfern wasn't also involved." He turned so his feet were on the floor. With his hands steadying my hips, he stood me up between his spread legs. "We need to move quickly." He looked over my shoulder. "Raya? Could you…?"

Two strong hands wrapped around my shoulders. "Come on Sky Girl. Let's get that blood-soaked dress off you and get you cleaned up." As she steered me toward the bathing chamber, Soren rose from the bed. He wavered and had to put his hand on the bedside table to steady himself.

"We need to confront the king," he said. "Gray, go spread word to my captains about the fight that's about to happen. I won't let Redfern win."

With a nod, Gray slipped from the room.

At the same time, I pulled away from Raya to return to Soren's side. "You plan to pull a sword when diplomacy is what is needed." I placed my hand on his cheek. His skin felt cool. And it still had a waxy, gray appearance. "You need to rest, not fight."

His fingers twined mine. "I'm fine."

"I can't tell if you're lying about your health to me or yourself."

He gave my hand a little tug. "If we return to this bed—after fetching clean sheets—we will not be sleeping."

"Ah…" My cheeks heated. "That lie was for me, then."

He bent down and kissed me fiercely. "I'm tempted to prove you wrong. Though, perhaps you'd have to do the bulk of the work again. You could straddle me and ride—" He pressed a deep but too brief kiss on my lips and then, lifting his gaze to the ceiling, he growled. "Goddess, how she tempts me like no other."

I chuckled. "That's on you, warrior boy. And I still believe you need to take some time to rest before picking a fight with your entire kingdom."

"If I don't fight, we'll lose more than just you."

"I could—" I swallowed down a lump of fear that suddenly blocked my airways. "—give you my blood."

"Not after you bled everywhere. Now, Raya, get Celestina into some appropriate court clothes. You'll all be coming with me to the throne room. One way or the other, we're going to settle things in a way that will keep my father or his lackeys from trying to harm you, Celestina."

Chapter 41

Prince Cullen and Princess Priscilla both converged on us as we entered the throne room. Raya had found a pale blue gown that had a matching ribbon that tied just under my breasts for me to wear. Soren had donned a pure black court suit. The cut followed the lines of his muscles perfectly. He looked both dangerous and delicious, especially with a broadsword strapped to his hip.

Raya and Gray were both wearing weapons, a pair of shorter swords that were strapped to their backs. They also had daggers tucked in their boots.

Going into the throne room armed was a colossally bad idea, but no one seemed to want to hear me tell them that. Gray and Raya seemed anxious but excited. Soren appeared resigned.

His weary gaze passed over his siblings to arrow in on the king who was seated on his raised throne on the far side of the room.

The princess jogged over to us. She looked as if she was heading straight toward me. Raya swiftly moved to block her.

"What is this, Raya?" Princess Priscilla honestly seemed surprised.

"It would be a good idea to leave, my princess." Raya paused a beat before adding, "Please, go somewhere safe."

The princess sucked in a sharp breath. She grabbed Raya's arm. "What's happening? Soren? What are you planning? And why are you all wearing weapons?"

"Take Raya's advice, Pris. And take that pain-in-my-ass brother with you as well," Soren said as he led the way across the room.

Neither Princess Priscilla nor Prince Cullen listened. They followed along beside us. As we moved through the room, filled with courtiers, I spotted several familiar faces from Soren's army. Mainly captains. A few were foot warriors. They were all impeccably dressed for a court appearance. And they were all armed.

The temperature in the room seemed to drop significantly as the true courtiers seemed to take notice of Soren and his armed men.

Someone must have alerted the King's Guards. Over two dozen, dressed and kitted out identically to Gray and Raya, streamed in through the doors behind us.

"We're outnumbered more than two to one, Soren," Raya warned.

He shrugged. "Seems fair. The King's Guards' training regimen is laughable."

"Hey!" Gray protested. "I designed the training program."

"They should have asked me to design it," Soren replied.

Redfern and the healer were bent over, talking with the king. None of them had noticed our approach or that the room was swiftly falling eerily silent. Queen Lenore noticed, though. She rose and nodded to a quartet of King's Guards that were stationed near the throne.

Soren reached over and took hold of my hand.

"Father," Soren called out when we were still several yards away. "I have a matter that needs discussing."

Redfern and the healer straightened. The king slowly sat back. He steepled his fingers in front of his lips. "So I've been told."

"I assume you've been told a great many things." He stopped at the base of the throne's dais. Princess Priscilla and Prince Cullen both bowed. I started to follow suit, but Soren's grip on my hand tightened, keeping me steady in place. He didn't bend a knee for his leader.

Neither did Raya or Gray. "I doubt any of them are true."

Redfern's entire body stiffened. "You call me a liar?"

"I am Your Highness to you," Soren said. "I am your crown prince, and you will address me as such."

The king waved Soren's demand aside with a loud sniff. "Let's not be distracted by a pissing contest. You've brought armed men into my throne room. Are you making a play for my crown, son?" The gentle way he said "son" sent a chill down my spine.

I hated the rift my presence in the kingdom was causing. Soren was willing to go to war with a father he obviously adored, and who clearly adored him.

If only Soren hadn't given me the order to not fall on any swords, ever. I would run myself through with the closest blade before letting Soren ruin his relationship with his entire family. I shuddered to think what it would do to Soren if this aggressive move resulted in the injury or death of a family member.

It would crush him.

Seeing him crushed would destroy me.

"*Please*," I whispered to Soren. "*Diplomacy.*"

The queen must have read my lips. Or perhaps her superior vampire hearing allowed her to hear me. Her eyebrows shot up to her hairline. "Redfern," she said. "Where do things stand with removing the collar from the girl's neck?"

Redfern stepped forward. He didn't look in our direction, which I took as a bad sign.

"Yes, Redfern." The king nodded. "Have you been able to come up with a way to remove the slave collar?"

"I'm sorry, Your Majesty. The magic binding the girl to slavery cannot be broken by me." He didn't sound that sorry. "I've consulted my books and sent letters to colleagues. There doesn't seem to be a way of removing it. Only the mage who cast the spell can break it."

"And she has no reason to do that," Queen Leona said in a soft voice.

"What if I killed Queen Beatrice?" Soren bit off angrily.

"Regicide is not a topic we entertain in this court," his father snapped. "Not even in jest."

"I wasn't joking," Soren said his hand moving to his sword.

"Killing the queen wouldn't matter," Redfern said. "The enchantment on the collar would outlive the queen."

"Then there's nothing that can be done," Queen Leona said as she settled into her chair. "I am sorry, Soren. I know you wanted to—"

"Oh, that's where you are wrong. There is something I can do." Soren turned to me. "Something I *must* do." He nodded to Raya and Gray. The armed men I recognized in the crowd moved to form a protective circle around us as Soren took both of my hands in his and knelt before me.

"Son, no!" Queen Leona leaped back to her feet as she cried.

"You cannot." King Devon rose from his throne.

I had no idea what Soren had planned or why it should upset his parents so much. "Celestina, my love, I—"

"She is not your mate!" his mother shouted.

"Think about this. You can only bind yourself to another once!" his father cried. "And once spoken, it's impossible to take back the oath."

He paused only a moment to glance up at his father. "She's bound to me in a way that cannot be undone. It's only fair that I bind myself to her in the same way."

"Guards! Stop him! He's not in his right mind! Use force if necessary!" the king commanded.

"Kill the slave girl!" Redfern shouted.

Steel clanged against steel as the warriors and guards clashed.

"Your sister and brother!" I tried to free my hands from Soren's. "They're in danger."

He refused to let go. "They can take care of themselves. Let me take care of you." He raised his voice to a shout to be heard over the thunderous dissonance of battle. "Celestina, you own my heart, my loyalty, my soul. I will serve you and only you for as long as there is breath in my lungs, for as long as there is blood in my veins, and for as long as there are stars in the sky. If you fall, so will I. This is my sacred vow, my pledge, my oath that I give to you and only you." His hands started to glow. That glow traveled through his touch, into my hands, and started to seep into my arms bringing a warm tingling sensation along with it. Tears filled my eyes. "From the first moment I met you as you fought against your parents to save the lives of the young princes under your care, I started to fall for you. As I watched you not only survive Mary but also win her admiration and friendship, I fell in awe of you. As I watched the blood seep from your neck after King's Guards attacked you, I felt the worst kind of fear for you." His hold on my hands tightened just a little bit. "Lady Celestina, I thank the horns of Galbraith for the gift that is you. And with these words, I seal myself to your life."

The room seemed to disappear as the glow that had spread throughout my body seemed to explode out into the space. The clamor of battle abruptly stopped. And gradually, gradually the brightness faded and the stunned room came back into focus.

Soren kissed my knuckles before rising to his feet. He kept hold of my hands as he turned back to the dais. "Father? Your move."

"Stand down!" the king ordered, he sounded defeated. His shoulders slumped.

The guards and warriors who'd already stopped fighting lowered their weapons. About a half dozen men lay scattered around us, bleeding on the shiny onyx floor, mostly from the King's Guards. Thankfully, none of them appeared gravely wounded.

Princess Priscilla pushed her way through the guards and warriors to wrap her arms around me. She hadn't suffered any visible damage from the fighting, I was glad to see. "Welcome to the family, Celestina! I've always wanted a sister."

"I don't understand," I said, my voice muffled since my face was buried against her chest. "Soren?"

"Don't strangle her." Prince Cullen gave his sister a nudge with his elbow. "Don't want to accidentally kill off both your new sister and your brother with one over-enthusiastic embrace. Don't know why Mom is crying. She's been after us for years to get mated."

"Mated?" I asked. I'd finally manage to wiggle out of the princess's embrace. "Soren?"

"The mating ritual was the best way to protect you short of starting a civil war. See, I listened to you. I used a little diplomacy."

"Very little." I swatted his chest. A battle had raged in the middle of the throne room…something that would have never happened in Queen Beatrice's court.

Soren didn't look bothered by any of it. "Besides—" He lifted my hand to his lips. "—while I don't consider you a slave. You are mine. You will always be mine. And I wanted to make damn sure everyone in the kingdom knows it." This last bit he said no longer looking at me, but at the king. "Princess Celestina will stand next to me in all that I do. One day, hopefully not anytime soon, she'll lead this land with me as my queen."

The room grew unnaturally silent as his words took root in everyone's mind. Including mine.

Princess. He'd called me his freaking princess.

I was a princess.

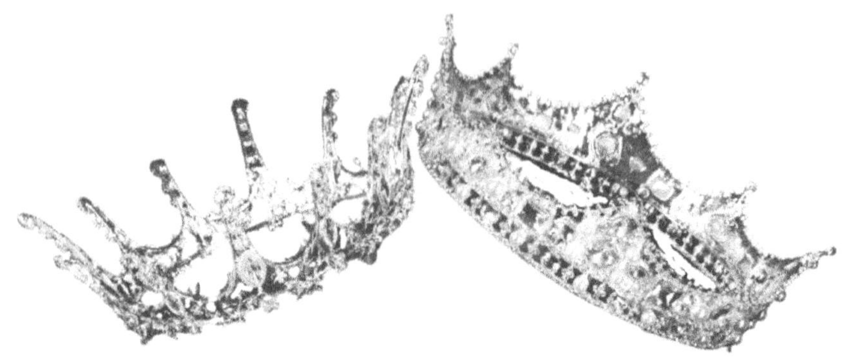

Chapter 42

"You tied your life to mine? In a way that can't be undone? Ever? What burst of madness? What kind of mind fever would make you do something so…so…damned idiotic!?"

"Why are you stalking around our chambers like a cornered mammoth cat?" Soren asked with considerably less heat. "I did what I did to avoid what would surely have been a devastating battle. I did what I did to keep you—"

"If I die, you die?" I shouted. I still couldn't wrap my head around why he'd do something so stupid, so reckless.

"I gave the kingdom the best reason for wanting to protect you." He gestured to himself. "Me."

Goddess, he looked so pleased with himself. I huffed a frustrated breath and turned away from him. As I did so, I caught sight of myself in a mirror. Raya had done a good job of taming my hair. And I looked refreshed, unlike Soren who still looked deathly pale from giving me too much blood. Dark bruises under his eyes underscored how close he'd been to dying.

He'd taken some of my blood back. My hand moved to my neck.

There was no sign, not even a pinkening of my skin, where he'd bitten me last night.

"When you bit me the first time, it left a mark." I turned toward Soren. "I was bruised for several days. But this time, there's no sign that you fed from me. Why is that?"

Soren's cheeks turned red. "You're not going to like my answer."

"Try me." My muscles tensed as I braced myself.

"Last night, I healed the bite marks with my tongue. It's simple enough to do." He mumbled the next part. "It's considered the polite thing to do."

"But…there was a mark? That first time? You didn't heal the bite?"

"No." He frowned.

"Why?"

His eyes darkened. He no longer looked embarrassed. He looked horny. Tired. But horny.

Men!

He stepped toward me. "Because Celestina." He put his hands on my hips. "I wanted the palace to see that I put my mark on you." He pressed his lips to mine. I melted more than a little from the heat and taste of him. Goddess, I didn't want to. Not when I was still angry with him. But my body's needs overrode my mind's wishes. "I wanted everyone to understand that you belong to me." He kissed me again. And it was a good thing he was holding onto my hips, because what his mouth did to me made my legs feel rather useless. "And, after what I did today, now everyone knows I belong to you, too."

And just like that we were back to talking about Soren making that ridiculous irrevocable bond with me. Without my consent.

"And that's how it works with mating? One party springs it on the other? Like, surprise! And everyone is okay with that? And the vows just go one way? In what world does that make a lick of sense?" My voice kept getting shriller and shriller, and there was nothing I could do to stop it.

"No, no, that's not how it usually goes. But you didn't need to pledge yourself to me because of the—" He pointed to the collar.

"And I needed to do something drastic to keep the royal advisors from convincing my father to take a sword to your neck. A feat I accomplished without spilling too much blood, without causing any deaths. I would think you'd be relieved. I listened to your advice."

"I do appreciate that you didn't go to war," I admitted. "But, Soren, if anything, this surprise one-way vow-taking of yours will surely convince the entire court that you're under my thrall."

He cupped my face in his war-hardened hands. "I am in your thrall."

I rolled my eyes and turned away from my desire to lean into him. "You know what I mean. Queen Beatrice's thrall. My goodness, Soren, even I'm beginning to wonder if she's somehow manipulating your thoughts."

"She's. Not." He sounded so sure of himself. It made me wish I could feel the same way. "Please, Celestina, let's not argue. Not right now. Not while the magic of our mating is still humming inside us." He started to pace. "You know that it's customary for couples to physically join after the vows are given. That's the only reason everyone has left us alone. And—" His eyes glittered "—I'm told that the lingering magic makes everything about the sex that follows that much more intense."

As much as I wanted to deny him, my body hummed with an arousal that demanded attention. "Only if you promise to rest afterwards."

"If you stay in the bed with me, my heart." He kissed me—his tongue mimicking the thrusting that would follow—as he took my hands and backed me into his adjacent bedchamber.

The beautiful dress Raya had found for me suffered the fate of all the others that came before it. It fell in tatters on the floor before we ended up on the bed, struggling to catch our breaths, with our limbs tangled together.

Goddess help me, I loved this man.

Erm…vampire.

Two days. That was how long he kept me in his bed. Loving me. Kissing me…everywhere. Feeding me strawberries and pastries that the servants left outside the door. And meat when we needed extra strength.

He fed on my blood. Not excessively. Not so I felt weak from it. Just often enough that thinking about it now made my body flush. I reached for his hand and, shifting toward him, positioned him until his fingers cupped that needy place between my legs.

"I like where your mind is going," his voice rumbled.

"You've corrupted me." Is this what happened when a human fell into a vampire nest? Part of me still worried that Soren was somehow twisting my thoughts around, turning me into a mindless, lustful beast for his use. A lifetime of warnings against vampires was hard to shake. Luckily, another part of me—the part that loved Soren for who he was, instead of fearing *what* he was—thanked the stars that we'd found each other. That was the same part that noticed the crease between his brows. "Not so corrupted that I don't see you're troubled this morning. What's wrong?"

"My parents have sent a note with each tray that's been delivered for the past two days. They're demanding we attend them." He rolled onto his back and groaned. "Goddess, I don't want to leave here. But I've left them alone with Redfern for too long already. It'll be dangerous to put them off any longer. They might turn against me, against us."

"Oh." I cuddled against his naked chest. I pressed a kiss to his clavicle. "Do you think we can delay—" I pressed a kiss to his chest. "—a few minutes longer?" I then kissed his rock-hard abs.

He ran his fingers through my hair. "Celestina."

"Hmm?" I shifted even lower so I could lick the tip of his arousal.

He groaned. "Woman, you don't play fair."

I smiled as I drew the length of him into my mouth. Instead of pushing me away, he fisted his hands in my hair and held me tight as he started to thrust. It was a potent feeling of power, knowing I was the cause of his loss of control. He growled my name and released my hair, giving me the choice of whether I wanted to keep my mouth on him as he came.

Afterward, much of his tension had eased from his expression. Seeing that I could have that effect on him made me feel even more powerful. I could do this for him. I could make him happy.

I playfully swatted his still-heaving chest. "Let's go face your parents." I moved to get out of our makeshift love nest.

"Oh no, you don't, princess. You're not getting away that easy." He grabbed me around the waist and tossed me facedown onto the bed. "You don't get to tease me like that and not give me the opportunity to return the favor." With one arm hand still snug around my waist, he kneeled behind me. After lifting me up, he nudged my legs apart and buried his head between them. With his tongue, mouth, and teeth, he worked my body until I was crying for release. With a smack on my bottom, he swirled his tongue inside me and then sucked on my clit, pushing me completely over the edge. My eyes rolled up into my head. My breath came in shuddering pants. My body continued to tremble and shake as he kept his mouth on me.

"Shit, princess." His voice rumbled against my most sensitive bits, which were now overly sensitive nearly to the point of pain. I cried out. "The way you just came for me has me aching for you all over again." He lowered me so my knees were on the bed again. With a quick movement, he proved how badly he wanted me by burying himself to his hilt inside me. His fingers dug into the soft flesh of my hips as he held me tightly against him. I shuddered and came all over his cock.

He pulled out and pushed in again, causing the throbbing between my legs to grow wilder. With no control over my body and feeling like I was sinking into an ocean of sensations, my fingers twisted into the bed sheets. I held on for dear life as he pistoned into me. Faster and faster. His hips slammed against me. When I tried to lift my head, his callused hand pushed my head back down to the mattress, keeping me at the angle that he wanted with just my hips jutting up in the air.

He gave a shout and exploded inside me, sending me over yet again. The moment his hands released my hips, my entire body collapsed onto the mattress. Soren, still buried inside me, fell with me, covering me like a heavy blanket. His chest heaved. With each labored breath, he whispered my name, "*Celestina. Celestina. Celestina. My love. My love. My love.*"

Chapter 43

While I showered, Soren directed one of the guards standing at the door to inform his parents that we'd join them for lunch. He also had a guard fetch Goldie, for which I was grateful. Goldie fussed and hugged and stuffed me into a sheath dress with a pearlescent sheen. She fixed my hair into intricate braids that looped around each other.

After joining me at the end of my shower, Soren donned a silver court suit with tall black boots. I noticed he slipped a dagger into his right boot when he thought I wasn't looking. His dark hair was tied into a queue at the nape of his neck.

Gracious, he looked delicious with the way the suit hugged his muscles. I placed my hands on his chest and kissed him, still not able to believe that this gorgeous man was mine. Mine to keep. Mine forever.

"Don't distract me," he said, pulling his lips away from mouth. "My parents will drag us from the bed naked if we don't show up. And if you keep kissing me like that, your dress will meet the same fate as your other clothes." In tatters on the floor.

He looked me up and down. A slow smile spread across his handsome face. "After lunch, and as soon as we get back to this room, your dress will definitely end up like the others."

"You know, you could just let me take it off," I said.

"Where's the fun in that?" He ran his hand through my braids.

Goldie swatted his hand away. "No touching until after lunch. I spent too much time making your princess shine for you to ruin it before she sits down with your parents." She pushed Soren toward the door. "Now, go and keep your hands to yourself, or else you'll answer to me." She threatened Soren with a wooden hairbrush in the same way Mary would chase the warriors with her oversized spoon.

I laughed as I followed Soren into the hallway. My laughter faded when I noticed that four of Soren's warriors—fully armed—were waiting to escort us.

"Are you expecting trouble?" I asked.

"One can never be too cautious," Soren replied easily, but his teasing good humor had been replaced with a warrior's hardness. His green gaze kept moving as we made our way in the direction of the king and queen's royal chambers with guards surrounding us on all sides.

Clearly, he was expecting trouble. And yet, who would dare try to harm me now that Soren had tied his fate to mine?

"Where's Raya and Gray?" I asked.

"After the battle in the throne room, I'm working to get them moved out of the King's Guards and into my command. Until that happens, I ordered them to keep to the military quarters. I'm worried a King's Guard might go after them in retribution for standing with us." He flashed me a sad smile. "We must protect the few friends we have."

"Everyone loves you, Soren."

The King's Guards who stopped us at an ornate set of golden double doors didn't look like they had any love for their crown prince. "Your men will have to wait out here," one of them said coolly.

"Who is in there, besides my parents?" Soren demanded of the guard who was blocking our way. Soren used that deep rumbly voice that made me want to do anything for him. Not in a way that the collar punished me. No, this was the voice that made every bit of me, all the way down

to my atoms, want to please him. Even though he wasn't directing his words to me, I shivered with a need to please him.

"The mage Redfern," the guard said, his voice flat and automatic.

I wondered why Soren had directed his question to that particular guard. That's when it hit me: vampires can't compel other vampires. At least a few of the guards at the door must have been vampires. Which meant that Soren couldn't simply compel them to stand aside and let him bring his warriors into the king's chambers.

"Redfern?" Soren's gaze flicked to the King's Guard who had to be a vampire. "The mage who called for you and the other the King's Guards to kill my mate? He's been invited to lunch with us? And you expect me to go in there unarmed?"

"Will all due respect, Prince Soren, we can't act against her, no matter what anyone says. Not after the vows snapped into place. The king has made that plain."

I hugged Soren's arm to keep myself from fleeing. I really wanted to run all the way back to Soren's chambers. I'd been safe there. And loved.

We'd both been safe there.

Soren looked down at me and sighed. "I should make them come to us."

I hurt for him. This was his family. His parents.

"Only you would bring a small army to lunch with his parents," Prince Cullen said with a chuckle. "I'm sure Mother will flip when she realizes she's not ordered enough meals to feed them all."

"There will be plenty of food. We're leaving." Soren barely spared his brother a glance. With a nod to one of his captains, he turned and started to walk away.

"Wait." The prince jogged after us. "What's going on? Mother was thrilled that you'd finally agreed to sit down with her and Father. We're to have a family meal. The first in too long. Pris is coming too."

"They also invited Redfern." Soren kept his pace quick.

"He is Dad's oldest and most trusted advisor. He has always come to all our family meals."

"Redfern is a danger to my mate."

A blush warmed my cheeks. The title of Queen's Lady had felt like a burden once Queen Beatrice had taken the throne. Nothing I ever did was good enough for her. I was always one step away from being the object of her next spectacle. And then the spectacle happened. She made me a slave. That title chafed more than I could ever explain. I'd thought that becoming Soren's mate would chafe just as much. After all, he'd made the vow without my consent. And now I was tied that much more tightly to him.

But hearing Soren call me "his mate" made millions of tiny dragons take flight in my chest. I loved him. And there was no doubt in my mind that Soren also loved me.

"Redfern is a mage with access to dark magics. I will not walk blindly into an ambush," he told his brother.

"Wait." Cullen charged forward to get in front of us. He wasn't wearing his glasses. He squinted as he looked at us both. "I'll get rid of him. If you promise to sit down with us without your freaking army, I'll make sure Redfern isn't in the room. Please, Soren."

Soren stared at his younger brother for so long, I thought he was trying to pull some kind of mind-trick vampire-move with him.

Which wouldn't have worked since Cullen was a vampire as well.

Soren squeezed my hand. "What do you think we should do, Celestina?"

It shocked me that he asked my opinion. How sad was my life up until this point that I never expected anyone to ask what I thought?

"Um…" I bit my lower lip as my thoughts scattered. It took several frantic moments to gather them up again. "I think we need to talk with your parents. The longer we put them off…it won't help matters. They don't like me. They think I'm controlling you. They'll blame me if you keep yourself away from them. Sitting down with them in their royal chambers might be the right move to show them that you're still willing to listen to what they might have to say."

"I'm willing to listen, but I'm not willing to do anything that'll put you at risk." Soren turned to his brother. Cullen, still squinting, slumped as he seemed to release the tension from his muscles. "Very well. Get rid of Redfern."

I winced when I took my seat at the king's table. Soren had held out my chair and was standing behind me. He moved preternaturally fast to squat down next to me.

"What's wrong?" he demanded. He looked ready to pull the plug on the lunch.

"*I'm sore*," I blushed as I whispered. I glanced down at my lap and the rawness between my legs. Goddess, if he kept at me like he had been, I doubted I'd ever feel comfortable sitting again.

When I looked back at him, his cheeks were tinged red. "Oh." He didn't sound the least bit sorry. I swatted his arm, though I wasn't sorry either.

He brushed a kiss against my cheek before taking his place at the round table to the right of his father. Soren had directed me to sit to the right of him. That had been the place reserved for Prince Cullen, but Cullen had taken one look at his older brother's expression and moved down to the next chair. Princess Priscilla gave me a hug before taking her place next to her mother. I believe I had been meant to sit next to Priscilla. Girls on one side of the table and boys on the other.

The private royal dining room was a large oval space with three sides of the room opened to the mountains and the ocean outside with tall floor-to-ceiling gilded arched windows. The fourth wall was covered in blue satin wallpaper.

The table, which could have accommodated twice as many as were gathered this afternoon, had been set with bone white ceramic tableware and gleaming silverware. A large vase in the middle of the table was filled with fresh fruit. I wondered if Lady Quell's father had supplied them. His indoor gardens must be glorious. I hoped I'd be able to tour them. I hoped I'd be able to do many things after this meal happened.

The king and queen entered after we were all seated. They were dressed in relatively casual clothes. The queen's flowing brocade gown looked comfortable. The king's suit looked like something a guildsman might wear to his job. Neither was wearing anything on their heads to signify their status, which I found interesting. While I'd only seen Soren with a crown once, he wasn't wearing one now. However, both Prince Cullen and Princess Priscilla arrived with diamond-encrusted coronets encircling their heads.

Was this common for what was supposed to be a simple family dinner? Or were Soren's siblings trying to make some kind of silent point? I wished I knew more about Fein court politics. Things in Earst had been easy. The queen was the absolute ruler. Anyone making a powerplay, like wearing a tiara to a lunch, would swiftly be put to death. At the table. Before the soup was served.

The king and queen greeted us, not personally, but as a collected group before they took their seats. As soon as they were settled, a bevy of servants swept into the room to place steaming bowls of fish soup in front of us.

I didn't realize how hungry I was until its spicy scent tickled my nose. Before I realized it, the spoon was in my hand and half my soup was gone.

Cullen chuckled.

"It's good soup," I said in my defense.

"We've not taken much time to eat these past couple of days," Soren added, his soup bowl already empty.

The princess giggled. The queen sniffed her displeasure. And the king hummed a bit as he slurped some of his own soup.

The table fell into silence again, mainly because the food being brought out was delicious. But also because the servants hovered. The king and queen wouldn't want the discussion that was inevitably coming to become gossip fodder in the back halls. Prince Cullen did talk a bit about his research. Princess Priscilla spoke about her work in rural clinics. Soren ate as if he'd never been fed in his life. After filling my stomach with soup, I picked at the rest of my meal. And the king and queen both ate moderate portions of whatever the servants placed in front of them.

As soon as the dessert—a delicious-looking sponge cake drizzled in gooey caramel and sprinkled with flower petals—had been placed in front of each of us, the king waved the servants away and personally made sure the door was securely closed. He then took out a key and turned it in the lock, sealing us in.

When he returned to his seat, he didn't even bother to pick up his fork, didn't pretend to contemplate how moist the cake looked, how sweet the caramel appeared. He sat back in his chair and turned to his right.

"Son," he said, his voice moderate in tone, almost gentle, "in all the years we have raised you, I have never known you to act selfishly until now. That stunt you pulled two days ago was unacceptable. The damage you did to the crown will give ammunition to our enemies."

Soren lowered the fork that was halfway to his mouth. "My actions weren't simply for myself. Protecting Princess Celestina protects the entire kingdom." Soren pushed his plate of uneaten cake away from him. "You, of all people, should have already realized the wisdom of pledging myself to her."

"What does he mean?" the queen demanded before I could. When the king pressed his lips together, the queen leaned forward to ask her son, "What do you mean?"

"Mother, you should know by now that I have never acted without considering all the consequences."

"That's not an explanation," I chided, not that anyone was listening to me.

The queen spoke at the same time. "You have always been a conscientious child. But that was before you fell under the spell of that…" She waved her hand in my direction. "Of that…"

Soren raised a questioning eyebrow.

The queen huffed. "Of Queen Beatrice's collar. Redfern says its powers extend to—"

"I'm not under Queen Beatrice's thrall." He looked at me and some of the tension eased from his expression. "I am, however, completely and utterly enthralled with the amazing woman seated here with me. She is my northern star, my sunrise, the calm before a battle. I would have joined with her no matter the circumstances."

My heart melted. Princess Priscilla sighed loudly, while the queen rolled her eyes.

"No," the queen said. "No, I cannot buy into your claim that this is a love match. Not when you rebuffed every potential mate introduced to you. All beautiful girls. All clever. All from well-respected families. Any perfectly suited to serve as your *northern star.*"

Soren took my hand and gave it a squeeze. "None of them were Princess Celestina."

The queen slammed her hand down on the table. "No. That's not good enough, Soren." Her voice grew sharper. I could see the frustration building in her eyes. "You told me again and again that you had no desire to join with any woman, not yet. Not while you're still acting as your father's sword. Life with an absent military spouse wasn't a life you would wish even on your greatest enemy, and certainly, you didn't want such a life for a delicately raised woman, especially not a woman you could develop soft feelings toward. Does this hasty mating mean that you're ready to set aside your sword? You wear a dagger to our lunch. So, I don't think that could possibly be the reason. What am I to think of this drastic change in your personality then? Is it caused by Queen Beatrice's doing?" She gestured toward me as she said *Queen Beatrice* with disdain. "That's what Redfern believes. He tells us—"

"I don't know what Redfern sees when he looks at Princess Celestina. Something evil, I imagine. A threat to everyone here. He's wrong. So wrong." Soren shook his head.

"He says she has magic. Apart from the collar. Is this not true?" the king asked.

"I don't have magic," I said, wondering why everyone was acting as if I didn't have the ability to speak.

"We don't know for certain if it's true or not." Soren glanced at me and then turned back to his parents. "And honestly, it doesn't matter, does it? As vampires, we have magic of our own. We're creatures that Princess Celestina has been taught her entire life to fear. And yet, she accepts me for *who* I am instead of fearing *what* I am. Shouldn't we try to do the same for her? Shouldn't my family try to get to know the woman I have pledged my life to instead of trying to decide whether or not she's some scaly beast that has tricked its way into our sacred lands?" He brushed aside one of those pesky lizards that had followed us from Earst to the palace.

"We're trying to protect you," the queen said.

"We have a duty to protect our country," the king said.

"What do you think I am?" I demanded. "What threat do you think I could possibly pose to anyone? You are all vampires. You're a kingdom full of vampires. And I'm…I'm just me."

Prince Cullen started tapping his finger on the table.

"I spent several hours with her the other day, and she seems perfectly harmless, delightful even. And she's good for Soren," Princess Priscilla said. I could have hugged her. "He's needed someone like her in his life for a long time now."

"A spy from another kingdom, you mean?" the queen demanded. "That is the last thing any of us—"

The door splintered with a loud crash.

Soren was on his feet with his dagger in his hand before the door fully burst open. The king and Prince Cullen weren't that far behind him. However, neither of them had weapons of any kind.

Princess Priscilla, I noticed, had grabbed a knife from the table before jumping up so hastily that her chair toppled over. The queen didn't move. I locked eyes with Soren's mother and remained in my chair as well.

"Redfern!" the king bellowed. "What is the meaning of this…of this outrage?"

"Country before self," Redfern said in a smarmy, cool voice that prickled my skin. "Country before all."

"Beast!" a scratchy voice shouted. "Beast!"

I knew that voice.

"I thought seers weren't welcome at the palace," I said to the queen, still keeping my sights on her.

"Needs must," she said with a shrug.

"Mother?" Soren roared.

"You did this?" Priscilla shouted.

"How did Redfern and this crazy woman get past the men I had posted in the hall?" Soren demanded.

"How did you get past my guards?" the king demanded.

"The same way I'm going to get past your son."

There was a flash of light. Soren collapsed to the ground beside me like his life had been ripped from his body.

The queen screamed.

I lurched out of my chair and dropped to my knees next to Soren. His eyes were open. He was breathing. But other than that, his body had turned as still as death. I peeled the dagger from his hands.

"This is treason," the king warned.

"This is saving the kingdom I've sworn to protect," Redfern corrected. "Step aside, or I'll do the same to you that I've done to your son."

Prince Cullen moved to stand between Redfern and me. Princess Priscilla, with the table knife still clutched in her hand, joined him.

"I'll take all three of you down," Redfern amended.

"No!" the queen shouted. "Only that Earstian slave. You told me you could remove the joining bond without harming my boy!"

"I'm cleansing the kingdom." Redfern shook his head. "Your son's infection already runs too deep."

"No!" The queen launched herself at the royal mage, knocking him down. "No! I won't let you harm him!" The two tussled on the ground.

"Beast!" the old, blind seer screeched. She sounded as if madness had taken hold of her mind. "The beast has returned! Burn it! Burn it or we will all be burned!"

"NO!" the king roared. He pushed his son and daughter aside and stood like a warrior prepared to fight to the death to protect his son…to protect me. "If the girl dies, we all die. Not just Soren. Not just the royal family, but everyone in the kingdom. The ground will be turned to ash. That is why Queen Beatrice sent the girl to us. She wanted Soren to kill her on Fein soil. She's not Queen Beatrice's spy. She's the queen's blade of death."

Chapter 44

The queen's blade of death.

That's what they thought of me? That's why Soren had joined with me? He'd told his father that it had been a selfless act. Had he made that vow and joined with me, not because he loved me, but to protect his kingdom?

No, no, I couldn't believe that. Soren had told his family he loved me. He'd called me his northern star.

I pushed to my feet.

He showed me his love in how he kissed me, how he touched me. I would not let self-doubt overwhelm me. Not now. Not when Soren needed me to fight for him.

Dammit. I wasn't a fighter. But when I looked down, I saw Soren's dagger clutched tight in my fisted hand.

"For the love of our kingdom, do not harm her," the king demanded.

Too late. Too late. The mage swung his fist at Soren's mother's head, knocking her unconscious. He then raised his hands. With a loud boom, his magic reverberated through the room. The king, Prince Cullen, Princess Priscilla, and the screaming old seer all collapsed to the ground as if they'd been knocked dead.

Redfern tilted his head to one side and glared at me. "How are you still standing?"

I shook my head.

His magic boomed like an explosion, louder than the first time.

I stumbled as I lunged for him. I couldn't let Redfern keep hurting Soren and his family like this. Who knew how much they could take of these magical assaults without suffering permanent damage.

"How are you still standing!" he shouted.

"I. Don't. Know." I plunged the dagger into Redfern's chest. It didn't go nearly as deep as I'd hoped. But it hit him hard enough to knock him off balance, enough to make him bleed. "Wake them up!"

"Not until you're dead!" He straightened and came at me.

I aimed the dagger at his throat.

Again, the sharp blade didn't sink into his body like I'd hoped. It cut into his skin but bounced back as if it had struck a rock. I couldn't understand what I was doing wrong. The warriors had made killing look so simple. This wasn't simple.

Blood squirted from his neck. Loads of blood. But the mage only appeared angrier than ever. He grabbed my wrist and, with a vicious twist that snapped bones, ripped the dagger from my hand. I cried out.

"Scream all you want. There's no one here who can help you," Redfern spat in my face.

His blood sprayed my face and beautiful gown as he wrapped his hands around my neck. I kicked and punched him. Still, he squeezed. Determination hardened his expression as he squeezed, squeezed, squeezed.

"*No.*" My growly voice that made the Fein nervous came out with my anger. "*No. You will not win. Soren will stop you.*"

As if summoned by magic, Soren was behind me. I felt the heat of his body, and the strength of his hands as he tore the mage's fingers from my neck.

"How——?" Redfern's cry of disbelief was cut short. Soren flung him across the room as if he were a lizard being flicked off the skirt of my dress. He hit the far wall with a sickening crunch.

I didn't have a chance to watch him slide to the ground. As soon as he'd flung Redfern, Soren had his hands on my shoulders and was spinning me around to face him.

"Where are you hurt?" He sounded breathless. "Where?"

"He broke my wrist, but—"

"Blood. There's so much of it." His worried gaze traveled over my bloodstained self. "Too much."

"It's his. All his. I tried to stab him, but I'm shit with a dagger."

His worried gaze softened. "You have to know where to strike. You'll hit bone otherwise. You're not strong enough to cut through bone, not with a dagger." His hands cradled my face. "Perhaps with a broadsword, you'd have enough leverage. But it-it's better to know where to strike." He dipped his head and breathed in as if taking my soul into his being. "The-the vulnerable places…" He kissed me.

His arms wrapped around me. It felt wrong kissing him like this. We didn't know if Redfern was truly incapacitated. His family was still on the floor, perhaps dead, all around us. The seer lay there too. Even so, I sank into his embrace, losing myself to the warmth of his lips.

I loved this vampire so much, my heart ached worse than my broken wrist. His hands traveled over my body. And goddess, my warrior knew where to strike all my vulnerable places.

I don't know how I managed to push him away before things went too far. As it was, the skirt of my soiled dress was bunched up around my waist, my legs wrapped around his waist, and we were both breathing as if we'd run from here to Earst and back by the time I peeled my lips from his and gave his chest a shove.

"Later," he promised and nipped me on the neck.

After we untangled from each other, Soren knelt next to his father. He shook the king's shoulder while I pushed my ruined skirt back down. The older man didn't stir.

"The spell," I said. "The mage cast it and is the only one who can break it."

Soren shook his father's shoulder again. "Please, wake up." The older man's eyes were open, but unseeing. He breathed, but shallowly.

"We need to rouse Redfern," I said. Redfern had explained how magic works after he'd examined my slave collar. Only the one who cast the spell can break it. "He's the only one who can wake them."

Soren shook his head. "We can't rouse him."

"Why not? He's right there."

Soren looked up at me with an expression of dismay. "Because he's dead. His neck snapped when his body slammed against the wall when I"—his voice cracked—"when I threw him against the wall."

"He's dead." And Soren's family was still cursed. Like the king, their eyes were open. They were breathing. It was as if they were frozen in place. "How long do you think they can survive like this?"

Soren plowed his fingers through his hair. "Hours. Maybe. With Redfern dead. Probably less."

"Then we need to find another mage." I started to run for the door. Soren caught my arm.

"How did you wake me?"

"What?" I tried to pull away from him. We couldn't waste a second.

"How did you wake me, princess?" he repeated.

"I-I didn't."

"You did. I was frozen. I couldn't hear but I could see. I watched as he put his hands on you, and I couldn't fucking move. It was hell. I couldn't stop him from hurting you. And then the next moment, I was able to get to you. How did you do it?"

"You were able to watch?" My cheeks burned like fire. Because if he could watch when he'd been frozen, that meant his family had watched as Soren— *Don't think about that.* "My growly voice. When I called out to you, my voice sounded like when I played with the princes. The voice that scares Gray. It just came out that way."

Soren gave a quick nod. "The voice that commands magical beasts. What if you can use it to command pure magic too?"

"I…I suppose I can try." I closed my eyes and drew in a shaky breath. This wasn't going to work. "*Awaken. Everyone who has been cursed by Redfern's magic, you are free. Awaken.*"

Even before I opened my eyes again, I heard the rustling of clothes. The princess was the first one on her feet. She still clutched the table knife and looked ready to use it.

"Redfern is dead." Soren closed his hand over his sister's and smoothly removed the knife from her grasp. "I killed him."

"Good." Her eyes glittered with rage.

By this time, Prince Cullen and the king had gotten to their feet. The old seer was on her hands and knees. She keened loudly, like she was in pain.

The king glanced at her and then at me before turning to Prince Cullen. "Go check on the King's Guards. See if they are recovering."

The prince started toward the door, but something must have caught his eye. He stopped abruptly. "Mother!"

The queen still lay on the ground. Prince Cullen rushed to her. The princess moved with that preternatural vampire speed and beat him to their mother's side. She dropped to the ground and cradled the older woman's head in her lap.

The king grew suddenly pale. He took a step toward his mate, but then stopped.

Soren grabbed my hand and gave it a tight squeeze. He'd turned as pale as his father. "Is she…?" he whispered.

"There's life." Princess Priscilla caressed her mother's cheek. "Barely."

"You can give her blood, and that'll make her well?" I asked.

Even before the words had left my mouth, King Devon was by his wife's side. He ripped open a vein on his arm with his teeth and pressed it to his mate's lips. The blood dribbled down the side of her face.

"If she's not strong enough to swallow, we'll lose her," the princess said.

Prince Cullen, on the floor next to his father, pulled at his hair. He looked as if he was about to completely unravel while watching the king's blood dribble uselessly down the side of his mother's face.

"She's swallow for me," King Devon said. His voice rumbled deep.

Vampires couldn't compel each other, and still, his voice sent the command. "Leona always swallows for me."

But her throat remained still. His blood continued to flow down the side of her face.

"We're going to lose her," Soren whispered. His hold on my hand tightened to the point of pain. *"And if she dies, my father will die."*

"No." I looked up at him. "She's magical. Vampires are magical." Goddess, I prayed this would work. It had to work. Please, let it work. *"Swallow, Leona. Swallow your mate's blood,"* I commanded in a growly voice I still didn't understand. I pushed as much intention behind the words as I knew how. The room seemed to sizzle with it.

The seer, still on her hands and knees, cried out as if someone had stabbed her. She had crawled across the room to get close to me. She looked up at me with those milky sightless eyes. "Beast," she groaned. "Destroyer."

She reached out. Her cold, bony hand wrapped around my ankle. I lifted my leg to shake her off. Her grip was surprisingly strong.

The princess, sounding so very far away, crowed, "She swallowed!"

I wanted to cheer. I wanted to celebrate with them. My arrival in the kingdom may have damaged their close-knit loving family dynamic, but they were all still alive. Over time, they could rebuild their relationship. As long as they all stayed alive.

"See what I see," the seer's voice scraped against my soul.

Darkness hit like a fist. I no longer felt the pressure of Soren's hand, only the seer's icy grip remained from *the before.*

I had been transported to *the now.* I stood alone on the edge of a cliff in the Yurdu Mountains that had called so sweetly to me as we'd neared Fein's capital city. An inky darkness infected the skies. Blasts of scorching air spiraled up toward me from the valley below. The City of Sukoon burned. All of it burned. Reinheart Palace had been reduced to a pile of smoldering blackened ash. Flames had engulfed the Palladian Central Library, devouring the books. Fires burned the fields outside the city walls. The trees in the forests burned. And the screams. They seemed to come from everywhere. Every living thing—*everyone I loved—*

in Fein was burning. Dying.

Already dead.

"Because of you." The old seer's crackling voice felt like claws in my already too-tight chest. "You cause this."

No. I would never...

The screaming. Oh, goddess, the screaming. The sound was so loud, so sharp that it hurt my ears.

And the screams? They were all coming from me.

Chapter 45

Five Days Later

Patty munched loudly on an apple as she lounged on the sofa in Soren's royal chamber. Her long legs were flung over the arms. "This is nice."

"You're a barbarian." Gray thumped her dangling feet with his arm. "Has no one ever taught you how to act indoors?"

"What? I'm comfortable." She took another bite of her apple and chewed even more loudly. Gray rolled his eyes. I chuckled.

Patty had been spending at least a few hours with me every afternoon. Inevitably, her visits coincided with when Gray was on duty, which seemed to irritate Gray to no end and kept me entertained.

Soren had left that morning to train with his men while I'd taken breakfast with his mother and sister. All evidence of the battle with Redfern had been cleaned away from the royal dining room. New carpets had been laid. The walls had been freshly painted.

After I'd lost my mind in that same dining room, Soren had been extra careful with me. He'd personally healed my broken wrist, even though I'd been terrified he'd give too much blood and would actually die this time. He promised that wouldn't happen again, especially not over a broken wrist.

He'd growled, *literally* growled, at the reasonable suggestion I drink someone else's blood.

He stayed by my side for three days, watching me as if expecting the screaming to start again at any moment. I suppose he had a right to worry about that. The first two nights I screamed in my sleep, when I could sleep, as the memory of that vision played out over and over in my nightmares.

And I looked horrible, with dark circles rimming my eyes from a lack of proper rest. Even though Goldie and Soren had filled his wardrobe with bright-colored dresses, I would wear black leggings and tunics like his soldiers wore and would spend hours at the Palladian Central Library researching omens, portends, and visions. There had to be a way to stop what I saw from happening. Unfortunately, there wasn't much written about the subject. And what I did read often contradicted each other.

What the authors of the books on the subject all seemed to agree on was that visions of the future were often murky and misunderstood. What I saw in the vision might not have been what would happen in the future. Gradually, with Soren's help in the bedroom, I slept better and felt stronger. But he still wouldn't talk about why his father had called me Queen Beatrice's blade of death. Whenever I asked him about it, he'd tell me not to worry because he had everything under control.

But did he? The vision the old seer had pressed on me seemed to suggest otherwise.

As the days passed, the horror of the vision gradually dimmed.

This morning, I even pulled on one of the gorgeous dresses Goldie had brought me. The fabric had floated around me like clouds when I entered the royal dining room.

This had been the third meal I'd taken with the queen since she'd tried to have me killed. And the first one without Soren at my side. I'd been nervous. But Queen Lenora, nearly fully recovered from her injuries, no longer looked at me as if worried I might plunge a knife into her son's heart at any moment.

I never told anyone why I'd started screaming in the middle of the dining room after the seer had grabbed me. I'd lied, telling them I couldn't remember why her touch had frightened me so strongly. I didn't want to add to their worries that I was a danger to them. I wasn't a blade of death, was I?

I suppose I should have told Soren about the vision. But I was working hard to convince myself that the seer's vision couldn't be right. I was simply me, Celestina from Earst. Bound with a slave collar. Unable to harm anyone.

The vision could even have been a trick the seer had used to scare me. Still, the memory of seeing all my friends die in a blaze of flames terrified me. It couldn't be right. It couldn't.

"Patty," I said, tossing her another apple. I was grateful for her visits. She kept my mind from visiting dark places. "What should we do today? The library? Shopping? Soren gave me the name of a dress shop where he's set up a line of credit for my use, even though I have enough gowns already to last a year."

Patty jumped up from the sofa. "Shopping. Definitely shopping."

"Um…" Gray moved to block the door.

Patty gave him a shove that didn't move him. "Don't tell me Soren doesn't want her to go. He wouldn't have told her about the shop and the line of credit if that were true."

"No. That's not it." Gray's brows creased. "I…" He rubbed his chin. "I've got something to tell you, Sky Girl. Something that's not…it's…it's not going to be easy to hear."

"What is it? You're worrying me, Gray." I perched on the edge sofa. Patty dropped down next to me and gave my hand a squeeze.

"Stop being so dramatic and spit it out," Patty said.

"Look," Gray said, turning even more serious. He started to pace. "Raya told me that I haven't always acted like your friend. And perhaps that's true. Perhaps I have let my…concerns…about the collar and what it might mean for our kingdom forget that you're a person with feelings. And I'm sorry about that."

I nodded. "I understand that you—"

He made a fist and continued on, his voice tight, "Here's the thing. I know something about the attack in town. I know that it was"—his fist tightened—"planned."

"I figured as much," I said. "The false letter I received lured me out into the town."

"It wasn't false." His face turned pink.

"What?" Patty jumped to her feet.

"Soren denied sending the letter," I said.

"Did he?" Gray asked. "Did he deny it?"

I closed my eyes and thought back to the time after the attack. Soren had said there was nothing to be picked up at the leather shop, not that the letter had been fake. But Soren wouldn't have sent me into danger. That would be, must be… "Impossible."

"I'm sorry, Sky Girl."

"I'm with our Sky Girl on this. Gray, you must be wrong." Patty sat back down and nudged me with her shoulder. "He's wrong."

"Okay, let's test this." Gray pulled out a sheaf of papers. "I'll write a command for you and sign Soren's name. Let's see if you feel compelled to do it."

I shook my head. "That won't work. I'll know it's false."

"Let's just test this. Prove me wrong, okay?"

I pinched my lips together. Soren wouldn't betray me. He wouldn't.

Gray wrote quickly on the same kind of paper that the forger had used. He folded it in half, just like the forger had, and then handed it to me.

I unfolded the note, read it, and smiled. "I don't care to bark like a dog. And I won't because I know this note is a fake."

"Okay. You proved your point. Then let's try this one." He pulled a note that had already been folded from the bottom of the stack.

I shook my head as I unfolded the note. It was the one I'd seen before. It still bore blood stains from my injuries on the day I'd traveled out into the city and had nearly died.

"This is the false note I thought Soren had written," I said frowning at it. "Why would you show it to—?"

The collar shot a painful jolt of compulsion down my spine. I jerked and then sprang to my feet.

"Why does the collar think it's real? You know it's not," Gray demanded as he watched me hurry toward the door. "Unless it isn't fake. Unless the prince actually wrote the message."

"Excuse me." I tossed open the door. "I need to go pick up a package from the leather shop."

"Stop her, Gray. She'll get hurt again!" Patty yelled.

Gray chased after me. "You don't have to go there. It's an old message. You already tried to go to the shop. You already know there was no package."

I wanted to scream at him that I knew that. I wanted to scream at him for tricking me like this. But what came out of my mouth wasn't a scream at all. Nor were they the words I wanted to say. "I need to pick up a package from the leather shop."

"Patty! Go get Soren!" Gray shouted over his shoulder. He grabbed my arm. "There's no reason for you to go back that way. It's not safe."

I knew that. I wasn't an idiot. My body may have been healed, but my mind remembered each terrible blow and the sound of my bones cracking. I didn't want to go anywhere near that horrid back alley shop. It was the collar that was forcing me to return. I had to go. I had to leave the palace. Now.

"I'm sorry," Gray said as wrapped his arms around me and held me in place. "I'm sorry. But I needed to prove to you that Soren sent you on that errand. He knew he was sending you into danger, and he did it anyhow."

"I have to go get that package." *There wasn't a package! It had all been a lie!*

"I'm sorry. I'm sorry. I'm sorry," Gray kept repeating. The collar made my skin feel like it was burning. I needed to get to the shop.

"Stop this!" The sharp command shot through me bringing both pain and relief. I stumbled as Gray loosened his hold on me. Panting, I looked up to find Soren standing in the middle of the hallway. A look of despair on his face.

"*Why?*" I gasped. The pain lingered even though the collar had stopped its abuse. "*Why?*"

He tightened his hands into fists at his side. "It's complicated."

"You sent our Sky Girl out there to be killed!" Gray shouted. "You promised to protect her and then you pull this shit? And then lied about it!"

"I...I didn't—" Soren's gaze flicked up and down the hallway. A few courtiers had stopped to watch as if we were the palace's latest entertainment. "This isn't the place to have this conversation."

He moved toward me, looking as if he might sweep me into his arms. He either read the look of fear on my face or the look of murder on Gray's. He stopped mid-step and held up his hands. Hands that had been so gentle with my body. Hands I had once thought would never be used to harm me. "My private apartments."

I tried to walk, but the emotional toll and the lingering pain wrought by the collar had me stumbling so badly, Gray ended up scooping me up into his arms. Humiliation burned hot in my chest as we passed warriors, servants, courtiers, and members of the royal family in the hallway. I wanted to close my eyes and block out their stares. But doing so felt dangerous.

Thankfully, we soon made it to the royal family's private wing. At this time of day, this part of the palace was nearly deserted. Our little parade ended in Soren's apartment. Patty flopped onto the sofa and buried her head in her hands. Soren paced while Gray placed me gently back on my feet. I looked around this room, the same room where Soren and I had shared our meals and made love. All the laughter, all the hope I'd experienced in this room now felt like a lie.

With an anguished sob, my legs gave out and I dropped to the hardwood floor.

Soren was on his knees in front of me in an instant. "It wasn't supposed to be..." He shook his head. "I would rather cut off my arm than see you harmed. But I…I…"

"How could you fucking do this?" Gray demanded. "When I handed that note to Sky Girl, I hoped she'd laugh and toss it away. I hoped I was wrong. Man, I thought I knew you. But apparently, you're shit."

Soren flinched as the words hit him. "I thought I could protect you." His voice was rough, like he had to pull them over gravel in his throat just to get them out.

"Protect her?" Gray laughed bitterly. "That's a load of crap, and you know it. Why would you do this to her? What made you think it would be okay?"

"I thought I was picking the least wrong of my options. The king…" He shook his head with frustration. "My father had threatened to tie you to a post in the far training field, Celestina, and have a guard horsewhip you."

"The king ordered her—?" Gray swore violently. "The king?"

"Why?" I gasped.

"I'm not sure the collar will allow me to tell you," Soren warned. "But you deserve the truth. I'll try my best to give it to you."

I steeled myself for the collar to choke me and then nodded.

"Whenever you've been hurt, whether it's the collar that's hurting you or someone else, dragons have been spotted in the sky," Soren said.

"Dragons?" Gray scoffed.

"Aren't dragons the stuff of fairytales?" Patty asked.

Soren kept his gaze locked on mine. "Gray, you were the one who told me that the collar reacted violently when Celestina had talked about dragons." He lowered his voice. "Let me know if the collar reacts to us talking about them, Celestina. And don't say anything. Just listen. I don't want this discussion to hurt you."

My heart started to pound a little faster. Could it be true? Could my dragons be watching out for me? My green dragon *had* come for me…saved me. Maybe… Maybe…?

"When the king heard about the sightings, he worried," Soren said.

"This is ridiculous," Gray said. "Who told him such nonsense? You?"

"Not me." Soren shook his head violently. "I thought I saw the shadow of one the day she was tossed into the ravine. And I have my thoughts on the matter. But I didn't say anything. Not to my father. Not to anyone."

"Thoughts?" I asked. The collar sent a sharp warning that left me pressing my forehead to the hardwood floor and panting.

"Dammit. I hate that fucking collar," Soren said as he rubbed my back. "I will tell you what I can. I promise. Please, try not to speak."

Everyone in the room stayed silent. Soren kept rubbing my back until the pain started to ease.

Finally, Patty whispered. "Didn't the Fein defeat the dragons at the beginning of time?"

"The story about the Fein fighting flights of dragons is a myth, a story to—" Gray said.

"It wasn't as long ago as the beginning of time, but yes." Soren sat back on his heels as I slowly pushed back up into a seated position on the floor. "The story is true. At least, parts of it are true."

My breathing was still rough. I worked hard to hide that I was suffering because I wanted to hear this.

"This land used to be part of the fifth kingdom, the kingdom of the dragons. The lands to the south belonged to the Fein," Soren explained. "There was a battle." He then told the same story I'd told the princes many times over. A tale about the age of the dragons. But there was a difference between Soren's story and the one I knew. In his, the humans weren't enslaved by the vampires. The humans, with the help of magical human-dragon hybrids, forced the vampires from their lands and into the wasteland that we rode through to get to the Fein capital city—the Rainbow Desert. The Fein, pushed into the dragon's territory, tried to live side-by-side with the dragons. But the dragons were fierce protectors of their treasure hordes and would attack the Fein relentlessly. The Fein, with nowhere to go, fought back. Eventually, they won.

"Dragons?" Gray dropped onto the sofa next to Patty. "They're real."

"This is so awesome!" Patty cried. "I knew Sky Girl wasn't lying when she told us about them in her valley!"

But where did they go? I wanted to ask. The collar sent a warning jolt in response to my thoughts.

"Shhh…I'm not done," Soren said when he noticed how I trembled from the pain. "The king learned about the dragon sightings. He demanded that, for the safety of the kingdom, we test it."

"That's why he wanted Sky Girl whipped? To see if her pain attracted a dragon?" Gray shook his head. "That's wrong."

"I agree. But he wouldn't budge. He said we had to put the kingdom's safety first." Soren growled. "I fought him on this, but I'm not the ruler. And I couldn't change his mind. That's why I gave him an alternative proposal."

"The note," Patty said. "You wrote it to lure her out of the palace and into danger."

"Why did you let her leave the palace?" Gray asked. "Just giving her the note and ordering guards at the gate to keep her from leaving would have done the trick, right? If what you're saying is true, the collar would have punished her enough that a dragon would have come."

"That was what was supposed to happen." Soren looked directly at me as he spoke. "I promise, Celestina. You shouldn't have been able to leave the palace. I hadn't counted on my sister ordering the guards to let you pass. By the time I'd reached the gate, you were gone. I tried to catch up to you, but"—he shook his head—"I couldn't find you until too late."

"You promised. You promised to never use the collar against me. You promised not to treat me that way." I wanted to curl up into a ball and sob until the room filled to the ceiling with my tears. But what would that accomplish? He'd torn out my heart. Not even an ocean of tears would be able to put it back.

"I shouldn't have done it," he said. "What I wish I had done was take you away from here, away from the reach of my father. What I thought was my responsibility to my people kept me from doing the right thing."

"Did they come?" Patty asked.

"Four dragons were spotted in the sky that afternoon. And the guards who were transporting Celestina to Sunjin were found…well, the parts of them that we were able to find were burned to cinders."

Four? Four had come? My dragons? That hadn't been a dream? But how did my green dragon even know I existed?

As silence spread out like an icy film across the room, Prince Cullen slipped into the room. His gaze flitted from my tear-stained face to Gray and Patty slumped on the sofa to Soren on his knees before me. "I see she's learned the truth," he said.

"Not entirely," Soren answered, his gaze hardening as if he was trying to give me some of his strength. "There are two more things I need to say. The first one, the king knows. The second, I have no proof, but it's something I believe in my heart to be true. For Celestina's sake, nothing I'm going to say can leave this room. Can you do that, Gray? Patty?"

"Of course!" Patty shouted. "We'll protect Sky Girl with our lives!" When Gray didn't immediately agree, she punched him in the arm. "Gray! You'll protect her!"

"Ow!" He rubbed his arm. "Gods, Patty. That's going to leave a bruise. Yeah, I'll not say anything."

I found it interesting that Soren hadn't asked his brother for his silence. And the way the younger prince watched me with his arms crossed and his head tilted to one side made me wonder if he didn't already know what Soren was about to tell us.

"First, I believe Queen Beatrice had planned to hand Celestina over to us all along. We have a strong army and are a threat to her kingdom. Remember how insistent she was that we not kill her right away? I believe she wanted us to kill Celestina on our own lands, triggering a catastrophic dragon attack that would severely deplete our strength."

The queen's blade of death…

Prince Cullen nodded. Clearly, this wasn't news to him.

Gray sat back and whistled.

"That bitch," Patty cried. "Sorry Sky Girl, but that queen of yours is evil."

I pressed my lips together even though I wanted to ask why, why would the dragons champion me? I was no one.

"The dragons want to protect you because I believe you are one of them," Soren said gently as if he had heard the question I'd kept tightly locked in my mind.

"Not just one of them," Cullen corrected. "*The one.*"

Chapter 46

The one.

I had no idea what that meant. And it certainly didn't feel right. I was one of the Queen's Ladies. Then a slave. And then Soren's mate. Not a dragon. *Never* a dragon.

"How is that even possible?" I asked. "It's nuts. The one." I lowered my voice and whispered the rest, *"The last moonlight dragon?"* Like in the stories? "A moonlight dragon is supposed to return from the Great Beyond. That's not me. I didn't appear from somewhere beyond this world. I was born to a mother, a human mother. Had a normal childhood. And now I'm a woman, a human woman. Not a very talented one, either."

Cullen leaned toward me. "You're coated in magic. Layers on layers. And it's not all Queen Beatrice's. The magic that belongs to Queen Beatrice and that collar is dancing on the surface. But there's another magic. Something that's been part of you for a long time. At first, I thought it was yours." Cullen shook his head. "It's that embedded. Likely cast when you were first hatched."

"First hatched." I looked over at Patty and laughed. I expected the others to laugh with me. "Come on. I think you're taking this too far."

Gray and Patty were both frowning at me. Soren appeared resigned. And sad.

Excitement danced in Cullen's eyes. "Someone in Earst wanted to hide you. Maybe even control you. Why do all the other kingdoms believe dragons are myths when you say a flight of them has been living outside your queen's castle?"

I opened my mouth to tell him that I'd been speaking the truth about the dragons when the collar sent a piercing shock through my system. I hissed a breath and curled in on myself again.

"And where did the dragons go when they left the valley outside the castle?" Cullen continued as if I wasn't roiling in pain.

"Enough!" Soren commanded. To me? To the collar? To Cullen? "Enough," he repeated, softer. His hand caressed my back, easing the pain. "We can't talk about this. Not with Celestina in the room."

I lifted my head. "But I need to know."

"No." Soren shook his head. "Not if talking about it kills you. And if it kills you, I die and so does everyone in the kingdom. We must be careful."

The horrifying images of the seer had forced on me flashed in my mind. We did need to be careful. Still, it grated that Soren had linked his life to mine.

"I didn't ask you to pledge yourself to me in such a permanent way," I complained.

"And I wasn't asking for your permission when I did it," Soren was quick to respond. He sounded angry. "I won't allow you to get in my way of protecting you. It's that simple."

Patty sighed loudly. "You have to agree that it's sweet how much he cares for you, Sky Girl."

"Not sweet. Irresponsible," I said as I managed to sit up again now that the collar had stopped punishing me. "Other adjectives come to mind, but I think I'll anger the collar if I state them aloud."

Patty snickered.

Gray, Cullen, and Soren all looked grim.

"I have parents," I said, wanting to disabuse them of this silly notion that I might be something other than me. Something that hatched from an egg. "Human parents. Nonmagical parents."

"According to my contacts inside Earst, the couple who raised you weren't your true parents," Cullen said as he sat crossed-legged on the floor next to his brother, who was still kneeling directly in front of me.

My parents weren't truly my parents? My *dead* parents?

"That doesn't mean they didn't love you," Soren said, his voice soft again. "I think they did…do."

"They're alive?"

Cullen nodded. "They're living in Tiburnia. According to my contacts there, your parents wanted to get you away from Queen Beatrice. They convinced the Tiburnians to attack Earst so the Tiburnians could take you, protect you."

I curled my hand into a fist. "And how did I repay them? I hit my father with a wooden sword."

"Even if you had gone with them," Soren said. "Queen Beatrice wouldn't have let you go so easily."

"No." That wasn't true. "She thought I was useless."

"No," Cullen said. "She feared what you could become. She feared you'd take over her kingdom. Or worse, that she might kill you in one of her rages. She needed to rid herself of you before that happened, before her anger issues brought the dragons back to destroy the kingdom."

"Starting the war with Earst was a foolish move on your parents' part. The Tiburnians wouldn't have protected you. They would have tried to use you, weaponize you," Soren said. "And if my father or anyone else in the palace believes you are what we think you are, they will want to do the same. Even with the bond between us, you aren't safe here, Celestina."

The one. They think I'm *the one.* The mythical—

"That's why her eyes sometimes glow like the moon, isn't it?" Gray said.

"I believe so." Soren took my hand in his. He rubbed circles around and around on my wrist with his thumb. I so wanted to lean into him, to take comfort from him. To trust him. "And why she was able to live in Earst in a room with no windows. She's a creature of winter."

Tears prickled at the backs of my eyes.

"What do I do?" I asked, feeling even more lost and alone.

Soren's own parents feared the destruction I could bring to their kingdom. How long before they came to the same conclusion as Redfern? How long before they ordered my execution even if my death meant bringing about their own son's death?

"Where do I go?" I wondered aloud.

I would have to leave the kingdom. If not for my own safety, for my friends'. The seer had been right. I wouldn't be able to stop the destruction that would come. But I could protect those I cared about. I could leave.

"First, it's not *I*," Soren said. "It's *we*. You and me. We're in this together. I stand with you from now on, no matter what."

"You can't make promises like that. You're the crown prince."

"Fuck my crown. I'm your bonded mate, Celestina. You're the beating of my heart. You're the reason I smile. If you can't stay here, I can't stay either." Soren pressed his forehead against mine. "Cullen can have the kingdom."

"Oh, no. Hell, no. Don't you go and lay that load on me, brother."

"Then Priscilla can take it. She'd love it. She's always going on and on about how the kingdom isn't doing enough for the common man, for the humans. She'd jump at the chance to be in charge and make the changes Father won't make."

"So that's settled then," Cullen said as if it were all that easy. "When are we leaving?"

"We?" Soren demanded.

"Leaving?" I asked. Where would we go? Where could we go that would possibly be safe?

Chapter 47

Cullen crossed his arms over his chest. "It's my connections in the foreign courts that will get you across borders."

"No," Soren said.

"I'm the only one who will be able to get us into the Tiburnian Castle safely," Cullen said.

"That's not true." Soren seemed determined to stop his brother from traveling with us.

"Yes, it is very true. Do you think Celestina's parents will welcome you when you bring their daughter to them wearing a slave's collar and bearing your bite marks on her neck? They will likely want to kill you. And as for the rest of Tiburnia, you did recently kill off a goodly percentage of their army. I don't think they'll be welcoming you with a friendly smile either, even if you do have a dragon on your arm."

"I'm not a dragon," I automatically corrected. The collar sent a burst of pain that had me doubling over.

"We need to get rid of that collar," Cullen said, blandly. "It's going to kill her."

"Oh, fuck me, why didn't I think of that?" Soren growled.

The two looked on the verge of physical combat. Soren could easily defeat his bookish brother. But I didn't want violence, especially not because of me.

I pushed past the pain of the collar so I could wedge myself between them. "*Stop this.*" I used my growly voice.

Was this my magic?

Was this my power?

Both men turned toward me. Their eyes widened as their hands lowered to their sides.

"Don't do that," Soren whispered with a shudder. "It's freaky."

"I wouldn't need to do it if you didn't get into pissing contests with your brother." I flashed him a sassy smile, while my insides shuddered.

Oh, my goddess.

I had magic.

I couldn't imagine anything more terrifying.

Or exciting.

I had *badass-warrior-controlling* magic.

I wish I'd known about this earlier. Like when I was still in Queen Beatrice's court. Would my magic have worked on her? Or did it only work on magical creatures like mammoth cats and vampires?

Soren held up his hands in surrender. A corner of his lips curled up in a rakish smile. "I like this side of you, Sky Girl."

While Soren was making eyes at me, Cullen sucker-punched his brother in the stomach. "I'm going to go pack my things, big bro. I suggest we leave on the next tide."

"Why are we sneaking out?" I whispered the question to Soren as we made our way down a narrow staircase that we accessed from behind a hidden panel in a servant's linen closet. It was the middle of the night. I had a small pack stuffed with clothes, toiletries, and the wooden dragon Soren had given me. My collection of sparkly rocks was hanging from its pouch at my waist. Feeling its weight made me feel stronger, braver.

Both Soren and I were dressed in our black tunics and leggings. One of Soren's black cloaks was draped over my shoulders. It was too big for me and nearly reached the floor.

Soren also wore his battle leathers. Weapons hung from nearly every surface of his body. I was surprised he didn't clank as he walked. But like a predator, he descended the stairs without so much as a whisper of his fabric.

I felt like a clomping beast beside him.

"Won't your family be upset that we sneaked away like thieves?" I was beginning to warm up to his mother and was already quite fond of his feisty sister.

"Even if my father hasn't guessed what you are yet, I doubt he'll let you leave so easily."

"He's afraid of the destruction I might bring. I would think he'd be glad to see me gone." After that terrifying vision, I knew I was glad to see me gone. I simply hated the thought of taking Soren and Cullen away from the family who loved them. *They should stay here.*

"Well, you might be right about my father wishing you weren't in his kingdom, like a ticking bomb ready to explode." Soren huffed. "But…" He shifted as if the conversation made him uncomfortable. "But I doubt he'd happily let me leave with you, even though I tied my life to yours, I have a feeling he's actively working on breaking the bonds that tie us together."

"You're the future of Fein." And his father loved him. Both of his parents seemed uncommonly fond of their children.

He shrugged. "My sister would bring about a better future than I ever could. She's a strong fighter, a clever diplomat, and a solid strategist. I'm only good at swinging a sword, a talent I'm sure will come in handy with what faces us in the future."

"I can think of a few other talents that'll come in handy," I teased, as I ran my hand down his arm. His steps stopped as he turned toward me. The bone-crushing strength his broad shoulders contained once made me afraid. But now, the sight of him made my body light up. His green eyes sparked in the glow of the lantern I was carrying, letting me know that his body craved exactly the same thing mine did.

"I'll be glad to use those talents on you as soon as we get aboard the ship, Sky Girl," his deep voice rumbled.

"I'll hold you to that, Warrior Boy."

"I'm no boy." He started down the stairs again.

No, he was all man…er…vampire. I stumbled as the thought hit me. It was amazing how I could forget that terrifying part of him. The Soren I knew didn't fit the warnings of vampires I grew up hearing, *except for the charming part.*

Was I under his thrall?

I was.

But was that really a problem?

We'd reached the bottom of the stairs. A door that looked as if it hadn't been used in the last century creaked as Soren pried it open.

He lifted the lantern from my hands and pressed a finger to his lips. He then motioned that I should go on ahead of him.

The damp, tangy scent of the sea welcomed us as we stepped outside. The distant creak of wood rocking against a dock was the first sound I noticed, followed by the soft lapping of water against an unseen shore.

"It's just down this path," Soren whispered. He'd extinguished the lantern, throwing us into darkness.

"I can't see a path."

He took my hand to guide me. "Your eyes will adjust."

Not far down the path, we met up with Gray and Raya.

"It's done," Raya said.

"What's done?" I asked.

Soren gave my hand a squeeze. "Just gathering all our gear."

That was a lie. I felt it in my bones. Raya had clearly meant she'd done more than just gather the gear and secure a boat.

I started to ask him about what Raya had done when Patty ran down the path, swinging a lantern and calling, "Wait up!"

"Oh, my gods," Gray grumbled.

Patty skidded as she collided with us.

Soren whipped the lantern out of her hands and swiftly snuffed the light while Raya caught Patty around the waist.

"I'm coming too!" Patty squealed.

"No, you are not, brat." Gray put his foot down. "It'll be too dangerous."

"Your parents will miss you," Raya said much more gently.

"But you'll need me. You're not bringing Mary, which means you'll need a cook. And I'm just as good at preparing a meal as Mary is." She huffed a breath. "Tell them, Sky Girl. Tell them you need me to come."

"I don't—" I started to say when a loud shout sounded from the palace gate.

"Halt!" a King's Guard cried.

"Stop them!" another shouted.

"I was hoping to avoid this," Soren grumbled. His grip on my hand tightened. "We're going to have to make a run for it. Raya, cover our flank. Gray, take the lead."

Gray cursed as he tossed Patty over his shoulder and ran past us as we ran toward the waiting ship.

Chapter 48

Oh, my goddess, we were going to be caught! Although we had a head start, it wasn't that much of a head start.

And ships—although I'd never been on one—I doubted they launched instantly. Didn't we have to wait for things like the wind? And the guards had arrows. We could be shot with an arrow.

We were so going to die. Or be caught. And then killed.

Queen Beatrice would definitely make an act like this against her into a long, painfully drawn-out, bloody spectacle. Soren's father, while not as hot-headed, wouldn't let someone in his kingdom escape with such an open display of treason, not even his sons.

My heart thundered painfully in my chest as I tried to keep up with Soren. Noticing how I was struggling, he scooped me up into his arms and picked up his pace.

"Raya?" he shouted over his shoulder.

"I already said it's done!" she shouted back.

What's done?

"Then why the fuck are we being chased?" Soren shouted.

"Give it a moment!" She sounded too calm for the situation.

"We don't have a moment. Not when there's the risk that Celestina might be harmed!" The ground below us blurred as Soren's grip tightened and he ran even faster.

A deafening crash shook the night. And then the shouts of what sounded like a thousand men.

"See!" Raya cried. "I said I took care of it."

Soren grunted. His steps slowed just a bit.

I peered over his shoulder and watched as his warriors came pouring out of the palace. They encircled the exterior. Their backs to us, they stood as a wall between us and the King's Guards who were trying to stop us.

"Your father should have never given you an army that you could use against him," Raya said with a laugh as she jogged next to us. We'd reached the docks. The three-masted dark ship creaked against the dock's wooden planks as they shifted under our weight.

"My father is grateful he gave my brother his army. Soren has created the most disciplined force in the four kingdoms," Cullen said as he waited for us to board the black ship. "He's lucky we're not taking his army with us."

Soren set me on my feet. His fingers trailed down my arm until they twined with my hand.

"Are you ready for this?" he asked, looking worried. "Are you ready to find out what your parents have to tell you?"

I glanced over at the wall of warriors keeping the King's Guards away from us.

"It'll be dangerous," he warned.

Soren was burning so many bridges for me. I started to protest. I started to tell him that he needed to go back to his family. But it was too late for that. He'd already cut ties with the family that adored him.

"I can't guarantee that collar won't try to kill you again."

I prayed I could prove myself, prove that his sacrifice wasn't made in vain. I prayed my love for him would prove worth this awful price. But how could it?

"Are you sure about all this?" I finally managed to get the words out.

He winced. "This is the only way, though I can't guarantee I'll be able to stop the collar from succeeding in killing you. I can't guarantee anything when I don't understand all the magics that are tied to you."

"But other than your brother you're leaving…everyone in your family." Would either Soren or Cullen ever be welcomed back into the palace after commanding the army to stand against the crown? Would they eventually hate me for being the reason they're losing their family? "Are you ready to leave your home and your family all behind?"

"Wherever you go, Sky Girl, that's where I belong." He kissed my knuckle. "Always and forever."

"Stop with all that mushy crap and get on this ship before we're all captured and dragged back to the palace with swords sticking out our chests," Cullen snapped. He then gave me a wink. "We have a tide to catch and a flight of dragons to find."

There was a story about a moonlight dragon I once heard when I was very young. It made me lose sleep for weeks. The storyteller had been an old woman with hair the color of the moonlight. I had remembered that especially, because I'd spent the entire evening imagining that she was the moonlight dragon, in human form, coming to teach us an important lesson. She told us about the last living moonlight dragon. It wasn't a warrior like the others who had died before it. The dragon had hatched from its golden egg only hours earlier and was resting in a nest of lavender and rose petals. The flight of dragons had left to go hunting at sun fall, as they did every evening. A fierce hellhound stood guard at the cave's entrance, protecting the future of all dragon-kind.

Dragons, the storyteller had explained, were creatures of habit and had never even considered leaving one of their own in the cave to protect the precious moonlight dragon. When they returned after many hours and with sated bellies, they found the hellhound crouched low, growling at the dragons who entered. He had blood on his muzzle and teeth. And had turned wild.

The great green dragon, who was the largest and strongest of the dragons, snapped the hellhound's neck in half while the other dragons searched desperately for the tiny moonlight dragon. Their hope for the future was nowhere to be found.

As the hellhound lay dying, it whimpered, for it didn't have the ability to speak or be understood. But it reached its paw toward the west and with its last breath howled mournfully.

Though the dragons didn't understand what the hound was trying to tell them, the smallest and swiftest among them, a pure black midnight dragon, shivered at the sound. She immediately set off, flying in the direction the now-dead hellhound had indicated. Miles and miles away, she picked up the lavender and rose scent of the tiny moonlight dragon as well as the scent of human blood…and magic.

And although the dragons searched endlessly for the last moonlight dragon, their precious hope for rebuilding their kingdom was gone.

As the moon rose over the ocean that night, our small band of friends sailed away from Soren's homeland and toward a destiny I doubted even the most talented of the storytellers or seers would be able to predict.

Epilogue
Princess Priscilla

Sweat glistened on my forehead as I stretched out on my bed. My body ached…in the best way.

Captain Tristan Fjors fell on the mattress next to me with a stated huff. He was, by far, the most handsome man to have ever guarded me. His muscular chest taunted me even now, begging to be touched some more. His blond hair was mussed from where I'd grabbed his head and held on while he'd buried his face between my legs. His King's Guard uniform made a rumpled trail from my bedroom door to the bed. Like always, our hunger for each other was so strong that we'd barely made it to my chamber before losing our clothes.

"We're lucky no one has yet seen us together like this." I lifted his hand and pressed my lips to the tip of his thumb. He groaned when I sucked that same thumb into my mouth.

"Would it be so bad if we were seen, *princess*?"

I loved how his deep voice rumbled when he called me princess. Like he scorned my position and only used my title as an insult. Gods, I was tempted to straddle him and start round two.

I suspected Tristan hated me—or at least he hated the life I was born into—which only made me want him more. I recognized how twisted that was. But after a life of being pampered and coddled and treated like I was entitled to every favor handed to me, I craved his contempt. It made me feel real.

"What happened to your promise to tell your precious father that you've been fucking a lowly guard?" he demanded as he pumped his thumb in and out of my mouth. He added his forefinger, roughly pressing it against my tongue. "Hmm?" He knew I couldn't answer him. But I liked it when he played rough with me like this, when he took control. "What's that, *princess*?" Again, how he said my title was dripping with delicious contempt.

I sucked his fingers with near-frantic desperation. He groaned. I might have handed him power over me, but that didn't mean I was altogether powerless.

"Princess, what you do to me…"

I smiled. With the lightest of pushes, I rolled so I was straddling him. His fingers slid from my mouth with a loud pop.

"I like what I do to you," I admitted, running my nails down his strong chest. "And I would like to shock the court with our relationship. But now isn't the time. Not with nearly losing my mother to that traitor Redfern. Not to mention Soren turned the army against my father, and my brothers abandoned the kingdom. I-I can't add to the pain those events must have caused my father." I kissed Tristan's chest. "But soon. I promise. Soon, I'll pull you out of the shadows."

Tristan chuckled. "Soren didn't turn his army against the king."

"Yes, he did." I'd watched in horror from my bedchamber's window as it happened. My heart had been in my throat, worried that Tristan might be harmed, that the kingdom might descend into a bloody civil war over Soren's love for Celestina.

Thankfully, it didn't come to that. Once Cullen's ship had sailed, the army stood down. The king forgave everyone. But my father had to be reeling from what Cullen and Soren had done. They'd betrayed him in the most public way possible.

"You're so pretty when you're angry." Tristan grabbed my shoulders and rolled so quickly that he knocked the wind from my lungs as he landed on top of me. He then kissed me deeply. "So very pretty." He nipped my lip. "And so very wrong."

"Wrong?" I groaned as he pushed into me.

"Your father knew all about Cullen and Soren's plans to leave." He pumped his hips. He had a talent for hitting the right spot. His hands tightened on my wrists so hard it would leave bruises as he held me immobile. I tossed my head back and lost myself in the sensation of being completely at his mercy. "Didn't you wonder why none of your healers were called upon after the fighting ceased?"

He moaned his release before collapsing on top of me.

"No one was harmed last night because the battle was staged," he panted.

"But…but Soren doesn't play those kinds of court games." I wiggled my arms, testing to see if Tristan would release my wrists. He tightened his grip on them. "He wouldn't even know how to play such a game. He's awful when it comes to diplomatic matters. Everybody knows that."

"That may be true." He kissed my breast. Even twice sated, desire rippled like a wave down to my still throbbing core. "But your brother is a brilliant strategist on the battlefield. Second to none. It's said he's playing a deep game."

"But for who?"

He bent to kiss my other breast. Before he could distract me, I tried to nudge him away. He gave me a wicked look, and then sucked my nipple into his hot mouth, giving it a twist as he did so.

I struggled against his hold on my wrists and against the weight of his body trapping me to the bed. I needed to think in order to understand what Soren had done. "Tris…"

His cock, which was still buried between my legs, grew hard again. He always liked it when I fought him.

"You're not getting away from me anytime soon, *princess*," he warned as he withdrew and then slammed back into me.

We both knew he was right. It would be quite a while before he'd be ready to find his release again.

After he finished playing with me, I passed out from sheer exhaustion. When I woke up, Tristan was still lying in the bed next to me. He had his head propped up on his hand as he watched me.

"Creeper," I said with a laugh.

"Tell your father about us," he pressed, which reminded me what we'd been talking about before we'd started round two…or was that round three? I'd lost count.

"I need you to explain what happened last night with the clash between the King's Guards and the army, because it doesn't make any sense. If the battle during my brothers' escape was just a show, and the show wasn't for my father, who was Soren trying to fool?"

"*Princess*," Tristan purred as if I should already know the answer.

A sick feeling twisted my gut.

"Don't tell me it was for Celestina." I liked her. She was both sweet and tough, a rare enough combination, especially within court life, which seemed to breed the most conniving females. I was thrilled at the thought of welcoming Celestina to the palace as my new sister. If Soren was doing something underhanded to trick the girl, I would rip him a new hole where a hole shouldn't be.

"Sorry, *princess*," Tristan said, not sounding sorry at all.

"But he performed the mating ritual with her. He confessed to loving her. He *does* love her."

"But, alas, that's exactly who the show was for. Talk within the guards is that Princess Celestina has ties to the dragons."

"Dragons?" I scoffed. "Didn't they all die out eons ago?"

"Apparently not."

I shuddered at the thought. While the history wasn't clear about what had happened so long ago, most believed that the dragons had once nearly killed off our entire race. The vampires had tried to live side-by-side with the dragons in their fifth kingdom, but it's said that the fierce moonlight dragons continued to relentlessly attack the vampires until my ancestors finally found a magical object that allowed them to kill all the dragons and destroy the fifth kingdom.

"There are still dragons in the world?" I whispered.

Tristan nodded. "Your father considers anyone with a connection to the dragons to be a threat to the Fein."

"So he sent Celestina away with my brothers? I still don't see the need for to stage a fake battle or have both my brothers leave the kingdom."

"Your father didn't send Princess Celestina away to get the dragons away from him, he sent your brothers to go with Princess Celestina to win her trust and to use her to gain control over the dragons. He wants to capture them and treat them like trained battle dogs. He wants to use them against our enemies."

No. No, the Fein haven't gone to war in over two generations. We were a peaceful society. We hid behind our country's walls to keep the humans from hunting us, from draining our blood…and from using *us* like trained dogs in battle.

We'd been hunted in the past. Our society still bears the scars of captivity. No, I refused to believe my father could condone something so hideous. And Soren, while he always put country before his own needs, he wouldn't do this, not to Celestina.

"There's no way my brother would go along with such a scheme." He loved Celestina. I was as sure of that as I was of my own name. He wouldn't use her as a tool to enslave the dragons.

Tristan clicked his tongue. "It was Soren's idea, *princess.*"

Thank you for reading
The Last Moonlight Dragon

The second book in the series is currently being written. You can read it as it is being written over on Kindle Vella. (This is an experiment with new technologies and reading along as the writer works. Oh, my!) Or you can sign up for my e-newsletter for updates on when the completed book will be published at www.dorothymcfalls.com

If you enjoyed this book, I would appreciate it if you'd help other readers enjoy it too. After all, most books are sold by word of mouth. What can you do?

Recommend it. Please help other readers find this book by recommending it to friends, readers' groups, social media, and discussion boards.

Review it. Please tell other readers why you liked this book by reviewing it.

Thank you!

About the Author

Dorothy McFalls was born in New York but raised in South Carolina. She makes her home in South Carolina. Though writing has always been a passion, she pursued an undergraduate degree in Wildlife Biology and a graduate degree in Public Administration and Urban Planning. She put her educational experience to use, having worked in all branches and all levels of government including local, regional, state, and federal. She even spent time during college working for a non-profit environmental watchdog organization.

Switching from government service and community planning to fiction writing wasn't as big of a change as some might think. Her government work was all about the stories of the people and the places where they live. As an urban planner, Dorothy loved telling the stories of the people she met. And from that, her desire to tell the tales that were so alive in her heart grew until she could not ignore it any longer. In 2001, she took a leap of faith and pursued her dream of writing fiction full-time. * *Dorothy also writes mysteries as Dorothy St. James*

Visit Dorothy McFalls at:
http://www.dorothymcfalls.com
http://www.dorothystjames.com

Books by Dorothy McFalls

Regency Romances
The Marriage List
Lady Iona's Rebellion
The Nude

Paranormal Romances
Taken by Moonlight

The Protectors Series
A Wizard for Christmas
Neptune's Lair
Mystical Seduction

Romantic Suspense
The Huntress

Books by Dorothy St. James

Read all of Dorothy's delicious Southern mysteries.

Ms. Starr's Most Inconvenient Change of Heart
(A Raven's Run Mystery)

The Beloved Bookroom Mystery Series

Book 1: The Broken Spine
Protecting the printed word can be deadly.
Book 2: A Perfect Bind
Secrets in a library comes at a cost.
Book 3: A Book Club to Die For
Getting into this book club is murder.

Southern Chocolate Shop Mystery Series

Book 1: Asking for Truffle
Death in a chocolate shop.
Book 2: Playing with Bonbon Fire
Beach music, spicy chocolates, and murder.
Book 3: In Cold Chocolate
Sea turtles, chocolate turtles, and a shot in the dark.
Book 4: Bonbon with the Wind
A hurricane, pirate's treasure, and a new batch of chocolates.

The White House Gardener Mysteries

Flowerbed of State
The Scarlet Pepper
Oak and Dagger

Birds of Paradise
(An Aloha Pete Short Story)